Select praise for *New York Times* bestselling author Maisey Yates

"Her characters excel at defying the norms and providing readers with...an emotional investment."
—*RT Book Reviews* on *Claim Me, Cowboy* (Top Pick)

"A sassy, romantic and sexy story about two characters whose chemistry is off the charts."
—*RT Book Reviews* on *Smooth-Talking Cowboy* (Top Pick)

"This is an exceptional example of an opposites-attract romance with heartfelt writing and solid character development.... This is a must-read that will have you believing in love."
—*RT Book Reviews* on *Seduce Me, Cowboy* (Top Pick)

"Their relationship is displayed with a quick writing style full of double entendres, sexy sarcasm and enough passion to melt the mountain snow!"
—*RT Book Reviews* on *Hold Me, Cowboy* (Top Pick)

Books by Maisey Yates

The Carsons of Lone Rock

Rancher's Forgotten Rival
Best Man Rancher
One Night Rancher
Rancher's Snowed-In Reunion
A Forever Kind of Rancher
Rancher's Return

Gold Valley Vineyards

Rancher's Wild Secret
Claiming the Rancher's Heir
The Rancher's Wager
Rancher's Christmas Storm

Copper Ridge

Take Me, Cowboy
Hold Me, Cowboy
Seduce Me, Cowboy
Claim Me, Cowboy
Want Me, Cowboy
Need Me, Cowboy

For more books by Maisey Yates,
visit maiseyyates.com.

MAISEY YATES

The Carsons Of Lone Rock

MIX
Paper | Supporting
responsible forestry
FSC® C001695
www.fsc.org

Published by
Mills & Boon
An imprint of Harlequin Enterprises (Australia) Pty Limited (ABN 47 001 180 918), a subsidiary of HarperCollins Publishers Australia Pty Limited (ABN 36 009 913 517)
Level 19, 201 Elizabeth Street
SYDNEY NSW 2000
AUSTRALIA

Printed and bound in Australia by McPherson's Printing Group

CONTENTS

Maisey Yates is a *New York Times* bestselling author of over one hundred romance novels. Whether she's writing strong, hardworking cowboys, dissolute princes or multigenerational family stories, she loves getting lost in fictional worlds. An avid knitter with a dangerous yarn addiction and an aversion to housework, Maisey lives with her husband and three kids in rural Oregon. Check out her website, maiseyyates.com, or find her on Facebook.

A Forever Kind Of Rancher

Chapter One

She was the most beautiful woman he'd ever seen. A vision dressed in pink, and somehow it made him think of strawberries, which got him to wondering if her skin tasted like strawberries.

She wasn't dancing, and she should be. Hell, Boone was wearing a suit, and he didn't much care for that shit. He didn't much care for dancing either, but this was the kind of thing you wore suits to, and danced at, so it felt like a crime she wasn't dancing.

It was his brother's wedding after all.

And he was damned happy for Chance. Really. He'd fallen in love and all that. Boone was in love too.

Had been for years. In a way that had left him cut open, hollowed out and embittered.

He respected the hell out of love for that very reason. He knew how intense it could be. How long-lasting.

He decided to remedy the fact that she wasn't dancing, because hell, he was in a suit after all.

He knew better than this. He stayed clear of her, except when he couldn't. He knew better than to approach her. She was forbidden. Because of what he wanted to do with her. To her. If all he wanted was a chance to say hi, a chance to shoot the breeze, they could be friends.

But it wasn't what he wanted.

It never had been.

Tonight this place looked beautiful, and so did she, and she was standing there alone, and that was wrong.

He ignored the warning sounds going off in the back of his head and crossed the old barn that had been decorated with fairy lights and flowers for his brother's big day.

"Care to dance?"

She looked up at him, and he saw it. That little spark of awareness that always went off when they were near each other. They saw each other way too often for his taste, and hers, too, probably. He loved it, and he hated it. He had a feeling she only hated it.

It only ever ended one of two ways. With her turning red and running in the other direction or getting pissed off and getting right in his face. As if one or the other would hide the fact that she wanted him. She did. He knew that.

Not that either of them would ever do anything about it.

They were too good.

Boone hadn't often been accused of being too good. But when it came to her...

He was a damned saint.

She lifted her hand, and the diamond there sparkled beneath the light.

"If he's not going to dance with you," Boone said, "you might as well dance with me."

And he could see it. That it was a challenge he laid out before her, and she wouldn't back down.

Wendy never backed down from a challenge. It was one of the things he liked about her.

That diamond ring was the thing he didn't much like.

And the fact that it meant she'd made vows to his best friend. Wedding vows.

Boone wanted his best friend's wife. And it felt so good he couldn't even muster up the willpower to hate it.

He didn't wait for her to answer, instead, he reached out and took her hand and pulled her up from her chair, led her to the dance floor, and tugged her against his body like they were friends, and it was fine. She looked over her shoulder, her expression worried. And that spoke volumes. Because they were friends, as far as anybody here was concerned. Because there was nothing between them, not outwardly.

But they both *felt* it. And that was what made dancing with her dangerous. He had known Daniel for a long time. He loved him like a brother. At least, he had. Before he'd married Wendy.

Daniel, as a husband, sucked. Witnessing that had started to damage their friendship. Boone had never been satisfied that Daniel valued that marriage.

He'd never witnessed anything concrete—if he did he'd be the first one to tell Wendy—but Boone had always had the feeling Daniel took his marriage vows as suggestions when he was on the road with the rodeo.

Not only that, Daniel missed a lot of his kids' milestones, not that Boone had any kids. Not that he was in a position to judge. It was only that he *did* judge.

Because he wanted what his friend had so very badly.

"What's wrong?" he asked.

He knew she wouldn't answer that. Because she wouldn't admit it.

Never.

And maybe they never danced. But they knew this particular dance well. They'd been doing it for fifteen years.

"Nothing is wrong," she said, linking her fingers behind his neck, and he wasn't sure if she was preparing to strangle him, or trying to keep herself from moving her hands over his body and exploring him.

"You look beautiful," he said.

She paused for a second. "Boone…"

"Where is Daniel?"

"Drinking," she said, looking up at him, her eyes defiant, as if she was daring him to comment.

He didn't have to. Instead, he moved his hand just a little bit lower on her back.

Her nostrils flared, and he even thought that was hot.

"If he's drinking, then he won't miss you."

And why the hell should Daniel have her anyway? He didn't fucking care about her. Boone was almost certain that every time he went out drinking with the guys, Daniel was screwing around with buckle bunnies. There was no way he was only dancing with them at the jukebox. Boone could never bear to stick around and find out, because he would have to tell Wendy, and his loyalty was supposed to be to Daniel, but he was at a point where he didn't feel like it could be. Not anymore. And he'd told himself he could not feel that way, and he couldn't act in the way he wanted to, because he had an ulterior motive. But now he didn't care. Right at this moment, none of it mattered.

"Come with me."

"Where?"

"Does it matter?"

Slowly, very slowly, she shook her head no. And he led her off the dance floor, out of the barn and into the night. And in one wild, feverish moment, he pushed his best friend's wife back against the side of the barn and pressed his mouth against hers.

Boone woke up with sweat drenching his body.

Dammit.

For a second, he let the dream play in his mind over and over again.

It was the sliding door. The other path.

The one he had decidedly *not* taken at his brother's wedding, when he had gazed across the barn and seen Wendy looking like a snack that night.

He hadn't even danced with her. Why? Because he'd known he was too close to losing control. But in his dreams...

In his dreams he held that pretty pink slice of glory in his hands. In his dreams, he had pushed her warm willing body up against that barn and tasted her mouth.

It was so real. It was so real he could scarcely believe it hadn't happened.

Damn it and him, to hell.

He was wrung out. It was all the sleeping in cheap-ass motels.

He missed home or so he told himself. Because it was better than missing a woman he'd never actually held in his arms.

He had bought himself a ranch, one that currently had no animals on it, with a damned comfortable bed in one of the rooms—a bed he hadn't brought a woman back to yet—in preparation for his life changing. He was on the verge of retirement, because... Hell. His brothers were all out of the rodeo, so he didn't understand why he was still in. He was the last one standing. The last one who hadn't left, who wasn't with the person that they...

Well. He had no idea what the hell Buck was doing. So maybe that wasn't fair.

Buck wasn't in the rodeo—he knew that much. But he knew nothing else since Buck had cut all ties with their family.

You have to face it, Buck. It happened. There's no use sitting down and crying about it, there's no use falling apart. You have to be realistic.

Not his favorite memory. The last time he'd seen his older brother. Eighteen months his senior and the heir apparent to the Carson Rodeo empire.

Not now, though. Now the heir was Boone.

Someone had to keep the legacy going. It was in his blood.

Because, after all, the Carsons were rodeo royalty.

He nearly laughed.

Rodeo royalty in a shitty motel. Oh well. That was the life. The royalty part came from the fact that they all had trust funds, something Boone had sat on until he got his ranch outright in Lone Rock, Oregon, where he would be near his parents and his brothers... Where he would finally settle... He supposed, because there was a point where the demands of the rodeo would get to be a little bit much, and he wasn't going to be bull riding past his fortieth birthday. He could, he supposed. He could keep going until he gave himself more of a trick back than he already had.

He could downgrade himself to calf roping, keep on keeping on, because he didn't know what the hell else to do, but he did feel like maybe there was a fine art to just quitting while he was ahead.

Except when his brothers had quit there had been a reason. There had been a woman.

He got out of bed and looked at the bottle of Jack Daniel's on his nightstand. Then he picked it up and took a swig. Better than coffee to get you going in the morning.

He grimaced, his breath hissing through his teeth, then he threw on his jeans and his shirt, his boots, and walked out of the hotel.

It was the third night of the championship, and he would be competing for the top spot tonight. Finally, for the first time in a long time, not competing against one of his brothers.

Not that he minded competing against them. It was all fine.

He wondered if Wendy would be there, or if she would have to be home with the girls.

And he had the feeling he had put more thought into Wendy's whereabouts than her husband probably had.

He spent the day doing not much. Had breakfast at a greasy spoon diner near the rodeo venue and didn't socialize, stayed in his own head, like you had to do.

He got to the arena right on time and cursed a blue streak when he drew the particular bull that he drew, because that bull was an asshole, and it was going to make his ride tonight a whole thing.

And then he saw Daniel from across the way, his friend tipping his hat to him, the ring on his left finger bright.

That was when Boone decided he wasn't going to let Daniel have *two* things that he wanted. He couldn't do much of anything about Wendy, but he'd be damned if he wouldn't get this buckle. It was only when it was his turn to get in the shoot that everything felt clear. That everything felt right. The dream finally wasn't reverberating inside of him when he got on the back of the bull—the bull who was jumping, straining against the gate.

Eight seconds. That was all it took. He couldn't afford to blink. Couldn't even afford to breathe wrong. Couldn't afford to have his heart beat too fast. Adrenaline could take him after, but not before. Before was the time for clarity.

Before was when everything became still. It was when he was at peace. At least, the most that he ever was.

It was damned near transcendental meditation.

He didn't question it.

And when the gate opened, the animal burst forth in a pure display of rage and muscle and he clung to the back of him, finding a rhythm. Finding that perfect ride. Because it was there. In every decision he made, and the way he followed all the movements of the animal. In the way he made himself one with him.

And maybe no other cowboy would relate to that way of thinking about it. For sure his brother Flint would laugh his ass off. But Boone didn't care.

There was a reason he was the last one in the rodeo, and it wasn't just because he hadn't gone and fallen in love. It was because no matter what he loved, part of him would always love the rodeo in a way he didn't think his brothers ever had.

Part of him would always know he found purpose there. And if he won tonight, he could leave being the best. And that was what he wanted more than anything. Quit while he was on top. Quit while he could still love the rodeo with all that he had, all that he was. To leave it wanting more. To leave himself wanting more. Because what the hell was worse than overstaying your welcome?

He couldn't think of much.

He'd set out to prove himself, and he was doing it.

So he rode, and he rode perfectly. And when that eight seconds was up, he jumped off the bull. He wasn't unseated.

And the roar of the crowd was everything he could have asked for. Except the one thing he really wanted. So he let it be everything. He let that moment be everything.

Nobody was going to outride him. Not tonight.

He was number one on the leaderboard and he stayed there, for the whole rest of the night, and damned if he didn't give the people kind of a boring show. Because nobody could touch his score, and he loved that.

In the rodeo, Daniel Stevens was second.

And hell, for Daniel that was probably enough. With the Carsons, all except Boone, moved out of the way, that was a damned high ranking for Daniel.

But Boone felt mean about it. Because he was number one, while Daniel was number two, and if Boone couldn't have the other man's wife, then it seemed like a pretty good alternative prize.

There was no question about going to the bar after, because the mood was celebratory, and the women were ready to party, and Boone figured it was just the right night to find himself a pretty blonde dressed in pink, one that would make the fantasy easy. He would lay her down in that bed he'd slept in last night, and he'd find himself back in that dream, make it feel real.

He didn't feel guilty about the fantasies anymore.

He'd been doing it for too long.

But when Daniel came up to him just outside the barn and clapped him on the back, he felt a little bit of guilt. Just a little.

"Hell of a ride," said Daniel. "You made that bull your bitch."

He frowned. "I don't work against him. I work with him."

"Whatever. Seems to work for you."

"It does."

One of the other riders, Hank Matthews, sidled up to both of them as they made their way into the bar. "Does that thing weigh you down?" Hank asked, pointing toward Daniel's ring.

"Oh, hell no," said Daniel, holding his hand up. "If anything, there's a certain kind of woman who likes it."

Boone let his lip curl when he looked at his friend. "Is that so?"

"Hey, don't worry about it," said Daniel. "Just having a little fun."

And after that, the intensity of the excited crowd broke up their group. Fans, male and female alike, were all over the place, and this was their moment of glory. There wasn't a medal ceremony, instead, they were showered with praise in the form of Jack Daniel's and Jesus. Free shots and a whole lot of glory to God.

It was normally the sort of thing he loved, but he was still distracted. That dream was in his head, and then what Daniel said about the wedding ring had gotten under his skin and stuck there.

He hadn't seen Wendy tonight, and it was kind of odd, because it was a championship ride, although they were pretty far off from their home base.

Still. He would've thought she might show up.

And there were women all over her husband.

Normally, Boone would be determinedly paying attention to his own prospects. Not tonight.

There were two women on either side of Daniel, both of them touching him far too intimately for Boone's liking. And then Daniel turned his head and kissed one of them, and Boone saw red. He was halfway across the bar, on his way to do God knows what, when a car alarm cut through the sound of the crowd and the music in the bar. The door opened and some guy came running in like the town crier. "Some bitch is going crazy out there on a pickup truck."

That was enough to send half the bar patrons pouring out into the night. And when a loud smashing sound transcended the noise of the alarm, Boone found himself moving out there as well.

He stood at the door, stopped dead in his tracks by what he saw. A black pickup truck seemed to be the source of the sound, the headlights on, casting a feminine figure into sharp relief. A slender silhouette with a blond halo all lit up by the lights. She was wearing a short, floaty-looking dress, and she was holding a baseball bat. Then she picked up the bat and swung it, and made the headlights go out, casting everything into darkness like a curtain had fallen over the star of this particular show.

"What the *fuck*?" It was Daniel, behind Boone, who shouted that. "That's my truck," he said.

"And I'm your *wife*," came the shouted replied, as the bat went swinging again, and dented the truck right in the hood. "I got you the deal that got you gifted this truck, by the way, so I think it's fair enough for me to vandalize my own property."

Wendy.

Somehow, he'd known it was Wendy. Or at least, his body had.

An avenging angel, looking beautiful and dangerous, and hell…he'd never wanted her more.

Daniel pushed past him, his jar of whiskey still in his hand. "You're being a fucking psycho," he said. "What the hell?"

Wendy advanced on him, her chin jutted out, fury radiating from her. "Tell me you weren't in there with another woman."

Daniel backed up, his face going bland. "I wasn't with another woman."

"I got the most interesting series of pictures texted to me today, Daniel. And it's definitely you, because I'm intimately familiar with your *shortcomings*."

"What the hell does—"

"Pictures. Of you. Screwing someone else."

"I never…"

"Save it. What's the point faking it? You don't have a repu- tation big enough to try and save it. Like I said. I know every detail of you just a little too well for you to try to tell me it's Photoshop."

And then Wendy stormed right up to Daniel, pulled her rings off and dropped them in his glass of whiskey. "Keep them."

"Baby," Daniel said, reaching out and wrapping his hand around her arm, and that was when Boone lost it.

He was right between them before he even realized he'd moved. "Get your hands off her."

"Boone?" Daniel asked, looking at him like he'd grown an- other head.

"I said," said Boone, reaching out and putting his hand around his friend's throat. "Get your fucking hands off her."

"She's my wife."

"And you put one hand on her while you're angry and I'll make her your widow. Step back."

"You should be defending *me*," Daniel said, as he moved away from Wendy. "You know I'd never—"

Boone growled. He couldn't help it. And it shut Daniel up good.

Wendy looked high on adrenaline, her eyes overly bright. And Boone wanted to grab her and shield her from all of this. From the onlookers, from everything. From the truth of the fact that Daniel just wasn't the man that he should have been for her.

Like you are?

No. But he hadn't made vows to her. And if he had, he would never have…

"I can't defend you if there's nothing to defend," he said.

Wendy looked around, and it was as if the reality of every- thing crashed over her. As if she suddenly realized what she'd done, and how publicly she'd done it.

Yeah, this was the kind of thing that got you on the news. And it was likely she'd only just realized that. And he wondered if she had driven all the way from California to Arizona riding high on anguish and anger.

He wondered if she'd even given it a second thought.

And now she was giving it a second thought. And third. And probably fourth.

But for what it was worth…

He moved near her, and she looked at him like she wished he would disappear. He didn't take it personally. She kind of looked like she wanted the whole world to disappear.

"Whatever you do," he said. "Don't regret *that*. Because it was damned incredible."

And he meant it.

"I don't have anywhere to go now." She looked numb.

"Sure you do," he said. "You can always come to me."

Chapter Two

Three weeks later...

If there was one thing Wendy Stevens did not want to do, it was depend on another cowboy. She'd learned her lesson. Some fifteen years and two kids too late, but she'd learned it.

She tried not to think about that night. The one that hadn't exactly covered her in glory. But it had covered the ground in shattered glass, and for a moment, it had made her feel satisfied.

For a moment, the images of her husband with another woman had felt dimmed, dulled, because all she had seen was the destruction she had caused to his truck. Technically, her truck.

Except you bought it with his money...

Well. That was the problem. She had given up her life in service to that man. She had acted as his agent, essentially, getting him endorsement deals and other things. He was good-looking. It had been easy to do. He was charming, that had made it easier.

Both of those things had likely made it easy for him to get women into bed too.

She was still reeling from the truth.

For a few days, she'd clung to the belief that he'd only cheated on her the one time. The time that had come with photographic (emphasis on the *graphic*) evidence.

She knew it was naïve. But it was deliberate. A form of protecting herself.

It hadn't lasted long.

Because once the floodgates of truth had been opened up, more truth had kept on coming.

Fast and swift.

More women had stories. Texts. Photos.

He'd *never* been faithful to her. Never even once. Their entire marriage was a lie. Everything they'd ever built in their relationship was a lie. She supposed the one thing she had to be grateful for was that he had been judicious in his use of condoms. One of the first things she had been worried about was what hideous disease the man had given to her, but he had sworn up and down that he'd had protected sex with all those other women.

As if that earned him some sort of commendation.

I would never do that to you, he'd said.

She hadn't even known what to say to that.

But she hadn't known what to say for a good three weeks now. That was the amount of time she'd given herself to clear up her life and find another place to go.

She had given everything to that man. When his career in the rodeo had started to take off, she'd discovered she had skills she hadn't known she possessed. She'd brokered all the endorsement deals that he'd gotten over the years. Her reputation was tied to his. Her career had been all about making money for him, and they'd put it all in one pot rather than having an official split because why would they ever need that? They were in love. They were forever.

The phrase *all your eggs in one basket* was suddenly far too clear for her liking, and yet there was nothing she could do about it.

Her eggs were in Daniel's basket.

She made a face. She did not like that.

"Mom?"

She turned to look at her daughter. "What?"

Fifteen-year-old Sadie looked at her from the passenger seat, and then twelve-year-old Michaela—Mikey for short—leaned forward. "Are we going?"

Wendy was at the end of a long dirt driveway. The one she knew would take her to help. The one she didn't want to drive down.

"Yeah. In a second. I'm just sitting here thinking about how little I like any of my options."

"You have our support," said Sadie.

"Yes," said Mikey. "It isn't your fault that Dad's an untrustworthy blight on humanity."

"Your vocabulary," said Wendy, rolling her eyes, but she was actually very proud, and beamed a little every time Mikey opened her mouth.

"It's because I read," said Mikey. "And also, because I binge-watch TV shows that are probably above my age rating."

"Let's just leave it at reading," said Wendy.

"I thought Boone was Dad's friend," said Sadie.

"He is," Wendy said slowly.

And she left out all the complications that Boone made her feel. She made sure to keep the pronunciation of those words as simple as possible. She made sure to leave any kind of subtext out of what she said. Because she had to. She had no room in her life for subtext. Not right now. And never when it came to Boone.

"So, why are we going to stay with him?"

"Because he offered." And he'd offered her a job. It was humiliating. But she didn't really have another choice. The one thing she had any kind of experience with before marrying Daniel was housecleaning. Boone said now that he was back from the rodeo, he needed a cleaner, and he had more than one house on the property, and more than enough room for her and the girls. She was in no position to turn it down. She had to take the offer.

Anyway, that night...

She kept seeing it. Over and over again. She'd been unhinged. But brave. And she couldn't help but admire herself. But also, she kept seeing the way Boone had put his body between hers and Daniel's. The way he'd been. Like fire and rage, and completely on her side.

And then the way he told her...

Don't regret it.

So she hadn't. Because Boone had told her not to, and maybe that wasn't healthy, but dammit all, she didn't have a whole lot of healthy available to her right now. Mostly she had disillusioned and confused.

"He didn't take Dad's side on this."

"Good for him."

"I admire his willingness to break with traditional toxic masculinity," said Sadie.

"Well, don't go giving that much credit," Wendy said. "He *is* still a rodeo cowboy. He just happened to...bear witness to some things."

The brief text conversation she'd had with Boone after her grand performance in the parking lot had confirmed that Daniel had been well on the way to cheating on her that night too.

At that point, she had known it was a routine thing.

Any guilt she might have felt eventually over smashing up the truck had been effectively squashed at that point.

There was no room for regret in the well of rage created by Daniel's own actions. If he didn't like the way she behaved, he should have been different. From the very beginning.

"I need something to get back on my feet. And I think we all need a fresh start. This isn't where we're going to stay forever but..."

"It's pretty," said Sadie.

She had expected her daughters to be a little bit angrier about leaving California than they were.

They'd lived in Bakersfield, and it didn't often feel like there was a lot happening there but heat and drought. They complained about both, often. And they seemed to be in places with friends where they were glad for a fresh start and a change of scenery. She couldn't help but wonder if some of it was the pain of having Daniel break up their family. And maybe leaving rather than having to tell everyone about it was easier. At least, that's how it was for her.

Their life had been quiet and stable. He might've been out chasing glory, but she hadn't been. To her, their life had been glory.

But it hadn't been enough for him.

She should've known.

He wasn't home all that much. When he was, they'd had a healthy sex life, but she had honestly just imagined that he was like her. That he turned it off when she wasn't there, like she did with him.

That's oversimplifying things, isn't it?

She gritted her teeth.

Maybe.

Maybe it was.

But she was happy for oversimplification right now. She needed it.

As if simplification didn't cause some of this mess in the first place.

So she started up the car engine and continued down the road that would take her to Boone's house.

When the house came into view, her stomach twisted. It was weird, because it was Boone. And she didn't need to go getting wound up about her own inferiority complexes, or her memories of growing up poor. Her memories of being a have-not in a sea of haves. Of her mother being the one who cleaned and now she was...

It wasn't the same.

Not because she was ashamed of her mother. She wasn't. She never had been. The difference wasn't in the work, it was in the person needing the work done.

Those people had all fancied themselves better than her mother. And that wasn't Boone. And it never would be. It wasn't why he had asked her to come.

He felt guilty, she knew that.

She also wondered how much he had known for all those years…

Well. You have plenty of time to talk.

Seeing as she would be living on his property and cleaning his house.

"Wow," said Sadie.

The house was beautiful. Even more beautiful than the one they had left behind in Bakersfield.

Their house had been elaborate. Because it was the kind of fancy Daniel liked. It had been positioned across from a field that was just empty.

And now she kind of felt like it was a metaphor. A dream house surrounded by a whole lot of nothing.

Empty. Like his promises.

She ached, and she couldn't quite work out exactly what she was feeling. If it was heartbreak or the sting of having been tricked. If it was betrayal or the loss of her marriage. Or simply the loss of her life.

She didn't know. Maybe it was all those things. It seemed like each moment one of those things felt more prominent than another. And then it would shift.

She didn't have time to think about anything shifting at the moment. What she needed to do was get her game face on.

She pulled the truck up to the front of the house and turned the engine off.

Okay. It was just Boone.

And something about that made her feel every inch a liar.

There was no *just Boone*. There never had been.

He'd been a particularly problematic thorn in her side for years.

Mostly because...

Of one moment. A very clear and terrifying moment—the minute she had first seen him.

She and Daniel had only been married for two weeks. It had been a whirlwind romance, and she'd been head over heels, and pregnant far too quickly, so they'd had a shotgun wedding, though Wendy had never felt forced.

She'd wanted it. She'd wanted to secure that life. She hadn't wanted to be a single mother. She'd found an easy man. A fun man. A happy man.

Her life had felt lacking in those things, growing up with scarcity was a feeling Wendy was very sensitive to.

Daniel had felt like excess. Excessive joy, excessive drinking, eating, happiness. She'd loved it. And when their love affair had had consequences...he'd been kind and he'd done the right thing.

He'd told her he loved her.

She'd said she loved him, because it was best if they did, and eventually she was sure she'd meant it.

And then she'd gone to the very first cowboy thing she'd ever done with him, and Boone had walked in, and it was like everything in the world had fallen away. Like something inside of her had whispered, *This is him.*

She had never in her life believed in the concept of the one. Ever. But right when Boone had come in, it was like the universe had whispered across her soul. That it was *him.*

She had never been so completely devastated by the impact of another person in all her life. He was ruinous. And glorious.

And the moment she had first seen him, she had wanted to *not* see him just as quickly.

Had wanted to go back to living a life where she had no idea Boone Carson existed in the world.

It was just easier if she didn't know.

When she was married to another man. Pregnant with that man's child.

She had told herself that all of it was silly. Boone was handsome, that was all. And she'd been surprised by the impact of him.

You didn't expect to see a normal man like that just…out and about in the world. That was all.

She was very, very good at telling herself that story.

She loved Daniel.

She had loved Daniel.

Did she still love Daniel?

Right now, she felt hollow.

She loved her daughters. She knew that much.

She let out a long, slow breath.

That was going to have to be enough, because it was going to be the thing that was driving her now.

She missed her anger.

It had been so bright and glorious and wonderful. And far too fleeting.

But it had fueled her for a while there and now she was just…

Well, she was at Boone's house.

She sucked in a sharp breath and killed the engine on the truck. She got out and the girls followed suit. Then she went around to the bed of the truck to start gathering their bags.

Boone walked out the front door.

"You made it," he said.

She stopped, and she wished she didn't feel like she'd been hit by a train, because she did. Just looking at him. She'd known him now going on fifteen years, and she couldn't understand how or why the man still did this to her.

"Yes," she said. "We did. Kind of a long drive."

"Not as far as Arizona." The corner of his mouth lifted.

She didn't smile back. "Yes." She moved to the bed of the

truck to grab her bag, but he started moving toward her pur-
posefully.

"You don't need to get anything," he said, and then he reached
into the back of the truck and plucked up her bag, her daughters' bags and a suitcase, which he lifted up over his shoulder.
"Your place is just a walk out back here," he said, gesturing
behind his grand house.

She stared at him. At the way he held all her baggage so
easily.

It was a very weird metaphor to be confronted with right in
this moment, and was it bad that she wanted him to carry it all?
Was it bad that she was tired? That she wanted him to carry her
worldly possessions in his strong arms and over his shoulders
because she was just so damned tired of…everything?

*Yes, it's bad. You need to figure out how to stand on your
own. That's your problem. You let a man carry you for too long.*

Well, that wasn't fair. Daniel hadn't carried her, but she'd
wound herself around him so tightly that cutting ties was painful.

Difficult.

But it wasn't the same as being carried.

But she figured she could also chill out and not see her lit-
eral baggage as a metaphor. Because physically Boone was
stronger than her and he knew where the house was, so why
not follow him?

"How was the drive, girls?"

"Good," said Mikey, "we played the alphabet game and also
discussed elaborate ways men should die."

"We didn't do that," said Wendy quickly.

"Wouldn't blame you if you did," said Boone.

"Not *you*, of course," Sadie said.

"Appreciate it, Sadie," Boone responded.

Boone had always had a decent rapport with the girls. It was
weird that right now it made her feel…lightheaded.

But Boone had been that fun uncle figure when he'd been

around, which had been often enough, and of course the girls enjoyed him.

It turned out their dad also thought of himself as a fun uncle. Which really didn't work when you were supposed to be a husband and father.

The path behind the house led to a cottage. It was small, with freshly planted flowers all around the front, and two hanging baskets with flowers on the porch.

It was beautiful. Small, she wondered if the girls would see it as a major downgrade. But right then...she saw it as salvation.

It was hers.

Theirs.

For now.

"Thank you," she whispered, her throat going tight.

She looked up at him, and her breath caught. His blue eyes were startling, arresting, there in the sunlight, and the way the gold played against the whiskers on his face did something to her stomach, low and intimate. His face was just...perfect. As if an artist had lovingly sculpted him by hand with the intent of making him the perfect masculine figure.

His jaw was square, his nose straight, his cheekbones so sharp she could cut herself on them. And then there was his body, which she'd spent a lot of time not contemplating and she surely wasn't doing it now, with her daughters present.

She freed the breath from the little knot in her throat and got herself together. She didn't need this kind of drama. Not now.

"This is so cute!" said Sadie, her voice going high, and the delight in her tone shocked and pleased Wendy.

"It's like a fairy house," said Mikey.

Wendy had to wonder if her daughters were being overly happy for her benefit, but then she decided she didn't care.

They'd been so supportive of her through everything.

If they'd been younger, she'd have tried to shield them. But the thing was, she'd sort of made the news.

"Scorned Wife Goes Full Carrie Underwood Song on Cheating Husband."

It was all over the country music news sites, given the rodeo circuit was sort of adjacent when it came to industry interest crossover, and also because, indeed, she had *sort of* had a certain set of song lyrics in her head when she'd driven across state lines.

Lucky for him it was more "Before He Cheats" and less "Two Black Cadillacs."

The article had actually made that point.

But because of that there had been no shielding the girls from the truth. She could have handled herself better, though she had a feeling there would have been some news about it anyway since Daniel was a minor—very minor—celebrity who both rode rodeo and had done some reality TV, so the breakup would never have stayed entirely between them.

"I'm glad you like it," Boone said.

He walked up the steps and pushed open the door and revealed a house that was immaculately put together. Everything in it was new. And she had to wonder if it had been furnished like this when he bought the place or…

She decided to stop wondering.

And just enjoy the experience.

Tomorrow she was going to get the girls off to school, and she was going to start work. She would give herself four weeks of this. Of taking Boone's help, and then she was going to need a plan. A real plan.

She was resourceful, and she was a hard worker, so she knew she would be able to come up with something. But it was hard to do when you also had deep wounds that needed a little healing.

And also had to be an adult and a mother when you just wanted to keep on being subject to the whims of your emotions. Being that woman, the one with the baseball bat, had been easier than being this woman. The one making plans and trying to hold it together.

But that was what she needed to do; it was who she needed to be.

For her girls if nothing else.

"I'll leave you to get settled," he said. "If you need anything, just give me a holler."

And then he put their things down and left them, shut in the little house that felt somehow indescribably safe, secure and... wonderful.

Like shelter from a storm she hadn't realized she'd been in.

Right now, she could rest.

Even cleaning his house for a few weeks would feel like rest.

And then she would have to figure out what to do with her life.

But until then, she was going to take the shelter he was offering. Since the man she'd made vows to had kicked her out into the elements.

So why not have this? Even just for a time.

"Why don't we get our things put away and then explore town?" she asked.

She knew Lone Rock was small, and the exploration wouldn't take long, but they needed to find some food, and a distraction would be good for everyone.

Her daughters smiled at her a little too bravely, and right then she hated Daniel. Because he'd done this to them.

"Great," she said. "This will be great."

"You did *what*?"

"I gave her a place to stay," said Boone, looking down the bar at his brother Jace, who was staring at him incredulously. His sister-in-law Cara leaned over the bar and stared at him as if she was waiting for more details.

"What, Cara?" he asked. "There's nothing to say."

"I don't believe that," she said. "The whole breakup was headline news, and he's your best friend."

"He is *not* my best friend," said Boone. "I *was* friends with him. More importantly, I was friends with the man I *thought* he was. But I didn't think he was out there betraying his wife every week out on the road."

"You really didn't know?" Chance, his other brother, who was seated next to his wife, Juniper, asked.

"No," he said.

And he left off the part about how he'd never *wanted* to know because it wasn't simple and never could be.

"Sounds unlikely," said Shelby, his other sister-in-law, from beside her husband.

Shelby and Kit had recently had a baby, but Boone's mother was always so happy to babysit that the happy couple could go out whenever they wanted. And were practically forced out by the well-meaning grandma even when they didn't want to go.

All his siblings—except Buck, as far as he knew—were coupled up now. And the only couples *not* present were his younger sister Callie and her husband, Jake, who lived out of town, and his brother Flint and his wife, Tansey, who was a famous country singer currently on tour. Flint was with her.

Talk about revenge songs, Tansey had written a hell of a song about her and Flint's first go-round that had made him infamous. Flint would probably have measured words for the whole situation since he knew how the media could whip up personal issues.

But Flint wasn't here, so no one was being measured.

"Good for her, I say," Shelby said to her husband. "But I'd leave your truck intact and take it. Your dick on the other hand…"

"Same," said Juniper.

It served his brothers right for marrying sisters who were as pretty as they were badass. Boone loved them. He loved it even more when they gave his brothers hell. His brothers seemed to get something out of it too.

His brothers had all married pretty badass women.

Bar owner Cara was no shrinking violet. And Tansey, well

she'd gotten rich with her revenge, and made his brother infamous in the process.

He thought of Wendy and how fragile she'd looked today. He'd wanted to tell her he'd done all that for her. The flowers, the new paint, the new furniture. He also hadn't wanted to say a damned thing because he didn't want her to think she owed him, and he didn't want her to thank him for something a man ought to just do for her because she was there and breathing and *her*.

He didn't want to do anything to crack her open when she was working so hard at holding it all together.

She was badass too. Hell yeah, she was.

She'd smashed the hell out of Daniel's truck.

But she was also wounded. And she needed to be taken care of.

He couldn't say he'd ever had experience with that, but if he was going to push the boat out on caregiving it was going to be now and it was going to be her.

"Did it really go down like they said?" Jace asked.

"It did," he confirmed. "But if you see her around, don't ask her about it."

Cara snorted. "We aren't feral."

Jace gave her a long look. "Well…"

"Okay, but we do know how to behave and not hurt people's feelings," Cara said.

"I know," Boone said. "But she's not going to be here forever. I'll talk to her more tomorrow about her plans."

Because if there was one thing Boone was certain of, it was that no matter how much he might want it to be, this couldn't be forever.

He might love her. He did love her.

But she was still married, and he didn't have the first clue how to…

He'd never had a real relationship, and there was no way this would ever be what she needed.

She had kids.

He had a ranch, which was a step into adulthood, but he didn't know how to do feelings and all that. It was one thing to carry a torch for a woman he couldn't have.

He was good with not having her.

One thing he wouldn't do was leave her uncared for.

He would make sure everything in her life was set to go just as she needed it to be, and then he'd let her go, because it would be the kindest thing.

She didn't need another project.

He wouldn't be the cause of any more pain for her.

If he was certain of anything in this world, it was that.

"She's with you?"

He regretted answering his phone as he walked out of the bar.

"Yes," said Boone. "And if I see you, I'll run you right off my property."

"What the hell, Boone? I thought we were friends."

"And I thought you were a husband, but it turns out you're just a little boy who can't control his dick."

"Boone… I'm sorry, I have to get her back. I royally screwed this up. I can't live without her and the kids."

The change in tone did nothing to sway Boone. Because he just didn't care. He wondered if Wendy would, though. Daniel was the father of her kids and all that. Boone didn't have kids, and the thought didn't sway or soften him at all. But he figured that could be because it was a connection he didn't especially get.

It maybe wasn't up to him to decide that Daniel should never speak to Wendy again. But he wasn't going to facilitate it, that was for damned sure.

"You should have thought of that before you cheated. Extensively, from what I understand."

"It was separate to me," he said. "I never thought of it interfering with what we had as long as she never knew. When I was home, I was always with her."

And I'm with her every time I'm with anyone.
I'm with her when I'm home. When I'm on the road.
Always.

He didn't say any of that. But he wanted to jump through the phone and strangle Daniel.

"She deserves better than you," Boone said, his voice rough.

"What? She deserves you?"

And that cut him deep because right then he knew Daniel wasn't as oblivious as he pretended to be. He only played like it when it suited him.

But of course he couldn't be as dumb as he played. He was a pretty big success and that didn't come on accident.

"No," Boone said. "But she does deserve someone who's honest with her."

"Is that why you brought her out to your place? Have you been screwing my wife, Boone?"

"When the hell would your wife have time to screw around on you, Daniel? She's busy raising your kids and holding your life together. Say what you want about me, slander me all you want, but don't project your bullshit onto her."

Boone hung up then.

He shouldn't have, maybe.

Because if Daniel was going to make up a story about him and Wendy it would probably only be reinforced by him hanging up like that.

But he just didn't care to speak to that asshole for another second.

He couldn't bear it.

Instead, he drove home, and when the phone rang again, he ignored it.

Chapter Three

The alarm went off too early and Wendy wondered at the wisdom of making the girls start school right away. Or at all.

If they were only going to be here a month…

But maybe they'd stay in Lone Rock for longer. Or maybe not. But it would be normal for them to have a school day and ultimately, that was what she wanted. For them to have something that felt normal.

She couldn't promise them a long time here, or forever or anything close to that, but she could give them something that felt like childhood.

She'd discovered last night that the fridge was fully stocked, and she wondered who had done all this. Boone? It didn't seem likely since he'd said he needed a house cleaner and had acted like he couldn't perform basic tasks without help because he was so slammed with setting up the new ranch.

Maybe one of his sisters-in-law had helped.

She'd have to thank someone for it. For the miracle of waking up to having coffee in the house and having bacon and eggs to fix the girls.

And she really didn't count on Boone showing up right when they were about to walk out the door.

"I thought, if you'd like, I could drive you because I know the way to both schools."

And she could have figured it out with GPS, she knew, but she very dangerously wanted to take this easier option.

Couldn't she? For just right now?

"Okay, if…if the girls don't mind."

"Sure," said Sadie, casually.

Because why would she care? This was definitely Wendy's issue, not her kids'.

"Yeah," Mikey said, reinforcing that thought.

The girls climbed into the back seats of the crew cab pickup, and Wendy got into the passenger seat. Suddenly, when he closed the door, the cab felt tiny, and she tried to remember if she'd ever been in such close proximity to Boone before.

She hadn't. She'd remember.

She did remember being at Juniper and Chance's wedding, because Daniel knew Chance from the rodeo and they'd been invited, and it had an open bar, he'd joked. She'd been sure then that he really wanted to support his friend's love and happiness. Now she thought it might have really been about the bar.

She remembered Daniel being out drinking and being alone at the big wedding reception.

She remembered looking up and seeing Boone. Looking at her.

Not just looking at her, though, it had been something hotter. Something deeper.

It had stolen her breath and made it impossible to breathe.

It had made her feel…

She had to stop thinking about that now.

She had to.

She kept her eyes fixed on the two-lane road and tried not to let the silence in the truck swallow her whole.

"Well, if you need anything or you need me to come get you, you can text me," she said, addressing both her daughters with an edgy desperation because she needed something to take over her awkwardness, even if it was a random comment she hadn't needed to make.

"Thanks, Mom. I'm sure we'll be fine," said Sadie.

"Or we won't be," Mikey said. "And it will either be a story of great triumph of the human spirit, or our villain origin story."

"I think we know which one it would be for you, Mikey," Boone said.

"Villain, for sure," Mikey said, happily.

The middle school came first.

As they drove away after Mikey got out, Wendy was struck by a feeling of loss and a sense of weird wrongness. She always felt that after summer break, and apparently a new school did that to her too. This weird feeling that she was leaving her kids with strangers. They weren't strangers. She'd had video meetings with the teachers before they'd come here, and the kids had had a chance to meet them too. But it didn't make it feel less weird.

She had the same feeling after dropping Sadie off.

But it was replaced instantly by the electric shock of realizing she was alone with Boone.

Alone with Boone, without her wedding rings. Without her kids.

Without anything keeping her from…

"So, what do you need done today?" she asked, because filling the horrible silence with words, any words, was all she knew to do.

"Oh, I'm easy," he said, slow and lazy and she felt it between her legs.

What was wrong with her?

Was this a trauma response to discovering her husband was a ho?

She would be able to write it off as that much more easily if Boone wasn't a preexisting condition.

Something that made her feel, deep down, like maybe she'd deserved for Daniel to betray her.

The thought made her feel like she'd been stabbed.

She hadn't realized she'd been holding on to that feeling. But she had been. Deep down.

She'd been attracted to Boone for years, and she'd done her best to avoid him. Not that avoidance had done anything to make the feelings go away.

She'd done her best to keep it hidden.

Maybe Daniel had known, though, that part of her had always been tangled up in Boone.

She needed to stop thinking about that.

Why did you come to him, then? Knowing it was this complicated, why did you choose this?

Because he'd offered.

That was all.

It was never all. It was never that simple with him.

She took a sharp breath. "I just want to make sure that I'm paying you back, because you're being so kind to me and…"

Tears welled up in her eyes and she hated that. Now she was crying? What was happening to her?

Why couldn't she just take what he'd offered, which had been work. And she'd been grateful he'd done it that way because if he'd just given her a place to stay it would have felt loaded, and like charity she couldn't afford to take, and he hadn't done that because he'd known. She knew he had known. That she couldn't take his charity, that she had to earn this fresh start.

That she couldn't feel like she owed him.

So why was she now falling into crying like it was a favor? Like it was personal.

They were both trying so hard to not make it that and now she'd gone and made it very, very weird, and she couldn't stop her throat from tightening, couldn't stop a tear from falling.

She hadn't cried.

Not once.

She'd gone from rage to determination and she didn't want to weep now. But it was the kindness of it all.

From a man she'd love to call just another rodeo cowboy.

A man she'd love to lump in with her husband.

But she just couldn't do that.

"I need to know what you want," she said, trying to get a handle on her emotions. Her breath. Everything. "Because you offered me work, and I do know how to keep house. Do you need a meal? Do you need something organized?"

"I just moved in, and there are a lot of things yet to unpack."

But the little cottage was perfectly set up.

"I can do that if you don't mind me deciding where things go."

"As long as you tell me where they end up, I don't mind."

"Okay, so what do you like to eat?"

"If you want to make me dinner I won't complain but do something you and the girls like and just make an extra portion."

She almost wished he was being high-handed. So she could get ahold of herself.

The kindness was almost too much.

You really can't be pleased.

Well, maybe in her position that was fair?

They pulled up to the house, and she realized she hadn't been conscious of where they were at all.

He killed the engine, but didn't get out of the car, and she did something foolish. Very foolish.

She turned her head and looked at him.

And it was like all the space around them became less. Like it contracted and sank beneath her skin. Shrinking around her lungs, her heart, her stomach. She couldn't breathe. She couldn't think.

She could only see Boone.

His blue eyes.

That moment at his brother's wedding when they'd seen each other across the room was suddenly alive again in her memory. Because they'd seen each other that night. They hadn't simply looked at each other for a moment across a crowded space.

The two things were different.

They were so different.

She hadn't truly realized it until now.

She tried to breathe, but she couldn't. Because everything in her was too tight. Too bound up in him.

Bound up in him...

And that did it. Like scissors cutting a string. Everything in her released.

Because she'd thought about being tied up in someone just recently.

It was the very way she'd thought about her relationship with Daniel.

She hadn't left to get tied up again.

She couldn't afford that, not ever.

She found herself practically dumping herself out of his truck, her boots connecting with the dirt and sending a cloud of dust up around her.

"I'll go get changed and then start work," she said, trying to sound bright, and like nothing had happened.

"Okay," he said. "Do you need me to show you the lay of things?"

"No. No you go ahead and get started on your day." She didn't want to wander around the house with him.

She wished she could pretend.

She wished she could pretend that her strange moments of attraction were indigestion. Or at the very least that they were infrequent, or one-sided.

But if she'd ever been able to trick herself into thinking her attraction to Boone wasn't mutual, he'd destroyed that with a glance the night of his brother's wedding.

Because that moment had contained so much deep truth, she'd had to turn away from it.

Because that moment had been filled with an acknowledgment they'd both spent fifteen years turning away from.

They'd been two seconds of prolonged eye contact away from

admitting it, for all those years. Never speaking of it wasn't enough. Because their eyes were determined to give them away.

Then the hitch in their breath.

And Boone...

She remembered him looking like the big bad wolf and the savior of the universe all at once. She'd wanted him to take a step toward her, and she'd wanted him to turn away. She'd wanted him to come for her, and she'd wanted to pretend she'd never even met him.

He'd taken a step.

And she'd taken one back.

And he'd stopped.

He'd listened to her. To everything she couldn't say. To the single footstep that had been her begging him to stop. To not take them another step further because it would be too far to turn back, and she'd wanted—she'd needed—to be able to turn back.

Just like she'd needed to jump out of the truck now, and he'd let her. She appreciated that.

The way he listened, even when she didn't speak.

"I'll just... I'll just go change," she said again. "And then I'll get started."

His face was like granite. Like at the wedding. "Okay. See you later."

She couldn't have made it any clearer that she didn't want him in her space today. She also couldn't have made it any clearer that she was attracted to him.

Attracted was a crucial descriptor. Because it was different from wanting.

He wanted her.

He wanted to take her into his arms and kiss her. He wanted to take her to his room and strip her naked and have his way with her.

He wanted her.

Like breathing.

More of a need than anything else.

She was attracted to him, and she did not want it. Not at all.

And he...well, he knew his place here. He was helping her. He cared about her, dammit all. And he was far too familiar with the fallout that happened when people didn't fulfill their obligations to the ones they were supposed to love.

She'd trusted Daniel and he'd betrayed that trust. Boone would never do that. He would never put her in a position where she felt obligated to him.

That wasn't why he was helping her.

He never shirked his responsibilities. Not ever.

He didn't leave people to fend for themselves.

That might be his oldest brother's way, it might be Daniel's way. But it would never be Boone's.

Some people might live in a fantasy world, and others lived with their heads up their asses. Not Boone. He was a realist, and he handled things. He didn't need to lie to himself or anyone else to get through life.

He'd been like that once. Someone who couldn't face the hard truths. It caused more harm than good, that was for sure.

He thought about that, a whole lot. The lines between attraction, desire, want, need and feelings. Obligation. All while he worked. Mostly he thought about her. Because she was in that house behind his, and it was the kind of proximity he'd wanted with her for a long time.

His phone buzzed in his pocket.

He pulled it out and saw Daniel's name again. "What?" he growled.

"Can you just ask her what I can do?"

"If she isn't answering your calls then there's not shit I can do for you."

"We went through hell together, Boone. Who was there for you when you were crying drunk over your brother taking off, huh? When you were the one who had to deal with your mama's broken heart because her firstborn ran off, after all the pain she went through losing her baby girl…"

"Don't talk about my family," he said. "Yeah, you were there for me when Buck ran off, I'll give you that. You were there when I was feeling squeezed by the family obligation he left for me, but here's what you're missing, Dan. Buck and I will never have a relationship again because he had a duty to this family, and he chose himself instead. I don't like it when people mis-use and mistreat people in their lives. When they fall down on their obligations. I can't respect weak men, and if you don't live up to your responsibilities, you're a weak man." He breathed out, hard, and his breath was visible in the early evening air. "You're a weak man, Daniel Stevens."

Then he hung up, because honestly.

He got into his truck and drove back toward the house. It had been a long day of chasing up permits at the county, mak-ing arrangements with contractors and going over the sections of land he could use for grazing, what he could irrigate and a host of other things.

Setting up the ranch wasn't going to be easy. But until his dad retired…

Well, he supposed he'd be taking over as rodeo commis-sioner in a few years. And he had to do something until then. Maybe after that he'd do what his dad had always done and hire out workers.

Buck had been the one who was supposed to do all this.

But Buck was gone.

Boone knew his brother had been through some shit, he did. But it was no excuse. At least not in his mind.

Even if you were going through something, you should be there for the people in your life. Your responsibilities didn't just…go away.

He'd told his brother that, the night before his brother had split town for good. Buck had been drinking, far too much. Like alcohol would erase the accident he'd been in. Like it might take away the horror of that night.

And Boone had snapped.

"You have a family, and you aren't dead. Stop acting like you're six feet in the ground with your friends. You aren't."

"It should have..."

"It wasn't! You're alive. Have some gratitude and get back to it. You have responsibilities."

And then he'd gone.

Boone had felt guilty about his brother leaving until he'd realized guilt was a waste of time. Time he didn't have to waste. It had been Buck's choice to leave. It was Boone's choice to deal with it.

There was no use getting lost in what-ifs.

Boone knew, from the outside looking in, people would probably think of him as a guy who didn't take much seriously.

They saw a cocky bull rider who could have a different buckle bunny every night when he was in the mood for that. They didn't see he was the one who held his mom while she wept on difficult anniversaries.

He was the one who took the brunt of their father's expectations onto his shoulders as the de facto oldest in the absence of the eldest son who had gone off to lick his wounds. A car accident the year Buck graduated high school had resulted in the loss of three of his friends, with Buck as the sole survivor.

It wasn't that Boone didn't get why that had fucked him up.

It was just...

They were all a little messed up. They'd watched their baby sister die when they were kids. So why not band together? Why not try to support each other?

That was what he'd never understood.

They'd been a support system, the Carson Clan, and never as close or as stable once Buck had taken his support away.

But his issues weren't the order of the day.

Today Boone wanted to make sure that Wendy was doing all right.

He pulled up to the front of the house and he smiled, just a little bit, when he saw the lights on in the kitchen. He wondered what it would be like to come home to her, and then he pushed that aside because it was a pointless little fantasy, and if he was going to have a fantasy it was going to be a big, dirty one, not a little domestic one about her in an apron holding a casserole pan.

Except he wouldn't even let himself have a dirty fantasy about her, not right now. She was too vulnerable, and he wasn't that guy. Not when her husband had proven to be such a horndog.

He wouldn't even go there in his head.

He walked up the front steps and into the warmth. This was his house. His home. He hadn't had one before, not really. It had been a place on his parents' property, and places on the road all these years, and it was all fine and good, but there was something surreal about walking into something permanent.

Nothing is permanent, Boone.

Yeah, he knew that. Not relationships with older brothers, or little sisters, or anything.

You couldn't trust a damned thing.

But when he walked in his house it smelled like heaven. And his kitchen was empty.

There was a plate sitting on the counter with foil over the top, and he assumed she'd done the cooking here, but took the rest back to her place and then vacated before his return which… was about right.

Attracted. Not wanting.

He lifted the corner of the tin foil and his stomach growled when the smell of roast and vegetables hit him.

Wendy might not be here, but a home-cooked meal was a close second. And when it made his mouth water, he could have it. So, there was that.

He opened the drawer in the kitchen island and took out a fork, and hunched over the counter, taking bites of food. And then there was a knock at the door.

His stomach went tight, and his heart did something he couldn't recall it doing before except when he was about to ride a bull in competition. "It's open," he said, around a piece of roast, and without moving from his spot.

"I didn't know if you'd be here yet or not."

Wendy. And she was lying. Because she'd probably seen him come in and that was why she was here. Because she'd wanted to avoid him. Except she didn't really.

He could relate.

She came into the kitchen, and she was holding a plate with something on it, but he couldn't look away from her for long enough to take in what it was. She was wearing pink. The same shade as the dress she'd had on at the wedding.

Her blond hair was in a ponytail, and she had on just a little makeup. Her cheeks were the same color as her dress, and so were her lips. Like a strawberry fantasy just for him.

Even though she wasn't for him.

There was something about it that made him want her more, and he had to wonder if that was just his body pushing back at years of being good.

Very few people would characterize Boone Carson as good. He understood that and he understood why.

Again, it was the bull riding, drinking, carousing, and on and on. But they didn't see all the shit he did *not* do. Like turn away from hardship in his family. Like running away. Like kissing his best friend's wife at his brother's wedding.

He deserved a damned Boy Scout patch.

Did Not Fuck My Friend's Wife.

Also knot tying.

He was good at knot tying.

He didn't get credit for the things he deserved to.

"I baked a cake over at the cottage while the girls and I had dinner, so I figured I'd bring you some."

Oh. Cake. That's what it was. He could see it now, even if it was fuzzy at the edges because he'd rather look at her hands holding the platter than at what was on it. But she'd made it, so he would eat it.

"Are you really eating standing hunched over a counter like a rabid wolf?"

"I don't think rabid wolves eat pot roast, I think they eat pretty women carrying cake."

He shouldn't flirt with her. But her cheeks turned pinker. So he considered that a win.

"Maybe just a regular wolf, then."

He grinned, making sure to flash his teeth. "Hard to say."

"You should sit down. There are studies on how you shouldn't eat standing up."

"Are there?"

"I'm pretty sure. It's something I'd say to my kids, anyway."

"Oh, well, then, I guess I'll consider myself chastened."

She glared at him. "I don't think you are."

"No. You need shame to feel chastened, I think."

"And you don't have any shame?"

He made sure to grin even wider. "None whatsoever."

If only that were true.

If only he didn't care so damned much about doing the right thing, and at this point it had nothing at all to do with Daniel. It was about her.

And that was immovable, as far as he was concerned.

"I really…" She closed her eyes for a moment, and he looked at how her lashes fanned out over her high cheekbones and felt a bit like his heart had lifted to the base of his throat, and his lungs right along with it. "I appreciate you doing this," she said, opening her eyes, letting out a breath.

It was like she released his breath along with it.

Then she walked over to the kitchen island and set the cake

plate on it. There was nothing more than a slim length of counter between them now.

She put her hands on the counter and examined them.

He did too.

Her hands, not his.

"Why wouldn't I?"

"Daniel has been your friend for longer than you've known me," she said. "You didn't take his side."

"There's no side here," he said. "To be very clear, I was done with him the minute I...that night, before you got there, he kissed another woman. I had never seen that before, I swear to you. And I looked the other way, I'll admit that. There were things I didn't want to know, because..." This was dangerous ground. They both knew it. "You know why."

"Do I?" she asked.

The words were too loud in the silent kitchen, even though they were practically a whisper.

"Yes," he said. "You do."

He cleared his throat. And took another bite of roast. Then he looked at her again. "I tried to keep myself out of your marriage. But I wouldn't have after I saw that, okay? I want you to understand. I was outright done with him the minute I knew he wasn't faithful to you. I told him so today."

"You...talked to him?" Her blue eyes went round.

"Yeah. He called. He wants you back."

She laughed. "Of course he does. I cook, clean and manage his career. I am an idiot who devoted years of my life to him and gave him two kids and asked for very little and when he wasn't with me, he was able to pretend I didn't exist. Who wouldn't want that woman back?"

She shook her head. "I'm not going to be her anymore."

He didn't have any place in this. Didn't have the right to lecture her, but he was going to do it anyway.

"Don't blame yourself. I didn't see it either. Like I said, I had some suspicions I shouldn't hang around and watch to see what he did with his evenings, but that's different than actually believing someone is a serial cheater. It's about him, and what he thinks about the people around him. How much he values them. Not how much value they have."

"Thank you, Boone," she said, though she didn't look at him when she said his name.

How many times had they circled each other like this?

There were so many moments over the years.

So many barbecues where they talked with a table between them and very little eye contact. So many rodeo events where Daniel would leave to get a drink and they'd be standing there, and it was like electricity. But the thing was, they'd never moved toward it.

They both knew it was there.

And that was the most unfair thing of all.

Daniel was the kind of guy who'd hump a table leg. He strayed just because he could.

Boone wanted Wendy in a way that went beyond anything normal, average or everyday. What he felt for her had been instant. It had been ruinous.

It had destroyed something in him he'd never built back up.

Desire like that wasn't common. It wasn't typical.

And the man standing in their way, the man who was still in their way because of the position he'd put Wendy in…didn't deserve the label of roadblock because he wasn't important enough. Because she hadn't meant enough to him.

What they'd resisted for the sake of responsibility was something you could write a song about.

And Daniel didn't resist a damned thing.

But even without any loyalty left to him, Wendy was facing starting over, with her girls. She was in Boone's care, and Boone would never take advantage of that.

"You're welcome. I promise when I eat the cake I'll sit down."

She did look at him then. "Good."

He started to move around the side of the island, he didn't

even think about it, but then he watched her eyes get round,
watched her posture go stiff, and he stopped.

If he got too close to her...

"Good night," he said, firmly.

"Good night."

Attraction wasn't the same as wanting.

He had to remember that.

Chapter Four

She felt breathless still the next morning, and all the way through taking the girls to school, and definitely when she walked cautiously into Boone's house to begin the day's chores.

There was quite a bit to do because the man wasn't settled into his house at all. There were boxes to unpack and things to organize and it was nice to lose herself in the satisfaction of a small task, easily completed in a short amount of time. Each little section—kitchen utensils, plates, cups, clothes, toiletries—was its own kind of satisfying.

It was also intimate, though, and she had to stop herself from running her fingers slowly over his T-shirts as she put them away.

Which was perverse behavior and she needed to quit.

She needed to focus on the fact that at least today, right now, there were small things she could make better.

Because Lord knew everything else felt like too big of a mess to even look at right now. So she closed the door on what she'd left behind, and what was up ahead, and she focused on folding Boone Carson's laundry.

That should demystify him.

He was the sexiest man she'd ever seen, and when he'd looked at her last night across the kitchen island and taken a step toward her, in the space of a breath she'd gone from being in that moment, to imagining what it would be like if he took her in his arms and...

Folding his socks should make that go away.

It was all fine and good to look at a man and think he was a sex god when you weren't handling his woolen boot socks.

Though here she was, socks in hand, still breathless.

This should be exposure therapy. She and Boone had had no choice but to try and avoid each other through the years. There were moments where she'd felt guilty for sharing a long look with him, because sometimes those looks were so sexually charged, they left her feeling more aroused than actual sex with Daniel.

It was a terrible thing to admit—or at least it had been.

And so she'd done her best to avoid ever acknowledging that sticky truth.

Part of her had wondered, though, if some of his appeal was that he was a fantasy. Daniel had always seemed affable and easy. She'd never thought of her husband as a bad boy—ironic—but Boone had seemed...edgy.

Raw.

There was something about him that called to unhealed places in her. To darkness she'd never felt like she could express with Daniel. He wanted his life to be easy. They had money and security in the grand scheme of things, so he didn't much want to hear about the way hunger pangs sometimes gave her flashbacks to a childhood of occasionally empty pantries.

How she'd had to mend the holes in her hand-me-down clothes.

How she'd spent her summer days alone in an overheated house because her mom had to work and there was nowhere else for her to go.

How, on those long hot days, she'd gotten good at hiding when the landlord came trying to chase down rent.

Daniel didn't like to hear about those things. They didn't matter. They were in the past.

She'd thought—more than once—that Daniel couldn't handle the idea that there were issues inside her that weren't solved by being married to him. He wanted to be everything to her. To have fixed everything.

It had never really occurred to her what narcissistic nonsense that was until that very moment, with Boone's wool socks in her hand.

She thought of Boone. The way he had looked last night. Intense and close. He was always intense. But there was usually something between them. Something other than a countertop. Her marriage. Her dedication to her vows. Her love for her husband. Because for all that she had wanted Boone from the first moment she had laid eyes on him, for all that it had felt significant and real and like something bigger than she was the first time she'd seen him, she had always loved Daniel.

She sat there, feeling the silence of the room pressing on her. Did she love Daniel?

No.

And it wasn't the infidelity that had done it.

Suddenly, it was like the truth was raining down on her, as if invisible clouds above had opened up and let it all come down.

They had been disconnected for a long time. She loved her life. She had loved their house in Bakersfield, even though it was hot there. Even though there was a big empty field across from them.

She had loved her routine of taking the girls to school. Of bringing them home. Cooking them dinner. She loved the freedom she had, the financial security that had come from his career as a bull rider and the way she had managed it. She had loved that her daughters didn't have empty pantries and long days at home by themselves. In that sense, she had been the happiest she'd ever been. But she didn't think she had been the happiest she'd ever been when he was home. It wasn't that she'd been unhappy when he was around, she just didn't think he was the main part of that happiness.

When he was away she could do whatever she wanted. She got to binge-watch TV shows and wear ratty pajamas. She had ice cream out of the carton and she took up the middle of the bed.

She was content with her fantasy life when he was away, and she didn't mind being by herself.

And none of those things were signs in and of themselves that she didn't love her husband. It was only that she could be a little bit more honest in this moment than she'd been able to in those first couple of days. She wasn't heartbroken. She had felt deeply wounded by the fact that she had lost her life. That she had lost these things she cared about so deeply. That her life had been compromised and shaken.

That she was thrown back into the space where she didn't know how she was going to survive. And she had never wanted her daughters to experience that.

She had never wanted them to feel any instability, and she was the most upset about that. And being betrayed. That had been a knife wound straight to her chest. That had been unconscionable. She really and truly hated it. She didn't like that she had been lying next to a man, making love to a man, telling a man she loved him, while he was able to take those hands, that mouth, that body and make love to another woman.

She would never have cheated on him. Not ever. She would've coasted along in this marriage that functioned primarily because…

Even though she had never betrayed him, she was in many ways functioning as a single woman when he was gone. And she had a feeling that was part of why their marriage had worked as well as it had.

He pretended she didn't exist when he was away, and she sort of did the same to him.

That didn't make her feel guilty, it just made her recognize that some fundamental things were missing from her marriage. And maybe that was why Boone had loomed so large in her fantasies.

She had done her best—her very best—to never fantasize about Boone.

She was *attracted* to him. But she didn't lie in bed when Daniel was away and think about Boone intentionally when she lay there and put her hands on her own body while imagining they were his.

Now sometimes he popped into her head, and she replaced him with Captain America because it was totally fine to fantasize about a man you weren't married to, but he really should be a man you also didn't know in real life. At least, that had been her arbitrary set of rules.

Every woman needed an arbitrary set of rules.

She did not need to follow those rules now.

Daniel had rendered them void.

That made her feel hot. She shifted, and she put Boone's socks down a little bit too quickly. Yes, she could fantasize about Boone now if she wanted to.

She didn't love her husband.

Suddenly, she felt dizzy. She didn't know if she was elated or if she was crushed by that realization. But she had been living a life she hadn't intended to find herself in. Daniel's betrayal was not the biggest issue with her marriage.

The problem was, they had met and they had fallen in love quickly. And Wendy had always been guarded. But he had gotten through her defenses with his charm. She hadn't been one for casual sex. She'd been waiting, and not because of any great moral reason, but because she was afraid.

He had gotten past all of that, and when he had asked her to marry him two months into their affair, she'd said yes. She didn't have anything else. Her mother had passed away the previous year, and she'd just felt so alone. So being with someone... To make a family, she had loved that.

And she had to wonder how much of it had always been loving that. Loving that she had someone. Someone she was attracted to, someone she genuinely liked—most of the time—but perhaps someone she had never actually been head over heels in love with.

She didn't want him back. She wanted the stability back. She wanted to be comfortable. But...

But if she were being perfectly honest with herself, she was thinking about more than comfort. That moment with Boone in the kitchen last night had been so electrically charged. And the way he had responded to it was... It was unlike anything else she had ever experienced.

Because he had been watching her. And more than that, he had seen her. He had responded to the way she had stiffened up, the way she had resisted.

And it was only because she knew if he had gotten any closer she would've kissed him. And more than that, she knew the minute she and Boone touched it was never going to stop at a simple meeting of mouths. Their clothes would be off instantly, and...

That terrified her. Because she was trying to start over, and she was trying to find something new. Because once she had imagined herself in love with a man because she had been at a crossroads in her life, because she had been afraid and insecure. Because she had thought it would be preferable to grab hold of the first man she slept with rather than be by herself.

And she didn't want to go from one relationship straight into another.

It doesn't have to be a relationship...

Now she really was being an idiot. She had to stop thinking about that. She had to.

She picked the socks back up and started folding again, and then she heard a sound downstairs. She stood up from the bed, the socks still clutched in her hand, and went down the hall, looking over the rail of the staircase down to the front door below.

Boone was in the doorway. He looked up at her, a cowboy hat placed firmly on his head. And right now, at this point in her life, the sight of a cowboy certainly shouldn't make her tremble.

"Hi," she said.

"Hi, yourself."

"What are you doing here?"

"I decided to come back for lunch today."

"Oh. Let me… I'll make something for you."

"You don't have to do that."

"I'm not taking charity from you," she said.

"I didn't ask you to."

"All I'm doing is very slowly folding your laundry," she said, holding up his socks.

"All right. Well, I hate to interrupt the very serious business of sock folding. But if you really want to make me a sandwich…"

"I really do."

She went down the stairs, and every step she took closer to him made her heart start to beat just a little harder.

Damn that man.

And damn her for being so…thrilled by it. She felt like a teenager. The kind of teenager she had never been. Because she had never indulged in flirtations, and she had certainly never experienced that wild, reckless feeling she heard people describe when they were in situations where no one was there to stop them from doing something stupid.

She felt it now. There was nothing to stop her from closing the space between them and wrapping her arms around his neck. There was nothing to stop her from touching him.

Nothing. Except for good sense. And the fact that there was no way she could carry on a physical-only affair under the watchful eyes of her far-too-perceptive daughters.

And there was no way she was going to put them through something like that when their lives had just been upended.

So yeah. Nothing stopping her.

It made her want to laugh.

She had behaved for her mother, of course, who had been deeply afraid of her becoming a single mom and struggling the way she had.

And now she had to behave herself for her daughters. Caught in between a mother-daughter relationship always, she supposed.

It can be a secret.

No. They would figure it out. That was just asking for the kind of sitcom hijinks she did not want to be embroiled in anymore. She'd reached her limit. Dirty pictures being texted to her of her husband's affair, and her busting out his headlights, were either a police procedural or high comedy, depending on how you looked at it, and she wanted no part of either.

"What's for dinner tonight?" he asked.

"Spaghetti," she answered.

He grinned, and she felt like he'd touched her.

She looked away and beat a wide path around him to the kitchen.

"I could get used to this," he said.

"I probably shouldn't stay more than a month," she said, reiterating what she'd told him before. On the phone. Before she had agreed to come.

"The cottage is awfully nice, and it's there for you as long as you want. Don't feel the need to move on quickly."

"I don't think I can stay for too long. I don't want to get… dependent."

"Is that really why?"

"That is the only reason we should discuss."

He nodded slowly. And she could see he was holding back. It was a strange thing to say. Because Boone was strong, and he was fearless. Because she'd watched him ride in the rodeo before, and he wasn't a man who ever hesitated. But there he was, holding back. And she knew it wasn't because of him. It was because of her.

Because he cared about how what he might say affected her.

And that touched her deeper than just about anything. Because she'd been married to a man who hadn't given a second thought to how his actions would affect her.

To what she felt, to what she cared about.

Boone cared.

"There's not a *should* anymore," she said.

Except there were. So many. And they both knew it.

"What's that code for?"

"Say what you're thinking."

"Be very sure," he said.

"I'm sure."

"You don't want to stay because you're afraid of what will happen between us."

She felt like a layer of her skin had been peeled away, but she nodded slowly. "Maybe."

"I don't think there's any maybe about it. It's been two days, Wendy. Two days and I swear to God if I come too close to you…"

"I know." She was suddenly desperate for him to stop talking. And she realized now why he held back.

"I won't, though, is the thing. I need you to know that. I recognize that what he did to you is going to have you messed up for a while. I don't want to be part of that. I don't want to be part of this… Hurting you. I don't especially want to have anything to do with him. You understand that?"

"Yes," she said.

"I would never do anything to take advantage of you right now. Or ever."

His words were raw. And the most real thing she had heard in so long. After so much bullshit.

"I appreciate that."

It was such a weak statement. And it didn't tell the whole truth. Or even part of it. *Appreciate* wasn't the right word for him. It never could be. It was much, much too insipid.

She felt torn apart looking at him. And mostly, it was regret. Regret that she couldn't afford to feel. Because she had the life she had. And the truth was, without Daniel in it, it was so good. She had Sadie, and Mikey, and they were wonderful. She would figure out what to do, and it wouldn't always be a struggle. She had confidence in herself now, confidence she didn't have when she'd been younger, and it hadn't been given to her by Daniel, so it couldn't be taken away by him.

She couldn't regret those things. And yet, she looked back on that moment when she had first seen Boone, and she felt… pain. This deep wish that she could go back in time with two doors in front of her. Two men. That she could walk toward one and not the other. If only those moments had joined up. If only they had been side-by-side.

If only Daniel hadn't been first.

But then she might not have confidence because of him, but she had made the steps she'd made in life in part because of her relationship with him, and she could never take him away and expect that she could have been the same person she was now.

So regret was pointless. But appreciation wasn't the right word either.

Because Boone made her feel bruised. And swollen with need. All kinds of it. And she felt…tired. And where before that exhaustion had made her want to let Boone carry her bags, carry her burdens, now it made her want to let her guard down. Because it just took so much strength to be near him and not get nearer. She hadn't realized how much strength it had taken all these years, but they were closer now. Closer than they'd ever allowed themselves to be, and that created a situation, or rather it exposed one she hadn't fully realized she'd been in.

She went to the fridge, and she got some mayonnaise. Some lunch meat. Then she got bread and tomatoes. And she began the very mundane work of making the man a sandwich. This was on the heels of having done the very mundane work of his laundry. She had none of the excitement with him. None of the electricity. And all of the chores.

And that should demystify him. It should make this feel as bland and dry as appreciation. As thanks for helping her out, and nothing more.

She got a knife out of the drawer and she began to spread mayonnaise on a piece of wheat bread. Truly, what could be more boring?

"I like a little mustard on that."

"Oh," she said.

She turned back to the fridge and opened it again, hunting around for the mustard.

"You said you wanted to make me a sandwich."

"I do."

"But you don't want me to tell you how I want a sandwich?"

"I didn't say that."

"But you're annoyed."

"I'm not annoyed."

Maybe she was. Maybe she had kind of wanted to intuitively guess exactly what he wanted on his sandwich. She blinked. That was a very odd thing to want. A strange thing to worry about.

"Listen," he said. "At the end of the day, I would probably like it however you wanted to make it. But if you want a little instruction…"

"Who says that I like to take instruction?"

"I'm sure you don't."

And here they were, standing in the man's kitchen in the middle of the day. The sunlight streaming in through the window. There was no sexy mysterious lighting. A broad shaft of light was going across his face. But it only made him look more handsome. He was the sort of man who could withstand being on a big screen with high-def. She was sure of it.

He didn't have a flaw in his features. He was perfect in every way.

And so even the broad light of day couldn't diminish it.

"Tell me, then. Tell me how you like it."

His smile shifted, turned wicked. And they might not be in a bedroom, but his eyes held the suggestion of it.

She took the mustard out of the fridge.

"Just make sure you've got a firm grip," he said.

"For God's sake, Boone."

"What? You wouldn't want to drop a bottle of mustard."

"I guess not."

"Give it a good squeeze."

"Boone," she said, not sure whether she wanted to laugh, or get irritated, or… If she was a little bit turned on. That was ridiculous.

"Just trying to help with best kitchen practices. You can lay it on a little thick."

She rolled her eyes because she decided faux irritation was better than melting into a puddle over this kind of thing.

She turned the bottle over and squeezed a generous helping onto the sandwich.

"Just like that, Wendy."

His voice was like silk, and the sensation it sent along her nerves was glorious.

"I don't need encouragement to make the sandwich."

"All right."

She got the tomato and sliced it, then laid it on along with some turkey. And then she handed him the sandwich with no ceremony. But when he took it from her, their fingertips brushed, and her breath was sucked straight from her lungs.

He looked at her. And he really looked. Saw her. Looked into her. He took a slow bite of the sandwich, and there was something about the way he did it, purposeful, and intense, that made the space between her thighs throb.

She shook her head and turned away from him.

"It's a good sandwich," he said.

"You're welcome," she said.

Doing housework for the man felt like sex. And that seemed unfair. Because it should defuse things. Everything. This reminder that he was normal. That he was a human. That he could never live up to whatever fantasy her body was convinced he would give. Because how could he? No man could. No man could live up to the ridiculous thing she had built up in her mind.

Or rather, tried not to build up.

"So you only want to stay here a month," he said.

"Yes. That was my thought."

"And what do you want to do after that?"

"I don't know."

He set his sandwich down on a paper towel on the counter. And then he grabbed hold of the loaf of bread and took two pieces out. "Do you like mustard, Wendy?"

"No," she said.

"Mayonnaise?"

"Yes."

"Okay."

And then, slowly and methodically, he began to make a sandwich. This one without mustard. And she could only stare at him because she didn't know why it made her want to cry. Because this was such a small thing. Because she was supposed to be working for him, and he was doing things for her, and she had made him a sandwich, and they could've easily made their own, but he was making one for her.

And it just seemed exceptional. Maybe it shouldn't. Maybe that was the biggest commentary on her marriage to Daniel so far.

That she wanted to weep as she watched strong, scarred masculine hands put turkey between two slices of bread.

He handed it to her, and she did her best to swallow the lump in her throat.

"Thank you."

"You're welcome."

She took a bite of the sandwich. "I don't know what I'm going to do," she said finally.

"But not this."

"No," she said. "Not this. My mother cleaned houses. It's a good job. It's a great job. I don't look down on anyone for any kind of work that they do."

"But you've been looked down on."

She nodded slowly. She felt exposed, and he could see that. Quite so easily.

"Yes. I have been. I grew up in a community where being the daughter of a cleaner made me a certain thing to other people. Mostly, the worst part about my mom's job was that sometimes the people she worked for tried not to pay her. And that would create gaps between paychecks. And she was never quite in a space where she could just walk away from that work, not while they were dangling money owed over her head. There was no protection. No rights. No power. It's the kind of thing you never forget. And I never wanted to be in that position. I never want my girls to be in that position. And here I am. We don't have a prenup or anything, and I know he's going to have to pay child support of some kind, but the truth is I earned so much of his money for him. Right now, I don't want it. I want to wash my hands of him and walk away. But I know that in the long run that isn't the best decision. I know it isn't going to serve me. It isn't going to serve my daughters, so it isn't the way I can treat this situation. But I want... I want to find myself. I want to *be* myself. Whatever that means."

"I know who you are," he said. "You're the woman that showed up with the baseball bat and smashed the hell out of that asshole's truck. Even though you could've gotten in trouble for it. Even though it destroyed a perfectly good vehicle. You've got a lot of passion. And you're right, you have a lot of what you have because of that passion. Because you got him all those deals, because you were so good at building him up. And what did he do with that? Tried to tear you down. If you need anger to motivate you, to kind of guide your way…why not use it?"

"Well, the problem is, I'm not all that angry right now. I'd like to be. But anger just implies a level of passion I'm not sure is there. I felt scorned. I felt tricked. And that made me mad. I felt disrupted. That made me mad. I'm not heartbroken, though."

Something in his eyes sharpened. "Really?"

"Really."

This was dangerous. She had tried to steer them back into something mundane. Tried to think about socks and turkey sandwiches, but he had gone and changed everything when he had made the sandwich for her.

Her husband had found it a turnoff for her to talk about her past. And yet here he was, listening to her, and he didn't seem turned off.

"No. Because I think that I love the life I had as a result of my marriage a lot more than I love my marriage. Or maybe seeing a picture of him quite literally sticking it in another woman did it for me. That could also be it."

"I'm sorry. It was a terrible thing."

"It was. But you know the truth… There have been very few moments in my marriage when I haven't wanted another man. You know that."

She was being so dangerous right now. So very dangerous. "And I might not have acted on it… But the truth remains… I was with Daniel and the whole time I wanted someone else."

"Yeah," he said, his voice suddenly gruff and strangled.

"I was poor," she said. "And I've been shaped by that. The way you saw me react to my divorce, it was all the anger that had built up inside me all those years. All that hunger. Because I know what it's like to have an empty pantry and I never wanted that for my girls. Because I didn't have a father growing up and I didn't want that for them either. So I clung to the shape of my life because it was the shape I wanted, even if the content was never quite what I had fantasized about it being.

It didn't matter. I found a man, and I thought that was going to keep me safe, so I clung to it. And even though I know better, I've seen better—in all these years I've learned I don't need him to keep me safe, I don't need him to make me money—I was afraid that by walking away from the marriage I was walking away from security. And so, when he ripped it out from under me, I was furious. Because I felt like he was taking from me the one thing I cared about the most. My security. That was why I was so angry."

"As you should be," he said.

"Does it bother you? To think of me that way."

"In what way?"

"Does it bother you to know that the woman you met, the woman who was dressed nicely, who looks like she's never known a struggle, isn't real?"

"Why the hell would that bother me? You're strong. And I like that about you. I always have. Did you really think I was responding to a certain brand of cowgirl boots? Did you think I was responding to the rhinestones on your jeans? I don't give a shit about that. It's your backbone. There are a lot of beautiful women, Wendy, but I haven't spent fifteen years fantasizing about what it would be like to get them naked. It isn't just how pretty your eyes are, or the shape of your mouth, though I think it's beautiful. It isn't just the way your tits look in what I assume is a pretty expensive bra. Though I like that too. It's not your ass. Though again, I like it."

His words were the single most erotic thing she'd ever heard in her life, and maybe that made her simple, but she didn't care. She just did not care.

"It was always the spark in your eyes. It was always that little bit of wicked in your smile. The way your ass moves because of the way you walk, which has nothing to do with the shoes or how expensive they are, but with the way you carry yourself. You're strong. And he never gave you any of that. And he does not have the right to take any of it away. No. Finding out that you were broke when you were young doesn't turn me off. It just explains what I saw in you already."

"He didn't like to hear about it," she whispered.

"He's a weak man," he said, restating it.

"And you're not."

"I'm just a man," he said. "I'm a man who wouldn't dream of turning away from my responsibilities, not on the level he has. But also, I don't take on shit I can't hang on to. I don't try to carry something I can't hold."

That felt like a warning more than a promise. And she should be grateful. Because she knew it was foolish to go straight from a marriage into another relationship. Hell, it was foolish to go straight from a marriage into Boone's arms, but suddenly it seemed like maybe it was a stupid thing *not* to do.

"Fifteen years," she said. "That's how long it's been since I walked into that bar and saw you," she said. "That's how long it's been since I…since I looked down at my wedding ring and wanted to take it off. I didn't want to do that all the time. Not for the whole fifteen years. But pretty much every time I was with you. I wanted to break my vows for the chance to know what it was like to have your hands on my skin, Boone Carson. Do you know what kind of insanity that is?"

He moved closer to her, his blue eyes blazing. And there was no counter between them.

"Yes. Because it's the same kind of insanity I felt since the moment I saw you. Forget friendship and all of that. Because I just wanted you."

"I had kids with him," she said.

"I know," he growled. "Do you have any idea how much I hated that? Knowing… Knowing just how tied to him you were. Your girls are great, don't mistake me. And I'm not saying that I should've been a husband or father or anything like that. But I am saying… Damn, honey, I wasn't gonna go here. I wasn't gonna touch you."

"You still haven't."

"I'm going to, though, you know that."

"It was inevitable. From the beginning."

"Maybe I should thank him. For being the one to blow it up. Because we don't have to."

She shook her head. "We wouldn't have."

"Are you sure? Because I'm not. You've been here two days. And here we are. Being just a little too honest."

"You made me a sandwich."

"So?"

"Yeah, I asked myself that same question. Why should that matter so much? Why is it so damned impactful that a man is showing me basic concern? Because it's what I've been without. Because I had a marriage, but just the framework of one. We were business partners, and sometimes I think we liked each other. We had sex, and it was fine. I gave myself to him when I was nineteen, and that was just that. I thought I had to stick with it. Because I didn't want to be pregnant and alone. Because I didn't want to have the life I grew up with anymore, and I didn't want that for my kids. I sure as hell wasn't gonna blow it up just because I wanted to tear some other guy's clothes off."

"I want you," he said. "I want you, and I understand that you don't want me."

She was immobilized by that. "What does that mean?"

"You're attracted to me, but you don't want it. You don't want me to take your clothes off. You don't want me to kiss your lips. You don't want me to taste every inch of you. And you sure as hell don't want me inside you."

She couldn't breathe. His words were tracing erotic shapes through her mind's eye, things she was never going to be able to unseat. To un-imagine.

"I don't understand…"

"Because if you did, you'd be across this room already. Because you know what's holding me back. It's you. I cannot be part of hurting you. And I cannot be part of taking advantage of you, and I sure as hell can't have you thinking you owe me.

And it doesn't matter that I know you're attracted to me. I know something is stopping that from becoming want, because if it was *want*, then the want is on both sides. And it would be enough to push us together."

"I have the girls. And I just think that if…"

And she knew that it was a lie. The moment those words passed her lips. Even thinking about whether or not it was smart and all of that, it was just excuses. She didn't want to get hurt. She didn't want to get burned by the intensity of the thing between them. She had discounted common sense once for a man, and ended up married to someone who had never been faithful to her. So this was all about fear. It was one thing to want Boone when she couldn't have him. It was quite another to have him and contend with what that might mean.

With where he might fit into her life, or with where she would want him to fit into her life even if he didn't.

But she knew one thing.

That she had fifteen years' worth of complicated regrets. Like trying to pick broken glass out of a piece of cake. And she just didn't want any more of that. There had been good things about her marriage. Even though she was hurt by it now. Even though it wasn't going to last forever. Even though it was over.

She had her girls. She had some work experience. She would find a way to use the things that her marriage had given her. Even as she moved forward without her husband.

But she didn't want Boone to be a regret. Not anymore. He'd been one, deeply, for fifteen years. And that was what she didn't want. More than anything. More than she wanted to be protected. More than she wanted Boone to be a safe space. And yes, when she had first shown up at the house, she had maybe wanted safety more than she wanted him. For a minute.

Because it was wonderful to have him remove the burden. Wonderful to have him give her a place to stay. Wonderful to have him carry her bags.

But she would leave. She would leave in four weeks, just like she'd said, and she would start fresh on her own. But she would know. She would know what she'd been missing all this time, and he would be resolved. She deserved that. She needed it.

"I do want you," she whispered.

She took a step toward him, her heart pounding. Nothing was stopping her. And she was giddy with that. Giddy with a sense of freedom and wildness.

And it was like years had been lifted off her shoulders. Not just the years of marriage, but the years that had come before it. The years of feeling like she had to be good. Better. To avoid ever stepping into the trap of poverty again. To avoid food insecurity and homelessness and all the things she had grown up so terrified of. The things that had shaped her. And yes, they had made her strong, but sometimes she was just so tired of being that kind of strong. She didn't want to do it anymore. And he made her feel, in that moment, like she could just be. Like there was nothing but now. Because there were three hours until she had to go get the girls from school. Because her wedding rings were gone, and her vows meant nothing. Because he didn't look at her and see somebody who deserved to be treated like less because she had been through something difficult.

Because he had listened.

And all those things combined to make her feel free.

And she knew what she wanted to do with that freedom.

Nothing was holding her back.

And for the first time, she reached out and she touched Boone Carson.

Chapter Five

Wendy's hand on his chest was so much more erotic than anything he ever could've imagined. His heart was pounding so hard he thought it was going to go straight on through his rib cage. And then she would be able to hold it in her delicate hand, and that would seem about right. That would seem like the appropriate fee for this gift. This gift of her delicate hand against his body.

They had been foolish to think it wasn't going to end here.

Maybe they had needed to be that foolish, for a time.

God knew he had.

He had needed to construct a ladder made of lies so they could climb up to this moment.

Because the truth would've sent them both turning away.

Thank God for the lies that had brought them here.

He wanted to savor the moment.

This moment *before*. When it was like storm clouds were all gathered up ahead, swollen with the promise of rain, but not a single drop had fallen. Where the air had changed to something thicker, more meaningful. Thick with promise.

The promise of her mouth on his.

In only a few moments he would taste her. And when he did, he was going to part her lips, slide his tongue in deep.

But he hadn't yet.

And it was the promise that kept him poised on the edge of a knife. That kept him on high alert. The promise of strawberries, the forbidden, and the need that had been building in him for fifteen years.

He was in no rush for the first raindrop to fall.

He could live in this moment forever.

Except then her touch shifted. Except then, she moved her hand up to curve around the back of his neck, the touch erotic, purposeful. Glorious. And the minute her fingertips made contact with bare skin, it was too much. It was electric. And all his control snapped.

The rain began to fall.

He wrapped his arm around her waist and brought her hard against him so she could feel him. Feel his need. Feel the way his heart was beating almost out of his chest, feel how his cock had gotten hard.

For her. His breathing was ragged, pained. And he knew she could hear that, feel that. The way his chest hitched, the way his breath tried to cut his throat on each and every exhale.

She swallowed hard, and brought her hand around just beneath his jaw, traced it, down to the center of his chin.

"Wendy," he whispered.

She licked her lips, and that was it. He lowered his head and brought his mouth down onto hers.

The impact of her mouth under his was shocking. He had kissed any number of women. More than he could count. Innumerable.

But that had never been this.

No woman's mouth had ever been this.

It was Wendy, and she was imprinted into every cell of his body.

Her mouth was so soft. And she didn't taste of strawberries. It was indefinable, wonderful her. It was nothing else. It never could be.

It had been the easy way out to imagine there was another

flavor to compare her to. Something he could hang on to on late nights when he was unsatisfied. A lie. And one he had needed. The same as he could lie to himself and say that having sex with a gorgeous blonde might do something for that need.

Of course, it didn't. Of course, it never could. Because that was just sex. And this was something else.

It was something more. Much more.

Sex was as cheap as vows that weren't kept. This was precious. Real. Deep.

It pulled a sound straight from the bottom of his soul like dying, like hope, like pain and glory and wonder, all rolled into one.

He cradled her head with the palm of his hand as he leaned in, took the kiss deeper.

His heart was pounding so hard he thought it might be a heart attack, and if it was, he would accept that this was his moment to go and be happy with it.

He'd ridden on the backs of angry bulls intent on grinding him into the arena dirt beneath their hooves. He'd won competitions and lost them. His sister had died. His brother had left. He'd felt his heart pound with adrenaline, ache with loss, burn with anger.

And this was somehow more, and better and worse, all at once.

It was new.

Boone had given up on ever feeling anything new again in his whole jaded life, but this was bright and shiny and wholly unique.

This was Wendy.

Not a kiss.

An event.

His mouth shifted over hers, and it nearly brought him to his knees. He tasted her, deep and long, and as much as he wanted this to go fast, to see her naked, feel her naked, be inside her, he also wanted this moment to go on forever. Just like that breath before the kiss.

He wanted everything all at once. The anticipation, the glory of need and the thunder of satisfaction.

But he didn't have the control to hold back, so he tasted her deep, though he kept his hand firmly on the back of her head, and the other wrapped hard around her waist, because if he let himself explore her...

It was Wendy who moved her hands over his shoulders, down his back, then his chest.

It was Wendy who let her fingertips skim down his stomach, and then skimmed his denim-covered arousal.

His breath hissed through his teeth, and he felt like she'd lit a match against him.

He lifted her off the ground, holding her heart against his body as he continued to plumb the depths of her mouth.

He knew what it was like to desire somebody. He knew what it was like to be physically aroused. This was past that. It surpassed everything.

This was something new altogether. Something intense and raw and more.

It was the thing he had always both craved and wanted to close the door on forever. Something altering and destructive that he felt far too familiar with.

Because how many times in his life had the landscape of his soul been rearranged? Torn apart?

He hadn't wanted to do it with her.

And yet, there was an inevitability to all of it. Something that couldn't be denied. And he wasn't going to deny it, not now. It was only that he was very, very aware this wouldn't simply be sex. But something more altogether. Something he had never experienced before.

It was Wendy.

And there was no use comparing her to anyone else. No use comparing the way his need for her tightened his gut, made his body so hard it hurt, made him tremble with the need to be inside of her. Because there was nothing worthy of drawing comparison to. There was nothing like her. And there never could be.

He moved his hands down to her thigh, gripped it and lifted her leg so it was bent over his hip, then he moved her back against the kitchen island so he could press himself against her, let her feel, at the center of her need for him, just how much he wanted her. She gasped into his mouth, and rolled her hips forward. "Yes," he whispered against her lips.

And he knew he could get lost even in this. And moving his body against hers fully clothed, like they were a pair of desperate teenagers. And he would find pleasure in that. Because already, he had found more satisfaction in his mouth on hers than any previous sexual encounter had ever brought.

Maybe this was delayed gratification. Maybe this was just the way it went when you wanted somebody for years and couldn't have them. Maybe this was the release of self-denial followed by action. Or maybe it was simply Wendy.

He couldn't answer the question, or maybe he just wouldn't.

He would leave it a mystery. Intentionally. Wound up in a tangle he could easily undo if he pulled at the right thread. He knew where the right thread was.

But there were some mysteries best left tangled.

And that was the truth.

But there was no need for deeper truths than the one passing between their lips now, and there was no need for honesty any deeper than the raw need that coursed through his veins. It was enough. And anything more was likely to destroy them both, and it would be nice if, at the end of all of this, they could stand on their own two feet.

Because he didn't want to reduce her, and maybe even more than that, he didn't want to reduce himself. He wasn't a saint, after all, and he had never claimed to be.

He was simply a man. One who was held in the thrall of the desire he felt toward the woman in his arms.

And even though he could've stayed like this forever, he didn't want something juvenile and desperate to mark the first sexual encounter between them. He wanted it to be her, and him, and nothing in between.

So he lifted her up again, and began to propel them both toward the stairs.

She clung to him, lifting her other leg and wrapping them both around his waist, holding fast as he propelled them both up, and then down the hallway toward his bedroom.

And he knew he would have to address the subject of barriers, especially because she'd been with a man she couldn't trust, and it was going to take a deep amount of trust to want to be with someone like that again.

And he would never violate her trust. Not out of desire, not out of selfish need. Not for any reason at all.

And he would never be lost enough in his own arousal to lose sight of her.

Because she was the reason. She was the answer to the question. She was the fuel for the fire raging through him now, so how could he turn his focus inward? He couldn't. Ever.

When they got to his bedroom, he set her down gently on the foot of the bed, and knelt before her, lifting his hand to cup her cheek. "I have condoms," he said.

"I have taken every test known to man recently out of an abundance of caution."

He nodded. "I trust you. But you don't have any reason to trust me."

She looked at him, her blue eyes seeming to go deeper than his skin. "I don't have any reason to trust Daniel. But you've never given me a reason to not trust you. You gave me a place to go, and I know you didn't do it so we would end up here. I trust that. I know nothing you did was to manipulate me. To use me. You've never been anything but honest with me, Boone."

"I want you. Without one. I don't want anything between us. But I will do whatever you need to feel safe."

"Well, I'm protected from pregnancy. So if…"

That did a weird thing to him. To his gut. Because the idea of Wendy being pregnant with his baby didn't make him scared or upset at all.

It made him feel something else altogether, and *that* made him a little bit scared. Made him a little bit upset.

"Good. Then we don't need it."

He moved away from her and stripped his shirt up over his head.

This was happening. And it was everything he wanted.

He just had to make sure he survived it.

Chapter Six

Wendy couldn't keep her eyes off his bare chest. He was the most beautiful man she'd ever seen. He always had been. Even with her doing her best not to examine the fine architecture of his body, she had noticed.

How could she not?

He was so glorious. So utterly perfect. And shirtless, he was... He was a phenomenon. He was the kind of stunning that could only be compared to a mountain range, looming in the distance, glorious and transcending all other natural wonders. Broad and brilliant, the musculature of his shoulders, his chest, his stomach...

She had always known the desire between her and Boone went somewhere beyond mere physical attraction, but for the moment, she just marinated in the absolute masculine perfection present before her. For he was something else altogether than she'd seen in person. That was for sure.

She was almost startled by the visceral reaction she had to him. By the wave of need that washed over her. She wasn't a stranger to sexual desire, or arousal. She enjoyed sex.

But it had never been like this. It had never been all-consuming. It had never been a driving need that washed out everything else, washed out her fear. Because she was the kind of woman who had been raised from a place of fear, because her mother had known she would need it in order to make her way in the world. Because her mother knew that a woman had to suspect everything and everyone. That a woman could never fully place her trust in another human being, because the moment she did that person could take advantage of her.

Yes, she had always been afraid. And so nothing had ever been able to carry her away, not completely. She had left herself fairly unprotected in her marriage, but even now, she'd known exactly how she would get away. And she had already made sure she and her girls didn't end up on the streets. And perhaps she was giving herself a bit too much credit when Boone deserved more of it, but still, she felt confident saying she had never let herself get lost entirely in any sort of passion, anytime, anywhere.

Except now.

There was no logical thought. Nothing rational or reasonable about this. It was just need. Raw and aching and torn from the depths of her soul.

She was empty, and she needed, more than anything, to be filled by him.

She leaned back on the bed, looking up at him.

His grin... That edgy, wicked grin she had always longed to have turned on her.

And nothing was holding her back now. Nothing whatsoever.

It was freedom, the kind of freedom that made tears prick at the backs of her eyes, the kind of freedom that made her feel like she might be on the edge of a cliff.

And normally that would scare her. She was afraid of heights. But not here. Not now.

Everything about this man said he would catch her.

She could jump. With all the wild abandon she never let herself feel, she could jump.

Because he was more than strong enough to catch her.

Because he was more than strong enough to make good on every promise the arousal he built inside of her created.

Yes. He was the man who had engineered this desire, and he was the man who would answer it.

Because Boone Carson was a man who kept his word.

Even when they were words he didn't speak with his mouth.

He moved his hands to his belt buckle, and everything in her stilled. He began to undo the leather slowly, and her body rejoiced.

He pulled the belt through the loops on his jeans, and methodically set it on the edge of the bed, right next to her. He kicked his boots off, the movements there slow as well, removing his socks and placing them next to the boots. He was doing this on purpose.

Because he didn't hurry to get up here, and now he was taking his time. She couldn't even be angry, because it was the single most erotic thing she'd ever experienced. An echo of the denial they'd been experiencing since they had first met, and yet now with the promise of that desire being satisfied.

His hands went to the button on his jeans, then slowly lowered his zipper. His pants and underwear came off as one, and the extreme pulse of desire that rocked through her core when she saw the full, masculine extent of him made her mouth dry. He was glorious. The most beautiful naked man she'd ever seen, even though she'd only ever seen one other in person.

He was perfection. He was everything.

She couldn't help herself. Or maybe she didn't want to. She licked her lips.

And he laughed. Enticing. Husky. He made her feel like maybe she was wicked too.

And for the first time in a very long time, she didn't feel like somebody's wife or housekeeper or household manager. She didn't feel like somebody's mother. She just felt like her. Her, if she hadn't been raised to fear everything, to hoard good things and be afraid of what might come tomorrow.

Just who she might've been. Who she wanted to be.

A woman. A woman with the capacity to desire perfection. A woman with the capacity to let herself hope.

All because of Boone Carson's gloriously naked body.

And if that wasn't a testament to the wonder of a perfect penis, she didn't know what was.

And she hadn't even touched him yet.

She put her hands on the hem of her T-shirt, fully expecting to undress herself, until his eyes met hers. "No." The command, the denial, was rough and hard.

"That's for me," he said.

"Okay," she said, her voice trembling slightly.

But she loved the command in his voice, and she didn't want it to go away.

He took her hand and encouraged her into a standing position, and then he grabbed hold of the edge of her shirt and pulled it up over her head.

His nostrils flared, his eyes going hot. "You're so beautiful. And I'm gonna tell you right now, I'm not going to have any pretty words for you. Just dirty ones. Rough. I'm not gonna write you poetry, because I just want you so damned bad. And that is the most flowery, beautiful speech I have. Everything else is going to get a lot harder. You okay with that?"

"Yes."

Because it was poetry to her since it was said in his voice. Because the heat in his eyes might as well be a sonnet, and the music he called up within her a symphony.

He could say whatever he wanted. He could do whatever he wanted. It wouldn't be wrong. It couldn't be.

And he made good on his word. As the layers of her clothes came off, he affirmed her with rough, coarse speech that made goose bumps break out on her skin. Her husband was a cowboy. He'd used all manner of rough language. He wasn't delicate when it came to words surrounding sex, but it was different from Boone. Because it was about her.

Because his language spoke to a level of desperation that healed something inside of her she hadn't even realized had hurt.

This idea that she hadn't been enough. That giving a man her body hadn't been enough. That loving that man hadn't been enough. That keeping his house, raising his children, managing his money hadn't been enough. That if doing all that wasn't enough to satisfy him, it meant there was a deep shortcoming within her she was never going to fix.

Boone made that laughable. He made it clear, so very clear, even to her, that the issue was Daniel.

Because if Boone could be reduced to trembling over the sight of her bare breasts, then maybe she was beautiful after all.

Then perhaps she wasn't wrong. Then perhaps her husband was just a bad husband.

And she had been a good wife. It just hadn't mattered to him. And never would, no matter what she did.

And so this weight that had been resting in the pit of her stomach from the moment she had found out about Daniel's infidelities evaporated. And then Boone took her pants off. Her underwear. And she was naked in front of him. This man she had wanted for so long, for whom her desiring had become as natural as breathing, so much so that she had managed to carry it around all these years, some days barely noticing it.

And now she could feel it. The way that it made her want to be wanted.

The cascade of all those years was suddenly pouring down over her, amplifying her desire. Her need.

She wasn't embarrassed to be naked in front of him, because she knew she had been thousands of times in his mind, and she could see from the heat in his eyes he wasn't disappointed. Far from it. And then he began to tell her. Just how satisfied he was.

And he was wrong. It was poetry. A field of dark desire dotted with bright, explicit daisies. And it was more than beautiful to her.

Because it was real. Because it was nothing held back. Because it was as honest a moment as she'd ever had in her life, and honesty was perhaps the biggest aphrodisiac of all right now.

Truth.

Unfiltered, unabashed.

And then he wrapped his arm around her waist and brought her bare body against his. And they were touching, everywhere. Naked, against each other. He was so hard and hot, and her desire for him was like a living thing. Demanding. Exulting. And she indulged.

She wrapped her arms around his neck and kissed him, gloried in the feel of her sensitized breasts moving against his hair-roughened chest. Loving the way his large, calloused hands moved over her curves, the way one cupped her ass and squeezed her hard.

Then delved between her thighs to tease her slick entrance.

She cried out as he pushed a finger inside of her, and then another.

Boone. She would never not be conscious it was him.

It wasn't about generic desire. It wasn't about that basic sort of human need that everyone experienced. This was singular. It was for him. About him.

And when he lifted her up and laid her down on the bed, he looked at her like a starving man. And he pushed her knees apart, kissing her ankle, that sensitive spot right on the inside of her knee, and up her thigh, slowly. His mouth was hot, and his eyes were full of intent, and even as she felt a vague amount of discomfort and embarrassment wash over her when he drew closer to the most intimate part of her, she couldn't look away.

Because she had to see it. She had to see Boone's mouth on her. And then it was. She gasped, arching up off the bed, her hand going over her own breast as she squeezed herself, greedy now with all the heat inside of her. And he began to lick her, deep and with intent, pushing a finger inside rhythmically as his tongue moved over the most sensitive part of her.

She was lost in it. In this new music inside of her.

He was an artist, and if he would make her his muse, she would consider herself fortunate.

She closed her eyes, finally surrendering to the overwhelming onslaught of pleasure, finally unable to keep them open. But still, she saw him. His face. His body.

Boone. She was overwhelmed by him.

His touch, his scent. And that realization, his name, him—that was what sent her over the edge, more than a touch, more than his skilled mouth. Just him.

And when she shattered, he clung to her tightly, forcing her to take on more and more pleasure. As he pushed her harder, further, through wave after wave, through a second climax that hit before the first had even abated.

And she was spent after. His name the only thing in her mind, the only thing on her lips. Perhaps, the only thing she knew.

"Boone," she whispered, as he moved up her body and claimed her mouth, letting her taste her own desire there, the evidence of what they had done.

His smile was more than wicked now. It was something else. Dark and satisfied, and everything.

He moved his hands up to cup her breasts, skimmed his thumbs over the sensitized buds there, then moved both hands down her waist, her hips, beneath her rear as he lifted her hips up off the bed.

"I want…"

"Later," he said, his voice jagged. "I need to be inside of you."

And then he was, in one hard, smooth stroke, filling her, almost past the point of pleasure into the gray space where pain met need, and it was wonderful.

He began to move, rough, hard strokes that pushed her further and further toward that shining, glorious peak again. Impossibly. Brilliantly.

There was no way she could come again. She had never in her life come twice during sex, and a third time would just be pushing it, except each and every stroke demanded it.

It was Boone. Inside of her. Tormenting her. Satisfying her. Creating within her an aching need that only he could satisfy.

And she could've wept with the glory of it. With the intensity of the new, building need in her that felt entirely separate from the need she'd had before.

Because this was about them. Being one. His body in hers. Intimate. Too much. Not enough.

She met his every stroke, and then he took hold of her chin and pressed his forehead to hers. "That's right," he whispered. "Come for me. For me, Wendy."

It was the desperation there, the fact that he wasn't talking dirty to her for the sake of a game, but issuing a command that came straight from the very center of who he was, out of the deepest, darkest desire. That was what sent her over. That was what shattered her. And it was nothing like her other two climaxes. This was like something sharp piercing a pane of glass, cracking and shattering it into glorious, glittering pieces. Making it into something almost more beautiful than what it had been before.

And then he followed her. On a rough sound, he found his own release, spilling himself inside of her, his body pulsing deep within. And she watched him. Watched as he was undone.

By her. By them. By this.

And all she could do was hang on to him in the aftermath. Clinging to his sweat-slicked shoulders as she pressed her head to that curve right there at his neck, as she tried to keep herself from weeping.

"Boone," she said.

"It's about damned time," he said.

And she laughed. Impossibly, because nothing felt light or funny.

Except it was just the truth.

It had been so long in coming, that it was nearly a farce.

Had it always been inevitable? She supposed there was no good answer to that question. The decision as to whether or not they would do something to violate her vows had been taken away from them. And they had certainly kept themselves away from any sort of temptation they couldn't handle for long enough that they deserved a medal.

But it had been taken away from them, the need to resist. And so they didn't.

Lying there with him felt inevitable.

But maybe it was Daniel's betrayal that had always been inevitable, considering he had never once seen a need to be faithful to her.

Maybe that was the thing that had always been set in stone: the failure of her marriage. Maybe it had been fate that day that had brought Boone into her path and said, *Here is the better choice.*

For all the good it had done. Because she had been so bound and determined to do the right thing, she hadn't taken the destined thing.

Except now, in the aftermath of what had been fairly spectacular sex, she was left with the reality that sex was hardly destiny.

It had been amazing. Surpassing anything she had even thought could exist.

But she still had all the things in her life to take care of. And kids to pick up from school in… She looked over at the bedside clock. Thirty minutes.

For a moment she had felt free of all her responsibilities, but she wasn't. Not really.

She still carried them all. She still had to be Wendy Stevens. Mother, a woman in the midst of a divorce.

She still had to figure out where she went from here, and what she did next. Not even three soul-shattering orgasms could take that away.

Because bodies meeting wasn't a promise. Not forever, not really anything.

And in the place she was in life, she could hardly ask Boone for promises.

He looked at her, and she wanted to.

But she didn't.

They had known exactly what to do.

It was funny that neither of them seemed to know what to say.

"I have to go get the girls. Soon."

"Yeah."

"I can't… You know I can't be over here at night."

He nodded. "Yes."

"I just can't have them knowing."

"I get that." He cupped her chin. "It's not gonna just be the once, though. You know that."

She could resist. She could tell him it had to be once. She could tell him that, for their own protection, they needed to keep it that way. That they had to be smart. But she would only end up back in his bed the next time they were alone in the house, and it would just make her a liar.

She wasn't going to do that. She wasn't going to insult them.

Because the truth was, she wanted him again even now, and if she wasn't on a time limit, she would probably be climbing on him.

Because she hadn't been able to touch him the way she wanted to, hadn't been able to explore him. Hadn't been able to taste him.

And she was just not in the space to build up a host of regrets. Or even a single new regret.

"I am going to leave," she said.

"You said."

"I'm not even divorced yet."

"You are in every way that counts."

"Except the legal ways. And I have to get through that."

"I get that."

"Thank you. For being here for me. I really appreciate it. I really… This is going to happen again."

"Yes," he said.

And then it was her turn to be bold. Because why get mis-sish now?

"I need to taste you," she said. "I haven't had you in my mouth."

He growled, and she found herself pushed flat on her back, a whole lot of muscled, aroused cowboy over the top of her.

"Careful."

"I don't have time," she said. "Because as wonderful as that was, I can't stop having my life just so I can please you sexually."

"Tease."

"It feels good to tease."

It felt good to be with him.

It was strange how natural it felt, sliding out from beneath the covers and taunting him with her naked body as she went to collect her clothes.

She just wasn't embarrassed.

And she wasn't going to pretend to be. Why take on shame she simply didn't feel? There was no point to that.

Now she just had to get through the rest of the day with her head on straight. She had to pick up her girls like she hadn't just been ravished. She had to get dinner made.

"I'm probably gonna go out tonight," he said. "Don't worry about saving me dinner."

And that felt... It hurt. It felt like he was avoiding her, and maybe he was.

"Oh," she said.

"I'll see you tomorrow, though."

"Okay."

"I can't have you again tonight," he said. "And I get that might sound outrageously selfish to you. But honestly, I'm not sure I have it together enough to be around you in front of the girls, or to... I just need some space."

She was shocked by that. By the honesty. By the blatant truth that had just come out of his mouth, a truth that exposed deeper feelings in him that she had thought he would be comfortable betraying.

"Oh."

She had wanted to be close to him because she felt needy right now. But he had a point. They needed to figure out how they were going to be around each other if the girls were in the middle of them.

And right now, they were on anything but normal footing.

"Okay."

"I don't want you to be hurt."

She shook her head. "I'm not."

"Don't lie to me, Wendy. There have been enough lies all around us, there don't need to be any between us. Not anymore."

"Okay. I was a little bit hurt. I thought you didn't want to be around me if you couldn't have me."

"Yes...but it isn't like that. It's not because I don't have another use for you. It's just because I don't quite know what to do with myself right now."

"Okay. That's fair."

And maybe a little bit more honest than she'd been with herself.

"I will see you tomorrow."

"Okay."

Chapter Seven

Walking away from her had been the hardest thing he'd ever done. But he had work to finish, and she had to get her kids.

Being honest with her about why he needed a little space had been the other hardest thing he'd ever done. Because it came too close to admitting the truth.

This impossible truth that he had no idea what to do with now that they'd slept together.

He had felt like he was in love with her for a very long time.

But that love had been impossible to act on. So it had felt... safe in a way.

Or at least abstract.

The truth was, Boone didn't know how to love somebody actively.

He knew how to do things for them. But he had no idea what being in love entailed.

He looked at the way his brothers had brought women into their lives, the way they'd rearranged themselves to have them. He didn't like the thought of that. Not at all. Because he'd rearranged his life so many times.

And he just couldn't take all that on right now.

Hell, more than that, he knew it was an impossibility. Wendy was going through a divorce. Wendy had kids.

There was something much heavier to the idea of trying to be with a woman who had been through so much, than if it was a woman he didn't know.

He knew her. He knew how difficult all this was.

He knew about her life, about the things that she'd been through. And about the responsibilities she had.

And he took all that shit very seriously.

So he decided to go out. Decided to go to the bar. And wasn't surprised to find his brother Jace there, since Jace's wife was working tonight.

"Hey," he said.

"Hey yourself."

"What brings you out on a weeknight?"

"I need a drink."

He could confide in his brother.

He could. He was still considering it when Jace looked at him just a little too keenly. "Woman trouble?"

"You could say that."

Because he had been considering telling his brother about it unsolicited, so he sure as hell didn't have it in him to lie.

"Wendy?"

"Yeah."

"You know, this just isn't a great time for her, I would imagine."

"It was a fine enough time for her to sleep with me."

"Oh. Well. I guess I shouldn't be too surprised about that."

"It's not a surprise," he said. It really wasn't. They wanted each other too badly for too long for it to be a surprise.

"What's the problem?"

"Life is just really messed up," said Boone. "I don't know how you ever let go of that enough to be with someone. Especially when everything they're going through is as equally messed up as the world around you. It was easy. To carry a torch for her knowing I could never have her. But the rest of it…"

"Yeah. I get that."

"She's in a bad space," he said.

"So you said," Jace commented.

"It's true though. And it's important I remember that. I don't want her to feel obligated to me."

"Bad news," said Jace. "When you have a relationship with somebody you do often feel obligated to them. It's not a bad thing. I think that's somewhere in line with basic human connection and empathy."

"Yeah, but I don't want this to be transactional."

"Fine. I can understand that. But if you do something for her and she wants to do something for you, that's not transactional so much as it is a relationship."

"She doesn't need one of those right now."

"And that's up to you to decide?"

He snorted. "I didn't say that. But I don't't…"

"Listen to me, and trust me. I say this as a man who talked himself into thinking he knew better what the woman in his life wanted than she did. That way lies disaster. If you actually care about her, you need to give her some respect. The respect that she knows what's going on in her own mind. At least that."

"I know she does," he said. "But just… You weren't there. You didn't see her marriage. Okay? I did."

"Yeah. You were friends with her husband. If you hate the guy so much then why—"

"I didn't hate him. Not everything about him. When we were hanging out on the rodeo circuit, he was a good guy. The thing is, he kind of taught me how to have a good time. I needed that. You know how things were after…after Buck left. I had to take on a lot. And it was heavy. And I threw myself into the rodeo after that because I knew it was so important to Dad. I found some things there that I didn't expect to. But Daniel is a fun guy. And he kind of gave me something to look forward to. He taught me how to enjoy what had felt like an obligation before. There were good things about him. But when he married Wendy, things did change." And he left out the fact that a huge part of that was the way Boone felt about Wendy. From the moment he'd first seen her. There was no way Daniel could ever have been good enough for her. Even if he'd been perfectly good after all.

It was just that he hadn't been. So that combined with everything else made it kind of an impossible situation.

"Our friendship has had some cracks in it for a while. And in the end, I chose her. I was always going to choose her. I…" He realized what he'd just said.

"How long have you had a thing for her?"

"Too long. But the timing is bad."

"Word of advice. The timing is always bad."

"No, it really is. And I'm… I'm not someone who just hopes because he wants something. Not anymore."

"Boone, listen. I know… I know Sophia—"

"It was a lesson, Jace. When an illness is terminal, hoping for the best is stupid. It's not charming." He took a drink. "It's been a long time. But I changed. I know better. And I can see clearly, without…without being a blind optimist. The timing is bad."

Jace shook his head. "I get where you're coming from. But when it comes to relationships, the timing is always bad."

"What the hell does that mean?"

"Because at some point, caring about somebody means getting over yourself. And that is a really hard thing to do."

He could understand what his brother was saying. But caring about Wendy had always meant denying himself. It had always meant caring more about her than about him. Of course it had.

He'd always been clear on what loving Wendy meant.

He could care, but he couldn't have her.

And if anything, it just reinforced what he had to do. And that was let her go at the end of all this.

Because that was what caring about her meant.

It meant not being like Daniel. Not holding her to him when it wasn't right. When it wasn't the best situation for her. That was what love was.

It was sacrificial.

So there.

"Well, that's the way I feel about her," he said. "Like my feelings can't be first."

"Great. Just make sure you don't decide for her what her feelings are. Okay?"

"Yeah."

Jace raised his hand, and Cara brought over a couple of beer bottles.

"Do you have a designated driver, Boone?" she asked.

"You have my permission to put me in a cab if I have too many."

"Good. I have to look out for you. You're my brother now after all."

It was weird, the way the family kept expanding. Especially after being so conscious of the contractions in their family for all those years.

But Cara was a sister to him. Another person who cared.

That sat a little bit uncomfortably in his chest, and he couldn't quite say why.

"My biggest problem now," he said, lifting his beer bottle and looking at his brother, "is figuring out how to act like what happened earlier today didn't happen, especially when her kids are around."

"Well, not that I know, but I assume kids are a pretty big dampener on the libido."

"Especially teenagers," Boone said. "Little kids you could get that past, but older ones…"

"I don't know, man. Sounds to me like you just stepped your boot into a whole mess of sexual tension snakes."

He laughed. "Yeah." He didn't laugh because it was funny.

He laughed because it was true. He laughed because the mental image that it painted was far too accurate.

He had gone and done it. The nest of sexual tension snakes had been there all along, and he'd known. Full well.

But it was like stepping in it had been the only option. So there he was.

And now he was going to have to get back to the task of taking care of her. And taking care of the girls. All while carrying on a blisteringly hot, temporary affair with her. Because the snakes had been stepped in. So there was no point going back now.

"I'll figure it out."

"Sure you will," said Jace, a little too cheerfully for his liking.

"Why exactly do you seem to be enjoying this?"

"Because a woman completely rearranged my life some years ago, and a few months ago, I was finally able to figure out exactly what that rearranging needed to look like. I'm glad to see you in a similar situation."

Except it wasn't the same. It never would be. But he didn't argue with his brother. He didn't have the energy for it. He had other things to save his energy for. If his time with Wendy was limited, he was going to pour everything into it. Absolutely everything.

She was so distracted. She needed to get her daughters through homework. And then she needed to get herself off to bed.

She managed that, just barely. But then she couldn't sleep.

She was completely consumed by her thoughts of Boone. And what had happened between them that day.

He was gone still, the driveway empty, and she should be completely okay with that. He explained himself after all.

And, anyway, he didn't have an obligation to her.

It wasn't about obligation, though. She just wished he was here. And when she saw headlights pull up into the driveway, she climbed out of bed and, without thinking, went out the side door of the cottage and walked toward his house.

It wasn't a truck; it was a car. And she stopped and stared at the unfamiliar white vehicle, not quite understanding what was going on until she saw the logo on the side.

He'd gotten a taxi.

He got out of the cab, and she saw him stumble into the house.

And without thinking, she went the same way he did.

"Are you drunk?"

He turned. "Tipsy. Not drunk."

"Okay. Why?"

"I was trying to make it a little bit easier to fall asleep, actually."

"Oh, Boone. Come on inside. I'll make you some tea."

"No. That is counter to my objective. Which is to not think about you. And definitely not to fall asleep with you on my mind."

He was a little tipsy. And she didn't usually find that kind of thing sexy. But here she was. She had a feeling she would find Boone's hangnail sexy. And that was a whole other kind of problem she'd never had before.

"In the house."

"I don't take orders."

"Why not?"

He grinned, and she found herself suddenly pressed up against the side of the house. "Because I like to give them."

Arousal crashed through her body. Yeah. She would really like to take orders from him. Though, that wasn't supposed to be what was happening tonight.

"And tomorrow afternoon when you're sober, and you come in for your lunch break, you're welcome to tell me everything your heart desires. But right now, I'm telling you to go in the house so I can make you some tea."

"I think you'd have more fun if you got down on your knees."

"For sure," she said, breathless with the desire that thought infused in her. "But sometimes you can't get what you want."

"I'm well familiar."

"Inside."

And this time, he obeyed her.

So there was that.

She found an electric kettle—which was surprisingly civilized of him, she thought—and plugged it in, flicking on the switch to start up the hot water.

"I appreciate that you got a cab. I feel like sometimes you guys are not so great with the designated-driver thing."

"You guys?"

"You rodeo cowboys," she said.

"Yeah well." He cleared his throat, his expression going stoic. "My older brother was in a drunk driving accident. He wasn't driving. But they were a bunch of boys that had gone out camping and drinking and... Anyway. He was the only one that survived. After something like that you take the whole thing pretty seriously."

"Oh. I'm sorry, Boone, I didn't know."

"Yeah. Nobody knows Buck. Because he took off so long ago. It really screwed him up."

There was something raw and unspoken in his words. A truth buried there she couldn't quite figure out. And he wasn't going to tell her. Not willingly. Not right now.

And that was okay. Because that wasn't supposed to be the point of this. But now she couldn't stop imagining the catastrophe, and the way it must have hurt everyone.

"Was he injured?"

Boone nodded. "Yeah. He was okay, though. I mean physically. But it's a small town. And people will define you by something like that. And everyone will know. You can't outrun it unless you leave. I know that."

"It must've been hard. Having him leave."

"Plenty of families don't live in each other's pockets."

"Yes. That is true. But I expect it feels different when somebody leaves because of something like that."

"I guess. Were you close to your mom?"

"Yes. Until she died. She died when I was eighteen. And then after that, I met Daniel. I expect I was looking for a connection."

"Yeah. Probably."

"We don't often do the best things for ourselves when we're feeling desperate." She closed her eyes. "That isn't fair. He was good to me. As far as I knew. I wasn't openly accepting poor treatment."

"I was trying to remember today, when my brother and I were talking at the bar, exactly why I used to like Daniel. It occurred to me that he was one of the most carefree guys I've ever met. And as somebody who was burdened with a host of care by the time I was sixteen, I liked being around him."

"That's what I liked about him too. I was always afraid. Always afraid of losing what little I had. Always afraid of when the other shoe was going to drop. I was always scared. And he never was. Not of tomorrow, not of his success vanishing, not of our relationship imploding, he just lived. And now, I feel a little bit betrayed. Because so much of that is just arrogance, isn't it? Thinking you're the center of everything, the most important person, and that nothing you do can compromise it. And here I thought I was maybe learning some kind of life lesson from him."

"There's still a life lesson there, maybe. He doesn't have to have had everything worked out for some of it to be true."

"I guess."

"Did he ever make you happy?"

"Yes," she said. "And I guess it was real enough. I guess."

"I can understand why it's difficult. To accept that any of it was real when it seems like he was lying all that time."

"Yeah." She poured the hot water into a mug and put a tea bag in it. "But I guess that's the thing. That was part of his arrogance. He didn't think I needed his fidelity as long as he kept it from me. And I think he didn't much see the conflict there. It's insane. It doesn't make any sense. But I think that's what he thought. And so in his way, I think he loved me. I just think he never really loved anybody as much as he loved himself."

"And that may be why he was so happy," Boone said.

That made her laugh. "That's fair. How happy can you be when you're worried constantly about the happiness of somebody else? When you love yourself most, your joy isn't completely tied to the feelings of others. Like it is when you care about others as much as you care about your own. For Daniel, ultimately your own happiness is what matters…"

"I expect that's the easiest way."

"I wouldn't want to live that way, though. Because I wouldn't have my girls. Makes everything hard. Because as difficult as it is to go through this separation, it's so much harder when you're worried about other people's happiness as much as you are your own. Or more. But then I think at least I know what it's like. To feel an intense amount of caring for somebody else. I think that's the depth of it."

"Yeah. I think that's the depth of it. When I was a kid, my sister died. You might know that."

"I didn't," she said.

"Well. Sorry to bum you out with my family history. But it was a long time ago."

"I'm sorry."

"Thanks. Me too. But you know, that was my first introduction to understanding just how badly love could hurt. But what can you do? You love your siblings. No matter what. And I couldn't turn off my love for my family just because we lost our little sister. So I learned how to kind of move on with it. I learned that you could love even though it hurt. The hurt is part of it. And yeah, I think the way Daniel loves, that's kind of something else."

"Narcissism?"

"Possibly."

"I'm very sorry to hear about your sister. And your brother. Do you see him at all?"

"No. And in some ways that feels harder to deal with than Sophia's death. Because he is still alive. He just doesn't speak to us. He is still alive, he just… He won't come to us for help. After everything we went through. As a family. He put my parents through losing another child, effectively. He lived, but he won't live. And I just can't wrap my head around that."

"This one isn't about me," she said slowly. "It's my mother's story. But she isn't here to tell it, so I'd like to. My father abused her. She loved him, she trusted him, and he abused her. Physically. Emotionally. And I know that the woman she was after him was different. No matter how much she wanted to go back. She just couldn't. And sometimes I wondered why she didn't go home. Why did she go out on her own and struggle? When she could have gone back, because she talked about her family like they were all right. But the issue wasn't them, it was her. She survived something she didn't want to explain to anybody. And she didn't feel like she could go back. And I think there was something sad about that. I never got to know my parents. But I also understand there were things that happened that were so traumatizing she just couldn't face people seeing how they had changed her. And I can't judge her for that. Maybe your brother feels the same. Maybe he doesn't want you all to see who he is. Because maybe in some way he does feel like he died. I don't know. And I'm sorry if I'm overstepping. It's just that I love someone very much who did a similar thing."

He was quiet for a long time.

"This is maybe a little bit of a deep conversation to have when I'm partway into my cups," he said.

"I'm sorry. I didn't mean to overstep. But I—"

"You didn't overstep. Hell. We had sex a few hours ago, I think you can give me some advice."

"It's not really advice. It's just you said you didn't understand, and I hope maybe you might feel less mystified. And even if it isn't true, even if that's not why he left, if he didn't tell you, well, then what can you do? But if having an answer, any answer—one that's about him and his pain and not you—helps, then you might as well choose to believe that one."

"Good point. I can't argue with that."

"You could."

Their eyes met. This felt dangerous. Quite dangerous. Because this was another thing they hadn't done these last years. They hadn't gotten to know each other. They knew each other in the sense that they saw each other around. She knew the quality of man Boone was because she saw the way he interacted with other people. Because they chatted in passing at different things when it couldn't be avoided, and they did their very best to never be self-conscious about the sparks between them. To never draw too much attention to all of it.

But they didn't do this. They didn't sit and have heart-to-hearts. They didn't talk about his dead sister or his missing brother. Maybe she had started it, trying to push him away by telling him about her childhood. It hadn't worked. And now she knew about his, and that was close to having a connection. It was close to something she should be avoiding. And definitely something she shouldn't want.

Definitely not.

"Yeah. But, why? I'd rather kiss you."

"That's probably not a great idea." But she was already leaning in, and when he kissed her, it was almost tender. Nearly sweet.

It could never be entirely tender, though, because there was an edge to the meeting of their mouths that she thought not even time would take away.

It was the wanting. And how long they'd lived with it.

But tonight, there was something glorious about it. An ache fueled by how much she wanted him, and by knowing tonight she couldn't have him. Because she needed to get back to the cottage, needed to get back to the girls.

Because one thing she really couldn't afford was for her daughters to discover she wasn't home. For them to wonder where she was.

So he was forbidden again, but only for a few hours. There was something illicit, in a glorious way, about that.

A fun way because it wasn't impossible, it was just delayed.

So she let the kiss get intense, hungry, and she gloried in it.

In the building desire between her thighs, and the reckless heat that threatened to overwhelm her.

His whiskers scratched against her skin, and she liked that too.

Yes. She really did like it.

And when they pulled away, they were breathing hard, and her whole body felt like it was strung out, ready to shatter at the slightest touch.

"Are you going to touch yourself tonight? And think of me?"

It wasn't a question, she knew. It was a command. Because that was who he was.

"Yes."

"Tell me about it."

"Okay."

"Send me a text and let me know exactly what you thought I might do. Because you know, 'you have not because you ask not.'"

"All right."

He kissed her again, once more, then picked up his mug and stood. "I'll head to bed."

"Me too."

And she did exactly as he ordered, and when her climax hit, she turned her face into her pillow and said his name.

Then she sent off a furtive text letting him know she had

completed the task. But when it came to what exactly she thought about? That was a lot more difficult. And in the end, she only wrote one word.

You.

You.

Chapter Eight

You.

He couldn't stop thinking about that. Couldn't stop turning
it over and over in his mind. Damn that woman.

Getting up this morning and heading to work felt like a farce
because he was living for that afternoon break. He was living
for their agreed-upon meetup. He didn't care about anything
else. He lost the ability to do it. He just wanted her.

He had waited all this time for her. And then last night she
had...

She had managed to stick a ruthlessly sharp knife blade into
that wound, and the painful cut had let out some of the poison.

He didn't know how she had done it. How she'd so incisively
given him a truth he needed, even if it wasn't what he wanted.

He didn't need for her to understand him in addition to being
the hottest sex he'd ever had.

He didn't actually need for her to be anything, and yet, she
was doing her best to be everything.

You.

And by the time the afternoon rolled around, his blood was
thundering.

He practically tore the door off its hinges when he got into the house, and when he saw her standing in the kitchen, bare-foot and wearing a sundress that came up well past her knees he just about wrote poetry. Or perhaps a prayer of thanks to whoever had invented the sundress.

It was a magnificent work of art. The creation he had never fully paused to consider or appreciate until this moment. Until he had beheld the glory of one on Wendy.

And he was done playing. He was done waiting.

They'd set their boundaries, and he'd made it very clear what he was doing, and what he wasn't doing. Because of that, he felt like he didn't need to waste time with pleasantries now.

"You look pretty. I want you on your knees."

"Here?"

"Yeah. Here."

But because he was a gentleman, he went over to the stove and took down a tea towel. Then he put the folded-up fabric onto the floor, cushions for her. Because he didn't want her discomfort. He just wanted a little obedience. He just wanted…

This was a fantasy he hadn't let himself have. And now he wanted it. And he wanted to hold on to it. Tight.

Slowly, she sank down to the floor, her knees coming down to the center of that folded-up towel.

In his kitchen.

Holy hell.

All this trying to stay clear of domesticity, and he was doing a great job twisting and perverting some kind of housewife fantasy.

But he liked it. He couldn't help it.

What did he want? Just from his life in general. What had he ever wanted? Past the glory of the rodeo. Past being the one who picked up the slack for people who let go of their responsibilities.

What was left for him?

Was he going to live alone forever?

The years, the long lonely years, stretched out before him, and he realized why he never thought past the rodeo. Why he had put off retirement. Why he had put off this—buying a house. Making a life outside the rodeo.

Because he was clear-eyed. Because he wasn't an optimist. Because he didn't do hope, or dreams, and that meant the future was...

He could hardly even see it.

And that was sad.

But *this* wasn't.

So he was going to push all that to the side, and just be here. With her.

Because all she needed was him. And all he needed was her. That was for damned sure.

He moved closer to her and undid the buckle on his jeans.

And he suddenly felt unworthy of the gift she was giving him. It had been a follow-through of the game they were playing last night, and now it felt like something he maybe didn't deserve.

But she was looking up at him with wide, expectant eyes, and he was powerless to turn away.

He shifted the fabric of his pants, his underwear, and exposed himself to her. She wrapped her hand around the base of his cock and slid her elegant fingers along his length. Then she moved in, taking the tip of him into her mouth, before sucking him in deeply. She was confident. And more than that, her enjoyment was clear.

She wasn't shy—her eye contact bold, the sounds of pleasure coming from deep within her throat intense and raw.

He pushed his fingertips through her hair, held her there, held himself steady.

He didn't think he would survive this.

Even in this, he was so very aware it was her. Even in this, it could be no one else. He felt honored. Which was such a weird-ass way to think of a blowjob. But it wasn't just a blowjob. Because nothing with her was ever that simple. And it never could be.

He was close. So close, and he didn't want it. Not like this. He moved away from her, and she looked dazed, confused.

"Didn't you like it?"

"I loved it," he said, taking her hand and lifting her to her feet. And he kissed her, open-mouthed and hot. "A little bit too much. I need you. To be inside of you. Because I've got a month with you, Wendy, and there isn't going to be enough time. I'm not wasting it."

Something that looked like grief danced over her features, and he did his best to ignore that. They stripped each other naked, and made it as far as the living room rug. He pulled her over the top of him, and thrust up inside of her. Let her set the tempo of the lovemaking this time. Let her have control. She flipped her blond hair over her shoulder, planted her hands on his chest and rode him, the view provided by the position making him feel like his heart might explode.

Then she closed her eyes and let her head fall back, small incoherent sounds issued from her lips creating a glorious soundtrack to his need.

Her climax came quick, and he was grateful, because that meant he could give her two.

As she continued to move over him, he pressed his thumb right there, to that sensitized bundle of nerves, and began to stroke her. She shivered, the second wave of her desire cresting as she cried out his name on a shudder and a shout. And then he followed her over the edge. It had been so much faster than he wanted it to be. But it had been perfect.

That woman. Damn that woman.

"Have dinner with me tonight," he said without thinking.

"I have the girls."

"Well, all of you have dinner with me tonight. I missed you last night."

"You left last night on purpose."

"I know I did. But I don't want to be alone in this house tonight, and I don't want to be without you, and I don't care if that makes sense."

"It's the sex talking," she said, throwing her arm over her face and rolling over onto her back.

"Sure it is. But it's great sex, so it can talk as loud as it wants."

"You're impossible, do you know that?"

"Whether I do or don't is sort of immaterial, don't you think?"

"No." She frowned and rolled over onto her stomach, propping herself up on her elbows. "I have a question for you."

"What is that?"

"Does anyone take care of you?"

"What?"

"Your brother left, and you made it sound like you got a lot of responsibility afterward?"

"Not a lot. It's just there were a lot of assumptions about Buck's place in the family. A lot of pressure for him to be great at riding in the rodeo, to help my dad with the ranch. He was the oldest, and then I became the de facto oldest. I had to pick up where he left off. But I already had my own place in the family, and nobody stepped in to fill that. So it was just a matter of doing a little bit of double duty. But I don't resent it."

"You're lying. You do resent it a little."

"Okay. Maybe. But like anything else, what difference does it make if I do or don't? It is what it is."

"Maybe. But if you admit your resentment, it might inspire you to figure out how to live your life a little bit differently, don't you think?"

"There is no different for me."

"Why not?"

"I don't deserve to be upset about Buck," he said, his voice hard.

"Why not?"

"Because I'm the reason he left."

Her eyes went round. "You...you're the reason?"

"I didn't mean to be. But he was...he was a mess after the

accident. Not physically. Mentally. It reminded me too much of other grief. Other times. The thing is, I know life is hard. But you have to be…you have to be realistic. You can't sit around hoping for things to be different, you have to deal with what's in front of you."

"And that's what you told him."

He nodded once. "Yes. It's what I told him. And the next day he was gone."

"Boone…"

"I don't deserve your sympathy, it's misplaced. But I don't feel guilty either. Buck was imploding, and he was going to do what he was going to do. I nudged him, I guess, with some harsh truth. But like I said, I don't wallow. I just deal."

She was silent for a moment. "Except for you dealing means…not even planning your future? Not wanting anything?"

"It's not quite like that. But I take things as they come, knowing there are certain expectations and I'm going to fulfill them."

"You're just going to ride bulls forever?"

"No. I'm retiring."

"Oh. Well. That feels like big news, Boone."

"I'll probably end up being the commissioner. After my dad retires. That's part of the deal. That was kind of supposed to be Buck's thing, but now it's not going to be. Because he's not around."

"What do you want?"

"I'm kind of uninterested in that bit of trivia. I don't care what I want. What I want doesn't really matter. What I want is secondary to what's going to happen. For my family."

"What you want isn't trivial."

He wasn't in the business of being self-indulgent, and there were limits to how deep he wanted to get into a conversation like this. But it was hard to hold back with her, so he didn't.

Because they were here, and she was beside him, naked and soft and the epitome of every desire he'd ever had.

"What I want has been trivial for years. No one asked me if

I wanted to lose a sister. No one asked if I wanted my brother to go through what he did. And most of all, since the moment I met you, Wendy, what I wanted hasn't meant a damned thing."

She looked down and then back up, a sheen of tears glimmering there, and he hated that he'd put them there. And he loved it.

Because it mattered, this thing between them. It mattered now and it always would.

"I don't like that, Boone."

"You know it's true. We had to do the right thing."

"We did the right thing," she said. She scooted closer to him and put her hand on his shoulder, then leaned in, her breast pressing against him. "And this is our reward."

She felt hollow and sad after her exchange with Boone earlier. *This is our reward.*

Was it? Was this all?

Was this it?

This furtive, intense sex that was trying to compensate for all their years of pent-up desire? Maybe that was all. Boone wasn't offering more. But Boone was also...

He was stoic and strong. He was commanding and he was so damned good.

All things that were beginning to indicate to her he was a champion martyr.

What I want is trivial.

He claimed he didn't blame himself for Buck leaving, but he clearly did. He seemed to almost relish things being hard.

He was good at being uncomfortable.

She would have said a bull rider had to be, but in the grand scheme of things, she didn't think Daniel did discomfort. Ever.

Eight seconds of physical pain, and then alcohol to numb the aftereffects. Sex when he wanted it with who he wanted it with, while his wife kept house and peace at home.

Not Boone.

He rode bulls, not because he wanted to—though he claimed

he'd found passion for it—but because he was fulfilling the destiny of his older brother, who was gone now.

He took care of his parents and worked to fill a space his dad wanted him in because he felt like he had to. Because of their losses, she assumed. It had started with his sister, that much was clear.

Even wanting her was an extension of just how happy Boone was to sit in discomfort.

He seemed happy enough to indulge with her, but there was a ticking clock on that indulgence. Wendy was starting to feel wounded by that. Crushed by it.

She was starting to question it.

Boone seemed to have made his peace with the pain in life. She wondered if he had any idea how to have joy.

Do you?

Ouch.

That was a dark question from her psyche she didn't really care to answer.

But then she picked the girls up from school and she knew the answer was a definitive yes. She knew how to have joy.

She had it in spades, even while she had something less than joy, and that might be one of the greatest tricks in life.

To be able to feel this immense pure joy while in the middle of such a massive shift. While in the middle of questioning everything she knew about herself and her life, and where she was headed.

"How was school?" she asked, once Sadie was buckled in and Mikey had finished a monologue about art class.

"Great," said Sadie.

Which was what Sadie would say no matter what.

"What was especially great?"

"Oh nothing." She sounded vacant, and guilt made Wendy's heart squeeze.

Had there been something going on at school that she'd

missed while she was busy being consumed by thoughts of torrid sex?

"What's wrong?"

"Nothing, Mom."

"I don't believe you."

"Well, I don't want to talk about it."

"Talking will make you feel better," Mikey said from the back.

"Shut up, Mikey, I'm not you!"

"Okay, that's enough. You don't need to tell Mikey to shut up. She's trying to be nice."

"She's being pushy, you both are. If Dad were here, he would know not to push me."

Because your dad doesn't care as much as I do.

Wow. Thank God she'd managed to hold back those words, because that wasn't fair at all. Daniel had been a dick to her, but when he was home, he was a good dad. The girls were mad at him right now, but they wouldn't always be.

Well, Mikey always would be a little. She had a pure soul that was rooted in honesty, and in some ways, Wendy thought her daughter was a little too like her. Like she wanted maybe a little bit too much from a world that was never going to give it. That made her unforgiving and rigid sometimes, and also made her say things to her grumpy older sister like *talking will make you feel better*, because she only ever said what she believed.

Sadie, though, would forgive him. Because Sadie wanted things not to hurt so much, and forgiving her dad would make that relationship hurt less.

Wendy needed her girls to be able to forgive him.

She needed to keep some of the spite to herself.

You have Boone for your spite.

Well, that was almost a worse thought. Boone wasn't her human crutch, and he sure as hell wasn't there to just listen to her endlessly complain about her marriage.

He would say he was happy to do that, she knew.

Because that was Boone entirely.

What did his feelings matter?

What did his desires matter?

She thought of him ordering her down onto her knees. With a cushion firmly in place for her comfort.

She turned her car down the driveway to the ranch, and had the sudden image of one of her first dates with Daniel, at a pizza parlor that had pinball machines. She'd watched him play for a couple of hours, and she'd thought then that she was so dizzy with her infatuation for him she might as well be one of the balls in the machine.

She felt like a pinball now.

Worried about her kids. Worried about their relationship with their dad.

Flashbacks to giving a blowjob to the hottest man she knew.

Ping. Ping.

And right into the hole.

"We're having dinner at Boone's tonight."

"I'm not in the mood!" Sadie wailed. "I don't want to be social. I just want to have a plate of food and go to my room."

Well, this was wonderful.

"You can have a plate of food at Boone's and then leave, no one is asking you to stay and chat all night."

"You can't just dump this on me."

"I can't just dump you eating dinner next door to the house we're staying in, with someone you like a lot, who has generously given us a place to stay?"

"Yes!" She said that as if it was obvious, and also as if Wendy was an actual monster.

"Fine, Sadie, I'll leave you a plate at home, then."

"You're leaving me by myself?"

She said that tremulously and angrily, and if Wendy weren't also overwrought, she might have laughed. "Unsolvable problem, Sadie," she said. She was often reminding her daughter that she loved to present her mother with a problem, then when given solutions, she had a ready spate of reasons they wouldn't work.

Which was fifteen and fair, she guessed, but why did everything have to be a struggle?

"I just don't know why we have to go to Boone's."

"Because he is my friend and I wanted to spend the evening with him, and he wanted to see you both because he hasn't."

"I want to go to Boone's," said Mikey. "I haven't even been inside the house and we've been here for four days."

That earned a growl from Sadie, and Wendy accepted that there would be no consensus. Which was just life and parenting sometimes, but she didn't like it especially.

She knew she could be a hard-ass about Sadie's attitude if she wanted to be. But the thing was, Wendy had an attitude about things a lot of the time too. She'd smashed Daniel's headlights in after all. And yes, it had felt deserved.

But she knew all of this felt real and deserved to Sadie.

Maybe also you feel a lot of guilt over the whole thing.

Maybe.

Which wasn't fair, it wasn't her fault.

Not the divorce…you wanting to spend time with Boone.

Yeah. Okay fine.

They got home and Sadie went straight to her room while Wendy started dinner with Mikey sitting at the kitchen table. She could have cooked at Boone's, but she would rather be here talking to Mikey while she worked, and in close proximity to the melting down teenager.

"I don't know what her deal is," Mikey said.

"She's fifteen."

"I won't act that way when I'm fifteen."

Her heart squeezed tight. *Oh, Mikey. You will.*

"Thanks, honey."

"What are you making?"

"Lasagna."

"Yum."

At least she was doing something right in Mikey's world. Right now, she'd take it.

And after she was done with dinner and it was time to head to Boone's, Sadie appeared in a hoodie, with her hands stuffed in her kangaroo pouch pockets and the hood firmly over her head. But she appeared.

"Lasagna?" she asked.

"Yes. I can dish you a plate and you can go back to your cave, or you can come over for a little while."

She shrugged. "I'll come over."

So they made their way over to Boone's with a big bowl of salad, a pan of lasagna and no small amount of resentment from Sadie, like a parade. If only a very small one.

Boone opened the door and grinned. "Thanks for the dinner party."

And she noticed Sadie was charmed by him, even if reluctantly.

The house was better organized now, even though they'd spent the last two days having sex, which had taken up a good portion of her cleaning time. Apparently when she was motivated she could get a lot done.

But to his credit, Boone had set the table nicely for them, and he had an array of soft drinks in the fridge, which she knew was for the girls.

"Thank you," she said softly, as the girls dished their plates and took their seats.

"How is everything?" Boone asked.

Thankfully Sadie didn't implode and Mikey took the lead, talking about her art classes and her new friends with a lot of enthusiasm.

It made Wendy feel conflicted because Mikey was clearly finding a group she enjoyed here, even after four days, and Wendy was planning on going somewhere else after the month ended.

You were planning on getting away from Boone's charity, it doesn't mean you have to leave.

No, it didn't.

But how could she live near him without…

Why was she so afraid of that? Why couldn't she entertain the idea of a future with him?

She knew why. She knew all the logical reasons why. You shouldn't go from being married to being with someone new, and the stakes were so high. Her daughters had been through enough and she didn't want to drag them through any extra instability. And it was possible she felt pressure to be the most perfect parent so they would always stay on her side.

Well. She wasn't going to win that game. She was the parent most actively parenting, so she was going to be the bad one sometimes and there was nothing she could do about that.

She looked across the table and met Boone's gaze.

And resisted the feeling of rightness that washed through her.

This had been a weird mistake.

A form of torture.

She hadn't thought it through.

Sitting around a family dinner table with him and eating all together. Seeing where he could fit into her life. Into the most important spaces of it.

"And how was your day?" he asked, now looking directly at Wendy.

She blushed. She could feel it. Her whole face went hot and she hoped—she really hoped—her children would continue to be the preteen/teenage narcissists she could generally count on them to be and not notice subtle shifts in their mother.

"It was good, thank you. And yours?" She nearly coughed as she took a bite of her salad.

"Best I've had in a while."

She almost kicked him under the table.

True to her word, Sadie melted away as soon as dinner was

over, but Mikey lingered, and Boone and Wendy ended up at the sink doing dishes while she chattered about the drawing techniques she was experimenting with, and how her favorite YouTubers did certain kinds of animation styles.

Wendy looked sideways at Boone, who looked down at her and smiled. Her shoulder touched his, and it was her turn to feel like she was in middle school.

Her stomach fluttered.

And without thinking she leaned in and brushed her arm against his very deliberately, which earned her a grin.

And another stomach flutter for good measure.

"But I really need to get some alcohol markers, because I think it would help with making the lines on my art crisper."

That jolted Wendy back into the moment. "Oh. Okay."

They finished up the dishes and she walked back to the house with Mikey.

"I really like Boone," Mikey said. "He's cool."

"Yeah. He is. I like him too." An understatement, but the most she was going to say to her twelve-year-old, who blessedly hadn't noticed any of the subtext happening all night.

Unfortunately, Wendy felt steeped in subtext.

And in the aching window into another life tonight had given her.

What would it be like if she stopped worrying about what she thought was smart, or right—in the context of what other people would say—and just went for what she wanted?

If she closed her eyes and thought of her perfect life, Boone was in it.

So why was she fighting that so hard?

To try and protect herself.

But that ship had sailed, along with her inhibitions, right about the time she'd first kissed him.

The only real question was if she was going to keep on letting her childhood, the pain in her past, Daniel, the pain of his betrayal and the years' worth of lies decide what she got to have.

Yes, it was fast. But it also wasn't.

Boone had been there all along, and so had her feelings for him.

She had kept them in the most appropriate place possible. She had been a good wife. She'd honored her vows.

But the feelings had been there all the same. Daniel had been a great reason not to act on them then. He didn't get to be her reason anymore.

She was her reason.

And because of how she loved she could trust everything to flow from there.

Because she loved her girls, and their happiness would feed hers. She could trust herself.

To make the best decisions she was capable of making—not perfect ones, but not wholly selfish ones either.

She just had to hope that in the end, Boone wanted the same things she did.

But if not...

She was strong. And she had a lot of things to live for, and smile for.

She knew how to hold happiness and sadness in her hands at the same time.

So, if she had to, she'd just hold it all, and keep living.

Chapter Nine

When his phone rang, he half expected it to be Daniel because he had heard from the disgruntled asshole more times in the last few days than he would like to. Actually just twice, but that was more than he would like, and he especially didn't want to speak to him after having incredible transformative sex with the guy's soon-to-be ex-wife. Not because Boone was ashamed, and not because he found it weird. It was because, as angry as he had been before, he was even angrier now. Wendy deserved better. She deserved a whole lot better, and he wasn't going to be able to restrain himself from saying that. Because she was everything.

It wasn't Daniel, however, it was Flint.

"Hey. Calling from your private jet?"

"She doesn't travel by private jet. She thinks that's problematic for the environment."

"Wow. Not because you can't afford to."

"She's very famous," said Flint.

"You don't find that threatening to your masculinity?"

His brother laughed. The sound deep and rolling across the phone line. "No. My masculinity is good. Anyway. Tansey and

I are coming into town tomorrow, and I was hoping we could get together for a family barbecue."

"Yeah. Sounds good."

That would be time spent away from Wendy, though. He could bring her, of course, but that would be integrating her into the family in a way that...

Hell.

"I hear your hesitation. I'm wondering if it's because of your houseguest."

"I don't have a houseguest," he said, mentally trying to determine which person might have told Flint what was going on.

"I talked to Jace," he said. "He mentioned you had Wendy Stevens staying with you."

"Not with me. Wendy and her daughters are staying in the cottage on my property, and Wendy is doing some work for me. I'm paying her, and I'm giving her a place to stay while she works on extricating herself from that situation with her cheating husband."

"Got it. And it has no connection whatsoever with your personal feelings for her?"

"Of course it does. I don't just go offering a place to any random woman."

There was no point lying about it.

"Yeah. Well. Maybe you should bring her."

"Yeah, I was thinking..."

"I know you were thinking. I could practically hear you thinking. But you might as well bring her. And the kids."

"That might be weird."

"It's only weird if you make it weird, Boone. Maybe you should figure yourself out."

"There's nothing to figure out. I'm not in any way confused about what's happening right now."

"Well. Good for you. You're the only one of us who's managed to get entangled with somebody and not be confused."

"It's not an entanglement. I've known her for a long time,

and she's a friend. She needs somebody right now. And I'm not going to lie and say there's nothing more happening. But, you know, I would never put pressure on her to make it too much. And that's the problem," he said. "Yeah. That's the problem. If I go inviting her to a family thing she might think I'm pushing her for too much too soon."

"Or she might be grateful. You should leave it up to her."

That was the second time he'd had that feedback from one of his brothers. The second time they had pointed out he was making the decisions for Wendy, and maybe he shouldn't do that.

He could understand. And he even agreed. Because he didn't think it was right to make decisions on a woman's behalf. But he was just... He could foresee issues here, and again, he didn't hold out blind hope something wouldn't be awkward when it was clear it would be.

Except not inviting her...

Dammit.

"Fine. I'll invite her. I'm looking forward to seeing you."

"You too."

He got off the phone, and decided to walk straight back to his place. And there she was. In all her glory. He'd already been back to see her today, already made love to her. And she was looking at him with wide eyes. "I have to go get the girls in, like, ten minutes."

"I could get it done in ten minutes."

Her cheeks turned pink. "I'm sure you could..."

"That isn't why I'm here. My brother Flint and his fiancée, Tansey, are coming into town tomorrow. We're having a barbecue and I thought maybe you and the girls might come."

"As in... Tansey Martin."

"Yes. Tansey Martin. I know she and their breakup are very famous. As is their reconciliation, since there are now songs about that, too, and about to be a whole album."

"My girls are going to freak out." She shook her head. "We

probably shouldn't go. Because it's a family thing, and they're just going to be starstruck."

"Oh, they are. Not you."

She laughed. "Okay. I will be a little bit, but I'll be able to control it. Because I'm an adult."

"It's okay. She brings that out in people. You can be starstruck. But also if…if it seems weird to you to come to a thing with my whole family…"

She frowned. "It's weird for you, isn't it?"

"I didn't say that."

"Your face said it. You don't want me to go."

"Wendy," he said, regret tugging at his chest. "I do want you to go. I'm honest, right? I'm being honest. I was just a little bit worried about some of the…"

"You're worried about getting too involved."

"Yes. Because everything feels great right now, but it isn't going to last."

"Why not?"

She looked at him, so open and trusting, and it killed him.

"You know why. I've still got some time in the rodeo left. You and Dan aren't even divorced…"

"That sounds like a lot."

"We don't need to get ahead of ourselves," he said.

"Don't pull away from me just because of all that."

He let out a hard breath. "I'm not. You're the one who said you wanted to leave at the end of the month."

"I might not leave town."

"Great. I'd love it if you didn't leave town."

Except that felt like something clawing at his chest, and he couldn't quite say why.

"Maybe we both just settle down a little bit. And I will come to the family thing, as long as you're good with it."

"I'm very good with it. Perfectly happy."

"If the girls found out Tansey Martin was going to be a thing at your parents' house and they weren't allowed to go…"

"You're welcome to be there. I'm sorry."

He looked at her, and he felt… Wounded. It was the strangest thing. He had messed that up. He hadn't handled it well, and he just had to wonder if in the end he was going to do more harm than good to her. It was the last thing he wanted.

Of all the things, he knew that. But she was just asking those questions. Why couldn't they be together? Why not?

There weren't simple words for why not. That was the problem. Maybe he'd been avoiding thinking about whether or not his plan was to end up by himself because he hadn't planned on finding somebody or because that was the way it was going to be.

The fact was, the one woman he'd been able to imagine himself being with was Wendy. And it had been one thing when she was with another man. One thing when she was married. That had been destiny. She was safe from him when they'd met.

And now, everything else was due to Daniel's shortcoming. It didn't count.

It wasn't a thing.

It meant he got to have her now. It didn't mean he had anything different up ahead of him.

He had to keep clearheaded about it.

"I'll see you later."

"Yeah. I… I probably won't make the girls come over and have dinner tonight."

"Hey. Fair."

"But they'll enjoy the family thing on Saturday. So. And I'll see you before then. I…"

"Yeah. I know."

"Okay, I'll see you."

He didn't move. She did, though, headed past him and out to her car. And somehow, he felt like he'd made a mistake. He just didn't know what it was.

Chapter Ten

She had underestimated how awkward it would be to load everyone up into Boone's truck again with the amount of tension she felt just looking at him.

She was sure even her narcissistic teenagers would feel the tension.

Surely.

They didn't seem to, though. It was only Wendy who was sweaty and nervous and far too hot as they drove from Boone's ranch at one end of Lone Rock, to his family ranch all the way on the other end and out the other side of town.

She was never half so grateful for how absorbed teenagers were in their own issues than she had been these last few days. Or maybe that was simply because she was so absorbed in her own issues. Maybe it wasn't a teenage thing. Maybe it had to do with life being exciting. New.

It was always like that for her kids. Bless them. It was like that right now for her. Bless Boone.

She looked at his strong profile as he pulled the car up into the front of his parents' massive home. Yes, things were definitely exciting with him. But somehow, not easy. And you would think that if you had wanted a man for fifteen years, the coming together would be the easy part.

But maybe that was the problem. Something was holding him back. And she could understand there were logical things. There were things that had been holding her back.

But maybe that was the problem. Maybe she had to go all in. *You've done that before.*

Yes. She had. She had gone all in with Daniel. But it wasn't the same.

It just wasn't.

Boone...

Maybe calling it love now, this early, was a little bit foolish.

But maybe she felt a little bit foolish.

Maybe she was foolish. Certainly jumping into bed with a man on the rebound was somewhat typical behavior, but falling for the idea that it might be something more? There was almost no chance of anybody making that mistake unless they were doing it willingly.

Willfully even.

But what if it wasn't a mistake? What if it was him? What if it was always supposed to be him? Or maybe, even more beautifully, it was supposed to be him now, and the way she had felt about him up until this point was essential to being brought here to this moment.

Maybe.

But as she stared at his profile, intently, she just knew something.

She wasn't entirely sure what. But it was certain and settled in her soul. And the one thing she couldn't do in response was hold herself back.

She had to be all in. She had to be his.

"Let's go in," she said.

"Yeah," he said, looking at her and forcing a smile.

Wendy felt heavy, but she got out of the truck, and the girls followed suit.

"Is Tansey Martin really going to be here?" Mikey asked her mom, her eyes large.

"Yes. Why would I say that if it wasn't true?"

"To try and beat Sadie out of her room."

"I would never try and beat Sadie with something as basic as a pop-country crossover star. Sadie is not that basic."

"I'm basic," said Mikey.

"Mom," said Sadie. "You make me sound like a snob."

"I'm not making you sound like a snob. You are a snob. But it's okay. You're fifteen. It's your right."

"Tansey is very nearly my sister-in-law. I assume you know about the song," said Boone.

"Yes," said Mikey seriously. "We watched the short film."

"You should make sure to tell Flint that. He loves it. He's a huge fan. It did great things for his life."

Wendy looked at him in warning. "Don't tell teenagers things like that. They'll do it."

"I'm counting on it."

"What are you supposed to do when there's just, like, a famous person there?" Sadie asked.

"You just, like, eat your hamburger," Boone said, grinning at her.

Sadie smiled, which was glorious for Wendy to see.

Boone was so good with them.

They had a dad. But Boone would make a great masculine figure to have in their lives. He was protective. He was fun.

She wanted him.

He would make her happy.

Or at least contribute quite a bit to her happiness. That would help everybody.

Just jump in feetfirst. You're already there.

The Carson family home was massive, and beautiful, with floor-to-ceiling windows overlooking the craggy mountains and rustic decor throughout.

It was filled with all the siblings—even Boone's sister Callie, who Wendy knew vaguely from the rodeo. That was the great thing. It wasn't a room full of strangers. She knew Boone's parents, and she knew all his brothers, even if only in passing.

She had spent enough time at the circuit to feel like they were family in many ways.

"And how are you finding the single life?" This question came from Abe Carson.

"I'm not technically single," she said, grateful her daughters were occupied across the room. Talking to Tansey, who was warm and wonderful and actually not at all intimidating.

"Philosophically," said Abe.

"Thanks, Dad," said Boone.

"I see," said Abe. "Well, hurry up and get that divorce finalized so my son can make an honest woman out of you."

Her scalp prickled. "Well, I am happy to move it quickly."

She didn't see the point in protesting. Because hell, she kind of wanted Boone to make an honest woman out of her. Or a dishonest one. She just wanted to be with him. And her parameters for what that could look like were becoming quite elastic. At first, she had been a bit concerned about her girls knowing she was sleeping with a man she wasn't married to. But if they had a relationship… She was willing to have a serious and grown-up talk about it. Because this was life, and it was messy. She was in a situation she hadn't chosen, but she didn't have to be miserable.

"Actually, Wendy is looking for some new work. You know she managed Daniel."

"She could manage you," said Abe. "And there are some other guys I know who would love to have competent representation."

"I'm not sure I'm going to be anybody's favorite, considering I just kicked their buddy to the curb."

"If they have half a brain then *he's* not their favorite. I've never had patience for a man who would go out for cheap ground beef when he had filet mignon at home."

"Seems to me," Flint said from across the room, "that it's the man with quality issues, not the woman."

"Sorry, son," said Abe. "I know I'm not woke."

"I don't think I'm woke," said Flint. "I just like women."

Wendy couldn't help but smile at the exchange.

They were a good family. Everybody involved was just… They cared about each other. And it didn't matter if they disagreed about things or saw things differently, they cared about each other. It felt different than what she'd imagined family might be. It had just been her and her mother after all.

And now it was her and the girls.

But even though she had a good relationship with Sadie and Mikey, it hadn't quite been this. Or at least, it had never quite been this between herself and Daniel. Because one thing she noticed was the way Abe and his wife interacted with each other.

There was an ease to them. And she didn't think she and Daniel had ever had that ease.

She looked at Boone. She wanted to feel it with him.

But she had a feeling if she put her hand on his, he would pull away, and she didn't want that.

She felt like they could have something easy and wonderful. If only they were brave enough to take the chance.

So she got up from her position on the couch and moved over to him, sitting next to him. It was a fairly unambiguous move.

No one said anything, but they all looked.

The other reason she couldn't go putting her hand on him just yet was the girls.

She needed to talk to them. At least, it felt like she should.

Not to get their permission, just to give them a warning. A heads-up. Her mother had never dated when Wendy was growing up, because her father had done such a number on her she had never wanted a man in her life again. It made Wendy sad, in hindsight.

And maybe the only way Sadie and Mikey would ever be able to understand Wendy wanting to be with somebody else was going to be in hindsight. Or maybe that assumption wasn't fair to them.

"We should go shooting," said Jace.

"What in the redneck?" Cara asked.

"It's a Carson family tradition. We love a good target practice."

Callie looked at her husband. "Will you stay with the baby?"

"Sure," he said.

"I'll stay with the baby," said Callie's mother. "You can all go shoot. I don't mind."

"Can I watch?" Mikey asked.

"Sure," said Wendy.

She had a feeling they were all going out for target practice.

"I guess I'll go," said Sadie, keeping an eye on Tansey, obviously curious about whether or not her new best friend was going.

"Sounds great," said Tansey brightly.

And so with that, they all trooped outside.

"We like to shoot up this way near this big gravel pit. It's got good secure backings so the bullets don't go drifting off anywhere they shouldn't."

"Good to know."

"My dad has extra ear protection in the shed."

"Oh good. So as far as adventurous activities go…"

"This one is occurring in a well-controlled fashion. No worries."

"I wasn't actually worried. I know you would never do anything to put yourself or the girls in danger."

He looked down at her, the exchange between them feeling weighty. Significant.

"I wouldn't," he said.

The girls were behind them, and so she didn't take his hand. But she did bump her shoulder against his, and he looked down, smiling. She smiled back.

"I like you."

He looked a little bit like she had hit him in the side of the head. "I like you too."

It felt pale in comparison to what she was actually feeling, but she didn't know how to say the other things. She didn't know what else to say.

It felt sharp and dangerous still. And this was the problem with never having been good at math. Order of operations was something she struggled with. She wanted to kiss him now. In front of everybody. Because there was a significant part of her that had already realized she had to go all in. That had already realized there was no going back. That had already realized she would never be able to quit him, never be able to forget him.

And there would be no protecting herself from any manner of heartbreak.

She would be heartbroken to lose him. Whether she told him she was in love with him or not. Whether she said she wanted everything or not.

Whether she did the important work of extricating herself from her marriage, and then tried to do some healing on her own, she was always going to come back to him. So she might as well... She just might as well.

Put herself out there. But there were ways that she needed to go about it. She knew that.

So she just smiled, and she kept *like* as the word, even though it wasn't enough. Not even close.

When they got up to the gravel pit, she and the girls put on ear protection and hung back while they took turns shooting things. Targets, yes, some kind of jelly target that healed itself. And also water jugs. Which did not heal themselves, but exploded grandly.

Mikey was very invested in the spectacle, and Sadie pretended to be just a little bit too cool. But ended up enjoying it all the same. Wendy could tell by the small smile on her face.

She felt a rush of euphoria right then. This could be their family.

Don't rush ahead of yourself and start glorifying all of this. They're just people. And they're not going to fix the difficult situation you're in.

No. That was what she had to be extra careful about.

Boone wasn't a crutch. He never would be. He was more than that.

And she felt…scared. It reminded her of old times.

She didn't like it.

But she really did want him and all these things that he came with. That wasn't so bad, was it?

She knew all these things he could do for her. All these things he had done for her.

And yes, she was working for him, but it wasn't the same.

She wanted to think of something she could do for him.

He felt so much responsibility toward everybody in his life.

And she didn't want to be just another responsibility to him. She wanted to be something more.

She watched as he shouldered the rifle, and she squeezed her thighs together, because whether she should or not, she was always going to find that hot.

Or maybe it was just him. And he could breathe and she would experience a pulse of arousal. Entirely possible. The man had an extreme effect on her.

He blew up the water jug with one shot, and she laughed and clapped. She couldn't help herself.

Maybe it was a little juvenile. But she felt juvenile, she'd already admitted that. This felt new. Wonderful. Terrifying.

And she wanted it. All of it.

They had target practice contests, and in the end it was their sister Callie who bested everybody. Afterward, they hoisted her up on their shoulders, while she screeched in protest, and Tansey, Wendy and the girls clapped. Cara pretended to be furious, while Shelby and Juniper made grand shows out of being gracious losers, since they had competed as well.

When they started the walk back, Flint was up with his sister, and Wendy lagged behind with her girls.

"I want to tell you something," said Wendy.

"What?" asked Sadie.

This was dangerous. Because the girls could make a big scene right here. But…she didn't really care.

Mostly because she just wasn't ashamed of any of it. If they had a bad reaction to it, they were going to have to deal with it.

"I just wanted to let you know that I…that I like Boone."

"Of course you do," said Mikey. "He's cool."

"No, Mikey. I… I *like* like Boone."

Both the girls stopped walking. "You're not serious?" Sadie asked.

"I am. And I wanted to tell you before…"

"Before what?" Sadie asked.

"Just before. That's all. Before anyone else."

"You're not even divorced yet," said Sadie.

"I know. I'm just being honest. And maybe it's premature. I don't know what's going to happen, if anything. Entirely possible *nothing*. But I just like him."

It wasn't Sadie who reacted. It wasn't Sadie who had an explosion. To Mikey's credit, it wasn't an explosion. But she put her head down, and she ran ahead. She wasn't quite in a group with anyone, but she held herself with her head down, and walked, and Wendy was too stunned to catch up with her. She felt frozen, and kept walking at the pace she'd been walking at before, uncertain of what to do. She really hated all the uncertainty.

"It's weird," said Sadie.

"I know," said Wendy.

"She'll get over it."

She looked at Sadie. "Are you over it?"

"I don't know. I think it's weird because… Because it hasn't been that long. But he's been really nice to us, and I know he makes you happy. You haven't been happy. And really, you shouldn't be. You left just a few weeks ago, and everything's been crazy, and you were not happy until we got here."

"But you're not especially happy here, are you?"

"I don't know. I do know that I wasn't happy back home either. I'm trying to be. But this is all weird, and it's a change."

"I want you girls to be happy. And I would never do anything to compromise that."

"That's the thing. I'm not sure there's anything you can do one way or the other. Sometimes we're just unhappy."

It was clarity from her oldest daughter that she hadn't really expected. But she could understand the truth there. They were teenagers. And she wasn't going to be able to make them happy. Not all the time.

"Okay. I accept that. But I do want you to know that I love you," she said. "No matter what. And all this stuff… I don't want it to make you afraid."

"What?"

"We haven't talked that much about what it was like for me growing up. But for good reasons, my mom was afraid of some things. And she made me afraid of them too. And I don't want my issues to become yours. I have them. Of course I do. And you can have your own. Like you said, you can't be happy all the time. Because you have your own life. I'm not in charge of that. But I love you, and I'm here for you. And to the best of my ability, I don't want the stuff I'm going through to mess with you. If you're miserable here, I want you to tell me. But I think I want to try to make a life with Boone. I don't know if he's going to want that with me."

"Okay. I guess that's…fair."

She could tell Sadie wasn't exactly overjoyed, but she didn't look upset or outraged either.

"I'll talk to Mikey."

"Maybe you should talk to Boone first," said Sadie.

"Well, what if Mikey can't deal?" She hated all this fear. This fear that made up her life. She'd been so certain that marrying

Daniel had gotten rid of it, but it hadn't. She was stitched together by fear, her whole life a patchwork quilt. Hunger, fear, then family, love. But the thread was fear either way.

She'd been so scared of losing Daniel, of losing her stability, and now she had. She was afraid of messing things up with her kids, afraid of losing Boone…

There was just so much to be afraid of. And it was what she'd known from the time she was a kid.

"Mikey is twelve," said Sadie. "I don't think you should go making decisions based on her moods."

"I could apply the same thing to you."

"I know. You shouldn't make decisions because of me. You're the adult."

She *was* the adult. But she was a freaked-out adult.

Still, she had to act like the adult.

And maybe as much as she wanted to be gentle with her kids right now, there was a merit in setting boundaries too. And in that, she supposed Sadie was right. Maybe she had to figure herself out first. She had a little bit of that epiphany earlier. But there was a certain amount of happiness she had to find before she could be the best parent.

This conversation with Sadie was confirming it. Removing barriers and obstacles she had put in her own way.

"Okay. I'll sort it out with Boone."

"He is nice. It'll be weird for you to be with someone that isn't Dad. But…"

"Yeah, life is weird. I guess if you've learned one thing from me, I don't want this to scar you, but it's not the worst thing to learn, it's that life changes. And sometimes the best thing you can do is just go with it."

So she was going to go with it. Whether it was smart or advised or not anything of the kind. She was going to go with it because it was her life. And it didn't matter what best practices were. She was living. And it was messy. Real. One of her kids understood, and one of them didn't. She wasn't going to get a one hundred percent buy-in here. She was just going to have to love them.

And herself.

And Boone.

And in the end she was going to have to hope it was enough.

Because fate might've put her in his path all those years ago, but fate wasn't going to make the right decisions for her now. Only she could do that.

She had resisted for a while. But what she wanted was going to require some work. So she was going to have to get busy.

Chapter Eleven

When Boone woke up the next morning, coffee was on in the kitchen.

And he could smell bacon.

It was Sunday, but he still had ranch work to do. He wondered if Wendy...

Yesterday with his family had been a whole trip. He had been so close to pulling her into his arms on multiple occasions, and yet he had known he couldn't. Because what was the point of it? But she was here today.

He walked downstairs, and there she was in the kitchen.

"Good morning."

"What are you doing over here?"

"I decided to make you breakfast."

"Thank you."

"You're welcome."

"Do the girls think you're having an early shift?"

"You're hilarious. It's the weekend. The girls aren't going to know anything until sometime after 10 a.m. But, anyway, I'm not worried about it. I told them."

"You told them?"

"Yes."

"What did you tell them?"

"Not that we were banging on every surface in the house, but that I liked you."

"That you liked me."

"Yes. That I *like you* like you."

"And how did that go?"

"Fifty-fifty. But I wasn't asking anybody's permission."

"Okay..."

She held up a hand. "You don't have to say anything."

"I figure I probably should."

"There's not much to say."

"Well. The thing is... I thought you were leaving in a month." He'd reminded himself of it every day. The reality of it. Of the situation.

She was still married.

She had kids.

She was leaving.

"I keep telling you, I'm not necessarily leaving. I appreciate everything you've done for me. What do you need?"

He looked at her dumbfounded. "What?"

"Boone, what do you need? You're retiring, you're starting this ranch. Do you want to take over the commission?"

"I told you, it doesn't really matter what I want—"

"Why not? Why do other people get all the consideration? Your father doesn't need you to take over the rodeo commission. That's about want. His. So why does it outweigh yours? Or why do your wants not even get to be up for consideration? I don't understand that. It doesn't make any sense to me."

"Because what the hell else am I going to do with my life, Wendy?"

"I was thinking about that the other day. And I was thinking about what your dad said. That I could represent the other cowboys. I know we didn't talk about that for very long yesterday, but I could do that. He's right. It's just a matter of going out and making the most of my connections. I'm really good at this. Representing people. I could do you too. But the thing is, opportunities don't just come to you. And I've understood that when it comes to agenting. But I haven't always been great about that in my personal life. And you're great. You're wonderful with the rodeo, you've got this property, all of that. But do you know... Do you understand that you can't just let life carry you down a current? You have to—"

"Yes I know that," he said. "I'm not just drifting. And I resent the hell out of the suggestion that I am."

"That isn't what I meant. I just meant you can't wait for things to fall into place. You have to get them. And you have to care."

"I care. I care so much that I have shoved everything I've ever wanted to the side. For my mother. For my father. For my friendship with your idiot husband."

"Well, Daniel isn't our problem anymore."

"He's the father of your kids. He is still our problem."

She shook her head. "I don't love him. I haven't for a long time. I don't love him, and I don't want that life back. I don't. It costs so much. And I didn't even realize it. It was so expensive to stay in that marriage. I thought it would be too expensive to leave it. But that isn't it at all. The real expense was in staying there. I wasn't happy. I liked being in that house by myself. I didn't like being in it with him. I didn't like *him*. I like being alone more. I convinced myself that I liked him, but what I felt was a holdover from what we used to have. What I liked, I think, was the part-time nature of it. I don't love him. And I was going to just...let duty or honor or the fear of change hold me there.

"I'm not sorry that I didn't do something disreputable. I'm not sorry that we didn't... I'm not sorry that I was faithful to him. I'm not. But I am a little bit sorry that I convinced myself somehow that doing the right thing would be what made me the happiest. When I say the right thing, what I mean was this idea of the right thing, this idea of what marriage vows were, this idea my husband didn't even agree with. I convinced myself it had to be the best thing, it had to be fate. It's not about fate. It was about fear. Fear of change. Fear of finding out if I left him, I'd have nothing, but that's a terrible reason to stay married. We get to make choices. And we get to demand more. We get to demand better. Anyway, I'm just... I'm deciding. And I'm here to have breakfast."

"Breakfast and demands. That's a whole thing."

"Well, *I'm* a whole thing. But I don't actually want to make demands."

"Except you want to know what I want."

"Let me care about that. Please. If you won't."

But he didn't have words. He didn't have anything. Nothing but a weird, pounding sense of panic moving through his chest, so he leaned in and he kissed her. Because it was better than talking. Because it was better than just about anything. Because when she asked what he wanted all he could think of was her, and everything else felt like details. Everything else felt like it might not matter.

He kissed her because she was what he wanted. Because she was everything.

Because she always had been.

He kissed her because it was like breathing.

It didn't much matter if it made sense. It had never made sense. He held her against his body, and growled.

"There's bacon," she said weakly.

"Fuck the bacon."

She blinked. "Okay."

He backed her up against the wall, kissing her, consuming her.

"I want you, Wendy. And none of it matters. None of it matters."

"Yes," she said.

Except that was wrong. It was wrong that he just... It was terrifying. Because it couldn't last. Nothing ever could.

He could already feel himself losing her. He could feel it in the dissatisfaction she was expressing this morning. In her asking for things he didn't know how to give.

He could feel it in the way his heart pounded when he tried to imagine forever, but could only picture his house empty.

He was losing her.

By inches.

Because that was what happened when someone was close to you. As close as a person could be. They had to start moving away at some point.

It was the natural order of things. An inevitability.

It was inevitable and he knew it.

He *knew* it.

It was just the way of the world. But right now, he was holding her. Firm against his body, and he was holding her so tight he was shaking.

And it would never be enough.

That was the other problem. When you cared about people, no amount of time could ever be enough.

There was no good cut-off point to a relationship. There just wasn't.

But sometimes things were terminal. And you had to accept it.

It would never feel like quite enough. And he was so unbearably, horribly aware of that as he pressed her soft body against the hard wall of his body and poured every ounce of his need into the kiss.

It was somewhere beyond need. It was desperation.

He stripped her shirt up over her head, but it got hung up on the apron because he couldn't think. Because he couldn't do things in the right order.

Hell. That seemed like a metaphor.

He untied the apron and threw it down onto the floor, taking the shirt with it.

She had on a sexy, lacy bra, not the normal kind of thing she wore.

And it was for him. And that mattered more than the bra itself. That she was wearing it for him, and he knew it.

All of this was for him. The coffee, the bacon, the sex. It was his.

And why did that feel terrifying?

Why did this feel like the beginning of the end? He didn't have an answer for that.

All he had was need.

So he kissed her like he was dying, because he thought he might be.

Because the idea of having to answer the question of what he wanted beyond what he'd already said seemed like a gallows.

And when he had her naked against the wall, he freed himself from his jeans and lifted her leg up over his hip and slid deep inside of her.

He watched her face as he began to move, as he moved deep inside of her, he wanted her. Wanted this. He wanted it to go on forever. But nothing ever did. Nothing ever did. His climax came on too hot, too strong, too fast.

He resented it.

And so he held back, bit the inside of his cheek so he could keep on going. Until she cried out, until her internal muscles pulsed around him. Until she was coming apart all over him, because he needed her to be as shattered as he was.

He needed to gain some control.

He put his hand between them, stroked her, brought her to climax again. He withdrew from her body, and sank to his knees, burying his face between her thighs and licking her until she shattered again.

He would do whatever he had to, to keep this going. Until he couldn't bear it anymore. Until he was so hard it hurt. Until the memory of what it had been like to be buried inside of her became too much, and he pulled her down onto the floor and over top of him, down onto his length, letting her ride him for two easy movements until he couldn't stand it anymore. Until he reversed their positions and pounded hard into her. Losing himself in this. In her.

Losing himself entirely.

And that moment felt endless. And over all too quickly.

And when she shattered again, he lost his own control.

He growled, letting go. Of everything. Absolutely everything.

And it felt like a loss when it was done.

And all she'd asked him was what he wanted.

But it had broken something inside of him.

"I love you."

And that was it. That was the beginning of the end.

Because this bright, white light tried to ignite in his chest and it was the one thing he could never accept. Not ever.

"Wendy…"

"No," she said. "Don't."

"Don't what?"

"Don't argue with me. Don't disagree with me. Don't make this harder than it has to be. You don't need to answer me right now, you don't. We can take our time. I'm sorry, I'm jumping ahead. But I don't know how else to let you know that I don't want to have a time limit on this."

"But everything has a time limit," he said. "Nothing lasts forever. It's better this way. If we can just decide on an end-point and—"

"It's been sixteen years. It's been sixteen years and I want you more today than I ever have. It has been sixteen years since you walked into that bar right after I married my husband and ruined my life, Boone. You ruined me. I have not wanted another man since. I haven't even entertained the idea."

"Except the man you were married to."

"That's different. It should have gone away, and it would've gone away. With time. You know, with the fact that I had children with somebody else. That I was supposed to love him and honor and cherish him for the rest of our lives."

"The only reason you didn't is because of him."

"I know that. I know that. You don't need to tell me why my marriage ended. You don't need to tell me what happened. I am well aware."

"I'm just saying, you were with somebody else and now you're not. And I'm an itch."

"Don't do that. Don't cheapen what we have. If you have to run away from this, then at least take it like a man. Don't belittle what we have. It's not fair. I deserve more than that, and so do you. Just be honest. Be honest about the fact that you can't cope, or that something's holding you back, or that you just don't feel the same as I do, but don't make it about me. I spent my whole life afraid, Boone. I'm just tired of it. I'm done. I don't want to leave a legacy of fear for my daughters. I don't want to be small and reduced because of something somebody else did to me. I want to live. I want to live, and I really, preferably would like to live with you. Yes, I came into this thinking there was no way it could be more now. How could it be? How could it be when you and I both know what a stupid idea it is to jump into a relationship at this point in my life? But I actually think it was stupid for us not to be together the whole time. Or maybe it wasn't. Maybe it had to be this. Maybe this is our timing. Whether it makes sense or not, maybe this is what's right for us. We didn't get here by betraying anybody, or by hurting anybody. We got here because it was where the road led us, and maybe that's okay. Maybe it's enough. Maybe that's what fate is. And now we have to grab hold of it."

"I love you," he said. "I do. I have. But it can't look the way that you want it to. It just can't. I'm not the right man to be in your daughters' lives. I don't want the responsibility. I have too much already, you know that. Because the thing is, I could never be Daniel. I could never go halfway. I can never mess up like that. I—"

"No. That's a lie, Boone. I know you. You can't love me and want to walk away."

"But I do. Because there isn't another choice. Not for me."

"Why?"

"Because everything ends. Everything. I can't live that way. If you're out there, and I love you, that doesn't end. But if you're here, if you're with me...you have to be realistic about these things."

She nodded. Slowly.

"I get it. Because I know what it is to be afraid. You're afraid. And you have every right to be. Life is crazy. And hard. You never know what's coming. But you can cling to what you want. You can fight for it. It doesn't have to be..." Suddenly something in her softened, even as she broke. "It's easier to want what other people want. To try and do it for them, because if you want something then you're the one that's going to get hurt. If you want me and you can't have me, you can love me but... You don't want me to love you. Because that's what you can't trust."

"That isn't it."

"It is. You don't trust me. You don't trust the world. Because it took a lot from you. You trusted your brother, and he left you. You were just a kid, and your sister died. Of course you don't trust in things to last. Of course you don't trust in people not to leave. Boone, I married a man because I felt passion for the first time, and then I was pregnant. And I didn't want to be alone. I entered my first relationship out of fear. Now I'm not afraid. And I'm not afraid to be alone."

"I thought she wouldn't die," he gritted out. "My parents told us she would. They said...they said the kind of cancer she had there was no chance. I didn't believe it. They were honest, but I couldn't deal with it. When she was gone I... I fell apart. I hoped. I hoped and I believed...past reality, and it damned near killed me and I knew I could never do that again."

She wanted to weep. For the boy he'd been. The boy that was still in him now. Who was afraid to hope. Afraid to love.

"Boone, it took bravery to decide to be with you. I wasn't running from something. I was running to it. It's different. And I know it is. And no, I can't promise you that the world won't continue to be harsh and hard. But I can promise you that I am in this forever. Because if my love was so easily destroyed, then I would've gotten rid of it a long time ago. But I can't. I can't. I love you. And it's only right now, standing here, that it feels like a clear sky filled with stars. It was always cloudy until now. My love was there, but it couldn't shine bright. I couldn't see it clearly. But now I can. Now I do. It's been love all along."

She could see in his eyes that he knew it too. It was the thing that terrified him. Knowing he was afraid didn't help this hurt less, but it did make her feel resolved. She wasn't going to be afraid. She wasn't going to flinch, not now. Because she could see the fabric of her whole life, stitched together by this fear. Fear of scarcity. Fear that there just wasn't going to be enough love to go around. That there wasn't going to be enough of anything. It had driven her into her relationship with Daniel, and it had kept her there. It had made her cling to the companionable, the unobjectionable. It had made her ignore any red flags that might've been there, because she didn't think she deserved to see them. Didn't think she could afford to. She wasn't going to do that now.

"We've both been given a lot of bad things," she said. "We have both been given a lot of bullshit. But we have a chance to have each other. We have a chance to have something new, something different, and I'd like to take that chance."

"I want you to be happy," he said, his voice rough. "More than I want anything in the whole world, I want that. But I can't…"

She looked at him, and she felt pity. "I can be happy without you."

Something flashed through his eyes, and she saw the contrary nature, the complexity of it all. He wanted her to leave him be because he was afraid. He wanted her to be happy, but he also didn't. Maybe he wanted them both to be a little bit sad all the time because they couldn't have each other, but they could have the possibility of it. Maybe that was the problem. If she was out there, away from him, he would be able to think about what might've been. Instead of trying and failing and knowing what couldn't be.

But he didn't understand that her love would cover all the failure.

"Sorry," she said. "But it's true. Because I have Mikey and Sadie. And that means I'll be happy. Because I have a life. Because I have skills. Because I am going to move forward in this work that I've enjoyed doing. Because I'm happy enough with myself. That doesn't mean a part of my heart won't be broken. My life would be better for having you in it. But I won't be miserable. I'll never love another man the way that I love you. I don't even have any interest in it. My life is full enough without a man. It will never be full enough without you, though. But life is complicated. In the same way I was able to be committed to my marriage while knowing the possibility of you and I existed in the world, I will be able to be happy if you can't get yourself together. You're not going to hold my heart hostage. Not all of it. A piece of it. Yes. You might hold my body hostage too. I think I'm set for sex. Unless it's you. So yes. Part of me will be crushed. Part of me will be devastated. Part of me will never get over you. But you can rest in the knowledge that I'm out there happy in the world. You can rest in that. And you can love me from a distance. We can have half. We'll be fine. We did it for all these years." She swallowed hard. "But why? Life breaks us enough, why should we break ourselves? Why, when all we need is a little hope?"

"I can't believe in impossible things anymore. I have to believe in reality."

"Why is a sad ending more believable than a happy one?"

He said nothing.

She dressed, slowly and methodically, and she began to prepare to go.

"Wendy..."

"Don't say anything else. Because you can't say anything

true. And I'm done with lies. I get that the lies are to yourself. But I just... I can't."

And when she walked out, she did cry. Real tears, falling hard and fast. And she felt like something in her chest was irrevocably cracked.

She stood there for a long moment, examining the difference. Between losing Daniel and losing Boone. Between knowing that it was over with him, and knowing it was over with Daniel.

The problem with Boone was he'd been there, a possibility, a distant fantasy, for fifteen years.

He had been the other part of her marriage. A piece of herself that she held back. Reserved for him. And now she'd given everything.

It was horrendous. And it hurt.

And she wouldn't trade it.

Wouldn't trade going all out. Wouldn't trade taking the risk.

She only hoped that in the end it was a lesson. If not for her, then for Mikey and Sadie.

That even if it was improbable, and even if it would hurt you, even if other people did not understand, you had to try for everything.

Because you were worth it.

Chapter Twelve

He didn't know what to do with himself. He had just done the dumbest thing he'd ever done in his whole life. And he rode bulls for a living.

He let her go.

You had to.

Why?

These were the rules he had set out for himself all these years ago, this embargo on hope, and now what were the rules doing for him? What had they gotten him?

He'd hurt the woman he cared for most.

And he'd devastated himself.

It hadn't protected him.

He felt like that boy, crumpled outside a hospital after being told his little sister was dead. He hadn't tried to hope and he still felt that way.

Because it won't last. It won't last.

And nobody understood that half as well as he did.

Screw Buck. Honestly. And cancer and everything else. Everything that had ever taken something from him.

He couldn't breathe.

He walked out of the main house, and stood there in the middle of the driveway, considering going to the cottage. To what end? Because what the hell was he going to do about any of it?

She was right. He was afraid. But he didn't know how not to be. And why did somebody like Daniel—heedless, reckless—get to have her? Treat her lightly, hold their love loosely and shatter it almost intentionally?

How are you any different?

Dammit.

And how was he any different than Buck for that matter? Who had run away rather than trying to sort it all out. Who had shut his family out, shut out everyone who cared about him.

How was Boone any different?

He wasn't different.

He'd just built a different wall around himself. He called it responsibility. He let himself believe it made him different than those he didn't respect.

It hit all the ways that he was the same.

He texted his brothers.

Because he had to fix this. He had to fix himself. And one thing he knew was that he couldn't do it alone.

But the biggest difference between himself and those men was that he was going to fix this.

He was going to fix himself.

Because otherwise, it was only hurting other people to protect yourself.

He wouldn't do that to Wendy.

Because he loved her. And if there was one thing he knew, it was that.

She agreed to meet with him. Finally.

This was the last little pocket of fear. The last foothold. She was done with it.

Because what did she have to lose? She went back to the house that night, and she texted Daniel, and told him she wanted to meet in the middle. So the next morning, she took the girls to school, and then got onto the road, headed a few hours west to where he was stationed—not their house, somewhere out on the rodeo circuit—and walked into the diner that he suggested, feeling oddly calm.

There he was. Her husband of all those years. She was still mad at him. It was impossible not to be. He'd lied to her. Nobody felt good about that. Ever. Nobody liked to be tricked.

But she wasn't in love with him, and she was clear on that. She wasn't in love with him, so it felt…it felt not painful in that specific way.

He looked up from the mug of coffee in front of him and half waved.

"Hey, Wendy."

"Hi. Looks like you got your truck fixed."

"I just got a new one. I mean I traded it in."

That sounded like Daniel. Why fix what you had when you could just trade it for something new?

They were different that way. It was sobering to realize. All the ways in which she had ignored this.

"I want to see the girls," he said.

"I'm not keeping them from you. I realize it might feel that way because I left. But you go this long without seeing them all the time."

"I know that. I know I've been a pretty shitty partner and dad. I mean, there's not even anything to say about what kind of husband I was. I don't know how to explain… But it was like I had two lives. And it just felt easy. To go from one to the other."

She almost laughed. "The sad thing is, I understand what you mean. It's just that I had a different life than you. But I pretty much felt like a single mom while you were away, and I kind of enjoyed the time to myself. I didn't think about you much when you were gone. And I thought that was healthy. To not miss you. To not be clingy. I realize now that maybe there was just something missing." She chewed on the next couple of words for a long moment. "I did want to be with someone else. I just didn't do it. I let that make me feel superior to you. But the truth is, my heart wasn't with you the whole time. And I'm not saying that to be hurtful or cruel."

"I know," he said.

"You know what? That I'm not trying to be hurtful?"

"I know you want someone else. I know you and Boone... I know there's something between you. There always has been."

And then she felt ashamed. He'd known that the whole time, and they never talked about it. All the things she and Daniel had never talked about. They hadn't had a marriage. They were roommates with kids.

"I'm not accepting responsibility for your behavior, and I want to make that really clear. But we were not good together. We didn't fight. We weren't ever toxic. The most toxic thing that happened was me breaking your headlights. But we shouldn't have been married. I thought because we didn't fight, because you weren't cruel to me, that there was no reason to leave you. But we weren't in love, Daniel."

"I loved what we had," he said, and he did sound miserable.

"I believe you. I did too. In a lot of ways. But there was something... We can have more. You'll find somebody someday that makes it unthinkable for you to be with anyone else. Someone you feel passion for."

"I guess I don't understand what that means. I wanted you. And that was real. It always has been."

"Just not enough to not want other people."

It didn't hurt her feelings; it didn't make her feel insecure. She had a man who wanted her in that deep, all-consuming, specific way. She didn't need Daniel to want her that way. Not now. It would've been nice if he had when they were married. More than nice. It would've been right. But that ship had sailed. And she'd moved on.

"I'm not with Boone, I would like to make that clear. It's not happening right now."

"You want it to."

"I do. I'm in love with him, Daniel. And I have been. I mean, I guess not really, because I didn't let myself know him well enough to have called it that when you and I were married. I tried very hard to protect our marriage."

"I didn't," said Daniel. "I'm sorry about that."

"You didn't. But I can't be mad, not about that specifically. I'm mad that you tricked me. I'm mad that I had to find out the way I did. But we were never much for honest conversations. So it had to get to a place where it came to that, I guess. I'm sorry. I don't think you were all that smooth. I just let you get away with it, because I wasn't paying attention."

"You were a good wife, though. I just didn't want to be a full-time husband. It's as simple as that, and I convinced myself I didn't have to be because what you didn't know wouldn't hurt you."

"I know you didn't want to hurt me. I actually know you're not a malicious man."

"I don't know if I feel all right about you being with Boone."

"Well, it doesn't matter what you feel. I have slept with him. Just so you know." A part of her, a small, mean part, enjoyed the bit of shock and hurt in his eyes. "He doesn't want to be with me, though. So don't worry about it."

"So you're just going to leave it at that? It's hard for me to believe he doesn't want to be with you after... He cut all ties with me over this."

"Boone has his own issues. And I'm not going to talk about them to you. I'm just letting you know the status of the situation. If it changes, and I hope to God it does, I'll let you know. But you and I need to be very clear with each other. And we have to figure out how to parent the girls. Because if Boone and I do end up together, there doesn't need to be a story from them or from you about how I tried to replace you. Not in their lives. You're their father. I want them to forgive you. I want them to have a relationship with you. Because the one good thing we did was them."

"It was. It is. I promise you, I'm going to do a better job. And I'm going to prove to them they can trust me as a dad."

"Good. For now, I'm staying in Lone Rock. I'm happy there. I need to find another place to live, but the girls are doing well at the school."

"I'm all the way in Bakersfield…"

"Not all year. And maybe you'll see fit to move, I don't know. Houses are cheaper up here anyway. You can get something big."

"I'll think about it."

"Okay. Well, I need to go because I have to drive back, and I have to get the girls from school. But I'm glad we could talk, Daniel."

"Me too."

"Maybe now that we aren't together anymore we'll be able to do that."

She said goodbye to him, and she didn't feel any pull to go back.

She hadn't thought she would, but it felt healing and clarifying to face him.

It was the right thing. She'd done what she needed to do for her daughters.

For herself.

When she got into her car and started back to Lone Rock, she cried. Because she still didn't have Boone, and she wanted him.

This was heartbreak. It was a strange thing. Her marriage had dissolved only a month earlier, and her heart hadn't been broken at all. It was losing the possibility of Boone that had done it. But at least she knew she could survive that.

She didn't have to be afraid of anything. And maybe in that small way, Daniel had done her a favor. He'd set her free from fear. And it was like that thread that had held her together—that thread she *thought* had held her together—all these years had suddenly vanished. And she didn't feel so much like a patchwork quilt now. She just felt whole. And like herself.

She knew that every choice she made from here on out wouldn't be because of fear.

It would be because of love.

That was a gift. And if it was all she took away...it would have to be enough.

Chapter Thirteen

"I need an intervention," Boone said.

He looked at Kit and Jace and Chance and Flint, sitting in chairs in a half circle, and folded his hands.

"Okay. For what?" Kit asked.

"Dumb emotional shit. Go. Fix me. How are you all in love? Tell me."

"Because there was no choice," said Chance.

"None whatsoever," said Kit. "I wanted Shelby for years, and once I could ever—

"I convinced myself that I didn't want Cara," said Jace. "But I was lying to myself."

"Great. How did you not lie to yourself? I'm familiar with wanting somebody for years. And not having them. Shelby was the same as Wendy. She was married to somebody else, so tell me how you fix it. Because you need to help me fix it."

"Wendy?"

"She loves me," he said. "I love her. I love her and I just... I imagine... What if I lose her? What if I mess it up?"

"Yeah. That's scary," said Kit. "It's damned scary. I got Shelby pregnant, so I kind of had to figure it out, didn't I?"

"But now you aren't scared."

"Shit, dude, I have a baby. I'm scared all the time."

"All the time," said Jace. "We don't even have kids."

"What?"

"Why do you think I broke up with Tansey? The first time. The last time. I'm never breaking up with her again, but it was because I was terrified," said Flint. "We had it hard."

"So hard," said Chance. "You never get over having someone in your family die like we did. Not really."

"Hell, I closed off all my feelings. My hope of anything. I didn't believe in miracles of any kind. Because that belief failed me when Sophia died," said Jace. "Which was why I didn't see that Cara was a miracle. She was another chance to find that kind of hope again."

"Shelby and I have both been through loss," said Kit. "She loved her husband. Chuck was a great guy. I know she would've loved him for the rest of her life. I also know that life is just... It can be merciless sometimes. But she got to love him for the amount of time she had him. Just like I got to love Sophia while she was here. And I will love Shelby, I'll love our son. No matter what. No matter the cost. Because it's worth it. It just is. Loving people has only ever made us better. So even though it hurts, we cling to that."

"But you're not...afraid?"

His brothers laughed. "Hell no. When you care about things life feels high stakes," said Chance. "I love Juniper more than anything else in the world. I'm not worried I'm going to mess it up, because it drives me. No, I can't guarantee anything. But she's the reason I wake up every day. My life changed because of her. And I don't regret a damned thing about it. I never could. I would never live a life where I didn't love her."

"But I just thought that if I loved her, and made her life better..."

"I would never live a life where she didn't love *me*," said Chance. "It's hard. When you've been through the kinds of things we have, it's really hard to accept the fact that you can't protect yourself. Because if you do, you're just living half a life. You gotta let her love you. You could have her, you could have stepkids, and kids. You can have a house full of love."

"It's just…it's so much easier to be a martyr about it." As he said it, he knew it was true. "To just tell myself I have all these responsibilities to people. To call it that is not love. To call it that and not… I don't know what to do about how unfair the world is. I don't know what to do with Buck leaving. With Sophia dying. I used to have hope, and it didn't get me anything so now I do things instead of feel them. I'm just trying not to grieve the losses I've already had. And trying not to ever earn any more grief."

"It's okay to grieve." That came from Flint. "It's another expression of love."

"It just feels risky."

"It is. But you have to ask yourself, what's life without risk? We are bull riders. We're a fucking metaphor. Accept it."

He laughed. "I don't think I'm actually all that brave. I'd rather throw myself on the back of a bull than… Than let myself hope. And have that hope get destroyed."

It was too vivid in his mind even now.

That burning bright certainty he'd had that Sophia would get better because the world couldn't be that cruel.

And then it was.

"But hope is what it's all about. I read that somewhere. Faith, hope and love. Without them, what's the point?"

He couldn't answer that. He didn't know what the point was without Wendy.

He needed her.

He needed her, and that was the truth.

And maybe that was the miracle. Nothing else seemed as terrifying now. Nothing but not having her. After living that way for all these years, he'd thought it was the safe thing. The easy thing.

But he wanted more now.

Looking around at his brothers, he thought more just might be possible. Maybe everything was.

Maybe that was healing. Maybe that was the miracle of love.

To live in a world, a broken, pain-filled world, and be able to want love, no matter the cost.

Suddenly it was like all the walls were gone. Torn down. Suddenly it was like he could see clearly.

This was life.

And it *did* matter what he wanted. What he wanted might hurt him. Might kill them.

But he wanted it all the same. And actually, maybe he would be the rodeo commissioner. Maybe not. He realized that none of it had mattered because all he really wanted this whole time was Wendy.

So he was going to have to win her back.

Wendy was just getting out of the car with the girls when Boone pulled up to the cottage in his truck.

"Wendy," he said, looking wild-eyed. "I love you."

She blinked. "Okay."

"I love you and I want to be with you. Fuck everything else. Sorry. Screw everything else."

The girls exchanged a look.

"Boone…"

"I love you." And then he pulled her into his arms and kissed her. Then she lost herself a little bit, it was impossible not to.

"Boone," she said, looking at Mikey and Sadie, who were staring at them both.

"Sorry," he said. "I'm sorry, and there's another part of this conversation," he said. "And it includes the two of you."

She had just been talking to the girls about how she'd seen Daniel, and how he wanted to see them. This was all very inconvenient timing.

But it was life. And it was happening. A lot of feelings, a lot of un-ideal sorts of moments clashing with each other.

"I'm not trying to take your dad's spot, because he's your dad. But I've known you since you were born, and I care about you. And I love your mom. And I'd be happy if you were all right with that."

"Everything is changing," Mikey said sadly.

"I know," said Boone. "And I don't like it, either, quite frankly. I just about messed everything up so I could keep some things the same. Because nobody likes change. I can't say that I've been happy all these years by myself. But it seemed pretty safe. And I was happy with that. So when your mom said she wanted to be with me, I said no. But I realized that I'm more afraid of not having her in my life. More afraid of not sharing a house with all three of you. More afraid of what the future looks like if you're not my family. I want you to be." He cleared his throat. "I… I have hope, Mikey. Even if I'm not certain. And I'm tired of living without hope."

And it was like Mikey realized for the first time that adults had feelings. Feelings and fears and all of this scared them too.

"Oh."

"I care about both you girls a lot," he reiterated, his voice hoarse. "I care about whether or not you're happy."

"I want my mom to be happy," Sadie said. "And you should be happy too."

"We should be happy," Boone said, looking at Wendy.

"Boone," she said, wrapping her arms around him and just hugging him. Because the connection between them had been more than sex. And she wanted to show him that now.

And also not make out with him in front of her kids. Because they were asking a whole lot of the girls, and she didn't need to traumatize them on top of it.

"What changed?" she asked.

"I accepted that there was always going to be some level of risk. I accepted that I had to let love be bigger than my fear. And you know what? I just don't feel afraid anymore."

And neither did she. Because the love inside of her was too big for that.

This was fate. Nothing less than waiting, stumbling through the darkness blind, fighting through all the issues they were beset by.

Grabbing hold of each other and refusing to let go.

It was that simple.

"I dreamed that at my brother's wedding, I crossed the room and kissed you," he said, keeping his voice low. "I dreamed it every night for weeks. And it's funny, I thought because you were off-limits there wasn't anything to learn from that except that I wanted you and couldn't have you. But there was. It was up to me to cross the room."

"And now it's up to us to hold on."

"I'm never letting go now. You know…you're the most beautiful woman I've ever seen."

"What's for dinner?" Mikey asked.

"Meatloaf," she said.

And it hadn't even broken the moment. Both girls went in the house and Wendy just stood there in Boone's arms.

Finally.

"I think this is going to work," he said. "I have hope. In you."

She smiled. "Good. Because I love you."

"That's all I need."

Epilogue

Welcome to Lone Rock...

He hadn't seen that sign in years. He wasn't sure if he felt nostalgic, or just plain pissed off.

He supposed it didn't matter. Because he was here.

For the first time in twenty years, Buck Carson was home.

And he aimed to make it a homecoming to remember.

* * * * *

Epilogue

Rancher's Return

To my wonderful children,
who are the greatest teenagers ever. There is
no greater job than watching you become yourselves.

Chapter One

Welcome to Lone Rock...

He hadn't seen that sign in years. He wasn't sure if he felt nostalgic or just plain pissed off.

He supposed it didn't matter. Because he was here.

For the first time in twenty years, Buck Carson was home.

And he aimed to make it a homecoming to remember.

"You look like you want to punch somebody in the face."

"You look like you got in a fight with your own depression and lost."

"You look like someone who hasn't learned to successfully process his emotions and traumas."

Buck scowled, and glared at his three sons, who were only just recently *legally* his. "I'm good," he said, as his truck continued to barrel down the main drag of Lone Rock, Oregon, heading straight to his parents' ranch, where he hadn't been since he'd first left two decades ago.

"Are you?" Reggie asked, looking at him with snarky, faux teen concern.

"Yes, Reg, and I wouldn't tell you if I wasn't, because I'm the parent."

"I don't think that's healthy," Marcus said.

"I think that somebody should've taught you not to use therapy speak as a weapon," Buck said to his middle son.

"You're in luck," said Colton, his oldest, "because I don't use therapy speak at all. Not even in therapy."

"Yeah, the therapy hasn't taken with you," Marcus said.

"Hey," Reggie said. "Leave him alone. He's traumatized. By having to go through life with that face of his."

"*All right*," Buck said.

It wasn't like he hadn't known what he was getting into when he'd decided to adopt these boys. But becoming an instant father to fifteen-, sixteen- and seventeen-year-old kids was a little more intense than he had anticipated.

When he'd left Lone Rock he'd been completely and totally hopeless. He'd been convinced he was to blame for the death of his friends, and hell, the whole town had been too.

After everything his family had already been through, he hadn't wanted to bring that kind of shame to their door. So he'd left.

And spent the first few years away proving everything everyone had ever said about him right. He had been drunk or fucked-up for most of that time. And one day, he had woken up in the bed of a woman whose name he didn't know and realized he wasn't living.

His three best friends had died in a car accident on graduation night, driving drunk from a bonfire party back to their campsite. He had also been drunk, but driving behind them in his own car. He had made the same mistake they had, and yet for some reason, they had paid for it and he hadn't.

They'd only been at the party because of him. All upstanding kids with bright futures, while Buck had by far been the screwup of the group. Their futures had been cut short, and for some reason, he had gone ahead and made his own future a mess.

That day, he woke up feeling shitty, but alive.

And when he had the realization that he still drew breath, and that he wasn't doing anyone any favors by wasting the life he still had, he had gotten his ass out of bed and gone into a rehab program.

But in truth, he had never been tempted to take another drink after that morning, never been tempted to touch another illicit substance. Because he had decided then and there he was going to live differently.

Because he'd found a new purpose.

After completing the rehab program, he had limped onto New Hope Ranch asking for a job. The place was a facility for troubled youth, where they worked the land, worked with animals and in general turned their lives around through the simple act of being part of the community.

Buck had been working there for sixteen years. Those kids had become his heart and soul; that work had become his reason why. And five months ago, when he had been offered the position of director, he had realized he was at a new crossroads.

There were three kids currently in the program who didn't have homes to go back to. And he had connected with them. It had been yet another turning point.

But that's when he had seen himself clearly. He had a trust fund he hadn't touched since he left Lone Rock. He had been living on the ranch, taking the barest of bare minimum pay. He had no possessions. He was like a monk with a vow of poverty, supported by the church. Though the ranch was hardly a church.

He used his paycheck for one week off a year, where he usually went to some touristy ski town, stayed in reasonable accommodations, found a female companion whose name he *did* know and spent a nice weekend.

But otherwise... He didn't have much of anything.

And he could.

He considered taking all his money and donating it to the ranch, but it was well funded by many organizations and rich people who wanted to feel like they were doing good in the world while getting a write-off on their taxes.

And then he remembered he had a unique resource.

His family.

He could give Reggie, Marcus and Colton a family. A real family.

Yeah, he was an imperfect father figure, but he had found that made it easier to connect with the kids at the ranch. Additionally, he had a mother and a father, six brothers and a sister. And they were all married with children of their own. He could give these boys a real, lasting sense of community.

And that was when he had decided to adopt those boys, buy a ranch in Lone Rock and reconnect with his parents. They had met on neutral ground, at various rodeo events over the summer.

His dad had been angry at first; his mom never had been. But he had explained what he had been through, what he had been doing and why he had been absent for so long, and ultimately, they had forgiven him. And welcomed him to come back home. He also knew they had done some work priming his brothers and sister to accept his presence. Or at least, the presence of the boys.

But...

He also had the sense all was not forgiven and forgotten when it came to his siblings.

Even so, he was looking forward to today's reunion.

At least he was pretty sure the sick feeling in his stomach was anticipation. And maybe some of the anger that still lived inside of him. At this town, at himself.

Well. Hell.

He supposed he didn't have a full accounting of all his emotions.

There was nothing simple about the loss this place had experienced all those years ago. His friends should be thirty-eight years old. Just like him. But they were forever eighteen.

He looked at his sons, sitting on the bench seat of the truck, with Marcus in the back.

It wasn't a coincidence that he had adopted three of them, he supposed. A more obvious mea culpa didn't exist. But then, he had never pretended he wasn't making as firm a bid for redemption as he possibly could.

Yeah. Well.

It was what it was.

"So we're meeting your whole family today?" Marcus asked.

"Yeah. For better or worse."

"You haven't seen them in twenty years," Colton said.

"No."

"God, you are so old," Colton said.

"Yeah. Really ancient," Buck said. "And feeling older by the minute around you three assholes."

"I do think you have more gray hair since you adopted us," Reggie said.

"I'll probably just pick up more girls with it," Buck said.

That earned him a chorus of retching gags, and genuinely, he found that was his absolute favorite part of this parenting thing.

Driving the kids nuts.

It was mutual, he had a feeling.

But he took it as a good sign that they felt secure enough to mess with him. They all definitely had their own trauma. Marcus didn't mess around using therapy speak by pulling it out of nowhere. He'd spent a hell of a lot of time sitting on a therapist's couch, that was for damn sure.

He turned onto the long driveway that was so familiar. But he knew everything else had changed. His parents had built a new house in the years since he had left. His siblings had been kids when he'd gone.

They were entitled to their anger, his siblings. They had already lost their youngest sister when they lost him too. And life had proven to be even crueler after that. So maybe his running off had been part of the cruelty, rather than the solution. Sobriety and maturity made that feel more likely.

But at the time, he had simply thought everybody would be better off without him. Hell, at the time that had probably been true. That was the thing. He had self-destructed for a good long while. He was pretty sure he would've done that even if he hadn't left.

So whether his family wanted to believe it or not, he really did believe that in the state he'd been in then, it had been better that he wasn't around. And then he had been afraid to go back. For a long time.

But his dad hadn't cut him off. His trust fund had still come available to him when he turned thirty. He supposed that should have been a sign to him. That he was always welcome back home.

But he'd left it untouched. Maybe that was the real reason he hadn't used it till now. He had felt on some level that he would have to reconnect with his family if he took any family money.

And it was the boys who had given him a strong enough reason to do that.

He followed the directions his mother had given him to the new house. It was beautiful and modern. With big tall windows designed to make the most of the high desert views around them.

"I didn't realize this place was a desert," Marcus said. "I thought it rained all the time in Oregon."

"In Portland maybe," he said.

"There's nothing here," Reggie added.

"There's plenty to do."

"Doesn't look like there's plenty to do," Colton said.

"You'll be fine."

"How come there aren't any cactuses?" Marcus asked.

He gritted his teeth. "Not that kind of desert."

"Are there at least armadillos?" Marcus, again.

"Still not that kind of desert," he said.

"What a rip-off," Marcus replied.

"I don't think you want armadillos, from the sounds of things. They're nuisances. Dig lots of holes in the yard."

Then, talk of armadillos died in the back of his throat. Because he was right up against the side of the house. He got out of the truck slowly, and the kids piled out quickly. And it only took a moment for the front door to open.

His parents were the first out. His mother rushing toward him to give him a hug. She had been physically demonstrative from the first time they had seen each other again.

"Buck," she said. "I'm so glad you're here."

"Me too."

"Hey," his old man said, extending his hand and shaking Buck's.

"You must be Reggie, Marcus and Colton," his mom said, going right over to the boys and forcing them into a hug as well. "You can call me Nana."

He could sense the boys' discomfort, but this was what he was here for. For the boys to have grandparents. To have family.

"You can call me Abe," his dad said.

And that made the boys chuckle.

He heard a commotion at the door and looked up. There were all his brothers, filing out of the house: Boone, Jace, Chance, Kit and Flint. Buck was about to say something, when a fist connected with his jaw, and he found himself hurtling toward the ground as pain burst behind his eyelids.

"Boone!" He heard a woman's shocked voice, though he couldn't see her from where he was lying sprawled out on the ground.

"Oh *shit*!" That, he knew was Reggie.

"Fair call," Buck said, sitting up and raising his hand in a "hold on" gesture. "Fair call, Boone."

"Violence isn't the answer, Boone," came a lecturing teenage voice.

"Sometimes it is," returned an equally lecturing different

teenage voice. "Sometimes a person deserves to get punched in the face."

"Maybe not right now," the angry female voice said.

Buck stood up. And looked his brother square in the face.

"Good to see you again, Boone," he said.

"Don't think I won't hit you again," Boone said.

"Hey," said his brother Jace, moving over to Boone and putting his hand on Boone's shoulder. "Why don't you guys punch it out on your own time."

"I don't have anyone to punch," Buck said. "And I'll take one. Maybe two. But no more than that."

Chance and Kit exchanged glances, like they were considering getting in a punch of their own. For his part, Flint looked neutral.

For the first time, Buck got a look at the woman who had defended him.

"I'm Wendy," she said. "I'm Boone's wife."

And he had a feeling the two lecturing teenage girls were Boone's stepchildren. His mother had filled him in on everybody's situation, more or less.

Right then, another woman came out of the house with a baby on her hip.

Callie.

His baby sister. Who had been maybe five years old when he'd left. He knew it was her. She was a mother herself. He had missed her whole damn life.

He was sad for himself, not for her.

There hadn't been a damn thing he could've taught her. He hadn't been worth anything at the point when he'd left. But he sure as hell felt sorry for himself. For missing out.

"Buck," she said. Her eyes were soft, no anger in them whatsoever.

"Yeah," he said, "it's me."

And he realized this whole reunion was going to be both more rewarding and more difficult than he had imagined.

Because his family wasn't a vague, cloudy shape in the rear-view mirror of his past anymore. His family was made up of a whole lot of people. People with thoughts and feelings about this situation. About him.

Hell. He had spent a little bit of time with the therapist himself.

"Why don't we go inside?" his mother said. "But no more hitting."

"Yes, ma'am," Boone said, looking ashamed for the first time.

This didn't have to be easy.

Buck was used to things being hard.

But he was home.

For better or for worse.

He was home.

Chapter Two

The first week of school was always a little dramatic, but Marigold Rivers didn't mind.

She loved that her daughter told her everything. That she gave her the rundown on all the drama. Hers, her friends', everyone's. Marigold had not told her mom anything. Because she had been a sullen and withdrawn teen still recovering from her brother's death and had kept all of her feelings and bad behaviors to herself.

She was thankful Lily didn't do that. Lily told her about all her classes, about all her crushes, about everything.

This week, though, had been light on the drama. Senior year was starting off relaxed.

Marigold was almost grateful for that.

Even as the idea of her daughter graduating in nine months made her want to curl into a ball and howl.

In some ways, she supposed she was lucky to be thirty-three with her daughter very nearly out of the house.

All the dating and everything she had mostly missed out on as a young mom could commence. She could travel. Could engage in wild one-night stands with hot mysterious Greek guys, just like the women in her favorite books.

Of course, in those books, the woman was usually virginal—lord, that ship had sailed—and usually ended up pregnant. Marigold had seen that film before. The guy didn't stick around.

Or, maybe it wasn't fair to compare the actions of a nineteen-year-old boy to the actions of thirty-year-old men who were billionaires. And fictional. There was that.

Whatever.

In a few short months, Lily would be off to college. And yes, there was anxiety associated with that. With applying for schools, financial aid, all of it. And, of course, worrying about whether or not Lily was acclimating to her new life, new friends, new environment. Marigold would be missing her so much that she would probably wish she was dead, but at least there would be freedom. Probably.

Mostly, she felt sad that this stage of her life was over already.

Being a teen mom had been hard. But nothing was harder than this—preparing to say goodbye.

She schlepped half the load of groceries inside and called up the stairs. "Lily, I'm home."

Lily drove herself to school now, and that had been a big adjustment too. Her daughter having freedom. Her own car. She had gotten her license a little late, because of course Marigold was paranoid about teen driving. And teen drinking. And teen sex.

Her family was a deeply unfortunate after-school special.

Her brother had decided to drink and get into a car with another boy who had been drinking. So many kids made that mistake. Her brother had paid for it with his life.

She'd had unprotected sex. She'd gotten pregnant.

And while she didn't think of Lily as a *consequence*—at least not these days—she certainly didn't want the same thing for her daughter.

As a result, while she did her best to be the kind of mom who fostered open communication, she was also…well, she had been very honest with her daughter about life's dangers.

She had tried to do it in a way that wasn't just about making rules, but that also explained her experience. She'd done a lot of work on herself since she was seventeen. After her brother died, she'd lost herself. She'd been angry. Looking for someone to blame—and she'd found him.

She'd never forget the day she'd confronted him in the middle of town, screaming at him, blaming him for her brother's choices. Something she realized now hadn't been fair. Her brother had been a ticking time bomb back then.

She'd been looking for something—anything—to make herself feel better. Older guys had made her feel validated. The attention she'd gotten from them had been a temporary bandage. And then she'd gotten pregnant.

She'd realized she needed her parents. She'd realized she needed to actually heal some things inside herself instead of simply trying to make herself feel better for a moment. She'd gotten good therapy. She'd started to live intentionally, instead of in a reactionary way.

Thankfully, she and Lily had a really open line of communication.

Their life had been a good one. It's just that it was changing.

Today's grocery haul was intense, as it always was. Her meal prep business had grown exponentially in the last couple of years. She had started making food as a means of supporting herself and Lily when Lily had been small, and now she was doing weekly meals for so many families in town she could hardly keep up.

But it was great. She got to do something she was good at, at home, in her modest house's certified kitchen, and make a decent living at it.

"Lily!" She said her daughter's name again.

There was still no answer.

She set the grocery bags on the counter and started up the stairs. She texted Lily on her way up, to see if she could get her attention that way. Odds were, she was sitting in her room with her earbuds on, but she most definitely had her phone, and she had her read receipts on, so Marigold always knew when Lily had seen a text from her.

No reading.

She frowned. She knocked twice on her daughter's bedroom door, and then pushed it open without waiting for a response. She was greeted by a flurry of movement. By Lily practically doing a dive roll off the bed, and a boy Marigold had never seen before in her life standing up quickly and pulling his shirt into place.

"What the... What the hell is going on?" she said.

And somewhere in the back of her mind was a calm, rational, *healed* voice that said she needed to react calmly so Lily would talk to her. That she needed to be rational, so her daughter wouldn't be shamed. So she would know Marigold wasn't angry, *just concerned.*

That voice was far in the distance, and Marigold was somewhere else entirely.

That calm, still voice had no hope in hell of winning.

In general, Marigold fancied herself somewhere between crystals and Jesus. A little bit woo woo, a little bit traditional. But right now, she was straight into fire and brimstone, do not pass the rose quartz, do not collect spiritual enlightenment.

"Who is this?"

"It's not what it looks like," Lily said, in the grand tradition of every teenager who had ever been caught doing stupid shit. But Marigold knew, she *knew*, that it was always what it looked like.

She'd had the positive pregnancy test at sixteen to prove it.

"Oh please, don't treat me like I'm an idiot," she said, and found that was what actually bothered her the most.

"I'm not. It's just it's not like... We were just..."

The boy was looking at Marigold with the appropriate amount of fear, so there was that at least. He was a boy she had never seen before, tall and exactly the kind of handsome tailormade to get nice girls like Lillian into trouble.

"Who are you?"

"My name is Colton," he said.

Colton. Of course his name would be Colton.

Colton sounded exactly like the kind of boy who would get you pregnant and disappear off to college, leaving you to deal with the consequences.

Her own Colton was actually named Christopher. Same dude, different font.

"Well, Colton, we are going to go have a talk with your parents."

"Mom!" Lily looked horrified.

She rounded on her daughter. "We're going to have a talk later. Have I taught you nothing? Have I taught you nothing about *safe sex*?"

"We weren't having sex," Lily said, looking filled with horror.

"Oh come on," Marigold said. "Do you think that's where he was going to stop?"

"Hey," Colt said. "I am very serious about consent."

Lily looked up at him. "So you mean that *is* what you wanted?"

Colton suddenly looked trapped. Good.

"It's what they all want," Marigold said.

"Mom," Lily said. "Can you please leave your teen trauma in the past?"

"No," Marigold said. "I can't. Because the result of my teen trauma is standing in front of me making more trauma. Let's go, Colton. I'm taking you home. Since I can see that your car is not here."

"Mom…"

"You're certainly not driving him home." And suddenly, she had a horrifying image of her daughter doing something drastic, running away or worse, if she were left unattended. "You're coming with us."

"Mom, I…"

"First of all, Lily Rivers, if you are going to mess around with a boy, you better do it when your mother isn't about to come home. Keep track of the time."

"Are you lecturing me now for not being sneaky enough?"

"I don't know. *Maybe*." Marigold had never been caught with a boy once.

"It's not like I thought you would care that much," Lily said. "I thought you would understand."

"Just come with me."

She led the two sullen, silent teens down to her car. They both sat in the back seat, and she didn't argue, even though part of her wanted to. "Give me directions to your house."

"I don't know the number yet. We just moved here."

"Are your parents home?"

"My dad is," he said. "I mean… I only have a dad."

"Okay," she said, doing her best not to feel sympathy for him. He was a sexual predator. Well. He wasn't a sexual predator. But she still felt wary of him.

"I can give you directions," he said.

"Good. Please."

She was filled with adrenaline. And anger. And she hadn't really thought through what she was going to say to Colton's dad when she showed up. Something along the lines of… *Keep your kid away from my daughter or I'll castrate him?* No. There had to be something less psychotic than that. Maybe.

She followed his directions out of town and off toward the mountains. Then she turned onto a dirt driveway, her car jumping around in the potholes. "You really live out here?" Maybe he was trying to get them lost.

"Yeah," he said. "I know, it sucks. There's not anything to do."

She heard him cut his sentence off just before the last word was out of his mouth, which was the only thing keeping her from leaping into the back seat.

She had spent all of Lily's life being both mother and father to her daughter. So it seemed completely right in that moment that she had felt very Liam Neeson. A particular set of skills, etc. But because she was a mother, her ultimate response had been less violent. Still, it included shaming him.

This felt like action, anyway, because when she was done with him, she was going to have to deal with Lily and having a very real talk about contraception and safety and all kinds of things she had sort of thought she had already done. Now she worried it hadn't been enough.

Finally, they pulled up to a very nice-looking, newly constructed ranch house backed by the mountains and pine trees.

"Well," she said.

And that was it. Because she didn't want to compliment the kid.

There was a gorgeous, brand-new truck sitting in the driveway too. So he was a rich kid. Likely why he thought he was entitled to whatever he wanted.

She felt no small amount of irritation regarding that.

She and Colton got out of the car, leaving Lily in the back seat, and Marigold walked up to the front door, Colton slowly trailing behind her.

"You can go ahead and knock," she said to him.

He did, looking at her out of the corner of his eye. She felt right then like her mom powers must be functioning at a really high level, because truly, this kid hadn't had to do a single thing she said, and he didn't especially look like he wanted to, and yet he was obeying.

She appreciated that she incited this level of fear.

She heard heavy footsteps on the other side of the door, and then it jerked open.

And her heart tumbled down all the way into her toes. Because she knew this man. This man standing in front of her with a tight black T-shirt, a cowboy hat and an expression too grim to be real. He was still outrageously handsome, but he had settled into his looks. No longer a smooth-faced, cocky teenage boy, he was weathered now. He was…

He was gorgeous.

He was also the man who had nearly torn her family apart. The man who had been the source of her unfettered teenage hatred.

Buck Carson.

The man who had killed her brother.

Chapter Three

Well it wasn't every day that a man ran into a living, breathing, potential *mea culpa*. But he supposed it was more common when one had committed sins on the level that he had, and when one had returned home, back to the scene of those sins, after twenty years.

It almost felt like poetry to see Marigold Rivers standing on his doorstep. What he didn't understand was why she looked shocked to see him, and why she was standing beside Colton.

"Can I help you with something?"

She was sputtering, like a fish that had been hauled out of the river by an angler's hook and flipped up onto the banks.

"I... I didn't expect to see you."

"I didn't expect to see you either, Marigold."

Her cheeks turned a very particular shade of crimson. The last time he had seen her cheeks lit up in red, she had been shouting at him. Full-throated, on the street. The angriest teenage girl he had ever seen, yelling at him about how he was responsible for her brother's death. It had felt good in a way. Because she had said what he felt was the truth when everybody else was dancing around it. She had finally taken the knife and twisted it, and he had exulted in the pain. Because it had been exactly what he needed. A good scouring, a flagellation much harder than the one he had been giving himself.

It had been the catalyst to him deciding to leave. Because his poor mother had also been standing by his side, because she had been through enough, and he knew she felt like the family she had worked so hard to rebuild after the death of her daughter was fracturing.

And it was his fault.

He hated himself for it. And so, after that scene, he had hauled his ass right out of town.

In many ways, he had found a certain kind of salvation thanks to Marigold.

He doubted she would want to hear that.

"I didn't know you were back in town."

"Really?" He frowned. "I've been back about a month. I would have thought the rumor mill would've been going pretty strong."

"Maybe people were just careful. Around me."

"Well. Perhaps. Though, then they open you up to a moment like this. Where you were bound to run into me without a moment's notice. I see you have my son."

Her eyes went round. "He's your son."

"Yes he is. Has he been causing trouble?"

"I… I don't even know how to… I…"

"What have you been up to, you termite?" Buck asked Colton. He figured he might get more of a direct answer from the young man himself than the decidedly flustered Marigold.

"It wasn't what it looked like," Colton said.

"Shoot, kid. That is the wrong thing to say to the likes of me. Because I'll be the first to tell you, whatever it is, it is always what it looks like."

That seemed to jolt Marigold out of whatever trance she was in. "When I came home from grocery shopping today, I went upstairs to check on my daughter. And found your son in her room."

And right in that moment, it didn't matter so much that the woman standing on his doorstep was Marigold Rivers. What mattered was the very clear and sudden realization that he had been thrown into the deep end of parenting, and this was something he had no idea how to navigate.

"You did what?"

"I have concerns," Marigold said. "And believe me, my daughter has agency, and I'm going to talk to her about it—"

But he wasn't listening. Not anymore. "Listen here," he said to Colton. "And you listen real good. This is a small town, and people talk. You go messing around with a girl, and she is going to get a reputation you're not going to get. Do you understand? The responsibility that she's going to bear will be so much bigger than yours. You have to be careful. Not just in terms of safe sex, but all these other things. Because no son of mine is going to walk around thinking he's exempt from consequences."

"Yes, sir," Colton mumbled.

"Get your ass in the house. I'm going to talk to Marigold for a second."

"All right," he said.

Marigold simply looked stunned.

"I didn't know... I was about to say that I didn't know you had a son, but I didn't know you were back here. I haven't known a thing about you for twenty years."

"Well, I only recently have a son."

"What?"

"I just adopted three teenagers. And I'm realizing right now that I'm maybe in over my head. I spent the last sixteen years or so working at a camp for troubled boys. And the thing about working at a camp for troubled boys is that there are no girls there. So there's a little less of this kind of thing. Not none, mind you, but at least nobody can get pregnant."

She looked stricken by that.

"Not saying that anybody here is going to get pregnant."

"She can't. She's going to college. She's going to get out of here, and she's going to do better than me."

"I'm going to talk to him."

"I… I can't believe this. I can't believe that this is the first boy she sneaks into her room."

"Listen, I know you have plenty of reason to hate me."

She looked away, and then back up at him. "I don't hate you. I recognize now that my reactions back then were… I was young. I was angry. But do the math on how old I was when you left and how old I am now. And the fact that I have a kid the same age as yours."

"You were still in high school when you had her," he said, not needing to do the figures to understand what she was getting at.

"I was. I got my life back on track. The pregnancy forced me to get things together, and it forced me to let go of the things that were no longer serving me. I'm grateful for her. I wouldn't change my life. But I don't want this for her. I want better."

"You know that if we try to keep them apart it's only going to be worse."

She bit the inside of her cheek and looked up at him with wide, amber-colored eyes. "Of course. Of course it will. Because then they'll think they're Romeo and Juliet."

"Yeah. And I didn't pay a lot of attention in school, but I know enough to know that ended badly."

"Just a bit."

"I'm sorry," he said. "But let's… Let's talk to them. About ground rules. And maybe… There is a beginning of the school year carnival happening down in town. Maybe they can have a date, and we can supervise."

"They're seventeen," she said. "Not seven."

"Sure. But they're on probation, right?"

"I guess so."

He let out a long, slow breath. "I suppose it's kind of big of you to not say you are extra suspicious of him because he's my kid."

"Like I said. I did my best to get over the past."

"Sure. But you were awfully angry the last time we saw each other."

"I also had a poster of Orlando Bloom as Legolas on my wall. So, things change."

"Have they?"

"Yeah. I'm an Aragorn girl now."

"I only vaguely know what that means."

"It's okay, you don't need to get the reference. But yes, things change. I have a teenager now. She's just a year younger than you were. A year younger than... Unfortunately, all of you were too young to take the blame. If it wasn't Jason's fault, then it's not yours."

He wasn't sure he had been looking for absolution. He didn't think he wanted it. Because holding the guilt close had accomplished a certain something in his life. And he didn't really mind that, when all was said and done.

"I actually don't need you to forgive me."

"Well, too late. I do."

That was irritating. He wasn't sure why. "I came back here to raise the boys. I mean, they're already mostly raised. But I wanted them to be around my family."

"That's a really nice thing for them."

"Thanks. I'll talk to Colton. You can talk to your daughter. And this weekend, they can meet up for the carnival."

"All right. That sounds like a plan."

"I guess I'll see you there."

"Yeah. I guess."

She turned and walked away from the door, and he was going to have to deal with Colton. But for just one moment, he reflected on the strangeness of this meeting. She might say that she forgave him, but that wasn't what he was after. Her walking up to his doorstep, walking into his life, must be a sign of some kind. That was the problem with going off on your own for twenty years. It didn't cure you of mystical thinking. If anything, that shit only got more profound. He had gone away looking for answers. Then he had found them. He had found purpose with the school, which had only deepened his certainty that there were times when a person stood at a crossroads and had to ask questions of the deepest part of their soul.

Hell, it was essential. And right now, he had a feeling this was meant to be. This was some essential part of his journey, and he had to pay attention.

He had a feeling that when they met this weekend, everything would become clear.

She got back into the car, her hands shaking. She was breathing hard. The events of the past hour didn't seem real, and it had all culminated with running into Buck Carson.

She *did* blame him for Jason's death. She just did. And as she sat there, trying to catch her breath, she became more and more certain of that truth. That no matter how much she had tried to get herself into a place that wasn't angry—into a place filled with forgiveness, filled with understanding and acceptance that some people were meant to have a short life, and sadly, her brother had been one of them—it was all only theoretical.

Because the person who had drawn the most fury and fire from her over the accident had left town, and she hadn't seen him for twenty years.

"Mom?" Lily's voice was tremulous in the back seat.

"I didn't kill him," she said.

"I didn't think you would."

"Sorry. I need a second."

This was one of those moments where she had to decide how up-front and honest she was going to be with her daughter. But if she wanted Lily to share with her, she supposed she had to share in kind. She tried to walk a fine line between being her kid's friend and her parent. They had grown up together, so their relationship was different from that of a lot of other moms and daughters. Sharing and talking had always been the method by which they understood each other.

"Colton's father is... I know him."

"What?" Lily leaned forward in the car seat. "How?"

"Well his dad was from here originally."

"He was?"

"He was...involved in your uncle Jason's accident."

"How?" Lily asked.

"Buck Carson, Colton's dad, was with Uncle Jason. Buck was driving in a car behind the one with all the boys in it. It's... I've been angry at him for a really long time. I blamed him. Because there was definitely... He was wild. He always was. He had a reputation for drinking. And yet I liked it when he was around. He was fun. Charming. Handsome."

"You were thirteen!" her daughter said.

So scandalized by an age gap. After being caught with a boy in her room. Kids today were a trip.

"Yeah. He didn't look at *me*, but I definitely looked at him. I think that's what made it worse. I idolized him. I thought he seemed like the fun kind of dangerous. But he wasn't. He was the dangerous kind of dangerous."

"Mom..."

"I'm not going to refuse to let you see Colton." Marigold started the engine. "I just wanted you to know what the situation was." She started to back out of the parking place, orienting the car so she could drive back toward the highway.

"I hear a *but* in that sentence."

"Yes. There are going to be ground rules and curfews. You are going to college," she said.

"I know. As soon as I can, I'm going to submit applications, and apply for FAFSA..."

"I want you to stay focused."

"Mom, I wouldn't... I listened when you talked about safe sex."

"I know. But no contraception is one-hundred percent and...

And there's no point getting attached to him. Not when you're going to leave."

"I guess not."

"That being said, I'm not telling you not to date him."

Lily screwed up her face. "You're not? Because it sounds an awful lot like you are."

"I guess I just… I want you to think about all these things. That's all."

"Why can't I just date? That seems normal."

"Of course it is. Of course. But you have never dated. So you have to admit, it's not completely out of left field that when I came home and suddenly there was a boy in your room, it felt out of character, and I want to make sure that you're not…going off the rails."

"Just because you did doesn't mean I will."

"I know."

She had tried to be the kind of mom her daughter could talk to, because she hadn't known how to talk to her own mother. That wasn't a failure for her or her mom. They'd both been grieving. Her own mom had lost her oldest child. And Marigold hadn't wanted to talk. She had wanted to get into trouble. She hadn't been levelheaded like Lily. She hadn't planned for her future. She had thrown herself into trying to forget her pain. She hadn't thought to plan even one step ahead, not like Lily.

The truth was, nothing scared her more than her teenage self. And when it felt like there was any chance that sort of behavior could pop up for Lily, it made Marigold feel unhinged.

She was her own bogeyman. Knowing exactly what she had gotten away with at sixteen years old, seventeen years old— that was sort of the ultimate consequence. A comeuppance she could never have imagined back then.

Maybe this was also a comeuppance of sorts.

"I just really like him," Lily said. "He's not like the boys around here. He's…"

"More experienced," Marigold said, knowing she sounded dry and suspicious.

"I guess. Maybe."

"But also exciting, I guess, because he's a stranger."

"Again, I don't know. I just know that I like him."

Well, it was a little bit galling that her seventeen-year-old was having the kind of fantasy love affair Marigold had built up for herself in her mind over the years, that Greek island fling. Meeting a stranger who made you feel something.

Yeah. She was a little too familiar with why that was compelling.

"We're going to take you to the carnival this weekend."

"What?"

"Buck and I agreed that it might be a good way for you to have a chaperoned date."

"A *chaperoned date*? I am not a toddler."

"No. But we need to set some rules and expectations. I don't… I don't want you getting too involved with one boy. I want you to date. Actually talk to him. Get to know him."

"Mom."

"Well. I want you to be safe and well protected."

"I'm going to college soon. You can't keep me from living."

"I don't want to keep you from living. I don't want you to shut down and not tell me things. But I know you. I know you really well, and today was out of character."

"Maybe he makes me feel out of character."

This was really testing her 'being an open-minded mother' determination.

But… It felt so important that she get this right. She didn't want to lose her connection to Lily, but she didn't want Lily to lose a connection to her future. Lily was going off to school; she was going to build a future for herself. And that would allow Marigold to build her business, her future, in the way she wanted to. Greek vacations optional.

"You can see him again this weekend. And then we'll talk

more. I just want you to tell me things. I felt blindsided by the fact that you hadn't even mentioned his name."

"I'm sorry," Lily said.

"It's all right. We'll figure it out."

She would. She would figure all this out. Because the truth was, she had been through much harder things than this.

Marigold Rivers was nothing if not tough and determined. And this would be no exception.

No matter that there was a Buck Carson-sized complication in the middle of it all.

Chapter Four

This was the most wholesome thing he had ever done in his life. Sure, he might have spent the past twenty years trying to find balance. He might have even tried his hand at being one of the good guys. But wholesome? That wasn't really in his wheelhouse. Which made him a good father figure for misguided teenage boys, he thought. Because after all the life experiences they'd had, wholesome was out of their reach too. At least, he had thought it might be.

But here they all were, dressed in their Sunday best, about ready to go to a school carnival of all things.

"You will make sure to get the dirt out from under your nails?" he asked, looking at the boys.

"I'm not an animal," Colton said.

"At least not an armadillo. Since there are no armadillos here," Marcus said.

"Shut up," Colton said.

"Yeah, you all look like you pass muster to me," Buck said. It wasn't like he made a habit of scrubbing his own nails or anything like that.

He thought about Marigold and ignored the tension stretching across his shoulders.

It had taken him a couple of hours after she left to realize how pretty she was. And to start to wonder about her. Really wonder. Not in terms of her being an emblem of potential salvation, but as a human being. Who had a seventeen-year-old daughter. His friend's little sister had always been a small, sunny presence, and she had been annoying. Chipper and buzzing around like a fly. He hadn't given her much thought. He had been nice, because you couldn't be mean to somebody else's brother or sister, that was just a rule. But she had been young, and primarily inconsequential to him. But she was a grown woman now. And it was strange on a few levels.

The first being that he hadn't seen Jason's family in all the years since the accident. Well, not since Marigold had yelled at him in the street. And the second being that because of the accident, Jason and his family had sort of frozen in place in Buck's mind. Because Jason was dead, so he hadn't gotten to grow or change or age. He was eighteen forever. Buck often found it strange that his friends were frozen forever in that place, graduation night, with a lifetime of possibilities ahead of them, while he was…getting old.

He had lines on his face. Calluses on his hands. New scars, in and out, that had torn through his flesh or his soul in all the years since his friends had been gone.

And Marigold was no different. She had grown, and she had changed. She wasn't the same person she had been all that time ago. She wasn't a child anymore. She was a mother herself.

It was a wrenching sort of joyous realization. Because at least Jason's parents had her, had a granddaughter.

And Buck's son was working on defiling her, apparently.

He'd had a pretty stern talk with Colton about possible consequences. Yet he had felt like an imposter, because he had practiced few of those things he was ranting against when he was a seventeen-year-old boy. Sex had been a game. It was a small town; there wasn't shit else to do. He had been part of the wilder group of kids.

The truth was, there was a narrative that he had somehow led those more upstanding boys into that wild space, but they had done a good job taking themselves there.

It wasn't that part of it that left him feeling guilty. It was being involved at all.

It was being the one who survived.

Because what he did wonder was if any of his friends would've done more than he did. For the world. For themselves.

If they were supposed to fall in love and get married and have children.

If they were supposed to cure cancer or climb the tallest mountain. Or maybe they wouldn't have done shit.

It was impossible to say. But it was the not knowing that got to him. It was the not knowing, and never being able to know. That was what kept him awake at night.

It was just a damned hard pill to swallow.

And then… there was the fact that she was pretty.

She was damned pretty. And he had done his best to ignore that. Because there was pretty, the kind you could appreciate, and then there was *pretty*. The kind that hooked its way deep in your gut, made you feel something down beneath your skin. Something that was more than just aesthetic appreciation. Attraction.

That was the dumbest thing he had ever thought. But it was rattling around inside himself.

He could not be attracted to Marigold Rivers.

"All right," he said. "Let's head out."

The boys loaded into the truck, and they started toward town.

The carnival was right off the main street with booths lining the sidewalk and string lights woven overhead. There were balloons and streamers and all manner of jaunty decor strung up about the place. It was a Fall Festival, early September so not Halloween as much as apples, gingham and myriad other things he'd never much associated with.

It was… It was like a small-town TV show. Or a Hallmark movie.

The Historic Main Street was looking brighter and more vibrant since he'd left twenty years before, with many of the buildings restored, including an old bed-and-breakfast at the very end of the street that belonged to his brother and his new wife. His sister-in-law also owned the saloon in town. The whole main street was practically a Carson parade.

He parked his truck up against the curb, and they all got out. He took out his wallet, and some cash, and handed it to the boys. "You can go meet school friends. And this is your money to spend."

"Gee thanks, Dad," said Reggie.

"You're welcome," he said.

It didn't bother him that they only called him dad when they were being sarcastic.

"Colton, you're on notice."

"What did he do?" Marcus asked.

Buck hadn't made a big song and dance about what Colton had gotten caught doing, because he didn't want to expose Lily to any kind of gossip, and on top of that, he hadn't wanted them to think Colton was cool.

"None of your business," he said, planting his hand flat on top of Reggie's head and giving it a scrub. "Just go about your business."

"Are you going to babysit me?" Colton asked, once his younger siblings had cantered off.

"I don't intend to. But I imagine I ought to be there when we meet up with Lily and her mother. Since you made a very bad first impression."

"So you realistically think teenagers are just not going to have sex?"

"It's not about what I think or don't think," he said. "But what I expect is that you will treat this place we've moved to with some kind of respect. That you'll consider Lily, her feelings, her future. Because you know what? I was the kind of ass who didn't. When you make consequences for somebody else, Colton, that's not something a good person can just walk away from. And you're a good person."

"You really think so?" Colton was looking at him with skepticism.

"Yes. I do. And you know...about my past. You know about the damage I caused here."

"Yeah. But it's not really the same thing."

"Maybe not. But you know what it's about, it's about prioritizing having fun in the moment over thinking about what that fun could cost. And I want you to be better than that. I want you to be different than that. I know you can be. I want you to be better than me. Because when I was your age, I did sleep around, and I didn't care if girls got their feelings hurt. I didn't care that my dad was busy. He was traveling around with the rodeo. My mom was...dealing with things. She had lost one of her kids. And then had another baby kind of late... It just... Nobody was really paying attention to what I was doing. There were too many kids and too many other things going on... At the very least, I want you to put her mom at ease. Show some damned respect."

"Yes, sir," Colton said, mumbling. But Buck counted that as a win.

They started walking toward the festivities, and he saw Marigold and Lily standing right there.

"Hi there," he said. "Good to see you again."

Marigold looked...beautiful, her red curly hair spilling down her shoulders in loose waves, her amber eyes glistening. She didn't exactly look thrilled to see him. But she had shown up. She had done that for her daughter, he was confident.

Her daughter looked a lot like her. Red hair, freckles. She reminded Buck a lot of her mother when she had been young. She reminded Buck a lot of the Marigold who had stood in front of him yelling and hollering and basically telling him he was a murderer.

A stark contrast to the woman who stood in front of him now.

"Go have a wholesome date," Marigold said.

"All right," Lily said, taking Colton's hand and leading him into the carnival.

"They seem unhappy with us," Buck said.

"Well. Too bad for her. I guess I'm not totally used to being in opposition to my daughter, but there's a first time for everything."

"Yeah. I guess I haven't been in opposition to the boys much. But that's a real thing with foster kids... They either test you and try to drive you away, or you end up in a honeymoon phase where they're trying to be good so they don't lose you. I would say the boys have been much more on the honeymoon track. So I guess this is kind of my trial by fire. At least, I hope it is."

He felt silly, and a bit naive, saying that. Because he knew full well that all three of those boys had been in much bigger trouble than being caught in a girl's bedroom.

"They've been through a lot," he said. "Colton... Listen, Colton's story is his to tell. He's a good kid. If I thought he was going to be a danger to your daughter in any way..."

"It's weird," Marigold said, taking a step back from him. "I have a hard time looking at you and seeing who you were. But if I think too hard about the Buck Carson I used to know, all of this feels like pretty strange things for you to say."

"I know. I get that. I don't exactly know why you would trust me. But I'm not lying to you. He's a good kid. Twenty years is a long time."

"Yes it is. It's a very long time. A lifetime. It's more years than my brother lived. We might as well address that. Because it is the elephant in the room, whether we want it to be or not."

"I have no problem hearing you out. If there's something you need to say." He hadn't exactly anticipated having this conversation standing at the edge of this carnival, but whatever needed to happen, he was just going to let it happen.

"I'm not angry at you. At least, I didn't think I was. But... I guess theoretical forgiveness is a lot easier when the person isn't around. But here you are. My brother is gone and you've had twenty more years on this earth." She shook her head. "So have I. And... I can't say that I feel entirely neutral about you. But I have a better appreciation now for how young you were. When I was thirteen you seemed like a grown man. But now my daughter is seventeen, and I know that eighteen is not grown. And I don't think you should have to suffer for something that happened all those years ago."

"But Jason did," Buck replied. "Jason, Ryan and Joey did. That's what it comes down to. We made a mistake. A youthful mistake. And because of that mistake they died, and I got a second chance. It was all a matter of being in a different car. Choosing to drive myself because I didn't want to sit in the back seat. Or whatever the reason was, I don't really remember. But I do know that what happened was not fair. You are right about that. There is nothing at all fair about the fact that a mistake for them was final, while for me it wasn't."

"You really have changed."

"I have. Because in the aftermath of their deaths, when you came and yelled at me in the street, it confirmed what I already thought about myself. And if I was the bad guy, then it meant I got to go off and continue to be the bad guy. I got to go off and continue to serve myself. Which was what I did. For a number of years, Marigold, I'm not going to lie about that. But one night I picked myself up, and I decided to change the way I was doing things. I decided to make living matter. I needed living to matter. I needed their lives to matter. I needed their deaths to matter. That's why I'm here now. That's why I have the boys."

"Three boys."

He nodded. "That's why."

"It feels so complicated."

"It is. But I came back because I thought it was all right for me to be back here now."

"What do you mean by that?"

"When I left, it was because I thought staying meant visiting hardship on my family that I didn't want them to go through. At least that's the story I tell myself to try and make it seem like I'm not totally selfish. But the truth is, there was an element of selfishness to it. Of course there was. I wanted to lick my wounds. And leaving allowed me to do it in a place where there was no accountability. I didn't want to come back until I knew I wasn't using my family simply as accountability. If that makes sense."

"It does," she said.

There. He had gone and vented his guts out after having been back for five seconds. "None of that is your responsibility," he said. "You don't have to forgive me, no matter what you said before."

"All right. I'll remember that. But I think we might have to be cordial because it seems our children like each other an awful lot."

"Yeah. They do. Colton was pretty mad at me for lecturing him. My one concern, and I am going to be really honest with you, is that Colton is not a small-town kid. He was not as well protected as I assume your daughter is."

She nodded slowly. Not for the first time, he looked down at her left hand. She didn't have a ring. He looked back up, and she was studying him.

"I'm not married," she said.

His mouth quirked upward. "You must be used to men looking at your left hand."

"I am. At least, enough that I know to recognize the question when it's being nonverbally asked. Her dad has never been in the picture."

"I see."

"Sometimes I wonder if I should work harder at reaching out

to him again. Because he went off to college. Or rather, he went back to college. I did let him know, but of course at the time… he didn't want to be a dad. It just seemed easier to let it go. So, from that standpoint, I understand what you're saying. Sometimes it does seem easier to just let go completely."

"Yeah. That's it exactly." He paused. "I don't have the whole world to offer those boys. I do have a trust fund from my father and a whole mess of extended family, and that seemed like something. Seemed like a good offering. A real offering. So I decided to come back. I'm not sure that I'm loving all the connections, though."

She laughed. "I imagine not."

"We can agree that this is not a comfortable situation."

"No it's not." She had a feeling they were talking about more than Colton and Lily, so she deliberately turned the subject back to their kids. "With Colton, what you're basically telling me is that you're worried he's more experienced than Lily?"

"Yes."

"He probably is. Lily has never dated anyone before. She has a mother who got pregnant at sixteen. The paranoia runs a little high in our household."

"If you don't want them dating, I can tell him…"

"No. I think what we discussed earlier stands. If we turn them into Romeo and Juliet, it's only going to get worse. I'm just going to have to try to keep talking to Lily. Keep her communicating with me. It's the best I can do."

"You have every right to yell at me, you know," he said.

"Would that make you more comfortable?"

"Yeah. Now that you ask."

"Then I'm definitely not going to yell at you."

His lips twitched. They regarded each other for a moment.

"So. Want to…walk around the carnival?"

"I don't know," she said.

"What else are we going to do? Anyway, then we can keep an eye on the kids."

That was true, but really he wanted to keep talking to her. She was right; he almost would've been more comfortable if she had yelled at him again. If she'd have picked up right where she left off years ago. Mainly because there was some part of him that still wanted to feel that guilt. That still wanted to feel that culpability for the accident. Because that guilt was his comfort zone. For a long time, he had acted out of a self-destructive place with that guilt. But he had stopped, and he had learned to use it as fuel. So maybe part of him was looking for more. Along with that extra bit of absolution. She felt linked to all that. He didn't want to lose touch with her.

"All right," she said.

The booths were set up on the sidewalks, in front of businesses. There were games and snacks and other things designed to appeal to teens, and all the proceeds went to fundraising for the school. There were caramel apples and balloon dart games. The kind of thing he never the hell would've gone to when he was in high school. He wondered if the boys were secretly enjoying this carnival, or if it felt really cheesy to them. But then, wasn't having something light and cheesy in your life a privilege?

Twenty years ago, he had been reeling from the death of his little sister. He had let it take the joy away from him. It was that loss that had put him on the road when his friends died.

So he had learned that the pain a person carried could hurt other people. No one was an island.

He had also learned that the ability to be happy was a gift.

"Candy apple?" he asked now.

"Oh sure," she said. "Why not?" She paused. "We're not on a date."

"No," he said. "We are not."

"Good. Just making sure."

"I don't think you can accidentally go on a date," he said.

"Well, I hope not. I'd hate to break my seventeen-year dateless streak."

"Seventeen years?"

"I have a kid. And yes, you can date when you have kids. But I decided that I didn't want to take the risk. Of having her get attached to somebody, and then having it not work out between us. It just always felt too volatile. I admire the people who do it. Who try to make that work. I just couldn't… I'd already had too many losses. And I didn't want to visit any on my daughter. At least none that I could help."

"Right." He felt sad for a second, because he knew the weight of those losses. He knew exactly what she was talking about. He had been part of that.

"Platonic candy apple," he said.

"That is allowed."

He bought the sticky, bright red apple for her, plus one for himself, and it was like being in an out-of-body experience. This strange kind of small-town moment he had never really experienced before. By the time his family had moved full-time to Lone Rock, he'd already been destroyed by the loss of his sister. So he had never really…done anything like this. Had never walked down the street with a pretty girl eating a candy apple.

He shouldn't be thinking of it that way now.

"So, what are your plans once Lily leaves home?"

"If you expect me to say *get a date*… Well. Maybe. It's not off the table. But the other big thing would be that I want to open a storefront for my business."

"What do you do?"

"Meal prep. I would really like to open a facility where people could come in and use it to do their own meal prep. I make the plan, they do the preparation. And I'd have a place to store more prepared meals so people could buy them for the week rather than being on my regular rotation. Which is what I do now—there are a certain number of families in the area who have me make their dinners for the week. I deliver them at a set time, and they don't have to worry about it. They just have to cook."

"That's pretty clever. I'll tell you, when I lived on the ranch for troubled kids, there was a cook. Three square meals a day, and I didn't have to think about buying the food, preparing the food, or what the food was going to be. That has been one of the harshest realities of adopting these kids and taking them away from the institution. I have to figure out what to cook for them."

"A lot of people hate it. I love it. I like figuring out how to work on a budget, how to make it as cost-effective and afford-able as possible."

"That's great. So you're looking for a building?"

"Yes. I… I mean, that's what I *want* to do. Because I need to do something with my time once Lily is away. But it's going to take… I don't know. A pretty substantial loan, and that scares me. When Lily was younger, I never wanted to get into any-thing like that because it would mean putting our house at risk. I would never do that, not when she was little. But I feel like I can maybe branch out now. Take more risks."

"You have a place in mind?"

She shrugged. "There's a building, just up the street. It's been empty for a while. I would have it completely gutted and renovated, and it would be so expensive—"

"You need an investor."

"Okaaay…"

"Yeah. Somebody to assume the risk up-front, and help you get this going."

"That sounds like a great idea. I have no idea how I would go about finding one."

"I could be one."

She blinked. "What?"

"Yeah. Why don't you let me be your investor?"

Chapter Five

Marigold was astonished. And thirteen-year-old Marigold was *appalled*.

She could not take this man's blood money. His guilt money. Under no circumstances. Her principled younger self was outraged. Her older self was trying to figure out if it was the therapy, if it was coming to believe that things were more complicated than she'd previously believed, or if the real issue was that she just really wanted to say yes. Because if he would invest, then she could do what she needed to do with the business. Without risking her house or any of the other things she had built. She wouldn't have to worry so much about Lily's scholarships covering absolutely everything. It was just...a miraculously good offer at a moment when she needed it most.

But he was Buck Carson.

You're eating candy apples with him.

She was. And if she was totally honest, when she had asked him if it was a date, it had felt a little bit like flirting.

He was *very* handsome.

Which felt like a psychotic thing to think—given everything. But she'd always thought he was hot, and also, the man standing in front of her didn't bear a resemblance to the boy she'd vented her grief on all those years ago. Not that he physically looked entirely different, but he was different inside. She knew it. She could feel it.

He had kids now. Recently adopted kids. He'd said *yes* to taking on all the trauma they might have. He was trying to actively parent Colton in this situation with Lily and...

It was far too easy to simply detach this older Buck Colton from the Buck she'd known back them.

Maybe because she was so different too.

The Marigold of twenty years ago had been fascinated by his wild streak. He'd been a bad boy. He'd seemed dangerous, and she'd liked that. In the years after, she'd burned herself out on bad boys. She'd learned her lesson, and well. She wasn't the same person she'd been.

It stood to reason he wasn't either.

She didn't know if she was being desperately naive in saying yes to anything. In even talking to him.

In doing anything other than punching him in the stomach and running away.

But... On the other hand, didn't he owe her *something*?

Not like that. But if Jason had been here, he would've been the best uncle. He would've been another positive male role model in Lily's life, and he would've offered so much in terms of support. He had been such a great older brother.

"Don't overthink it. I want to help. I have money. I have a trust fund. And I want to invest in your business."

"But..."

"Yes. Because I feel guilty. Okay? It's because I feel like I owe you. I do. There's nothing wrong with that, is there?"

"I don't know."

She really didn't. Maybe because even inside it felt mixed-up.

"What happened back then was bad. It was a tragedy. There's no way to shift it into something it's not. It was awful. It *is* awful. We can't change it. We can't fix it. But I have dedicated my whole life to figuring out how to make something grow out of the charred earth the accident left behind. To try and make it mean something. When you showed up on my doorstep yesterday I thought..."

She stopped walking and turned to face him. "You thought what?"

"I thought it was my chance to fix it."

He meant it. He wasn't lying. He absolutely felt that way. It was clear he thought this was a chance for him to make amends.

Did she want him to be absolved?

She didn't feel the way that she once had about him. She thought she had forgiven him, and she had put all her complicated feelings off to one side. She had a daughter to raise. She had a life to get on with.

When her grief surfaced, she didn't let it have teeth.

She didn't allow anger at somebody else to mix with the moment, because she wanted the moment to honor Jason.

It was different with Buck there, though.

It was very, very different.

"Yes," she said, before she could think about it anymore. Before she could overthink it. Because there was no right answer here.

She could be angry at Buck forever, and maybe part of her would be. But it wouldn't bring Jason back. It wouldn't bring back Ryan and it wouldn't bring back Joey.

He was trying. He had lived on a ranch for troubled youths. He had adopted three boys who needed somebody.

It still didn't bring them back.

So whether she hated him forever or scorned his money and his help, that didn't make a difference.

Her refusal wouldn't fix anything either. Maybe it would make her feel morally superior, but it wouldn't actually solve any of the problems she had.

She would have to make sure her parents didn't find out, though.

She didn't know how they felt about Buck. They had never talked about it.

She had gone off the rails, and then she had gotten pregnant, and everybody had rallied around her. Since then, her parents had devoted themselves to being the best grandparents on earth. But that didn't leave a lot of space to talk about grief.

That was all right. Because in some ways it was easier. She didn't have to carry their grief along with her own. Maybe that wasn't fair, but it was the truth.

"I can't commit myself to working too much before Lily leaves..."

"But we can get construction started. We can make a business plan, get permits—all that stuff takes time. It would be good if we could start as soon as possible."

"You're just now back in town. You have your family, other commitments. Why do you want to throw all in with me?"

"I already told you."

"You feel that guilty."

He let out a long, slow breath. "More complicated than that. I think this was what was meant to be. I... I don't ignore gut feelings. Okay? I really try to sit with them. I try to listen to myself. I try to see what God or the universe or whatever the fuck is out there is telling me. And it was telling me something when you came to my house yesterday."

"It wasn't just telling you that our teenagers have wildly racing hormones?"

"All right. It was definitely telling us that. But I think there's a point to be made here—this was meant to be in some way."

"You can still believe in fate?"

She had trouble with that one. Because she had a hard time believing her brother was meant to be gone. She had a hard time with people saying things like: it was his time. Because how could it be an eighteen-year-old boy's time? How? There was nothing just about that. There was nothing fair about it.

She had a very hard time believing anything that even hinted it was meant to be.

And she would've thought he could understand that.

"Maybe not fate. What I do think is that sometimes we get pulled up. By the scruff of our neck. By the divine, I guess, and it's up to us whether we listen or not. I try to listen now."

She couldn't argue with that. Because she related to that experience. When she had found out she was pregnant, it had been like a divine hand reaching down to redirect her. It had been like a total shift in the way she saw things. But she could have chosen a different way. She hadn't had to keep Lily. She hadn't had to change. But she had heeded the feeling. Maybe that was what she felt now. A tug. Telling her she had to take his offer. This opportunity. Because it mattered. Because it was going to mean something.

Or at the very least it was going to make her life easier, and surely that wasn't a bad thing.

"Well, it's good for me. Though I suppose we need to come up with all kinds of official terms and conditions."

"Of course. I'll send them over to my lawyer. I just did an adoption, so I'm more familiar with the legal system than I'd like to be at this point."

"They aren't brothers, are they? I mean biologically." She felt clumsy asking the question, concerned she'd done it in a way that didn't respect the bond they all shared. But she was more curious about his life, about how everything had come together to create that family, than she wanted to admit.

"No. They were all three at the ranch for a while, and none of them were going to a home. Reggie..." His expression suddenly went remote. She saw his throat work. "His mom got killed by her boyfriend. Along with his younger sister. It happened while he was at the camp. If he had been home, he would've been gone too. That poor kid."

Sympathy tightened her stomach. "Oh. Wow. That poor boy."

"When you meet him, though, don't be soft on him just because he's been through shit. He doesn't like that. He doesn't want pity."

She understood. It was hard when everyone knew something bad had happened to you. They were so careful. Sometimes so careful they decided not to speak to you at all. Reggie had a fresh start here. In some ways, that must feel good.

Buck knew too. And Buck had to find ways to help his son with his grief.

"That must be… That must be so hard," she said.

"It is. The kids come with a lot of baggage, but so do I."

She had to admit that it really did seem like he was trying to do the best he could with what he had. That he was trying to take a tragedy he had experienced and turn it into something good.

"Why don't you walk me up to your building?"

"It's not *my* building yet."

"We can put an offer in tomorrow if you want."

"Really?"

"I can pay with cash."

"It's expensive."

"Do you not realize that my dad's rich, right? My siblings and I all have huge trust funds."

She did sort of know that, but Buck had been gone and she'd assumed he'd been cut out of the cash flow.

"He still gave you money?"

"Yeah. I guess he always hoped I would come home. But I hadn't spent a penny of it. Not until I bought the ranch here."

"You already bought the ranch, and you *still* have money left over?"

"Yes. And I don't intend to live a life of excess. I intend to send these boys to college. I intend to get my ranch up and running. But I'm investing in your business. I'm not just dumping money into something."

"I don't know that it's going to earn much back."

"It will."

They walked down the street until they arrived at the vacant building. It was large and empty, once housing a department store when this street was a thriving thoroughfare during the gold rush. In recent years, the economy had picked up because more and more people were moving to Bend and pushing tourism out into Eastern Oregon, an area which had been desolate all the years before. And the town of Lone Rock itself was growing. Bend was so trendy it had become expensive, so moving to an outlying area that wasn't terribly faraway was seen as a great compromise by a lot of people. That meant the odds of her growing her business were good, and the real estate market was still competitive without being overinflated.

The building was still a mint green color with gold trim, and she loved how cheerful and old-fashioned it was all at once. It was easy for her to imagine different workstations where people could prepare their food. And a big commercial kitchen for her.

"This is it," she said.

"It's great," he said. "Really great. I love it."

"You do?"

"Yeah. I think you could really sell people on the community aspect of coming in and preparing meals together. Instead of it being drudgery, it would be a fun night out with your friends."

She loved that. She hadn't even really thought of that direction. She could furnish drinks, cocktails, coffee. She really liked the idea because for so much of her adult life she had been isolated. She'd had a daughter at a much younger age than anybody else she knew, and she was consistently a baby next to the other parents at Lily's school. And while she was relatively friendly with a few of the moms, most of the mothers of graduating seniors were ten to fifteen years older than her. The idea of community really appealed to her.

Maybe because it had been elusive for so long.

Maybe because she'd felt outside of it even before she'd had Lily.

Back when she'd been the sad girl whose brother was dead. And then the slut who would go with any guy that asked.

"Listen, if you want to, I wouldn't mind if you added me to your meal prep rotation," he said. "I'm dying trying to cook for these kids."

For some reason that made her stomach get tight. Made her heart throb. "I...yes. I'd like for that to be one of your investment perks."

"You don't have to do that."

"Maybe not, but it'll be a while before this is making enough money to cover what you're proposing to put into it. So let me at least make food for you."

"Fine. But I'm paying for the groceries."

"Okay. I want to do this. I mean I really do. I said yes because I didn't want you to change your mind, and not really so much because I felt totally on board. But now I do. I mean I really do."

"Good," he said. "I'm glad. I'm glad that you're on board for this."

"My parents...."

"Right. Shit. You want me to talk to them?"

"Not right now." She wished she was brave enough to talk to them. About Jason. About Buck. About Lily dating Buck's son.

But it was like the words froze in her throat whenever she tried.

Before her brother's death, her house had always been loud and fun, filled with Jason and his friends and their mom making food for everyone.

When he'd died, it had been so deathly quiet, and she hadn't dared speak above a whisper. When she was home, she tried not to speak or feel anything. She went out and she partied and she made up for all that quiet then. And came home with her parents none the wiser.

Until she'd gotten pregnant, of course.

Then they'd all figured out how to speak again.

But it was about new life, not about death. About Lily and what was best for her and what Marigold could do to be a good mom, not about losing Jason.

They didn't talk about their loss.

Marigold didn't know how to, not with them.

"All right," Buck said. "It's an awfully small town, though."

"I know. I will talk to them. I will. I just… I need to figure all this out."

"Seems fair. And you have yourself an investor, Marigold Rivers."

He stuck his hand out, and she really had to think about that. But then she took a breath and clasped his hand in hers. It was rough. Hotter than she had imagined it would be. And for some reason, it made her tremble. And maybe now wasn't the best time to reflect on the fact that it had been nearly eighteen years since a man had had his hands on her body.

"You have a deal," she said, breaking the handshake as quickly as possible.

They were already going into business together. She wasn't going to muddy the waters by feeling attracted to Buck Carson.

There were lines. And this was one she was never going to cross.

Chapter Six

After the boys went to school the next morning, he contacted Marigold. "You ready to go down and make an offer?"

"Yes. I called a buyer's agent this morning."

"Perfect. We'll go take a tour, and then we can put in a formal offer."

"All right. I'll meet you down there."

"Sounds good."

He felt a bit like he was having an out-of-body experience when he got into his truck and started driving toward Lone Rock. He had been here a month, and it was starting to feel okay that he was home. Starting to feel familiar. Starting to feel like home, but it was still complicated. Sometimes it was like being in a time warp. Other times it was like he had never been here before in his life. Like he was a stranger.

But he was very firmly rooted in the here and now when he pulled up and saw Marigold and the real estate agent already standing in front of the building.

Her hair was so bright, like radiant copper. He hadn't realized just how guarded she'd been when she was talking to him, because there was an easy pleasantness on her face that he had not seen before as she looked at the other woman on the sidewalk.

He parked his truck against the curb across the street and got out. Instantly he saw the tension rise in her body, saw her shoulders go tight. The corners of her lips pulled taut.

"Hi."

"Hello, I'm Louisa Ramirez."

"Buck Carson." He remembered what they had discussed, her desire that he be more of a silent partner. He looked at Marigold, but she didn't seem bothered that he had introduced himself.

"I'm excited to show you that—" The phone rang, and Louisa looked down at her phone. "Just one second."

"Sorry," he said out of the corner of his mouth while Louisa took the call, turning away from them. "I know you wanted me to keep this on the down-low."

"You don't need an alias. I just don't want it spreading around before I figure out how to approach it with my parents. Louisa is new to town, though. Your name won't mean anything to her."

That was a novelty. Not being notorious to somebody in this small town.

Being back the past month hadn't been as rocky as he'd thought it might be, but it had still been a *thing*. Some of his brothers were easier on him than others. Boone was still pretty angry and stood by the punch he'd thrown when Buck had first arrived.

Some people in town recognized him right away. Some didn't. Some genuinely just thought he was one of his brothers from a distance and waved like they knew him. He always waved back.

The principal of the high school was a guy he'd graduated with, which had made him feel desperately old. But the man had been friendly enough to Buck when they'd talked about the boys and their individual situations.

This small town was a mixed bag. And he didn't hold it against the people who didn't quite know what to do with him.

"All right."

"Sorry," Louisa said, turning back to them. "Childcare. I had to make sure everything was okay. You know, the day care calls and your heart stops."

"I do know," said Marigold. "Even though it's been a while."

"Of course you do. Anyway. I'm going to go ahead and give you a tour of the inside. It's in great shape—it has been completely gutted, with new flooring, new walls, new electrical and new plumbing. It's a complete blank slate."

"Perfect," he said. She looked over at him in censure. "What? I mean, it's up to you, but it seems perfect."

"But it's up to me," she said.

"Of course," he said. "It's up to you." Gradually, over the course of their inspection, he realized Louisa was treating them like a couple. But why wouldn't she think that? And, since Marigold didn't want him to make a big deal out of their business partnership, he thought it was probably for the best that he not go making pronouncements. He didn't know if Marigold was noticing the subtle tone of everything. He supposed it didn't matter.

They finished the walk-through without incident, but he kept his eyes pinned closely to Marigold's face.

"We'd like to make an offer," he said.

She looked at him, and he thought she might want to scold him again for making the decision, but he knew she wanted it. That he could see plain as day.

"Yes," she said slowly. "We would."

He didn't see the point in offering under the asking price, so when they got the paperwork to make the official offer, he went ahead and put it in as it was.

"I'll take this to the seller," the agent said.

"Thanks," he replied.

They walked out of the building, and that left him and Marigold standing on the sidewalk.

"Thank you for that," she said.

"Not a problem. Do you know of any good contractors around here?"

"Yeah. I do. There's a couple that seem to have a really good construction business, ones that I've only heard good things about."

"Excellent. Then once the offer is accepted, we'll line that up."

"We have to, like, get permits and stuff?"

"That too, but we're going to need a concrete plan, and the contractor will pull those permits for us."

She squinted. "So you've done this before."

"I helped with some renovations at the ranch years ago, so I'm familiar with the logistics, yeah."

"I guess I needed a partner more than I realized." She looked at him for a moment, and it felt like their eyes locked together, for just a moment. His gut went tight. She looked away quickly. "Okay. I guess we're doing this."

"Yeah."

"So…" She squinted. "Lily wants to have Colton over to study. And she swears that they're actually going to study."

"Oh. Well. Sounds believable."

She snorted. "I told her they have to leave the door open in the room where they're studying the whole time. Also, I was wondering if you wanted to come over and work on the plans for this."

"Better idea. Why don't you guys all come out to my place, and we can do the planning there? There's more room, and the kids can sprawl out in public areas, but still have some quiet for studying."

"Oh. That's great. If we do that, let me do dinner. I'm very efficient at dinner."

"I'm not going to say no to that."

"Okay. It sounds good."

"Yeah. Still not a date," he said.

"No," she said. "Still not a date."

Lily was a little bit irritated with Marigold at co-opting the study night, but her daughter seemed pleased to go to Colton's house. Like it would give her a window into this boy she liked, and it would probably be enjoyable.

"I mean, I haven't gotten to go inside," she said.

"No, and now you will. But not into his bedroom."

"*Mom*," said Lily.

"Well. His dad and I both thought this plan would be a good idea."

"Right."

Marigold needed to explain to Lily everything that was going on. She had mentioned that Buck had offered to invest in her business, and for all that she had been uninterested in the topic, Lily had seemed happy for her.

"To be clear," Marigold said, "I am not dating his dad."

Lily's face contorted in horror. "Why would I have ever thought you were?"

A good question. As Marigold had schooled herself into a sexless paragon. She had fashioned herself into a puritanical version of a mother. Not a woman. A mother. She had never gone on a date, not in Lily's whole life, so why would Lily assume that of her now?

Marigold had mentioned dates several times in regards to Buck Carson, and she couldn't pretend that she didn't know why.

She was attracted to him. He made her heart beat just a little faster, but the problem was that with every heartbeat there was a little pain as well.

He was inextricably linked to her brother's death. That was an old wound, but one that had not been tested in quite this way in a very long time. Well. Ever, really.

She had distance and perspective. She had age and wisdom. But that was about it.

She also had very large gaps in experience, and a whole lot of peaks and valleys in her personal development. She was a mother. She had started a business. She had raised a child to this point. She had bought a house and made a budget.

All her experiences with men and sex were the experiences

of a teenage girl. And maybe that was why she felt slightly teenage now. Attaching herself to the most ridiculous man she could have possibly attached herself to.

Or maybe the problem was that old attraction simply died hard.

She had always felt an attraction to him. Even when it had been a young and innocent fascination. Back then, he had been the boy who had the power to ignite her fantasies. Now he had evolved into the man who could apparently stoke a flame that had grown cold after so many years of neglect.

So maybe she was projecting when she continually mentioned dates. She was going to have to stop that.

"Well, it isn't, I just wanted to make it clear."

"It's worse than a date," Lily said. "You're supervising me."

"You made yourself worthy of supervision, Lily."

Lily scowled.

"All right. Let's just get there and see how it goes. Anyway, his house is bigger, and you were excited about seeing the house."

"Yes, yes."

Teenagers really were so mercurial. But normally, Marigold wasn't the subject of Lily's changing moods, so she couldn't say that she'd noticed so much. Or been bothered by it.

That felt significantly different right at the moment.

"It is a really nice house," she said as they pulled up to the large, modern dwelling.

"What does he do?" Lily asked.

"You didn't ask Colton?"

"I did. He said his dad used to work at a camp for troubled kids. Which is how he ended up adopting Colton. But that doesn't make any sense. Because I know everything is more expensive than you could possibly believe, and that you don't get paid good money for being a decent human being. This house is billionaire money. This is scamming other people's money. And yeah, you don't get that kind of money helping kids."

"Colton's grandfather is the commissioner for the rodeo."

"Really?"

"Yes. You don't really know the Carsons, but they were a big factor when I was growing up. They moved to town right before I started middle school. And they brought a lot of money with them. They had a lot of kids too, and they infiltrated every single school around. You couldn't ignore them."

"I don't know the lore," Lily said.

"Well. That's the lore. Abe Carson is the bigwig of the largest rodeo organization in the country. They travel all over the place putting on events, he has made a massive organization and he has tons of money. And what Buck said was that they had trust funds. All the kids."

"Wow. Must be nice."

"Right?"

"So that's what he used to buy this?"

"Yes."

"I guess at least a good person got the money."

It was interesting that Lily saw him simply as a good person. But then, why should she see him any differently? Jason's accident was theoretical to her. He had been gone long before she was born. And all Marigold could really say about Buck's connection to the accident was that he had been there. Everything else had been innuendo.

About the way he might've influenced the evening. It wasn't actually fair. Not if she stepped back from it.

It didn't make the wound less tender.

But that was all it was. Tender.

Such an old pain now. Dull and aching.

They got out of the car.

They walked up to the door together this time, rather than Marigold going alone, being on a warpath, and Marigold rang the doorbell.

Colton was the one who answered. "Come on in. My dad said you were making dinner?"

"He is correct. I'm offering dinner in exchange for the use of the house for studying. Since we decided not to do it over at our place. But I hear tell that you have a lot more room."

"Yeah. That is true."

They walked into the house, and Lily and Colton went off into a sitting room to the left. She heard noise coming from the kitchen and popped her head inside. "I just have a couple of bags to bring in," she said.

Buck was facing away from her, standing at the sink. His shoulders broad, his waist tapered. He was… He was gorgeous. It was problematic.

She realized right then that maybe she wasn't a paragon when it came to not dating so much as no one had ever been interesting enough for her to upset the delicate balance she had with her daughter. She had never met a man who tempted her to risk anything.

She had thought she was just super responsible and enlightened. She had been a little bit self-righteous about it, truth be told. Yeah, on the surface, she'd tried to pretend she was okay with how everybody else lived their own lives, but actually, she had let herself get very up her own rear about the whole thing, and she could see now in that moment just how ridiculous it was. Because Buck Carson was bad on every level.

Getting involved with him would be wrong.

And she was tempted.

Because he was compelling. Beautiful.

He turned to face her, and the hard, stark lines of his expression took her breath away.

Those blue eyes, chiseled cheekbones and square jaw. It was like he was carved out of granite.

And suddenly, her fingertips itched to trace the lines there.

She was so screwed.

She couldn't pretend it was just a lack of male interaction. Because she was around men all the time. She lived in the world.

There were plenty of single dads at the school. And they didn't make her feel like this.

She did wonder if there was some kind of sickness in all this. If she had some thwarted feelings from the past where he was concerned, and that was informing everything now.

"Yeah," he said, grabbing a dishrag and drying his hands. "Sure."

He did not look domesticated, and yet the vision of him in the kitchen doing the dishes like this was domestic. There was something about the contrast that was... Too much. Way too much.

"Just a second."

She scurried outside and grabbed her bag of groceries, bringing it back in. "I thought I would make us stew. I have a loaf of bread that I made this morning."

"Sounds great," he said.

"Yeah. It will be. I am a great cook."

"Glad to hear that."

"Especially since you're going to benefit from that cooking."

"Also, it's related to the investment that I'm making."

"True."

Silence fell between them, and she covered it up with movement, briskly making her way across the kitchen and beginning to unload the grocery bag. "I'm going to need a knife and a cutting board."

"Pretty sure I know where that is."

"If I find it faster than you, I'm going to shame you."

"The good thing about having a sister-in-law who owns a bar is that a lot of times I just pick up hamburgers from there."

"Oh, I mean, the burgers at Karen's place are good, but come on, not if you have them *that* often," Marigold replied.

"Do you actually go to the bar?" he asked. "There's not an embargo on my whole family?"

"No. Nobody..."

"Nobody wanted to punish the whole family because of me?"

"Basically," she said, feeling regretful. "Listen… I don't want to make you feel bad."

"Oh. I get something out of feeling bad. Or have you not noticed that yet?"

"You're awfully self-aware."

"It's one of my better qualities. But then, that's also a side effect of having been on my own for a long time. Nothing to do but think about myself. A form of narcissistic healing."

She snorted out a laugh. "I'm actually kinda familiar with that."

"Right. Single parenting?"

"Specifically, when I was pregnant."

"Tell me about that," he said, getting his cutting board down and putting it on the counter.

"Why?"

"Because I'm interested, Marigold. And I want to know. Because…we're doing this thing together. Also, I like you. I'm trying to get to know you."

She squinted. "Why?"

"Misplaced guilt, probably. But if it doesn't bother you, it doesn't bother me."

"Doesn't bother me." She took a breath and took her butcher paper–wrapped steak out of the bag and began to carefully take the paper off. "After Jason died, I didn't know what to do with myself. I wanted to disappear and I wanted attention. I wanted to explode, and I wanted to hide. I loved him. My parents were really going through it. Of course they were. They lost their son. I started rebelling in small ways. But really, the way I was able to get all those needs met was men."

"Boys, you mean."

She laughed. "I wish. No. I liked them slightly older. I didn't really want to sleep with somebody at my school."

"When you were fourteen?"

"Usually they were nineteen or so. A lot of times I wasn't honest about my age. Okay, anytime. Granted, it didn't come up. I don't think they cared. It was just the way I found this false feeling of control and power. And then it really came home to roost. Because I got pregnant. And he was headed off to college. He didn't want a baby. I realized I needed the baby. Which is maybe a terrible reason to have a baby, but I wasn't making the best decisions at the time, as we have established."

"And you had a bunch of assholes ready to take advantage of you being so lonely."

"That's the world, Buck. We make weird, bad decisions when we're in pain, and someone is always willing to take advantage of those reactions and traumas. I own my part in that. But you know, it's not any different from what we all did to you. We were angry. Collectively, as a community, and you were the survivor, so you became the scapegoat. Because nobody could yell at the three boys who had made the same decision you did. To get behind the wheel drunk, to get in a car with somebody drunk. To spend graduation night wasting their potential. The truth is... I was probably angry at Jason. But he was dead. So yelling at you was a replacement."

"Maybe." He looked sad. Thoughtful. That he still carried the grief of it all made her feel... Not better. That sounded mean. But she felt a kinship to him she had never imagined she might feel. "That whole period of time was a dark one for me too."

"So you mentioned."

"I had to hit rock bottom before I changed. I mean, I really had to."

"I think I would have too. If not for Lily. I think I narrowly escaped rock bottom. Some people would consider getting pregnant at sixteen rock bottom, I'm sure. But for me, it was the hand up that I needed. It was the only thing that was ever going to reach me."

"And now she's headed off to college. That means you did something right."

"I hope so. That's all you can do with kids, Buck. Hope. Hope you did the right thing. Hope your best intentions matter. Because sometimes they do and sometimes they don't. You hope the good you do outweighs the bad. The mistakes."

"Thanks," he said. He was silent for a long moment. "It's heavy. The way having kids makes you see things differently. The way being close to kids, even if they aren't yours, changes the way you look at your own life. Even when I was just working at the ranch, looking at those kids made me feel, for the first time, an appreciation for how young we were back then. But especially now. Looking at my boys. I feel old. And they feel so, so young."

"It's difficult," she said. "Because being a teenager should be a time when you're allowed to be stupid. But you and I both know that, depending on the stupidity..." She swallowed hard. "You just can't take some things back."

"No," he said, his voice rough. "And I'm trying to figure out how to impress that upon them while..."

"Not crushing them?"

"Yeah."

"I relate to that."

Again, she realized she had more in common with him than not.

It was such a strange realization.

Because she had thought he was an enemy. When in fact he was an ally.

"We just have to do our best."

She was chopping vegetables when he spoke again.

"You know. I lost my sister."

She stopped. She had vaguely known that. That the Carsons had lost a child before they moved to Lone Rock. But there were so many of them, and the loss had been abstract, so she had never really considered their grief. That it meant she and Buck had both experienced the loss of a sibling.

"You did," she said. "I'm sorry. I never really thought about that. I was... I'm really sorry that I blamed you."

"I'm not telling you that to make you feel sorry for me," he said. "I don't need or deserve pity of any kind."

"Yes. You do. Because you have really been through hell with all of this. And you had been through hell before all this too."

"I had a therapist diagnose me with survivor's guilt," he said. "And I thought that was the dumbest thing. Because why should you be in pain because you survived? I just don't get it."

"I think everything is just hard. And maybe part of the problem is trying to decide who's allowed to feel bad about what when… Life has a way of breaking us all down."

"Right. Cheery conversation," he said.

"Well. We don't exactly have a cheery shared history."

"True."

Suddenly, giggles erupted from the other room. He grinned. And it made her stomach go tight.

"I guess we're building a different shared history right now," she said.

"I guess so."

Chapter Seven

She put the stew on to simmer, and the scent that filled the kitchen was heavenly. He was damned glad he had enlisted her to help make meals. Because this was making his house feel like a home in a way it hadn't before. But there was also this… pull toward her. A pull that was not at all homey or in keeping with the conversation they'd had earlier.

He was actually pretty astonished to discover everything they had in common.

He hadn't expected that.

But even deeper, harder, was the attraction he felt toward her.

She was beautiful. He wanted to know more about her. He wanted to know everything about her.

And that was… That was the dumbest thing in the world. He had just adopted three boys. She had her daughter, ready to go off to school. Their kids were dating, and there was no guidebook.

For any of this.

When he called the boys for dinner, they definitely made a big song and dance about the food being better quality than they were used to getting from him. That was fine. He couldn't dispute that.

Marigold looked amused.

"Are you animals actually going to introduce yourselves?"

"Oh," said Reggie between mouthfuls of bread. "I'm Reggie."

"Marcus," said Marcus, not looking up from his stew.

Colton treated Marigold to a smile that was a little bit too smart-assed to be called polite. "We've met."

"Yes. We have. I'm Marigold. Lily's mom."

"We don't have to call you Mrs.?"

"No," she said. "First of all because I'm not a Mrs. and second of all because I like my first name just fine."

"Fair enough," said Marcus.

Lily looked marginally uncomfortable, but then, he couldn't blame her. He could think of few things that would've horrified him more as a teenager than having to sit down at a table with the family of a girl he was making out with, and he imagined that unease transferred across gender lines pretty equally. Colton, for his part, didn't seem to be having a problem at all, but Colton had an outsized amount of confidence for a boy of seventeen.

Likely, that was what attracted Lily to him. It was also what made Colton a potentially devastating heartbreaker. Buck also knew that from experience.

He had been a little bit *too* good at getting girls to fall in love with him. Not so good at getting anyone to *stay* in love with him, because he couldn't back up that charm with actual substance. Not back then.

Not that he had any evidence he could do it now.

Not that he had ever tried.

The odd one-night stand didn't exactly foster emotional maturity when it came to things like that. He liked to believe he had garnered maturity in other ways. But as far as romantic relationships went…

He looked up, his eyes connecting with Marigold's. Yeah. He didn't need to be looking at her when he thought about things like that.

"How are you settling into Lone Rock so far?" she asked brightly, looking around the table at all the boys.

"It sucks," said Reggie, chewing loudly.

"Boring," said Marcus, giving it a thumbs-down.

"I don't mind it," said Colton.

"Why do you think it's boring?" she asked, looking directly at Marcus.

"Because it is," Marcus said. "Respectfully."

"Is there a respectful way to call something boring?" Marigold asked.

He shrugged. "I figured I would give it a try."

"What kinds of things did you like to do back where you came from?"

Marcus squinted. "At the ranch? Or at home?"

He felt a small, strange kick in his stomach hearing Marcus refer to where he'd been before as home. But he supposed Marcus would feel that way. Because he had grown up in Cleveland, which was different from the ranch for troubled youth and different from Lone Rock, and Cleveland was what he thought of when he thought of home. Even if it had been inhospitable in a lot of ways. Even if he had spent years bouncing from house to house.

"Either place," Marigold said.

"There were always kids to run around with at home," Marcus said. "You could go out on the street and find whole group of them. Go play basketball."

"You can do that here," she pointed out.

"I guess. But I don't know any of the kids here. And I don't have a basketball."

"I can get you one," Buck said. "I didn't know you wanted to play."

He shrugged. "I didn't play at the ranch."

"Why not?" Marigold asked.

"I don't know," he said, looking down.

Buck had a feeling he did know. But he wasn't going to push.

He realized then that while he had experience with loss and with pain, even with leaving home, he didn't fully understand what it was like to be uprooted without your consent. To feel like everything was out of control. But these boys did.

Reggie's mom was dead. He didn't know his dad, and that made going home impossible. Maybe Reggie could get back to the house he had grown up in, but he would never be able to get back to the people. That was tragic. But Buck hadn't really given a lot of thought to the fact that home, in the traditional sense, still existed for Marcus and Colton. Their parents were alive. The system had separated them. And yes, the addictions and flaws of their parents had separated them. But the grief it must have created inside them to have *home* out there somewhere, and yet still out of reach...

"Do you like baseball?" Marigold asked.

"I do," said Reggie. "My mom used to take us to Fenway sometimes. When I was little."

"My brother played baseball. He loved it."

"Does he still play?" Reggie asked.

Buck's stomach dropped. But Marigold didn't look upset. She didn't look at Buck either.

"No," she said. "My brother died. But baseball is still a good memory."

"Oh. My mom and sister died," said Reggie. "But I think baseball is still a good memory for me too."

"I'm sorry, Reggie," Marigold said. "I know how hard it is to lose a sibling."

Buck knew some people might feel like they were witnessing a sad moment, but the truth was, everybody at this table had experience with loss. That was why the boys had a solid sense of dark humor, and it was why Buck never scolded them for it. Because they had seen the real ugly things in the world, and there was no need to protect them from that. Not when they had lived it. With that in mind, he knew this was a profound moment. One that meant something.

Because Marigold was identifying with Reggie, not pitying him.

Because Reggie didn't have to be afraid to talk about loss. It wasn't bringing down the room. It was something they all understood.

Buck had talked to Reggie about how he had lost his sister when he was little. To have both adults in the room truly understand him on that level was probably a unique experience.

"Maybe we can play some baseball," Buck said. "I'm bad at it. But there is a pretty good baseball team at the high school. The basketball team is terrible. But maybe they could use somebody who knows how to play."

Marcus looked thoughtful. "I dunno. Maybe I could learn how to play baseball."

Well. If you wanted a fresh start, that was fair enough.

"I don't want to play sports," Colton said. "There's already too much homework. Anyway, I'm a senior. I'm not going to be here that long."

"Do you have plans to go to college?"

"Buck says I have to go," Colton said.

Buck couldn't readily read the tone there. If Colton was happy about it or still annoyed. Colton had certainly never planned on going to college, not when he had been a kid in the system. But Buck was determined to give him the opportunity. If he didn't like it, if he failed out, that was fine. Buck just wanted him to have the chance.

It was amazing just how much this felt like a family dinner, when that was... Ridiculous.

They finished up, and she thanked him for the invitation. He thanked her for dinner. They said goodbye like they hadn't spent the last couple of hours having a deep conversation. Like they had just been adults interacting while their kids were studying.

"I'm meeting with a contractor tomorrow to discuss plans for the building," she said. She looked down. "I wouldn't feel comfortable doing that without you. Considering you need to approve that…"

"Sure," he said. "Sounds good."

Now he was going to see her tomorrow.

But that was good. He was listening. To his intuition, which said there was something here. Something he needed to accomplish through his reconnection with Marigold.

And so he was bound and determined to do it.

Chapter Eight

The next day, Buck put on his cowboy hat, a button-up shirt and a pair of blue jeans and went down to the local diner, where Marigold had said they were meeting the contractor over coffee and pancakes.

The boys were at school, and that meant Buck could focus on this project. He was also working toward getting the ranch prepared for cattle. But there was some time now between planning and when it would actually execute, so he didn't need to worry about it today.

When he walked into the diner, he saw Marigold, sitting at a table with her red hair pulled up into a ponytail and a deeply contemplative expression on her face. She had a legal pad in front of her, which he thought was cute and old-fashioned. She was holding a pen.

He gestured toward the hostess, who had been about to seat him. "I'm with her."

And then he went over and positioned himself across the table from her.

"Guess we're early," he said.

"Yeah. You want a coffee?"

"Sure. I'd never say no to that."

The waitress came by, and he ordered coffee, waiting on food until the contractor showed up.

"So basically, you need a kitchen," he said, a way to get her talking.

She nodded, and then started to explain the layout of the space. Buck really did think it was a great business idea.

"How did you get involved in this, anyway?" he asked.

"Well, I was cooking anyway. I wanted to be able to work from home so I could be with Lily, and I knew I was going to have to get creative because I didn't even graduate high school."

"You didn't?"

"No."

He knew a moment of anguish. Because her brother had died the night of his graduation. Because Buck had let his own life get derailed right after that. And it had carried back to Marigold. Who hadn't even had a graduation. The ripple effect of tragedy was an alarming thing.

Especially when he knew he could trace his own behavior back to losing Sophia, his youngest sister.

He swallowed hard and looked down at his coffee. And just a moment later, a man approached the table carrying a large binder. "Marigold," he said. "And you are?"

Buck stood. "Buck Carson."

The contractor reacted to his name. And Buck evaluated the guy as about his age. He wondered if they had gone to school together.

"I'm Jackson. Delaney."

Oh right. They had. They hadn't really been friends, because Jackson had been a jock and Buck had been a fuckup. So. One of those had been required to maintain a certain grade point average. The other had not.

"Didn't know you were back in town," he said.

"Yeah. I am. I moved back a month or so ago."

"Definitely didn't expect to see you with Marigold."

"Oh. Well. Jackson," she said, reaching across the table and putting her hand over the top of his. Buck felt his hackles rise. And he couldn't even quite say why.

Oh bullshit. You know why. You like her, and you don't want her touching anyone else.

Sure. But that was nonsense. What did it matter?

"I really would appreciate if you kept this to yourself for now. Buck and I ended up meeting because of our kids. His boys are at the school now. And Lily and Colton are... They're dating. So, we... reconnected." She repeated that part. Probably because it was difficult to distill all of this. Probably because it still made her feel uncomfortable. And fair enough.

"I told Buck about my business idea, and he offered to invest. But I am not ready for that to be public information."

"Oh yeah. Of course, but you're sitting here in the diner with him."

"I know. It's not cloak-and-dagger. I just... I don't want my parents to know yet that I am doing this with him. I'm going to talk to them."

"Listen, I'm not going to spread around what's happening. For a second thereabouts I thought maybe you were dating."

Marigold laughed. Too loud and too long, and her cheeks went red. "No. Absolutely not. But you know... You know how kids are. And ours like each other. So what can you do?"

Jackson snorted. "Nothing. I mean, I know that well enough. If I was in charge of who Elizabeth dated, her roster would look a lot different."

Buck felt the need to defend Colton, but he knew it wasn't the time. Or the point. So they got to work discussing everything. And by the time it was done, he felt certainty in his gut.

When Jackson left, he turned to Marigold. "I'd like to talk to your parents."

"What?"

"I'd like to talk to them about this. And I'd like to extend... I don't know if an apology is the right word. Because being sorry about what happened is never going to change it. But I don't want to create a situation where you have to hide, and... I need to build these bridges with everybody. I accepted that when I came home."

"I don't know that that's totally fair," she said.

"Listen, I don't actually need absolution on the level you seem to think I do." He took a breath. "I've lived in a state of self-pity for a long time. You don't get anything accomplished. But I find that guilt, and the driving need to make up for the fact that I'm alive while they are gone, has turned me into a better person. I know that's a double-edged sword. Because it almost doesn't seem fair to have the chance to improve myself when they don't. When they don't get to grow and change."

"The truth is, you didn't cause that accident. The truth is, if you had been riding in the car, you would also be dead. The truth is, you didn't make anybody drink."

"Yeah. That is the truth. But the truth doesn't serve anybody. Not half as well as a villain does. It doesn't even serve me as well."

"So you just... You're just happy to be the scapegoat because it does something for you?"

"It makes me worth a hell of a lot more. And I can't deny that it matters."

"Let me... Let me call them."

She got up from the table and went outside. He watched, as she wrapped one arm around herself and put the phone up to her ear. She bit her thumbnail as she waited, and he couldn't take his eyes off her. She said hello, chewed her bottom lip. Beyond that he couldn't quite tell what she was saying.

She looked upset. And then resolved. Grim. She nodded her head. Then she hung up her phone and walked back inside.

"Okay. We'll go over there."

"All right."

The thought didn't scare him. Because the worst-case scenario was that her dad would shoot him. And if that happened, he would be upset for his boys, but his family would take care of them. Support in any scenario was one reason it had been important that he give them this whole network. He didn't want his boys' happiness, their security, hinging only on him.

So really, even the worst case didn't much worry him.

He felt like he had been living on borrowed time for the past twenty years. Also, he didn't sincerely think her dad would kill him.

"Should we go together?"

"Sure," she said.

"I'll drive my truck."

He remembered their house. A small, modest place right in town that had always felt quintessentially warm and familial to him. There was something about the smallness of it. It gave off a sense of togetherness. They were a nice family. They always had been.

"I don't know... My parents and I have never really talked about any of this. They didn't want to upset me. You know my mom was there when I confronted you..."

"Yeah. Don't worry about it. I don't need you to protect me from whatever they feel. They're allowed to feel it."

She nodded. "I actually want to protect them."

"I get that too."

They got out of the car, and walked up to the house together. He let her knock. When the door opened, both her parents were standing there. Jim and Nancy. They'd been the nicest people. Always welcomed the whole group of them into their house. Fed them, laughed with them.

It felt appropriate to say nothing. He didn't know why. When he looked at them, it was with all the awe and reverence he felt when he walked into an old church. A hushed quietness and a sense of something he couldn't quite define.

This really was staring down the past. Nancy was looking at him like she wasn't sure what to make of him. And then she took a step forward and reached her hand out. Her fingertips connected with his face, softly. She traced a line on the side of his mouth. And her eyes filled with tears. "He would be your age now."

He felt that, like a punch to the gut. A real, profound connection to that grief. As if it was fresh and new.

He nodded. "It's been a while."

"He would probably have some gray hair," she said.

"Maybe so." He could hardly speak around the lump in his throat.

And then she did something he didn't expect. She stepped forward and wrapped her arms around him. "Just let me hug you," she said. "For a second."

Buck had been through a lot. He'd cried about the loss of his friends. He'd cried when he got drunk and fucked-up on dark nights after that. But he'd not cried since he'd gotten sober. He had stopped indulging in self-pity. But this time, when he felt tears sting the backs of his eyes, it wasn't self-pity. It was the bittersweet ache of knowing he was giving her a chance, just a moment, to feel like she was hugging her son. It was realizing he was an emblem of the past in this moment in a different way. One he never had been before.

When she released her hold on him, he looked over at Jim. The man didn't say anything. But he nodded twice.

"Come on in," Nancy said.

They walked into the house and took a seat on a blue faded couch that he was fairly certain was the same couch that had been here twenty years before.

"What is it you have to say, Buck Carson?" she asked.

"I moved back to town about a month ago," he said. "I thought it was time. Time to stop running. Time to reconnect with my family. I adopted three boys, and they're teenagers."

"Lily is dating the oldest," Marigold said.

He waited for them to get upset about that. But they didn't react. Then he explained the business partnership. And how it had come up.

"But mostly, I wanted to say what I couldn't say back then. I'm very sorry. For what happened."

Nancy shook her head. "Nobody should bear the blame for that, Buck. Nobody. You were all too young to know how your actions could hurt you. It was a terrible thing. It still is. I grieved all the things my son could've had. But those eighteen years, that was his life. And I have also worked very hard to look back on that life as a wonderful, joyful thing. He had friends he cared for very much, and you were one of them. You were part of why his life was good. You weren't just a part of the end of it."

Buck sat there, completely astonished. This wasn't just forgiveness. It was something else. It turned him into someone with the capacity to heal and not just hurt. It changed all the memories. Everything he had ever thought about that relationship.

It changed everything.

"Just one minute," she said.

She got up off the couch and walked out of the room. And no one said anything in her absence. When she came back, she was holding a baseball glove. He recognized it right away. Jason had played for the school. He had loved it.

"Lily doesn't play baseball. But you said you have three sons. Do any of them play?"

"They haven't really had the chance yet. They... They all had it pretty tough."

"Do any of them want to learn?" Jim asked.

"You know, they might." It hurt to speak.

"Because I miss..." Jim cleared his throat. "I miss that. Throwing the ball around."

"Well, I'm no good at it," Buck said. "So if you want to..."

"Yes," Nancy said. "That would be wonderful. Take this glove and tell them they can use it."

She handed it to him, a precious, sacred object. And when he touched it, his throat went tight. "Thank you. I will take very good care of this. So will the boys."

"Well, they don't have to be too careful with it. They're kids. And a baseball glove is meant to be played with."

He saw that with clarity all of a sudden.

That they were kids. No matter that they were teenagers. They were so, so young.

He'd been young at eighteen too.

"Thank you."

When they walked back out of the house, he didn't know what to say. It was as if a weight had been lifted off him. One he had been clinging to for a long, damned time.

Marigold didn't speak at all, and when they got into the truck, he noticed there were tears sliding down her cheeks.

He looked over at her. "I didn't expect that," he said.

"Neither did I," she said. The tears fell fast. He had to fight the urge to reach out and wipe them off her face, because he shouldn't be that familiar with her.

"You thought they were angry with me."

She nodded. "Because I was. Because so many people in the town were. But… She's right. You were a good part of Jason's life. And you haven't gotten to see yourself that way, and that's not fair. He was more than one tragic accident, one bad choice. And if he's more than that, then why can't you be?"

He felt something calcified inside of him crack, fall away.

"You're a good dad to those boys. I could see that last night when we had dinner. I could see how much they love you. You know, my brother had a great family. A wonderful life. Too short, but wonderful. I don't let myself feel happy for that often enough. When you told me about poor Reggie… He's a kid who hasn't known enough happiness. I'm glad he's knowing it now."

"Yeah," he said. "I have to tell you, I didn't expect this when I came back here."

"Did you want people to condemn you?"

"A little. My brother punched me in the face. I thought that might set the tone."

"He did?"

"Yeah. It's… It's getting better. He carried a lot of very spe-cific resentment about being left to be the oldest. To carry all the responsibility."

"Well, we all fall victim to that, don't we? Making other people the bad guys in our story." She laughed. "Sometimes I wonder if Lily's father was never as much of a villain to me because I already had one."

"How can that guy not be a villain?"

"I think because he didn't matter. Anyway, my parents are… They're wonderful. And they're great grandparents. My dad has been a fantastic father figure to her. She didn't need the loser that I had sex with one time. And I didn't need to be tied to him for the rest of my life. I'm grateful, in some ways, that he and I had a clean cut. Yes, some things were harder. But being with someone you don't care about, that's not going to make it easier."

"I don't know. The more I sit with that the more I just think maybe your family has a supernatural capacity to bend around a person's limitations and create as kind a story as possible."

She smiled. "That is an interesting way to put it. I appreci-ate it. And now there are no secrets. I have to remember that I shouldn't try to protect them. We didn't talk about you all this time because I was trying to protect them and they were try-ing to protect me. I think it would've been better if we had just been honest." She let out a long breath. "Holding on to anger is exhausting. It's a relief to let it go."

He wasn't so sure about letting go of guilt. Because it had been such a key, driving force for him.

Guilt was a comfort, really. It had been the thing that had ultimately pulled him out of the pit. Maybe that was a messed-up truth, but he had often felt that there were certain things some sorts of people had to be extra careful of. There was a reason he didn't drink now. Not even in moderation. It was, in his opinion, a crutch he was prone to leaning on far too much.

Not everybody was so careful.

Maybe guilt was a crutch too. But he wasn't going to wake

up face down in a ditch because he had overindulged in guilt. So there was that.

But what had just happened in Marigold's parents' house was one of the more profound things he had ever experienced. So maybe there was value in being changed by it. In moving forward differently than he had been. Maybe.

Right now, they were starting something new. Something fresh.

For the first time, it really did feel like something good was growing from all that charred earth. And he had Marigold to thank for that.

Chapter Nine

She had been delivering meals to Buck once a week for the past two weeks. Every time she saw him, it got less jarring in one sense and more complicated in another. Because he was gorgeous. And it wasn't a simple impersonal observation. It was something she felt. Every time she passed the bags of food from her hands to his, every time she was near him. He was becoming more and more himself to her.

Buck as he was now, and not the version of him she had yelled at in the streets, or even the version she had philosophically forgiven in his absence all those years earlier.

They also had conversations that filled in the gaps of the last twenty years.

Tonight, she was intent on dropping the food and leaving. Quickly.

But as soon as she showed up, so did her daughter's car, which was carrying not only her and Colton, but Marcus and Reggie as well.

Marcus and Reggie tumbled out of the back seat while Lily rolled the window down.

"Can we go to the movies?" Reggie asked.

"All of you?" Buck asked.

"Yes. Colton and Lily said we could come."

"Are they buying you a ticket for an R-rated movie?"

"Buck," Reggie said. "My life is an R-rated movie, man."

"That didn't answer my question."

"They're going to a cartoon," Colton shouted.

"We are not," said Marcus.

"Whatever," said Buck. "Fine. You can go to the movies."

"Send me money on my phone," Colton said.

"Fine."

"We need popcorn and stuff," he said.

"So, you need a hundred dollars, that's what you're telling me," said Buck.

"I wouldn't say no," Colton said.

Lily, for her part, looked appropriately chagrined.

"You can buy your own ticket," Marigold said.

"She doesn't have to," said Colton.

"Apparently my son is being chivalrous with my money." Buck smiled. "Get out of here, you heathens."

And that left the two of them standing there, by themselves.

"You want to come in?" he asked.

Did she want to come into the house where it would just be the two of them by themselves? She found that she did, perversely. But she also felt like she probably shouldn't. Of course, her feelings could be entirely one-sided. That was most likely. Also, they were adults. They were not hormonal teenagers who needed supervision to be alone in a room together. That was Colton and Lily.

Another potent reminder of why nothing was ever going to happen between the two of them.

There was ruining your kid's life, and then there was ruining your kid's life by having the hots for her boyfriend's father.

Wow. What a horror show.

"Sure," she said. She stepped inside, almost to prove that she could. Almost just to prove that there was no real bogeyman here. There was no lack of control she needed to be worried about, no attraction that was beyond the both of them.

It was just silly to think in those terms.

"You want to stay for dinner? You and Lily, when she gets back. I have a feeling they're all going to be overfull from what they're eating at the theater."

"Sure."

"I have these great preprepared meals," he said.

She laughed. She laid the bag on the counter. "I mean, there's a little bit of work yet to do."

"I can help."

"There's not much to it. We just need to put the chicken in the oven, along with the roast vegetables. Since there's time yet before they'll return."

"Sounds good."

She started getting the ingredients out. And compulsively, she began to put away the other preprepared meals she had brought, because she was here, so she might as well.

She could feel him looking at her.

"Sorry," she said. "I probably overstepped."

"No," he said. "You haven't overstepped with anything."

"The permits got submitted," she said, taking a deep breath and wondering if the subject change seemed too weird. But there was something so warm, so lovely about being in here with him, and she was pushing against that reflexively. Against the feeling of contentment that had begun to bloom in her chest.

Maybe that was silly. Because over the last couple of weeks Buck really had become a friend. He had brought the boys to her parents' house to throw the ball around with her dad. Now the boys were considering trying out for the baseball team at school. Buck was part of her life. It might be unexpected in a lot of ways, but it was definitely reality. So maybe she just needed to stop being awkward.

"Glad to hear it," he said.

"Oh yeah. I am especially glad. I can't believe it, though. I can't believe that everything is progressing. I just… A month ago, I wouldn't have thought I would be here."

He looked around. "Specifically in my kitchen?"

"Well. That too." She paused for a moment. "It's a good thing. Because Lily is going to college."

"I know." He grimaced. "I do worry. About Lily and Colton. And the logistics of that relationship."

"I know," she said. "So do I." She took a breath and tried to ease the knot of tension in her chest. "He's a really good kid, Buck. Apart from being in my daughter's room that first day I met him, I mean."

"Yeah. Well. He is a good kid. A little bit feral, but he's trying."

"I know. I don't want either of them to hold each other back."

"Neither do I. But they don't seem to have an angsty, over-the-top teen romance thing happening. I mean, they're going to the movies with Colton's younger brothers."

"Yeah," she said, smiling.

It really was the most wholesome, lovely thing. The way Buck and the boys had formed a family. The way Colton took care of Marcus and Reggie.

"I don't mean… Just to be very clear, it isn't that I don't think Colton is wonderful. I do."

"No, I know. Lily is a great girl. You've done an amazing job with her. I can only hope that I do half as well with the little bit of time I have… That is the only thing. I wish I had more time to parent Colton."

"I know you don't know this," she said softly. "Because you left home at eighteen and didn't really have contact with anybody, but parenting doesn't end at eighteen. Colton is going to need you a lot when he's off to college. And he's going to need this place to come back to. Your continued support when he's not technically a kid anymore, that's going to mean the world to him."

The corner of his mouth tipped upward into a smile. "I hadn't thought of it that way."

"I mean, it's a great way to continue to show that when you took him in, it was forever. I imagine he hasn't had a lot in the way of stability."

Buck shook his head. "No. Colton was put in foster care when he was three. He got bounced around all over the place for years before his mom lost parental rights. And then... He was running away from foster homes all the time. He got caught with drugs he was selling. And that was how he ended up at Hope Ranch."

Sympathy made her chest tight. "That poor kid."

"Yeah. He was fifteen when he came to the ranch. Alone in the world. Angry. He's had two years of stability. Compared to all those years without it."

"It's amazing what a difference it makes."

"I just wish... You know, it's one of those things. I just really wish I could've found them earlier. But in order to do that I would've had to find myself earlier. And I wasn't there yet."

"But you were at the ranch for sixteen years."

He chuckled. "Yeah. And for a while, that was just triage. Me trying to stop the bleeding so I could stay standing."

"I need a cutting board," she said.

"Right here," he said. He moved toward her, and then reached up into the cabinet above her head, bringing his chest right up against her, and when he looked down, the breath exited her lungs in a gust. He was so close. She could smell him.

He smelled like cedar, dust and hay.

She wondered about the plans he had for this ranch. He had mentioned a little about them a couple of times in passing when they were planning different things for her business. But she found she wanted to know more about him. And at the same time, she realized she also wanted to draw closer to him. She felt dizzy with it.

He seemed frozen there. He wasn't grabbing a cutting board. He was just standing there. His hand pressed against the cabinet above her, and her eyes drifted to his forearm, well muscled and glorious. To his mouth again, down to his broad chest. His lean waist. Highlighted perfectly in the maroon Henley shirt he was wearing.

"Buck," she said.

A warning, an invitation—she wasn't exactly sure.

But his name tasted like moonshine that neither of them allowed themselves to drink anymore. Intoxicating. Forbidden.

Then suddenly, he grabbed the cutting board and took a step back. "Here," he said.

"Oh," she said, taking it from his hand.

Their fingers didn't brush. He was very careful to make sure they didn't.

He cleared his throat. "Anything I can do to help? I thought all the prep was done."

"I decided I wanted to add a little bit more garlic. That's all. It's in the suggestions in the recipe, but since I'm doing it..."

"You shouldn't do it. You already did all the work."

"I don't mind. It's my job. And cooking is easy for me. Probably a lot easier than watching you stumble through the motions."

"Well, I have stumbled through the motions when you're not here."

"Yes," she said. "But crucially, I don't have to see it."

"Harsh," he said.

Their gazes connected, lingered for just a little bit too long.

She didn't know what to do in a situation like this. She hadn't wanted to kiss a man in a very long time. And the truth was, she wanted to kiss Buck Carson.

But it was inconvenient, and it was foolish.

"Stop looking at me like that," he said.

Well. He was going to make hiding it pointless.

"Sorry. I'm trying to figure out exactly what to do about it."

"About what exactly, Marigold?"

"Don't make it weird," she said.

"I'm not making it weird. But I am asking you. Honestly."

"No you aren't. Because you know exactly what I was thinking."

"Tell me."

He was daring her. The sensual challenge in his voice ignited something in her stomach.

How was that possible? Only a few moments ago, their kids had all been in a car in the driveway, and they had been bantering with them. It had all been so parental. And for her, being a parent had meant separating herself entirely from sexuality.

Or maybe that separation had been about protection. Not just protecting Lily, but herself.

Because she had only known how to use sex in a really unhealthy way. It hadn't been about pleasure; it had been about oblivion. Attention. It had never been about love; it had been about loss. About the emptiness inside of her. And she just hadn't wanted to work any of that out with her daughter around watching it.

He made her want to try. Because right now, they felt cocooned. Right now, this felt like a lovely, secret moment.

She wanted to take his dare. She wanted to find the part of herself she had put away so long ago and take it back out. Look at it. Examine it. See if it still shone as brightly as it had then. Because that was the thing. She could have regrets about the why of all the things she had done, but there was something wonderful about being young. And a little bit wild.

Both she and Buck had put away their wildness so effectively. And maybe that's what she was seeing when she looked at him. When their eyes caught and held. Maybe she was seeing the remnants of that wildness, a little spark.

It made her want to test it. To try it.

"Well, I was thinking about kissing you."

He made a sound, adjacent to a growl, and it left her feeling thrilled. Excited.

"That would be a very bad idea," he said.

"I know. That's why I didn't do it."

"But you mentioned it."

"After intensive questioning," she said.

"Because you were being so obvious."

They stared at each other for a long moment. She tried to take a breath, but she found the air in her lungs was frozen. And in a voice she barely recognized as her own, she heard: "Just once."

Maybe this was a gift to the girl she had once been. The girl who had idolized him. Who had thought the sun and moon hung on his smile. The girl who had been so devastated and damaged after that accident that she had lost pieces of herself. Maybe it was a moment to give that girl a small fantasy.

Because hadn't she been endlessly responsible? She had. She had made nothing but the best decisions every day of her life since Lily was born. And they had this small window. This couple of hours where nobody was here, where no one was watching them, and she just wanted to make one choice that was self-indulgent. Some might call it bad.

But they'd been so good. How could it be bad?

That was how she found herself taking a step toward him. And he didn't move away.

She put her hand on his chest and startled. He was so hot, so solid. She could feel his heart raging beneath her palm.

It had been so long since she had touched somebody else like this, and the last time she had, it hadn't been the same. It hadn't been slow. It hadn't been deliberate. She had wanted to be carried away from the moment. Right now, she wanted to linger in it.

She didn't want to forget who she was. She remembered. Every year, every mistake. Every version of herself that she had ever been. She allowed all of those Marigolds to enjoy the moment. Because in that moment, she was flooded by a rush of forgiveness. Not just for him, but for herself.

For the foolish things, the hopeful things, the wild things, the self-sacrificing things and the indulgent things.

Because she was all the decisions she had ever made, good

and bad. And one didn't take away from the other, and none of it defined her either.

She moved her hand slowly down his chest, to the firm, flat ridges of his stomach. She stopped at the waistband of his jeans, her breath catching hard.

Then she reached her hand out to his face, tracing a line along his square jaw, relishing the sensation of his whiskers beneath her fingertips.

"You... You're so..."

"Shut up and kiss me," he said.

She didn't have time to respond, because he wrapped his large hand around the back of her head and pulled her in close, his mouth firm and hard against hers as he claimed her with an intensity that was unlike anything she had ever experienced before.

His body was so hard, his hold so tight, so perfect. She wrapped her arms around his neck and gave herself over to the kiss. Learning how to do it all over again. She followed his rhythm, parted her lips, and when his tongue touched hers, she gasped. Then sighed as he went deep, luxuriating in the slick friction of it.

He moved his hands down her back to cup her rear, and she arched forward instinctively, reveling in his touch.

She didn't know if this counted as one kiss, because eventually he was kissing her neck and back to her mouth again, then down to the curve of her breast.

She gasped.

He lifted her up off the ground and placed her on the counter, stepping into the space between her legs and deepening the kiss.

She wrapped her legs around him, realizing she was pushing this further, faster than she had meant to. But it was instinct. It was needed. So many years of not being held, not being touched.

She wondered then if she had been acting out of any sort of great restraint, or if she had been punishing herself. She had decided she didn't deserve this. This magical alchemy of human connection. The glory of a man's hands on her body.

Suddenly now she wanted it more than she could remember wanting anything.

More than she could remember wanting to breathe.

Nothing was simple about this. He was Buck Carson. Their son and daughter were dating. Their connection was loaded. Like a stick of dynamite. But then, so was this. This need.

She gave back everything he was giving. He growled, and when his hands moved to cup her breasts, a sudden rush of reality crowded in.

"Wait," she said.

"What?" he asked, his voice deep, his words slurred.

"We can't. Colton and Lily are dating. We are business partners, there is so much... There is so much stuff."

He took a step away, letting out a deep breath. Then he looked up at the ceiling.

"What are you doing?"

"Trying to recite the alphabet backward."

Her eyes dropped to the front of his jeans. "Oh," she said.

He winced. "Yeah."

"I... I'm sorry. I haven't been with anybody in a long time."

"It's been a fair amount of time for me too."

"Seventeen years?"

He had to laugh. "No. But still. A while." He let out a slow breath. "And even if it had been yesterday, it wouldn't matter. Because you're you. And I have been attracted to you since the day you showed up practically towing Colton by the ear. It's you. It's not the celibacy or the fact that it's forbidden or anything like that. It's just you."

She'd had no idea how much she needed to hear something like that until he'd said it.

To not just feel desired, but special.

It had been a long time since she had felt anything like that, too. Maybe she never had.

"This is a really bad idea," she said. "I mean, not the one kiss. That was wonderful. But anything else…"

He looked at her, and there was fire in his eyes.

"Don't look at me like that," she said.

"I believe I just said that to you, and look at where we ended up."

"Definitely not preparing dinner." She took a deep breath. "Do you know why I've been celibate since before I had Lily?"

"I could take a few wild guesses."

"It felt easy in some ways, to not have her dad around. I felt like I was blessed with a lack of complication. That meant she was my daughter and I got to raise her on my terms. The idea of bringing random men into the life I so carefully made for her, for me, I couldn't bear it." She decided not to mention any of her errant thoughts about the possibility of it being a punishment. Like she had cut herself off for being overindulgent. "And she's leaving in just a few months."

"I understand that. But you aren't with her all the time."

"Aren't you listening? I don't like complicated. Maybe because I had my fill of complicated a long time ago. You have to understand that."

He nodded slowly. "I guess maybe I should. But I was never trying to make my life simple. I think I don't know anything *but* complicated. I mean, I just adopted three teenage boys, so obviously simple is not my wheelhouse."

She laughed. "I get that. But…"

"Yeah. There's a lot of people who could get hurt."

She nodded. "Yes. There is."

"The thing is, nobody will get hurt if nobody knows."

She hadn't even considered that. "What would that even look like? Do you mean… If we just…"

"It's entirely possible to keep things only physical."

"Well, that's the thing. Our lives are kind of enmeshed. And that makes it difficult to be only physical."

"Friends with benefits. I hear that works."

Wow. That was an incredibly tempting offer. But she had to wonder…much like when she was on the cusp of that same feeling she'd had when he had first offered to help her with her business.

Wondering if she was just doing moral gymnastics because really, she wanted to take him up on the offer.

Everything felt too high stakes.

That was the bottom line. She couldn't go playing around with her daughter's first relationship. With her last few months of her daughter being at home.

Are you still making excuses?

She didn't think so. But when she looked at him, her heart beat faster, and that reminded her of scarier times.

More exciting times.

But scary, all the same.

"The kids will be back soon." She let out a long, slow breath. "Thank you for… That was actually the first time I've done anything like that for a long time. As you know. And it was really, really nice."

"And the sky didn't cave in," he said.

"No."

She had so many questions. About how he had conducted his life for these past two decades.

Not the stuff she knew—where he had lived, the work he had done. She wanted to know about his sex life. About his relationships. Because she was standing on the edge of those things, and she wished she could understand what made him think he could just be her friend with benefits. She also knew that talking about it was dangerous. That they needed to get back on less precarious footing.

So she didn't ask him. She just decided to finish cooking the chicken. And by the time the kids got home, she could only hope they didn't look like they had been caught with their hands in the cookie jar. She sort of felt like she had been, even though time had lapsed since they'd given in to that kiss.

Their eyes met across the table, and she decided, within herself, that whatever happened, they were going to be friends. And that was it. That was going to be the solid foundation by which they built everything. Their business... And everything.

After they'd driven home, she looked over at Lily. "Did you have a good time?"

"Yeah. I had a great time. Colton's brothers are really cute."

"They're not that much younger than you."

"No, but they seem like it. I don't know. They're nice kids."

It was funny to hear Lily talk about a fifteen-year-old and a sixteen-year-old that way. She supposed it reflected how mature her daughter felt at this point in time. How ready she was to be seen as an adult. Yes. Her life really was changing.

And Marigold thought about that kiss...

No. She was resolved.

And yet, friends with benefits...

She ached. She really did. Because what if they could do that? What if they could have a relationship nobody knew about but them? One that didn't complicate things. One that just eased both of their needs a little bit.

You would never let yourself have something that nice.

That very disturbing thought echoed in her head for the whole rest of the evening.

Chapter Ten

Buck's head was still reeling from that kiss. Hell, his whole body was on high alert. He hadn't slept a wink. He had ended up taking a cold shower at one in the morning to try and spite his overactive hormones. It really was a hell of a thing. And he was supposed to see her today on a matter of business.

Yet nothing inside of him felt ready to discuss business. What he wanted to do was take her in his arms again. Kiss her senseless.

How had that happened?

But he hadn't been lying when he had told her it was about her. About how much she made him feel.

About how much he wanted her.

It had been like that from the moment she had first appeared on his doorstep. And maybe that was the real reason he had kept her close. Maybe he was full of shit. Maybe it had never been about trying to follow his gut instinct. Maybe it had always been about wanting her. Maybe atonement was just an excuse.

That made him feel guilty.

And he would be lying if he said he didn't like the guilt. It was his comfort zone.

Right about now, he felt like Marigold's lips were his comfort zone. Where everything was that he had ever wanted.

He wanted to kiss her again, strip her bare—

"You passed the school driveway, Buck," Reggie said.

"Dammit," he said.

Colton laughed.

"Well, you're going to get your driver's license, and then they're going to be your responsibility," he said.

"I never said I didn't want my license," Colton said. "I think you don't want me to get it."

Well. Colton wasn't entirely far off. Driving was a fact of life. It wasn't like he had a long-standing hang-up. And he had been fine yesterday when Lily was driving the boys. Alcohol had played a factor in the accident that had taken his friends' lives. That aspect wasn't something that could be ignored. But...

As much as Colton was responsible—and he had become responsible in these last couple of years with a little bit of guidance, and having the chance to not live in chaos—Buck knew how stupid teenage boys could be. In a pretty damned haunting way.

"I do want you to get your license. It'll make my life easier. But there are going to be so many ground rules."

"I know, I know."

Buck turned around in an auto parts parking lot and headed back toward the school. He summarily booted the boys out of the truck and then headed on down the road toward Marigold's place.

He hadn't been to her house yet.

He thought it was strange that he was looking forward to it. To seeing what sort of life she had built for herself and Lily. He knew it would be warm. Inviting. Well ordered. Because Marigold herself was all those things.

When he pulled up to the house, this theory was proven to be true. It was small, but well ordered, with a neat garden area in the front, and a porch with a rocking chair and a wreath on the door.

When she had said that she'd set out to make an entirely complete life for herself and Lily without Lily's father, he hadn't entirely known what that meant. But he got it now.

She was self-contained. Entirely happy without a man.

Well. Almost.

He thought again about that kiss. It had been absolutely incendiary.

Maybe they could...

Maybe.

Because he'd never had a sexual entanglement that got emotional. And she clearly didn't need anything emotional from him. That was the perfect arrangement as far as he was concerned. A woman who didn't need anything from him but physical pleasure. Because he could do that. He could give that.

As part of being a marked man, a man who had to go through life atoning, he had made it his business to be the absolute best lover possible. He needed the women he had sex with to come twice before he got close to the peak of pleasure. It was part of putting more out in the world than he took away.

He wanted to make Marigold come even more times than that.

He gritted his teeth and got out of his truck, made his way toward that cute, neat front door.

School carnivals, a passel of teenagers, meeting her parents, this adorable house. All of it stood in stark contrast to the riotous, sexual thoughts making their way through his head.

It was like the deepest, darkest part of himself was rising to the surface and making waves that didn't belong in a beautiful, placid lake.

Wholesome.

That described so many of the interactions they'd had since he'd come back to town.

And then he'd kissed her.

Which had been anything but wholesome.

And what he wanted now was anything but wholesome.

He was about to knock when the door opened. There she was, her red hair wild about her face. Her eyes wide.

"Dammit," he said.

She stepped back, and he stepped in, closed the door firmly behind her and pulled her into his arms. He was kissing her before she could say anything. And she melted against him, kissing him back with a ferocity that didn't even surprise him, because the wild look in her eye when he had approached her, said everything he needed to know.

He could read her. It was so goddamned annoying. It would be better if he hadn't known. If he didn't see the sensual need in her eyes when he looked at her. But he did. Because it was the same need that echoed inside of him.

Because, for some reason, they felt that for each other on the same level. Because for some reason they felt...inevitable.

Was this it?

That day she had come to his door with Colton—was it all leading to this?

Well, his dick would like to think so. But that seemed... Well, it didn't really seem like atonement. Because it felt a hell of a lot like pleasing himself.

He would put her needs first. He would put *her* first.

She wrapped her arms around his neck, her fingers pushing up through his hair, cradling the back of his head, moving down his back, and he did the same to her, feeling those wild curls, her petite frame, moving his hands all the way down to the delicious curve of her ass.

She was so gorgeous.

She was unlike any woman he had ever wanted before. Simply because she was her. Maybe because he knew her.

Maybe because he cared.

It wasn't about a generic desire to score points with the

universe, but about wanting to see her experience pleasure at his hands.

This was an entirely different experience to any he'd ever known.

Friends with benefits?

Yeah. That was what it would have to be. Because they were business partners. Because of the kids. Because no one could ever know that this had happened, least of all Colton and Lily.

Shit. That would make him the worst dad in the entire world. Scamming on his son's girlfriend's mother. The absolute worst. And Colton would have every right to disown him. Or punch him.

So no one would ever know.

No one would ever have to know.

That fueled him now. Made this feel darker, more glorious. Surrounded by her adorable house with gorgeous knickknacks. She had a shelf full of birds wearing scarves. And he wanted to strip her clothes off and see every inch of her bare skin. Right in front of those birds.

Maybe that was the whole point of it. That they had thrown themselves into this other reality. One where they tried to be acceptable. One where they tried to be neat. One where they tried to be better than they were. Better than their darkest, wildest impulses—but neither of them were. Because maybe no person was. And maybe they weren't two different things, or two different kinds of people. Maybe everyone had this inside of them.

They had suppressed it. They both had. She sure as hell had. But it was still there.

And it was pretty damned glorious.

"I want you," he growled against her mouth.

"Yes," she breathed.

"God help me," he said.

He lifted her up off the ground, her legs wrapped around his waist as he started to carry her up the stairs.

"You know where my bedroom is," she said.

"I'll figure it out."

He was resourceful that way.

"I don't have condoms," she said.

Everything stopped for a moment.

"I have one," he said.

Just one. One he always carried in his wallet for emergencies, even though it wasn't like one-night stands broke out without careful planning on his part. And there hadn't been one since he had adopted the boys. But he made sure to religiously replace that one condom, so it never went past its expiration date and didn't spend too long being exposed to the elements or anything like that.

He was safe.

"Oh," she said.

"It's a safety measure," he said. "I wasn't planning this. It's just…"

"Right," she said.

"Are you judging me?"

"No. I'm glad."

"Good," he said.

He claimed her mouth again, marveling at the fact that he could be thirty-eight years old and this on edge. That he could be this intent on having her.

That he could want her so very much.

He felt like a teenager. They were even having discussions about condoms.

He wanted her so much.

He brought her into the bedroom. He was certain it was hers. And because she didn't protest, he knew he was right. It was neat as a pin, like everything else in the house, her bedspread an adorable gingham. He was going to strip her naked on that gingham and do unspeakable things to her.

He set her down at the center of the mattress and stepped away from her, stripping his shirt up over his head.

Her eyes went wide. "Damn," she said.

"Thank you. That's awfully kind."

"It's hardly kind. A simple damn doesn't do justice to those muscles. I feel spoiled."

"Not as spoiled as I feel. Believe me. Because you are... I don't have any gentlemanly words for it, Marigold. I just know that I want you. More than anything. I can't explain it. Because it's something that goes beyond words."

"I don't need words. You can just show me."

So he did. He stripped off his jeans, his boots and socks, everything, and let her see how hard he was for her. How much he wanted her. Her eyes kept getting rounder and rounder.

"It's been a really long time," she said.

"I'll be careful," he said.

"Thank you," she responded.

He moved over the top of her, kissed her neck, slowly, very slowly, stripped the sweater from her body and unclipped her bra. She was as beautiful as he had imagined she would be. Even more so. Because he hadn't been able to imagine the exact ripe colors, the perfect softness and roundness.

And now he did. He cupped her breast, slid his thumb over her nipple. Watched her arch against his touch. Watched as her face contorted with pleasure. She was so beautiful.

So beautiful.

He growled, kissing her neck, kissing down to the plump curve of her breasts, taking one nipple into his mouth and sucking hard.

Then he moved down the rest of her body, gripping the waistband of her skirt and tugging it down her thighs, taking her underwear with it.

She arched against him, and he held her down against the mattress, parting her legs for him so he could taste all that glory between them.

She was wet for him, and she tasted like heaven.

He gripped her so tight, she couldn't pull away from him. She was whimpering, crying out, and he could feel her whole body draw tight like a bow as she got closer and closer to the peak.

"Yes," he growled against her. "Come for me."

He felt her shatter against his mouth, and he kept on going, pushing two fingers inside of her as he did, as she unraveled completely. There on that sweet little bedspread.

And she was still the responsible, well-ordered mother of a teenager, but her hair was spread out on the pillow like a ring of fire, and her lips were swollen, her cheeks pink with desire.

He was still a man on a mission to be redeemed, a man with a black mark in his past so profound he didn't think he could ever erase it. A man trying to do right by three teenage boys, a man whose head was filled with plans for a new ranch and plans for the future of the kids he had just taken on.

But he was also wholly here with her. And she was with him.

They were all the things, all at once.

His chest burned with it all.

He moved up her body, kissing a trail along her soft skin, before kissing her mouth, putting his hand between her legs and wringing another climax out of her.

Then, only then, did he reach for his wallet.

"Are you ready?"

"Yes," she whispered.

"Good," he growled.

He tore open the condom and rolled it over his length, before positioning himself at the entrance to her body. Then he tested her readiness.

"I'm good," she said.

She gasped as he filled her, and it was tight. But she seemed to want it. Seemed to glory in it. Just as he did. She wrapped her legs around his waist and clung to his shoulders as he began to move.

It was like a baptism. By fire, by grace, by Marigold, and he couldn't get enough.

Because it was everything, and so was she.

He held on to his own climax as long as he could, gritting his teeth, biting the inside of his cheek to create enough pain that he wouldn't lose it completely.

And then finally, finally, she shuddered out another climax, and he embraced his own.

He growled out her name as he let the pleasure take him, and then everything was still. Quiet.

She let out a long, heavy sigh.

"Oh, I feel so much better," she said.

And then she laughed.

He withdrew from her, lying on his side. "Me too. But I'm glad that it's mutual."

"Was that really stupid?"

"I don't feel stupid. I feel fucking amazing."

"Me too," she said. "I don't want to… This doesn't have to be dramatic. I just… I haven't been with anybody in a long time, and I don't want to get married. I don't even want to have a boyfriend. I don't want to share my house with a man."

"Great," he said. And he couldn't quite pinpoint why an element of what she said made him feel a little dissatisfied.

"I just want… I want this. This that just happened. I like you. I know you came here to work with me. And we can do that. Now. We can talk about business. And then we can get dressed and go to our respective houses. Maybe we can even have dinner with the kids again. But they don't need to know."

She echoed every thought he had about this. It seemed perfect, and it seemed completely logical.

He loved it.

What wasn't to love?

"Friends with benefits," he said.

"Yes," she said. "Friends with benefits. I think it's a great idea."

"Fantastic," he said.

"Yes," she agreed.

"All right. So let's go over what we need to go over about the business."

"I'll go get my binder."

He chuckled, and lay back in the bed. Wholesome. Almost. Everything was going to work out fine. They both knew what they wanted, and what they wanted was essentially the same thing. There was absolutely nothing that could go wrong here.

Absolutely nothing.

Marigold was trying to chop celery, but she kept spacing out.

And when Lily came home, Marigold startled at the sound of the slamming door, like she hadn't been expecting it. Because she had forgotten where she was. She might have forgotten who she was. The afternoon felt like a complete and total fever dream.

He'd come to her house, they'd had sex, and then they had lain in bed and pored over her planner like they weren't naked, and then they had ended up making out, and he had to run to the store to buy a box of condoms. Which they had made good use of.

They had made love and worked on their plans off and on for the whole day, until it was time for him to go and get his kids from school.

And she felt... Changed. Which wasn't how friends with benefits was supposed to go, she was sure. But she didn't know if there was a woman alive who could keep her head on straight when she was being thoroughly...rustled by Buck Carson.

She paused for a long moment.

Buck Carson. He was the object of so many complex emotions in her life.

This friends-with-benefits situation felt like acting out against the past. Against the pain she had once felt, against things that had been taken away from her.

And maybe it was acting out.

Yet, he had proven he was safe.

They wanted the same things. He was investing in her business. They had a connection that transcended sex, but sex was an equally strong connection. And neither of them wanted it to be romantic. Today hadn't been romantic.

She paused again.

"Mom?"

She snapped back to reality for the second time in just a few moments. She had forgotten that her first jolt was the door closing, which meant Lily was home.

"I'm in here," she said.

"I wanted to go to Colton's house for dinner tonight?"

"Sure," she said.

"You don't have to come," Lily said.

And that made Marigold feel sort of hurt. Also, she wanted to see Buck. Which was silly.

She tried to smile. "Okay. I won't. That's fine."

"Are you okay?" Lily asked as she made her way over to the fridge, opened it and took out a sparkling water. She popped the top on the can and stared at Marigold suspiciously.

"I'm very okay," she said.

"Good. Glad to hear it."

"Well. I hope you enjoy dinner at Colton's. Did you talk to Buck about it?"

"I don't know. Colton did."

As if on cue, Marigold's phone rang. Buck's name appeared on the screen, and her heart tried to race up her esophagus and out of her mouth.

"Hi," she said, answering the phone almost immediately. Lily was staring at her.

"Hey," he said, his voice soft as velvet, like hands against her skin. She shivered. She looked at Lily out of the side of her eye and then studied the celery she was chopping. "Lily tells me she wants to come to your place for dinner?"

"Yeah. I know I have those great prepared meals but I was thinking of grabbing a pizza for the kids to throw in the oven, and maybe you and I could go have dinner somewhere else so we aren't overrun by teenagers."

"Yeah. That sounds good."

"I'll come get you after Lily arrives at my place."

"Okay. See you then."

"What was that?" Lily asked.

"Oh, Buck just thought maybe it would be more fun if you guys were at the house by yourselves. I mean, with Reggie and Marcus, obviously. We aren't leaving you in the house alone."

"Oh," Lily said.

"He and I are going to go have dinner somewhere else. It's not a date."

She felt her face getting pink.

"Mom," Lily said. "You're blushing."

"I don't think I am," she said.

"You are literally bright red."

"I am not. Because there's nothing… I am just going to dinner with him so you can have some time with Colton."

"I don't know. I think you're weird about him."

"Yeah, I'm a little weird about him, because we have a strange…connection. Okay? We have a strange connection, and I don't really know what to do about it. I'm still figuring it out. Grandma and Grandpa were wonderful when they met him, and when I explained that you were dating Colton, and that he was helping with my business, but there's just a lot of history there."

"Did you ever date him?"

"No. I was thirteen, remember? I did not date him."

"Did you like him?"

"I told you that I thought he was handsome. But that's not the same thing as having a crush."

"Do you like him now?"

"I'm thirty-three years old," Marigold said. "I don't have crushes."

"You would be allowed to have crushes," Lily said. "I

wouldn't care if you did date. I mean, not Colton's dad, but I wouldn't mind if you dated."

"I never wanted to do that," Marigold said. "Because I like our life the way that it is."

"But I'm leaving soon," said Lily.

"Yes. You are."

Lily frowned. "I mean… I like Colton. A lot. And he makes me feel things…" It was Lily's turn to turn pink. "It's really bad timing, isn't it?"

Marigold thought about the afternoon she had spent in bed with Buck. "I don't know. Maybe. Lily, I was worried about you getting hurt. I still am. And of course I'm worried about safety and responsibility and pregnancy and all that kind of stuff, but the truth of the matter is, Colton seems like a really good kid. And if he's good to you, it doesn't matter if it's forever or not. Maybe what he's teaching you is what a good boyfriend looks like. So that when you're lonely and away at college, and you like somebody, you don't accept less than what you feel right now."

Lily looked sad. "Maybe."

Marigold wondered if it was the same for herself. The sex that she and Buck had today had been transformative. Better than any she'd ever had, but of course that was the difference between having sex with teenage boys and having sex with a thirty-eight-year-old man who knew what the hell he was doing.

There had been such a gap in her experience—this was a teachable moment. Because Lily was right. Things were changing, and she was leaving. So that meant… It meant that Marigold should figure out what her future could look like. Maybe someday she would want a relationship. Maybe someday she would want to fall in love and get married. That would be… Well, it wasn't something on the horizon just yet.

She couldn't see past Buck being in her bed.

But maybe today was a learning experience. She would never

settle for less than what she had felt in his arms. Because after knowing that existed, why would she?

She would never settle less for less than the insanity that had gripped them both when he had come to the door.

Why would she?

"Well, have fun at your dinner," Lily said.

"You too," she said.

And she felt just a little, tiny bit guilty that she wasn't being totally honest with her daughter, but there was no point to that sort of honesty. Lily didn't need to know that Marigold was having a sexual revolution.

If she was relieved that Lily left in time for Marigold to get dressed up for said dinner, well, that was just the way of it.

By the time Buck got there, she was wearing a skintight dress and more makeup than she normally bothered with.

"Wow," he said. "You look beautiful."

He moved in and kissed her, and she didn't stop him. There was nobody here.

But as he deepened the kiss, she did press on his chest. "I'm hungry," she said.

"Me too," he growled, kissing her neck. She shivered.

"For pasta, not your penis."

He stepped back and barked a laugh. "Well, you have a way of putting a man in his place."

"I'm not trying to," she said. "I'd like to have dinner. Also, I'm too nervous to go having sex when the kids could just appear at any moment. Or at least, my kid could. When she's in school, great. But otherwise... We have to be careful."

"Yeah. I hear you."

"All right. Pasta."

"Just tell me where the best place is, and I'll take you there."

She picked her favorite restaurant, because she could, and the two of them got sparkling water, slightly to the chagrin of the waiter, she could see.

"You can have wine in front of me," Buck said. "I don't care."

"It's fine. I don't really drink much. It reminds me of…bad times. So, it's not really a relaxing escape for me."

"Fair enough."

"I wanted to thank you. For earlier today."

"No. The fact that it left you craving fettuccine instead of more of me doesn't exactly feel like a standing ovation."

She looked at him, feeling a shiver go down her spine. "I am craving you. But I'm also trying to be reasonable and rational."

"I think I might be incapable of that."

They ordered their entrée, and her stomach went tight. She really did wish this dinner would end with a kiss at her door. And her inviting him in.

She really did want him again.

"This is not a date," she said, looking resolutely at her menu.

"Of course not," he said.

They got their entrées and bread, and talked more about business, rather than steering the conversation back into the personal.

She looked down at his hand, the way it gripped the fork, and thought of the way he had touched her.

"So, you do have to tell me."

"I have to tell you something?"

"Yes. How has your…love life worked, exactly, for the last twenty years?"

"Oh, now you have questions."

"Yes. Because you are very, very good."

"Well. Thank you for the compliment. I… The honest truth is that when I was kind of off the rails there for a few years, it was a lot of sex. Mostly anonymous. I… I didn't care, about anything. I didn't want connections. I wanted oblivion."

"I relate to that."

"But after I started working at the camp, it wasn't that simple. Everything I did had to be a lot more…deliberate. I had leave every year, and every year I would take myself off somewhere faraway, to a tourist spot, find a woman and spend the week with her."

"Really?" She hated that woman. Whoever she was. Whoever she had been for all those years.

"Yeah. I mean, not for the last couple of years. I was deciding what to do as far as adopting the boys. I was realizing I needed to make some changes. Sex was more of an itch to scratch, I guess. Kind of like leisure time. It felt good and relaxing. I made it my mission to make it as good as possible for every woman I was with. And that made me enjoy it too."

"I see." Was that what she was? A sex vacation?

"No," he said, like he had read her mind. "It's not the same as you. You're different. Before, I never cared who the woman was. Blonde, brunette, slim, curvy. Didn't matter. Just somebody to be with for a little bit. It was the companionship, the touch—that was what mattered. With this, it's you. Because I haven't felt the need to go out and find anybody since I adopted the boys. And I didn't go out and find you. You found me."

"Right."

She held his gaze, and she felt something in her chest expand.

She didn't need to have feelings for him. She really didn't. It would be a mess. An absolute mess. And so would she.

"There's a big barbecue happening at my parents' house this weekend. Colton wants Lily to come."

Marigold closed her eyes. "I really do worry about them."

"Yeah. We all have to go through some heartbreak, don't we? And hey, maybe they won't. Maybe they'll go off to college, and it'll feel natural for them to let go of each other. Or maybe they won't. Maybe they'll find their way back to each other."

"Maybe." It felt so loaded, him saying that.

Was that what *they* were doing? Finding their way back to each other?

Don't romanticize it. Just friends with benefits.

"Anyway. I thought it would be nice if you could come. I could introduce you to my parents."

Her heart slammed against her breastbone. "Why?"

"Because," he said. "We're doing business together. Also, your daughter is dating my son."

"Yeah. Okay."

She wanted to go. That was the thing. And maybe it felt like a bit of a letdown that he didn't want to introduce her to his parents because she was special, or whatever else it could've been.

But, it also didn't feel like a letdown. It didn't.

Because she just wanted to spend time with him. And the reason didn't much matter.

They finished up their dinner and walked alongside each other back to the truck. It felt hideously awkward to not hold his hand. They had never held hands before, so she couldn't fully explain why it would feel awkward, but it did.

She let out a long, slow breath, as she settled into the passenger seat and let him drive her back to her house.

He walked her up to the front door, and she felt a tense pause inside of her. Her breath hitched; her heart lifted. Right then, she heard the sound of tires on the driveway. Lily pulled up alongside Buck's truck, and Marigold froze.

"I guess that's good night," she said.

"Guess it is," he said.

He waved, like they hadn't just been about to kiss. "See you this weekend, at least."

"Yeah. See you then."

He started to walk back to the truck and greeted Lily as she headed toward Marigold.

"Great timing," Marigold said, smiling.

"Yeah."

"Did you have fun?"

"I had a great time. He invited me to come out to his grandparents' house this weekend."

"Well, I hope you don't think it's weird, but I got an invitation also."

"It's not weird."

"Great. That sounds just great."

Chapter Eleven

Buck kept scanning the pandemonium of the yard, waiting to see if she was going to arrive. It was an unseasonably warm September, and they had set up tables outside for their barbecue dinner. His brothers were talking and laughing, and occasionally, even Boone almost smiled at him.

There were kids. So many kids. Toddlers and teenagers scampering around the place.

But he was waiting for Marigold to get there. And suddenly, her car rounded the corner, and both him and Colton stood up. Wow. He was acting like a teenager. Because he looked just like his son.

"Lily's here," he said.

"Yeah," Buck said, rubbing his chest. He had missed Marigold so much over the last few days. All he had wanted was to go to her house, get in bed with her. Take them both to the places they'd gone when they'd made love that afternoon.

He needed her again. So badly, it made his jaw ache.

But there just hadn't been a chance. Yeah, the kids were in school all day, but they both had inconvenient things like jobs.

He was getting the logistics worked out for the ranch. And

the build for her new facility. And she was continuing to do the job she had already been doing.

When Marigold got out of the car, he couldn't say it was only his body that was affected by the sight of her. It was everything. She made his heart beat faster; she made everything in him feel like it was on red alert. That woman. Good God, that woman.

Colton was halfway to them before they finished getting out of the car entirely. He didn't have any of the self-possession that Buck did. Buck knew how to play it cool. Buck...was walking toward them too, and he hadn't even fully realized it.

"Can I help carry anything?" Buck asked, as Marigold got out and opened up the back of the car, taking out a basket.

"If you really want to," she said.

"I live to serve."

Her cheeks turned pink, and he knew exactly what she was thinking of.

"You know I do," he said.

She elbowed him in the stomach. And he laughed.

Then realized that Colton and Lily were watching them.

"You know, she *is* my best friend's younger sister," he said. Like that explained the familiarity. And not that he'd hooked up with her.

It felt good to say it like that. Like she was still Jason's sister, instead of it just being in the past. And Jason was still his friend. Like he had never lost the right to call him that.

They walked back over to where his family was, and he made introductions: Lily as Colton's friend, and Marigold as Lily's mother and his business partner. He had already told his family all about them, and about the fact that he was investing in the business.

Obviously, he had not told them that she was his friend with benefits. Because that was just between them.

Marigold had brought a basket filled with rolls and a couple of different cakes to put on the table for dessert. They paired beautifully with the barbecued brisket, hamburgers and sausages that his father had grilled up.

And even though Buck had been back now for a little while and had experienced family gatherings like this before, this felt different. Significant. Complete in a way that nothing else had.

He looked to his right, at Marigold, and wondered how much of it had to do with her.

Then he looked back at his food.

His sisters-in-law took to Marigold immediately and spent the whole dinner talking her ear off, while Lily was easily chatting to Boone's stepdaughters, who he intuited she already knew from school.

He stood up to go get another helping of food and just about ran into Boone at the serving table.

"Hey," he said.

"Hey."

He nearly got a smile out of his brother.

"Marigold is nice," Boone commented.

"Yeah," Buck said, frowning. "She is."

"You seem to like her quite a bit."

"What's not to like? Anyway, she's my business partner, and of course Colton is dating Lily." How many times had he said this exact thing to different people over the course of them working together, even in conversations with her? An easy, well tread justification for why they spent time together. For why he liked her.

It was the damnedest thing.

"Seems like you've been settling in pretty well," Boone said.

"Yeah. I guess. And the bruise on my face is healing."

"Sorry about that," Boone said, clearing his throat. "My wife informed me that it wasn't an appropriate way to greet my brother."

"I don't know about that. You had your feelings. You were entitled to them. I'm not going to pretend that my behavior in the past was...honorable."

He had talked to all his brothers quite a bit since he had come back. But Boone least of all. And they hadn't addressed the way they had greeted each other. And he wasn't sure—was that what was happening now? Maybe there was just enough distance between that moment and this one. Or maybe somehow the difference had to do with Marigold. He couldn't quite figure out how, but he felt different because she was here.

And maybe Boone could sense that.

"I felt like you left everything to me," Boone said. "All the grief, all the responsibility. Everything. And I... Believe me when I tell you, a certain part of me gets off on that shit. I'm a champion martyr, Buck. I was in love with my best friend's wife for over a decade." He looked across the space, at Wendy, who was currently talking to Marigold. "I wanted her, and I couldn't have her. And everything in my life felt like a struggle. I think I wanted it to feel like one. But you were my bad object. The person I blamed all of it on. Well, not Wendy being married to somebody else, but all the other stuff. I've dealt with a lot of things over the last few years. I have Wendy now. But apparently, I was still carrying around a little resentment toward you."

This felt comfortable. Being resented. Buck kind of wanted to thank his brother for it.

"Hey. I don't blame you. What I did back then was selfish. And at the time, I really did believe you were all better off without me here. It's that kind of depressive thought that sends you down really dark roads. And I went down a pretty dark road. But when the fog finally cleared, I realized how selfish it had been. At that point, I'd been gone so long I didn't know how to come back. That was selfish too. But part of me really was afraid I was going to disrupt whatever you all had put back together in my absence. I didn't want to do that. I threw myself into my work, but it was when I adopted those boys that I really understood... Family is important. It makes a huge difference to these boys and..."

"You can say it makes a difference to you," Boone said.

"Of course it does."

"Are you glad you're back?"

He felt like he was being jabbed in the stomach with a red-hot poker. "Yes. Of course I am. I missed you."

Emotion tightened his throat. He really didn't like how close to the surface all his feelings were now that he was home. Now that he had kids. Now that he was...trying to be healed. Whatever all of it was...it was creating a damned difficult way to be.

Maybe that was part of why he had avoided coming home for so many years. Maybe that was why he had stayed away. Because somehow he had known that, if he came back here, he was going to feel things. Everything. And yes, he had done a lot of work on himself, but he had also spent a lot of time living a life that allowed him to control what people knew about him, what he talked about and when and what he allowed as far as emotional closeness.

Everything was more volatile here. Everything had been more volatile since he had adopted Reggie, Marcus and Colton. Because there was no control when it came to caring for kids.

They were mean to you, they were wonderful to you, and you loved them all the same. They jerked you around, endlessly. They made you feel like you would cut off a limb to be there for them. To do whatever they needed.

The experience had left him raw and vulnerable, frankly, and coming home had only made it worse.

He'd missed his family.

And he grieved the loss of those years. That was perhaps the hardest part.

Because the loss was his fault. It had been his choice.

And that was something that transcended the guilt he was comfortable with. It overrode the self-flagellation that made him feel most at ease.

"I missed you. And more than that, I wish like hell I hadn't stayed gone for as long as I did. I regret that. I missed so much of your life. So much of Callie's. So much of everybody's. I'd like to say I regret most that I left you with all that responsibility, but hell, I regret the most that we weren't close. That we have a relationship to rebuild now, because I shattered it. Because I didn't just..." He closed his eyes. "I lost my friends. And I felt helpless and responsible for that. But maybe feeling responsible was a way to find some place for all that anger to go. Because it's just such a helpless, infuriating feeling. Losing people you care about like that. I hated it. I still do. And I hate this. I hate that the end result of everything that happened was losing time with my family, even if it was my own choice. When I know how short and fragile everything is."

"Yeah," Boone said, looking down. "I mean, I get that. I'm mad at you about that. And I still feel some resentment sometimes toward... Wendy's ex, I guess. For all the years I couldn't have her, because he was wasting her time. But mostly... When you get something good, you kinda gotta just take it. I have Wendy now, so what's the point of being angry about all the years I didn't have her? What's the point of being full of resentment? I have what I want."

"I don't quite follow."

"You made your choice. I can't even say it was a bad one. Because who knows what would've happened to you, who knows if you could have healed the way you did, if you hadn't made the choice. You wouldn't have ever met your boys. That you don't regret, do you?"

"No," he said. "Of course not."

"Exactly. So... Yeah, parts of this were hard. And there are always going to be things to regret. But those were the decisions you made. So here we are, all together now."

"Yeah. I guess we are."

"You like her," he said, gesturing toward Marigold.

"I... Of course I do. She's my friend. She's Jason's sister. There's a lot of baggage there."

Except that felt like the smallest piece of what they were. They understood each other. Because they had both been through difficult things. It was more bonding than baggage, and not in a traumatic way. It was something he would never be able to explain to another person. He wasn't sure he would ever fully be able to articulate it to himself.

"No. Come on. You know what I mean. You're into her."

Buck flashed back to kissing her. "Yeah," he said. "I am."

Because there was no point lying when he was sure his desire for her was written all over his face. When he was sure his brother knew him better than that.

In spite of the distance. In spite of the time they had spent apart.

"What are you going to do about it?"

"Are you asking about my sex life?"

"No. I don't give a shit if you're sleeping with her or not. What I want to know is—are you going to let yourself have her? I'm not talking about physical stuff."

Boone was talking about love.

And it was all fine and good for his brother to believe in that sort of thing. For himself.

But Buck… He couldn't see a way forward with love.

"I'm just… Whatever we can have, for as long as we can have it, that's what I'm here for," he said.

"Because?"

"The kids are dating," he said.

"Right. So you're going to give precedence to a couple of teenagers' first relationship over what could be the real thing?"

"No. I… That isn't it. There's no way to say this without sounding like a vampire in a teen movie. Okay? But there are just some things that can't be fixed. There are some scars that leave you too…messed up to move on from."

"Yeah. You're right. You do sound like a vampire in a teen movie. Ridiculous. The thing is, Buck, it's your life. I'm not really sure why you'd choose to live in hell when you're alive and could choose something different."

He grimaced. "It is not that simple."

"Well. I'm glad you're home. How about that? And someday, I hope all of you comes home."

"What does that even mean?"

"It means as long as you keep part of yourself hidden away, you're not really here. You're not really living. Enjoy your food."

And Boone walked away, leaving Buck standing there wishing his brother had just punched him in the face instead.

Chapter Twelve

The next few weeks passed in a level of bliss Marigold wasn't used to. She spent time with Lily, made plans for her new business expansion, did her job and always found time to make love with Buck while Lily was at school. And it was in those times, those stolen hours, that a part of herself began to grow again. A part that had been stunted, reviving itself in a way that she hadn't imagined was possible.

She felt lighter. She felt more herself. In touch with all the parts of herself, not just the part that was Lily's mom. Not just the part that was a businesswoman or a responsible citizen of Lone Rock. She was a woman. And in Buck's arms, she felt like one. Really. Truly. Wonderfully.

And when Lily came home saying they needed chaperones for the fall festival dance, Marigold felt honored. That her daughter wasn't embarrassed by her and actually wanted her to attend a school function. That felt amazing. Really and truly wonderful.

So she agreed. And the next day, when she was lying in bed with Buck, she found out that Colton had asked him to chaperone as well. Which meant they were the two primary chaperones of the fall festival dance.

"That's hilarious," he said, laying his head back against the pillow, naked and proud and glorious.

"Why?"

"Because it's so public, while we're sneaking around. We are not complying with the rules."

"We are also not teenagers," she said, swatting him on his broad chest. He really had the best chest. Hairy and muscular and yum.

"Right, right. Can't wait to stand there next to you, trying to be good and proper."

The idea sent a thrill through her.

"Yes. And we will be."

"Maybe I should bring you a corsage."

He rolled over so he was above her, and she arched up and bit his lower lip. "Maybe you should."

So when he did, she shouldn't have been surprised. They drove separately and met outside the school gym. He was dressed in a suit, and the sight made her heart drop into her feet. She was in a sparkly dress that went down to her knees, trying to look fancy, but not like she was trying to look young. Even though she was.

"Your corsage, madam."

"You're ridiculous," she said.

"Am I? Or am I romantic?"

She wasn't supposed to want him to be romantic. But it made her heart sing. It made everything inside of her lift.

She really did kind of want the romance.

And she didn't know what to do about that.

They walked into the gym together, and she had the corsage firmly on her wrist. Bright pink roses and baby's breath. She tried to imagine him actually going into a flower store and buying this, but he must've done it.

Colton had brought one for Lily. And she was almost entirely certain that Buck had insisted. She wasn't really sure if kids gave each other that kind of thing these days generally. But clearly Buck thought it was important.

"Wow," she said, surveying the scene that could best be described as teen hormones crashing into teen emotions. In other words, a lot of a lot.

"I don't miss being a teenager," he said.

Which was somewhat ironic, all things considered.

"Yeah. Not really."

"Even Marcus has a date," he said.

"He does?"

"Yeah. He was excited about it."

"That's cute."

"Sure. Cute. Terrifying. What was I thinking getting into kids at this level? Having to worry about sex and pregnancy and all that kind of stuff."

She barked a laugh. "I don't actually know. You're an idiot. Or a glutton for punishment."

"Do we have to worry about Colton and Lily sneaking off tonight?"

"No," she said. "She's actually meeting up with a group of her girlfriends afterward, and I have confirmed this with their mothers. Because obviously I'm well acquainted with subterfuge. It's one thing to say you have plans, but I require proof. Also, I can track her cell phone. It is so much harder to be a kid these days."

"Damn," he said. "What a nightmare. Your parents can actually verify where you are?"

"Yes. I mean, you could leave your phone at a different location, but they won't do that."

"No," he said, chuckling. "They won't. Imagine being that connected all the time. What's the fun in that? We used to get to run absolutely feral."

"Yeah. Look where that got both of us."

He lifted a shoulder. "Yeah. Fair." He cleared his throat. "My brother said the other day that you can't do too much second-guessing of your decisions. I mean, not when the decisions lead you to good places. I regret that I left home. But I don't regret adopting the boys."

She nodded. "Yeah. I get that. I regret my behavior after my brother's death. I don't regret Lily. And that's always a really tricky thing as a parent. To try to make it very clear to her that I want her to have different...different paths available to her than I did, but to also make it very clear that I don't regret being her mother."

"I don't envy you that."

"She's a good kid. I just have to be thankful for that every day. This has actually been...probably the most difficult part of our relationship. Because she's trying to be a grown-up, and I don't want her to be. And at the same time... *I'm* trying to be a grown-up."

"Yeah. Well. Do you regret that you...have to do this? Be a parent?" He looked at her, his eyes intense.

She shook her head. "Of course I don't. I'm happy."

"Me too."

They spent a portion of the evening guarding the punch bowl and dealing with some mild bullying and a little bit of drama around two girls who came in the same dress. But otherwise, it was a pretty quiet evening. It was strange to be in the gym of the old school. She had been a different person back then. So had he.

And they had never been in it together. But here they were now.

The DJ onstage announced it was time to play some oldies, and she died inside when the first song was one that had been popular when she was in middle school.

"Did you hear that?" she asked. "We're oldies."

"Well, I'm offended," he said. "But I have always liked the song."

"It's a good song," she said, as the sweet vocals filtered through the gym. There was nothing to dislike about Sixpence

None the Richer, and this one had been popular at school dances back then for a reason. The demand to be kissed was of course inside half the kids in this gym. Now and then.

A universal need.

"I think we should dance," he said. "All the better to supervise these kids."

"Really?"

"Yes," he said. "Really."

He held his hand out, and...she didn't have the strength to say no. Because she wanted to touch him. She wanted to be held by him. She wanted him.

He pulled her up against his body, and she felt herself melt. They moved in time to the music, their eyes locked together, and she could no longer deny that she wanted romance. Or, maybe she didn't want it. But they were having it. It was happening. This wasn't friends with benefits. It was something more. And she wasn't sure if she had the strength to turn away from that. Because it was so beautiful.

He twirled her and brought her back to him, holding her like she was precious.

And all the years that she had spent feeling like someone who was on probation—like someone who didn't deserve everything, like someone who had damaged herself, and her life, with her choices—melted away. Because he didn't look at her like she was a consolation prize. Like he cared for her, but it was a shame she had been such a slut when she was a teenager. Like she was great, but it was a shame she came with her daughter.

Never. Not once.

He looked at her like she was precious. And it made her heart just about burst.

"Marigold," he whispered, against her ear. "I think this might be a date."

She pulled back just slightly and met his gaze. "Yes. I think it is."

Chapter Thirteen

Lily looked over at her mother and Buck. The suspicion that her mom had feelings for him had been getting more and more certain every week. Her mom said no, but she blushed when his name came up. She looked giddy whenever he called.

Lily recognized it, because it was how she felt when she thought about Colton. But...the more she thought about it, the more she was sure her mom wasn't going to do anything with Buck if Colton and Lily were dating. Because her mom had always sacrificed for her.

Lily was leaving for college anyway. She was seventeen. You didn't marry the first guy you ever made out with. The first guy you ever let get to second base. You didn't marry that high school boyfriend, because you had to go do things.

Her mom hadn't gotten to go do things. And she was counting on Lily to go away and make something of herself. She had sacrificed so much in order for Lily to do that. And now her mom was getting ready to sacrifice wanting the first guy that she had even shown any interest in for Lily's whole life because Lily happened to be dating his son. A dead-end relationship that she knew wasn't even half of what Buck and her mom could have.

She put her hand to her chest and wished it didn't feel like her heart was breaking and moved away from Colton, stepping outside the gym, trying to catch her breath.

She was grateful she had made plans with her friends. Grateful she had decided she wasn't going to do something crazy like sleep with Colton tonight.

Her eyes filled with tears, and she shook her head, didn't let them fall.

Colton followed her out the door. "What's wrong?"

"You see them?"

"Who?"

"Buck and my mom."

"Oh yeah. They were dancing. So?"

"She likes him. I mean… They like each other."

"You think so?"

"Yes. And… I think there's something going on between them. I have thought that for a while."

"Why didn't you say anything?"

"Because I thought I was being crazy. And… I didn't want to mess this up. Us. But the truth is… We can't be together."

He looked like she had hit him, and she felt horrible. She felt like the villain.

Breaking her own heart.

Breaking his.

"My mom has sacrificed everything for me. Absolutely everything. And I think your dad would make her happy. But she keeps telling me that nothing is going on between them, and she so clearly… I think she's in love with him. And she doesn't want to disrupt my life or my relationship with you, because if they get married, then I'm going to be your stepsister."

"Why are you saying this?"

"Because it's true. It's real. It's happening." She took a deep breath. "We're going to college anyway. We are not going to end up together, Colton. This was… It was great. And you were great. There's nothing wrong with you. But it's not the right timing. And I think… I think because of them it's never going to be."

"You're really breaking up with me at a dance?"

"We don't have to be broken up until after the dance ends," she said. "We could have one more dance."

Colton's face looked stony. "No. We can't."

"Please don't be mad at me. Please. I like you. I care about you. And if our parents end up together then…"

He swallowed hard. And it was like he suddenly saw all the potential problems with all of this. They could never get to where they hated each other. Not if they were going to be stuck together as part of the same family, forever.

"Okay."

"Let's go back to the dance."

"Sure."

But there was something terribly blank in his eyes. And when he touched her hand, it didn't feel the same.

But that was a good thing. It wasn't supposed to.

She had made the right choice.

Because her mom wouldn't tell her what was going on, she'd had to try to figure it out and handle it herself. Try to fix it.

So she had done the best she could.

Chapter Fourteen

Lily was safely off with her friends before the dance ended, and Marigold breathed a sigh of relief when the last of the kids filtered out of the gym.

She felt Buck approach, and she turned to him. Her heart lifted, lodging itself in her throat. He was just so…handsome. She wished she could see a way out of how complex all of this was. But there were just so many reasons for what was between them to not be the big romance. And yet it was beginning to feel like one.

She wasn't sure what to do about that. The best thing to do would be to stop sleeping with him.

Yet she didn't want to. Hadn't she done enough behaving?

She didn't want to behave.

She had lost this part of herself for so many years, and she felt like she was awash in new tones of color ever since the two of them had first kissed.

She couldn't go back.

"I told the boys I was headed to my parents' house. That I wouldn't be home."

"Oh."

"I lied to them," he said.

"You lied to them?"

"Yes. Because I'm a very bad man. And I would like to spend the whole night showing you exactly how bad."

That was so cheesy. She shouldn't respond. But she was responding to that. Because she knew about his brand of wickedness, and it lit her skin on fire. It lit her soul on fire.

"Are they going to be all right by themselves?"

"Colton is seventeen. They'll be fine. I just have to drop them back at home."

"Okay," she said.

"I'll meet you back at your place."

She drove home, giddy and fizzy. They had a whole night to themselves. The luxury was almost impossible to take on board. Normally, they only had stolen moments during the day.

She wanted to sleep with him. Share the bed with him all night. Let him hold her.

She had ordered some sexier underwear, since this new situation had developed where she actually needed it. So she took the extra time she had to herself to get a bit of a performance together. She found a red lace bra and panties, and put a red silk robe over the top of it. It was a little a cliché, but men were simple. Buck was very simple, in the best way. She didn't worry about being sexy enough for him. He seemed happy no matter what she was wearing, or not wearing.

She had never really been in... She hesitated to call this a relationship. But it was the closest thing. The same man, a man she talked to, a man she knew, a man who had gotten to know her body as she had gotten to know his.

When he knocked at the door, she hopped in place a couple of times, trying to get the excitement more reasonably distributed through her body so she wasn't shaking when she went to kiss him.

She opened the door. There he was. Tall and perfect and beautiful. The exact delivery she had been hoping for.

"I can't believe we have all night."

He stepped inside and closed the door behind him. He didn't grab her and kiss her like he normally did. He took his time. Slowly, he put his hat on the peg by the door, took his jacket off and hung it there too.

And she was mostly naked.

It was erotic, if a little bit irritating, because it seemed imbalanced.

But instead of commenting on it, she just untied her robe and let it drop down to the floor.

And she could see that whatever he had been intent on doing, he'd lost his resolve completely when he saw her body.

His eyes were like a blue flame, and she felt his own need echo inside of her.

"Well I'll be damned," he said.

"Do you like it?"

She sounded more hopeful than she had intended to. A little more insecure. She wasn't normally insecure. But she did want to hear how much he appreciated her. It was like he had opened up a well of need inside her that she hadn't known previously existed.

It just felt really good to have someone who seemed to want to spend time with her. To have someone in her life who thought she was beautiful. To be touched, casually and intimately. Intensely and softly. He was everything, all the time.

And she was used to carrying all the things by herself.

But not with him. Not with him.

He closed the distance between them and began to kiss her, deep and hot, carnal.

It didn't even feel strange anymore. To be everything—every part of herself—that she contained. To know she could have this wildness and still be the Marigold she wanted to be. To know she could be sexual and sensual and responsible and good all at once.

She began to unbutton his shirt, pushed it off his shoulders.

She kissed her way down his body and knelt down in front of him, slipping his belt through the buckle.

He grunted as she exposed his hardness to her touch and then, leaned forward and took him in her mouth.

She felt wicked. In the very best way.

Luxuriating in this, in him.

She wanted to give to him.

It was like a dam had broken inside of her. And she knew one thing above all else. She didn't have a place inside her that was angry at him. Not anymore. She didn't have a place inside her that grieved her brother separately from everything else in her life. Just like she didn't have a place inside her that was only good and responsible or a secret chamber where she kept her sexuality. She was everything. Everything all at once. And only when the intensity of those emotions, the certainty of what she felt, was free to flow, to be, could she see the truth.

Yes. Everything was complicated. Yes, *they* were complicated. But she was falling in love with him all the same. It could never be physical only. Because she had too many feelings for him.

She had made him her bad object once.

She had been slightly concerned for a moment that she was just making him a good object, rather than a whole person. But that wasn't it. He wasn't the one who needed to change. She was. She had closed off so much of herself because of fear. She had been the best mother she could be. She loved her daughter. She put all her ferocity, all her care into that relationship. But she hadn't tried to make friends. She had never tried to have relationships. She had been so careful with her parents.

It was all just trying to protect herself. From bad feelings. From difficult feelings. Trying to be healed when… There was healing to be had, she believed that.

But perhaps more than healing, she wanted to be brave enough to try and dig deep and find a purpose in the tragedy that had happened. Not to make bland comments about how it was God's will, or it was Jason's time—she didn't believe that. It was a mistake. It was a bad thing that happened. And if she could go back and choose it all over again, of course she would never shorten her brother's life in the name of her personal growth.

But she didn't get to choose it.

What she got to choose was what she did with it now.

She wanted to love Buck.

She wanted to be a great mother.

She wanted to be a good daughter.

She wanted to be a businesswoman. Someone who mattered in the community.

She wanted to be everything. She wanted to be bold. She wanted to risk. She wanted to care.

She poured all of that into him now. Into pleasuring him.

Everything.

And right when he was on the brink, he gripped her and pulled her to her feet, branding her mouth in a searing kiss. "Marigold," he said, his eyes wild.

She was pretty sure she had done to him what had just happened to her. That all the walls were down, that everything was flooding out.

That he was everything.

The good man and the bad one. The one who had made mistakes and the one who had spent years trying to correct them. The one who had been made a scapegoat when he didn't deserve it. The one who had hurt his family. The one who had loved his family.

The boy she had been attracted to then. The man she loved now.

She took his hand and led him up the stairs.

Brought him into her bedroom.

They fell down onto the bed, and he stripped her the rest of the way, rolling her over so she was sitting on top of him. Then he handed her a condom packet.

She tore it open, rolling it over his hard length and positioning herself on top of him.

She took him in, inch by inch, relishing the feeling of joining, knowing that she cared for him. Or rather, enjoying the immense, incredible feeling of not trying to hold anything back.

She clung to his shoulders, clung to him. Rolled her hips in time with her need, riding them both to completion, their harsh cries of pleasure mingling together as they both found their release.

She collapsed over him.

"Stay with me," she said. "All night."

"Of course," he said.

The complicated stuff was just going to have to work out. It just was.

Because she wanted him.

The question was, how big of a risk was she willing to take to have it all?

The last thing Buck expected to see when they tumbled down the stairs the next morning to get coffee was Lily and Colton sitting there at the breakfast table, looking like two disapproving parents.

Marigold stepped behind him, holding her robe closed, and he felt like clutching his own nonexistent pearls at the fact that they had been caught by their children.

"Good morning," Lily said, looking sideways at Colton.

Colton took a sip of the coffee, looking at Buck disapprovingly. "You didn't come home last night," he said.

"No," Buck said. "But I told Marcus to let you guys know something came up."

"You did," Colton said. "You weren't honest about where you were. You said you had to go to Grandma and Grandpa's. Is this Grandma and Grandpa's, Buck?"

"It isn't," Buck said, giving his son the most deadpan stare he could manage.

"I didn't think so. It's very disappointing behavior."

"Well, very sorry for disappointing you."

"We just want to know that you're being safe," Lily said.

Marigold sputtered. "Excuse me?"

"Emotions can run high in these situations, and it's very important to know that you're making good choices. Your health and safety is very important. As is your future. Mom, you're about to start a business, and given that, you know it's not a good time for you to have a baby."

"A baby!" Marigold looked like she was going to faint away.

"Well, accidents happen," Lily said.

"And on that topic," Colton said. "Buck, anybody could see your truck was parked in the driveway all night. You know how the neighbors will talk. And it is much more difficult for the women in these situations than for the men. People are very judgmental."

"All right," Buck said. "That's it. Enough."

"Don't take that tone with me," Colton said. "Sorry," he said, "it was for the bit."

"Well the bit is *done*," Buck said.

"You just should've told us," Lily said. "Instead, we had to figure it out by watching the two of you at the dance last night."

"Which anyone could have done," Colton said. "Because you were putting on a performance for our entire school. How do you think we feel about that?"

Marigold pushed forward. "I'm sorry," she said. "I didn't mean to…"

"Don't worry about it, Mom," Lily said. "I'm not mad. I just wish you would've told me."

"I thought it was too complicated."

"There's no complication," Colton said. "We broke up."

"What?"

"Yeah," he said, shrugging his shoulder. "A while ago. We're just friends now. And we're going to college at the end of the school year. It's not that deep."

Buck stared at his son. He didn't think Colton was being honest at all. There was a strange kind of detached way he was talking that Buck recognized a bit too clearly from when he had first met Colton at the ranch.

It was the way he responded to trauma. And Buck didn't like that at all.

"What we wanted to say," Lily added, "is that there's no reason you two can't...do your thing. Date. Whatever this is. You're adults. And yes, we wanted to give you a hard time, since you gave us a hard time too. But whatever reason you have for hiding it... You just don't need to anymore."

That was such a strange sensation. Getting a blessing from their kids. And yeah, he supposed that did mean they didn't have to hide it anymore. But that also meant they needed to come up with a different label for it. Which he had been pretty aware of for a while now. There were feelings between them, and those feelings transcended the physical. They had for a while. Last night... Last night had been transformative in a way he hadn't been anticipating. It had changed things.

But he still didn't know... He still didn't know what he wanted. Or what it meant.

He just knew that he cared about Marigold, and he wasn't ready to let go of whatever this was.

"Well," Colton said. "Lily and I will leave you to it."

"You will?" Buck asked.

"Yeah. We're going to go out and get pancakes. See you later."

Colton stood up, and Lily followed, and they walked out. Leaving Buck and Marigold alone.

"Well. I guess... We weren't being as secretive as we thought."

"I need to talk to her."

"You just did," Buck said.

"She can't just be okay with the fact that her and Colton broke up."

"Sure she can. They're young. Like she said, they're going to school."

"I just don't believe it."

"How about we deal with the two of us for five seconds. What about that?"

She turned to look at him. "And what? What are we?"

"I guess we have to answer that question. Because we don't have the excuse that we did fifteen minutes ago."

"What excuse is that?"

"That it's too complicated because of the kids."

He wasn't sure he wanted to go there. Wasn't sure he wanted to take the conversation in this direction, but he was doing it. Because he was pretty sure it wasn't fair to be bringing this up when he didn't think he could answer the question either.

Can't you?

"I keep thinking about it," Marigold said, looking at the back wall.

"What exactly?"

"Us. This." She shook her head. "We had a good reason to keep it a secret. There were a lot of complications. You went and talked to my parents. We discovered that wasn't really a complication. Our kids came here and talked to us, and now that's not really a complication. So where is the complication exactly?"

"I'm not following."

"It's us. It's us, or there isn't one. I don't know. But I realized something last night."

He felt everything in him go tense. "What's that?"

"I think I'm in love with you, Buck. And I say that as somebody who knows how scary life is. I say that as someone who has spent so many years protecting myself that I don't even remember what it's like to be…fearless. And young. My foundation, so much of me, is based on loss. And I told myself for a really long time that I was just being responsible. By not bringing men into my and Lily's lives. That I was being respectful and careful by not talking to my parents about you or Jason. You left town. I withdrew in a different way. I made myself into a different person, and I cut a lot of myself off. And last night it was like... It was like I realized that I was feeling everything for the first time."

His heart hammered.

Everything in him felt stuck. Sick. He didn't want to hurt her, not in any way. But he also didn't think he could give her what she was asking for. Because with love, came a set of responsibilities he had never once managed to live up to in his life.

He was trying. He had adopted the boys. But dammit, to throw a relationship on top of that? Another kid?

He had abandoned his family. Nothing in him was...

He didn't deserve this.

And above all else, he couldn't handle it.

"What exactly do you think you want?" He asked it carefully. Slowly. Because he was making assumptions. He was jumping to conclusions. And she didn't deserve that.

"Everything. Nothing less. I didn't want to fall in love with you, Buck. You are the most inconvenient person for me to fall in love with." Her eyes filled with tears, and he wished he could say something to make it better. Except he was the one making her cry. He was the one who was going to make it worse. He was the one who was going to break everything.

So there was nothing he could say. There was nothing he could do.

"Of course you didn't," he said, his voice rough. "Nobody would."

She shook her head. "No. It isn't because of you. It's because of me. Because I told myself you were absolutely the worst person to fall in love with, but what if my perspective was all wrong? It's a terrible thing, trying to figure out how to categorize your brother's death. Trying to figure it out while you're all laden down with the stuff life throws at you. And at the same time, people say all these things to you. Well-meaning people say the most horrendous things. About how it was meant to be.

About how he's in a better place. But I always wanted him to be here with me."

"Of course you did," he said.

"It's just, because of that, I really resisted looking for meaning in what happened back then. Like finding any meaning there was a betrayal. Like it diminished the loss. But not accepting what it meant, that was just me fiercely holding on to pain I didn't need to hold on to. I think I can believe both things now. That Jason should be here, and that because he isn't here there were certain things I had to learn and accept. Certain ways I had to grow. And certain people I am connected to. Forever." She made eye contact with him, her gaze like an arrow. "You. I think you are one of the only people in the world who could possibly understand me. My pain, what I've been through. I think you're the only person, other than my parents, who felt the impact of that loss. But you do."

"Yeah. Because I'm complicit."

"You're not. And you know that."

He did. But something in him was desperately seeking a shield to throw in front of her words. And taking responsibility for her brother's death was a big, easily accessible shield.

She was quiet for a long moment. "I can't help but notice that you're not saying it back."

That stuck him, right in the gut. The truth of the matter was, he couldn't say it back. But he also couldn't deny that he did love her.

He loved her.

He had fallen in love with her over the course of these weeks, months. And it wasn't just working together, sleeping together, these family dinners, seeing her with his family. With his boys. It was everything. It was the way she smiled, the way the sunlight caught her hair. It was the way she made him feel. Like anything was possible.

But he knew it wasn't.

Because he knew what he was.

He was the man who had left his family for twenty years. He was trying to make up for it. He was trying to be new, trying to be better, trying to be different. But he wasn't. Not yet. And he maybe never would be.

And so he couldn't say that he loved her. He couldn't promise her a future. He couldn't promise her anything.

"Now you don't have anything to say."

"I can't."

"You know, there was a man who once told me he paid close attention to what the universe was trying to say to him. To his intuition. The checks in his gut. Where is that man?"

"I'm listening to my gut," he said.

"And your gut says you can't be in love with me?"

"My gut says we can't make a future out of this. My gut says I went way too far off the path to get back on it now. I'm sorry. I wish things could be different. But I have Colton and Marcus and Reggie, and I am trying to make up for the fact that I have been a bad son and a bad brother for two decades. I am trying to make up for the fact that…"

"I don't believe that. I don't believe any of it. You know what I believe? You need your guilt. Because it's your security blanket. Without it, you're afraid of what you'll become. But I know you don't need it. You're a good man, Buck Carson. I don't care what anyone in this town used to say, and I don't care what my thirteen-year-old self said to you in the streets all those years ago. You don't need guilt. This is why you didn't want to accept my forgiveness. You wanted to come home and have everybody throw stones at you. All the better if your own family would've picked up the rocks. Because then you can insulate yourself with that guilt. You could say you were right to be gone. Because everybody hates you. Is it that bad to find out people are actually happy to see you? That we actually want you?"

"I just can't do this."

He turned away from her, and he walked to the door. He got his coat and his hat from the peg. And he felt like a damned coward. He felt like he was doing the same thing he had always done.

But sometimes it was for the best.

Because just like back then, he knew leaving was the right thing to do.

Was it the right thing to do?

He gritted his teeth, and he walked out the door.

But Marigold followed him.

He made his way to his truck and opened the driver's side door, but she kept on coming.

"You are a coward," she shouted.

"We don't need to perform this for the neighbors," he said.

"Why? Because we are so evolved now? Because we've changed? Because I'm not thirteen anymore, so I don't get to yell at you in the street? I will. If that's what it takes for you to understand. What's the point of growing up if you don't grow up? What's the point of all this? Of being so good. Of both of us being so damned responsible. What is the point of any of it? I'm letting it all go. I'm giving it away. I'm not responsible. I'm not good. I am heartbroken. And I am angry at you. For throwing all of this away, for throwing us away. How dare you."

"You don't understand," he said, slamming the door shut again. "I'm trying to protect you. You're right, you have done a lot of work. And what am I? Nothing. No matter what I do I am never going to be able to erase the way I messed things up. My parents are old. My siblings grew up without me. They had to take care of everything while I was off licking my wounds. I didn't apologize to your parents, I didn't apologize to Ryan's parents, I didn't apologize to Joey's parents. All I did was take all my hurt and stuff it down deep inside of me. I made it all about me. That's who I am. When everything is terrible, I make it about me. And it is only my guilt that finally dragged me out of it. It is only my guilt that finally made me take a good, long, hard look at myself and say that if I was still breathing, I better the hell make it count, because my friends were dead, and

I was wasting my chance at life. Yeah. Guilt pulled me out of rock bottom. And I'm sorry if you don't understand why that worked for me. But it did."

"You're more than that," she said. "This is your sign. This is your other opportunity. To look around at yourself, to look around your life and ask why are you breathing?"

"For those boys."

"Breathe for yourself too."

He shook his head. "I can't."

"You are the biggest catfish on the planet," she said. "Because you are so charming and so handsome, and it is fake. Inside, you are a mess. The same mess you were when you left. You haven't grown at all. You're just hiding behind something different. Now it's this facade of the benevolent martyr. How nice for us. And how nice for you. You can roam around in a philosophical hair shirt for the rest of your life and never have to take a risk again. Because you're already dying. So what are you afraid of? Living. That's what you're afraid of."

"Maybe," he said, feeling like he'd been stabbed straight through the chest. "But you know, a lot of people are afraid of bad things happening to them. I'm afraid of the way I seem to make bad things happen to other people. And I don't know what to do about that fear."

It was the truth, even if it was a little overdramatic, even if it didn't entirely make sense. He knew. He understood. He felt the truth of it, burning there at the center of his chest. There was something in him that was just rotten and wrong, and if he didn't control it… If he didn't control it, then everything would be ruined.

"Maybe it's best this way," he said. "Best if you don't understand. And you just hate me."

"We're business partners," she said, clearly exasperated, broken, and it was his fault.

"That's not going to change. I won't go back on my word."

"Is that the game you play? You make all these commitments

that you can't get out of, and then you tell yourself that even if you withhold your heart, you're doing the right thing? Is that the point of you following fate?"

He knew it wasn't. He knew what she said wasn't totally true. Except, maybe when he had adopted the boys, he hadn't anticipated loving them like he did. Really loving them like his own sons.

But he just... He just couldn't do more.

"You'll thank me for this later."

She bent down and picked up a pebble, as he got into the truck, then threw it at the door as he pulled out. He heard it hit; it dented.

He unrolled his window. "Are you nuts?"

"If I am it's your fault!"

Well. That said it all. And that was why he had to go.

So he kept on driving, until he couldn't see her anymore.

Chapter Fifteen

When Lily came home, she was the immediate and total focus of Marigold's feelings, because what else was she supposed to do with all the pain building up inside her chest.

Certainly not feel it.

She almost laughed at that. At herself for being so ridiculous. At everything.

"You're really okay?"

"I said that I was," Lily said.

"Well, I just I know breakups can be hard and…"

Lily frowned. "Are you okay?"

She realized that she probably looked a mess, and that her mascara was running.

"I'm good," she said.

"Did something happen with Buck?"

"Lily… This isn't about me. It's about you. And the fact that you chose to do something rash because you were worried about me."

"That wasn't why. I was thinking about what you said. About the fact that I'm going off to school, and you're right. How am I supposed to go off and have new experiences if I'm obsessing about a guy back home. I like Colton, and I didn't want things to get dramatic between us. So now they don't have to. It's not a drama."

"Oh."

She wouldn't know what "not a drama" was like. Since every time she tried to feel something, apparently it was a drama. It ended with screaming in the streets.

"Lily... Buck and I broke up."

"You broke up?"

"Yes." She sighed heavily. "I wanted more than he was ready to give. And you know, this is why I worried about you. You and Colton. It isn't about maturity, it's about the fact that this kind of stuff can be really dangerous. I'm thirty-three, I should have it together a little more. It's not like I'm totally inexperienced with men."

Lily grimaced. Because what could be more horrifying than having to hear about your mother's past sexual experiences? Even if implied? Nothing.

But if Marigold had to be a cautionary tale, then she would be.

It would at least make this heartbreak feel like it had a point.

"Well, you know you were born somehow," Marigold said. "So don't grimace at me."

"I'm just... Mom, are you okay?"

"No," she said. "I mean, I'm going to get out of bed and I'm going to do things, and I'm going to be your mom, and I'm going to be myself, but I'm hurt. It's been really, really difficult these last couple of hours. So I don't know what it's going to be like going forward. I really thought we had something. I thought he was in love with me. Anybody can get hurt when there are bodies and hearts involved. And so if you take anything away from this, I just want you to take away that…this is why I was worried about you. Because it's hard for me to go through. And I would never want to see you in this kind of pain."

"I don't want to see you in pain either," Lily said. "How can he not be in love with you? You're the best and you're amazing. You are the sweetest, nicest, most caring person I know. You're the best mom. You have done more for me than I can ever thank you for. You're just... You're wonderful. And if he doesn't realize that, then he can go straight to hell."

Marigold should probably correct Lily for speaking out harshly, but she wasn't going to.

"I don't want you to be jaded, and I don't want you to be armored," Marigold said. "But I do want you to be aware that... Love can be... Well, it can be *this*."

"I'm sorry." Lily wrapped her arms around Marigold. "He should appreciate you."

"Thank you. I want you to remember too, Lily, that love can also be *this*." They parted for a moment, and she felt a little glimmer of hope inside her, a little shaft of light shining through the gross darkness. "We have had a lot of love. And we have a great life. Nothing was ever missing. How could it be, when I have you? The greatest daughter in the world. I'm so proud of you."

"Thanks, Mom," she said.

"I'm going to be okay."

"Are you going to date other men? Are you going to go wild when I leave?"

"Maybe," she said, trying to smile. "Probably not."

"It would serve you right if you did. I'm very sex positive, Mom. It's your body. You can do what you want with it."

She tried to contain her grimace. "Thank you. I didn't need to hear that."

"Well, I don't want to know about it. I'm just saying...

Times have changed and women are allowed to express themselves that way."

"Thank you very much," Marigold said. "Someday, I will regale you with stories about how I am a slut of the old ways, my child. But you're not ready for that yet."

That earned her a look of horror, which she decided to call her one win for the day. Well, other than the fact that no matter what happened, Lily loved her. And so all wasn't lost. It couldn't be.

But when she left Lily downstairs, Marigold threw herself across the bed and wept. Because all might not be lost, but a big piece of her heart was.

And she didn't know if it was ever going to grow back.

He was trying to fix fences, but mostly, he was just hammering his thumb. He cursed and chucked the hammer across the field, and Colton picked it up and handed it to him. He looked up and saw that Reggie and Marcus were standing behind him.

"Here, you dropped this. Dumb ass," Colton said.

Buck looked up at his oldest son, who was glaring at him like he'd just clubbed a baby seal. "Excuse me?"

"You heard me," Colton said, his eyes full of storm. "I didn't stutter."

"What did I do?"

"You broke up with Marigold," Marcus said, stepping forward, even angrier looking than his brother.

Buck wasn't about to be lectured by a half-grown piglet who'd never even touched a woman. "Yeah. I did. For her own good."

Reggie howled. "For her own good! Do you hear yourself? You sound like a chump."

"Listen," Buck said, his voice hard. "Men and women are different and—"

"You sound like you have a *podcast*," his youngest added.

"What the hell does that mean?"

"Do you feel insulted?" Reggie asked.

"Yes."

Reggie narrowed his eyes. "Then you know what it means."

Buck stared at his boys. "I'm serious. She is an amazing woman. And she deserves somebody who… Who is better than me."

The three of them exchanged glances.

"She does? But we don't?" Marcus asked.

"That's *not* what I said," Buck said.

"It kind of is, though," Marcus said. "A little bit. Why are you not good enough for her, but *we're* supposed to live with you?"

Those little rats. That wasn't what he was saying at all, and it was different, and they ought to know it. He was sort of tongue-tied trying to figure out how to explain that it was different, but it was.

"I... It's *different*. Romantic stuff is different." He decided to go with that very articulate explanation.

"Is it?" Reggie asked.

"You're a smart-ass, shut up."

His words didn't have any heat; they sounded petulant even to him. And Reggie was not deterred.

"*Seriously*, Buck. You meet a nice woman. A beautiful woman. We all like her daughter—sorry Colton—and you break up with her. We could've had a *mom*."

It was the slight break in Reggie's voice at the end that got him.

That stabbed him clean through the chest. "That's not... That's not fair. You are an emotional terrorist," he said.

"Maybe you deserve it," said Marcus. "Maybe you deserved a little bit of emotional terrorism for the shit you put her through."

"I'm not trying to hurt anybody," Buck said. "I'm a mess, okay? That is a documented fact. In high school I drank too much, and I was adjacent to that awful accident. I frankly should've been in it. Everybody in town blamed me. Then I abandoned my family."

"So what? That's all you are? You just do stuff because you feel guilty and you feel like you have to make up for it?"

"Yeah. That's why I do stuff."

It was why he had to. To try and be better. To try and atone.

"Ah. So we're all part of your redemption scheme. You just feel guilty. See, you adopted a bunch of sad foster kids so you could try to right your balance with the universe." Reggie looked angry now. "Good thing my mom died, I guess, and my sister too. What a big help to you. It made it really easy for you to earn some points on that one. I was an extra sad case."

This was going all wrong.

"Reggie, that's not what it is."

They were all looking at him. All angry.

"I love you," Buck said. "I didn't expect it. I can be honest with you about that. I thought... I thought it would be like taking care of you as campers. But it's not. It hasn't been. I'm your dad. And I love you, and guilt has nothing the hell to do with it. You knuckleheads. You're not just mine right now, not just mine because...because I feel like a mess, and I wanted to do something to make myself feel better. You're mine because you were meant to be. Because the whole fucked-up road I took to get to Hope Ranch led me to you. And I was supposed to be there, even though a whole bunch of stuff around it wasn't supposed to happen. Adopting you three was one of the few good things I did. I listened to my gut. And then I ended up... You changed my life. If not for you, I wouldn't have come back here. I never would've reconnected with my family. That's not guilt. It's love."

Colton blinked, then looked away, a muscle in his jaw twitching. "Sounds to me like you don't really need the guilt."

And all Buck could do was sit there, shell-shocked. Because it was true. It wasn't guilt that kept him with the boys. It was love.

Guilt wasn't what kept him going.

He thought of his choice to leave his family. There had been misguided love there, even if the choice had been wrong. He had acted from a place of love. Flawed love. But...

Every day with the boys he saw what flawed love could do. Why wasn't he willing to try that with Marigold?

Because you're afraid. Because everything she said is true.

His heart caught hard in his chest. Yeah. That was true. He was afraid. He was afraid of letting go of his guilt. There was a reason he hadn't gone to see Joey's and Ryan's parents. There was a reason he was holding on to those shields.

Because they protected him, not because they protected the people around him.

Because he was afraid he could never be worthy of her love, and if he accepted it and he lost it...

He had never felt weak. He had felt a lot of things, but never weak. Yet in this moment, that was how he felt. Like nothing more than a coward.

And that was unacceptable.

"I've got to fix it," he said.

"Great," said Marcus.

"But I've got to fix *me* first."

"Shit, bitch," said Reggie. "We don't have that kind of time."

"Maybe not all the way. But I have to... I have to do something."

"Maybe you should make a list. That's what my therapist used to say to do."

"Okay. I'll make a list."

So he did. He spent the day writing down what he needed to do, who he needed to talk to. He started at Joey's old house. Joey's mother let him in. His father had died five years earlier. She didn't condemn him.

Then he went to Ryan's place. And as he talked to Ryan's parents, he released the guilt. He realized he was the only one holding on to it.

And then it was time to go to his own parents' house.

"What brings you here?" his mother said, smiling.

"I want to say that I'm sorry. I really am so fucking sorry. I'm so sorry that I missed so many years. And I really want you to forgive me. Because I want to be different. I don't want to feel this way for the rest of my life. I want to be more than grief. And more than mistakes. And more than good deeds trying to cover up everything broken inside of me. I want to be better. And I want... I want to be able to love a woman the way that I should. I love Marigold. I want to have a future with her. A family. I messed up big-time with her. I realized not too long ago it's because I'm such a mess."

"Hell," his dad said. "Son. We are all a mess and none of us makes it through life without getting messier than we were when we were born. I spent years feeling regret over how you left. Wondering what I could've done better with you."

"So did I," his mother said.

"No," Buck said. "Don't feel bad. It was my decision to leave. I was the one who couldn't handle it."

"And I feel like, as your parents, we should have done something different to make it so you knew you could stay." His dad cleared his throat. "That's life."

"What if we all just stopped blaming ourselves? Because there's no room for regret. I mean, I have it. A bunch of it. For all the time I missed, but..."

"But you have your boys."

"Yes. And I hope that I'll have Marigold. And if so, then what it took to get there... It would be worth it. Somehow all my bad decisions led me to the right place." He thought long and hard about that intuition in his gut. And he realized, that was the thing that had been leading him all along. More than a gut check. Divine intervention. Because it was nothing short of miraculous that with everything he'd done wrong, so much was right.

"I'm just thankful," he said.

"I think that's a pretty good start."

He nodded slowly. And when he went outside, the sun felt different. Warmer. He couldn't change his past. He couldn't go back and make better decisions. He could only make good ones going forward. And give thanks for the fact that he had been given so much in spite of himself.

Chapter Sixteen

Marigold was bustling around the new building, her dream significantly less beautiful than it had been only last week. What did it matter now?

This was the problem with love, she thought. With opening yourself up. Then beautiful new kitchens didn't feel as significant as they should.

She'd been dreaming of this, and now her dreams felt dim. Which infuriated her. Her dreams were not dim.

But for a moment, she'd thought it was possible to have it all.

Now anything else felt less.

Damn that man for making her life feel like less.

She was about to go into the back room when she heard the door open. Then she stopped and turned around, and there was Buck, standing there backlit against the sunlight.

Like a knight in shining armor.

A hero.

Light and color and everything she'd been missing, in his black Henley and his blue jeans, his cowboy hat on his head.

No. He ruined this, remember?

But she didn't care. Because she wanted him.

And because everything they'd talked about, everything

they'd been working through these past few months, was all about the fact that you had to be able to move on from bad choices.

That the end wasn't final, if you didn't let it be.

"I need to talk to you," he said.

Her first instinct was to protect herself. "Why? Haven't you said everything there is to say?"

"No. Because last time we talked I left off something really crucial."

"What's that?"

"I love you. I loved you even when I was telling you no. You're right, I never said I didn't love you. I loved you that whole time. But I couldn't figure out how to keep myself safe and how to love you. That's what it comes down to. I told myself all kinds of things. That I didn't deserve love because of the way that I had abandoned my family. That I couldn't be trusted. But I spent twenty years disconnected from everyone and everything. On purpose. Until those boys came into my life, I had forgotten how to really love. I knew how to atone. I knew how to do good things because guilt motivated me. But those boys changed me. Yet with you, I tried to do the old things. I tried to revert to type. But having my boys look at me and ask if I only adopted them because I felt guilty… Hell no. Of course not. And that's another thing. I'm trying to be a role model here. I'm doing a bad job at it. Because what I'm showing is that if you make a mistake you have to make yourself pay for it for the rest of your life."

"You didn't make a mistake. You didn't cause that accident."

"I don't mean the accident. I mean leaving. I mean not staying. But I was too hurt. I was too messed up. I told myself that everybody would be better off without me. I believed it. Because I… I just hurt so damned bad. So much of this, is just actually being afraid of hurt. And not knowing how to share myself. Because what I know how to do is run away. I reverted to type. And I'm sorry. You didn't deserve that."

"Why don't you let me decide what I deserve?"

"But I want to take care of you. I want to be better for you. I want— I'm an idiot. Because the reason you came to my door that day had nothing to do with business. Or atonement. Or even sex. It was love. That was it. That was everything. From the first moment. The first moment I saw you. I just knew that I couldn't let you walk away from me."

"I love you."

"I love you too."

"I want it all," he said. "I want to get married. I want to move in together, I want to share space. But I do understand if you can't do that before Lily goes college."

She nodded slowly. "I'll have to talk to her. It is her last few months at home."

"Of course."

Because loving each other meant loving all of it. Loving him meant loving all his baggage, all the boys. And loving her was the same. And they both understood it. Because they understood each other.

She had thought for a long time that she was healed. In some ways, she had been. Healed enough to do right by her daughter, healed enough to be a good mom. But she was finally healed enough to be herself.

And that was an incredible gift.

Epilogue

Welcome to Lone Rock...

The day Buck moved Marigold into his house they passed that familiar sign.

All of Marigold's belongings were in the back of the truck, and they were ready to start their new life together. They would be living in sin before the wedding. And Lily had said she didn't mind moving out to the ranch before graduation, which meant they were going to be one big happy family before she and Colton left for college. Reggie and Marcus especially had completely latched on to Marigold as their mother, and she was giving them absolutely everything.

He had never felt more in awe of how beautiful life could be. He had spent way too long thinking about how cruel it could be.

"You look happy," Marigold said.

"Of course I am," he said, slinging his arm over the back of the seat. "I'm in love."

And for the first time in twenty years, Buck Carson was well and truly home.

* * * * *

Rancher's December Miracle

Chapter One

Escaping teenage heartbreak was usually pretty easy. Step 1: leave your hometown. Step 2: don't go back, and if you do, stay out of *his* favorite haunts.

Don't go to his favorite bars, don't drive past his house.

Very basic stuff.

It was much more difficult to do, however, if your great teenage heartbreak also happened to be your stepbrother.

And that was the essential problem that faced Lily Rivers every time she came home.

He was family. So she should be used to it.

When their parents had first moved in together, they had been seventeen. They had cohabitated for eight months. And then blessedly they had gone off to college. Which meant they were mostly confined to interacting during holidays.

The problem wasn't that he was mean to her. It was that he was fine. Aggressively and totally fine.

And why shouldn't he be?

They had dated for a couple of months when they were teenagers. He had been her first kiss. Her first…well, she was a little fuzzy on which base was which. They hadn't had *sex*, but they had done *stuff*.

Stuff she couldn't get out of her head. Stuff that haunted her. Made her wake up in a cold sweat.

With her heart pounding and her body aching and...

And then she had gone and imploded their relationship by breaking up with him because she could see that her mother was into his father, and the rest was history. She had told him their relationship was probably doomed—and it had been.

She had also told him it was very important they not get into a situation where their dating got so serious that if they ever broke up it would be impossible for them to be around each other.

That had been the smart thing to do, all things considered. The responsible thing.

And anyway, she had been so certain they were young, and they would find other people, and that would be that.

It should've been that.

That was the problem.

Well, the real problem was that nothing had faded. Time hadn't pushed the way that Colton made her feel into the recesses of her memory. So every single time she had to gear up to do a big family thing, she felt...

Like she was being skinned alive.

She didn't need to ponder that now. Not while she was driving on extremely slick and windy roads. It was so cold. Usually the coast was a bit more temperate in Oregon, but it was freezing, and so were the roads. It had started snowing when she was inland, and she'd paused to check the weather in Lone Rock, where her parents were coming from, and had seen that it was snowing there too.

It was a little more festive than she was looking for.

She turned up the radio and started to sing. Trying to drown out the intensity of the feelings rolling through her.

She was twenty-three. She really should be over it by now.

Colton had moved back home after graduation. He had gotten a house in the mountains near his dad and her mom and was working on their ranch.

She had decided to stay in Eugene. She had gotten a job there as a researcher, and it was decent work. She had aspirations of someday reinvigorating the museum in Lone Rock and working as an archivist there, but that was a someday fantasy.

And she would have to contend with *him* if she moved home.

Of course, she would be closer to her mom, to her other two stepbrothers and to her little half brother and sister, who had been born during her first and last year of school.

It wasn't anybody else's fault that she couldn't get over him. It was dumb. Because it wasn't like she was in love. How could you ever call something like that love? It was juvenile. It was… *He* was… She was going to calm down.

She was very chill. Of course she was.

She breathed a sigh of relief when she pulled up to the family beach house, because the road conditions had been slowly twisting her nerves.

The ice. Definitely. The twisting was *not* due to thinking about Colton.

The house itself was practically a tourist attraction. Strange though it was. But legendary country music star, Tansy Martin, was Lily's aunt by marriage and had written her breakout hit there. Which happened to be a devastating breakup anthem about Lily's uncle by marriage. It was a whole weird thing.

The family often went to the house at Christmastime, and this year was no exception, although only her mom, stepdad and stepsiblings and half siblings were coming. Only. Like that wasn't a massive and significant number of people.

The house was beautiful as ever. A glorious two-story home with stunning views of the Pacific Ocean, the majestic rocky Oregon beach below, the waves against the rocks deafening, even from where she sat in her car.

She could see a tree through the window, twinkling brightly, and Christmas lights going strong all around the outside. Her parents always had the house decorated for their arrival, and it gave her a profound sense of homecoming, even if it wasn't her home, technically.

It was traditional. And lovely.

She was the first one there, which was somewhat blessed. It gave her a chance to gather her thoughts. To get her emotions together. Sometimes, when she thought about Colton, she imagined her feelings bubbling up, boiling over, and she just needed to turn the heat down on them to get them back in their proper place. She imagined herself doing just that. Turning down the heat on the burner. She took a breath, then another. She got out of the car, and the mist enveloped her, the scent of the sea. She took another breath.

She was regaining control of herself. She was finding her center.

She did not have to think about what it had been like when she used to make out with Colton. *Before* he had been her stepbrother.

Really, it was just bad luck. How many people did that happen to? Meet a guy, get bowled over by your chemistry, have your parents end up falling in love.

She sighed and took all her things out of the trunk of her car, one bag with all her supplies and another with all her presents for her family, and closed the back of the car, heading toward the house. She entered the code and retrieved the key from the lock, letting herself in and taking a breath of the pine-scented air.

It really was *Christmas*.

She walked slowly up the stairs and cracked open the door to her bedroom, which was just as she had left it last time they'd been here. Her dark red bedspread, velvet and seasonal, was spread out on the mattress, with round, fat pillows propped up against the headboard.

She'd seen a movie when she was a kid called *A Little Princess*, and there was a scene where one of the girl's rooms had been transformed for Christmas as if by magic, with warm shoes and cozy blankets and finery.

Lily always felt that way coming to this house. Coming into this room.

Like it was a magic miracle that could all disappear in a puff of glitter.

It made her ache.

It was such a strange thing. She and her mother had lived hand to mouth for most of her childhood. It had been comfortable, and it had been nice. Her mother was such a hard worker.

But her stepdad was *rich*. His whole family was rich. They had multiple houses. Her aunt Tansy had a private jet. It was just a whole new kind of life, one she'd been thrust into when she was seventeen. She'd gone to college not long after, so she dipped in and out of this life, and she'd never gotten used to it.

She knew that her stepbrothers were just as overawed by it as she was most days. They had been adopted by her stepdad when they were teenagers, so the change to their lives had come around when it had come to hers. In that sense, they were united. If she didn't feel so awkward around Colton, she might feel a kinship to him.

He, however, didn't seem to feel any awkwardness at all. Not that she could see. But then, maybe that was because Colton wasn't awkward, ever.

No. He was just hot. Overly confident in all things. It was deeply annoying. Because she just didn't feel like she was… It was hard to articulate. He seemed to have taken to everything in his whole life better than she did. He was gorgeous. Self-assured. He seemed to step into his role in their family with ease. He had become a Carson effortlessly.

She still felt very much like she had been grafted onto the tree, not because of the way anybody treated her. Of course not. The Carsons were wonderful. But she just mostly felt like the girl who had been raised by a single mother, whose dad was an absolute dickhead and who had lovely grandparents who lived in a modest house on a regular old street.

It still felt like she was going to a museum when she visited the Carsons. With their massive mansion in Lone Rock, and yet...

And yet there was something reassuring about this place. She couldn't quite pinpoint why.

Her phone buzzed, and she took it out of her pocket.

She had missed a call from her mother.

She wrinkled her nose, and then hit the button to call her back. She started to walk down the stairs with her phone to her ear.

"Hello?"

"Hi Mom," she said. "Sorry. I got here safely, the roads were sketchy but I'm fine. I just put my bag in my room. I don't know why my phone didn't ring."

"Thank God. Because apparently the highway between Lone Rock and the coast is closed."

"What?"

"The road is completely impassable."

She'd been coming from the north, and her family was coming in from the east.

"I don't..." Her head was spinning. She didn't want to spend Christmas without her family. Surely it would clear up in the next couple of days.

She heard tires on the gravel driveway out front.

"Hang on. Somebody's here." She craned her neck to try and see out the front door window. "It might be... Did you get food delivery?"

"Yes. And Christmas dinner is going to be catered." They always did that. They got a fully cooked meal delivered.

Her mom did meal prep for a living so the holidays were a time when she absolutely didn't prep anything.

"*Surely* you're going to be able to get here for Christmas."

This was starting to feel like a bad holiday special.

"I don't know. It's going to depend. They can plow the road, but I imagine it's going to take several days to clear since it's both the snow and the downed trees, and that's if the weather behaves itself. We got about an hour from home and had to turn around, and from what I heard it was even worse up ahead."

"I really want to see you," she said.

Her mom's voice softened. "I know. I really want to see you too. It won't feel like Christmas if we aren't together."

Lily was expecting a knock at the door, but there wasn't one. Instead, the handle turned. The door opened, and her heart dropped into her toes.

Because of course her whole family was stuck. Of course her whole family couldn't get here.

Except for Colton Carson.

The bane of her existence, the love of her life.

Her stepbrother.

Chapter Two

Colton felt tension migrate up his spine the minute he walked in and saw Lily.

He should be over it.

He would *never* get over it.

Because the thing about Colton Carson was, he didn't let go of a damn thing. He kept careful record of every transgression that had ever been committed against him. By somebody in the system, by anyone he had met when he had spent time on the ranch for troubled youths, where he had first met his adoptive father, Buck.

By any kid who had ever been mean to him at school.

Yeah. He kept track of that shit.

He never let them *know* it. It wasn't his style. But he didn't forgive, and he didn't forget.

His stepsister, Lily Rivers, was at the top of the list of people who had transgressed against him.

The way she had broken up with him the night of their fall dance senior year had fucking devastated him.

Not because he didn't have real problems in life. He sure as hell had known enough suffering by seventeen to make grown men cry.

But that was the problem.

He had thought he'd finally found everything he'd ever wanted.

A girl who really saw who he was. Who thought he was worth whatever trouble he came with.

But she had bailed the minute things had gotten complicated. And the worst thing was, he still had to see her. The worst thing was, he had to smile at her, and he had to pretend that everything was all good when it was actually all bad.

It was just that he was very, very good at pretending.

He hadn't shown her how badly she had hurt him, not the moment she had broken up with him, not ever.

He was good at that. He was good at it from years of being bounced around the system. He was good at it from years of having people treat him like garbage to be taken out to the curb and picked up and dumped at the next waste site. That was foster care, at least that was his experience of it. It was a shit show. And he had gotten real good at being the ringmaster.

He acted unbothered. He acted like he didn't care.

It made you believe your own bullshit sometimes. Made you buy into the idea that maybe you didn't care. And that made things a hell of a lot easier.

So he smiled. Because he knew it would confound her. Because it always did. "Lily. Great to see you. No one else is here yet?"

"No," she said. "Actually, no one else is coming."

He stopped. He had had dreams like this. Fuck. Those dreams were not anything he needed to think about right now. Those dreams were X-rated. And he tried very hard to never telegraph that he had an X-rated thought about his stepsister... Ever.

Sadly, he did have those thoughts, all the time.

That was why he was still so angry.

Because in all these years, he had never met a woman who fired up his imagination quite like her.

And he had seen her first. He had seen her before Buck had

ever seen Marigold, who had ultimately become his stepmother, and the only real mother figure he had ever known. It wasn't that he resented their relationship. How could he? It had created this wonderful stable home environment for him, on the one hand.

On the other hand, it had taken the woman he wanted most in all the world and placed her off-limits.

Or maybe, she had placed herself off-limits and that had just been a convenient excuse.

His mind often toggled between those two potential truths.

He mostly thought she just must not care. Because she had cut things off, and it had been so easy. That had been her first solution. Not just talking to her mom.

That, he would never understand. Not when they had been...

Well. He had thought he was falling in love. Clearly she hadn't been. That wasn't his issue to sort out.

"Why not?"

"The roads are closed."

"What the hell?"

"Weren't you driving the same roads?"

He shook his head. "No. I'm actually coming from Portland. I had some things I had to pick up."

"Well, the road from Lone Rock is blocked. There are downed trees, inclement weather. Apparently it's a whole snowpocalypse."

"They promise one of those every year and it never happens."

"I'm aware," she said.

He chuckled. "Right. Nothing out there really looks like snowmageddon to me. A lot of hysteria and no white stuff."

"Sure, but this isn't Portland, city boy." A silly jab, and yet one she couldn't resist making. Made extra silly by the fact that he now chose to live in the mountains in Lone Rock and she was the one who lived in Eugene. "The fact of the matter is, the ground here is soft, and when you add heavy, wet snow or ice, the trees just kind of crumple like wilting movie starlets in the 1930s. Across the roads."

"There's an image."

"Anyway. Guess we're here."

"Yeah. Guess we are." He looked around. "So." He was determined not to make it weird. She didn't get to be the one that looked cooler and more collected.

He really wished he could get it together and find somebody else. But he couldn't help but notice she hadn't either.

She'd never brought home a man for Christmas. That was something he thought about more years than he didn't. But someday, Lily was going to swan into a family event with a guy on her arm, and he was going to have to figure out what the hell he was going to do about that. He blamed his psychological trauma on the fact that he hadn't managed to let go of her. Part of him had wanted so desperately for all the good things he got when he first moved to Oregon to be permanent.

At least that was what he told himself.

Because there was no way he was just still in love with her.

Hell, a seventeen-year-old didn't even know what love was. And perhaps, the case could be made that a twenty-three-year-old maybe didn't know what it was either, but that meant he certainly hadn't been in love. And he could hardly claim to be in love with a girl he hadn't even fucked.

Not that any of the women he'd been with since had done anything to erase the memory of her kiss. He had tried to jump right back into what he knew.

Sex with no connections.

He had become sexually active at far too young of an age. But he basically ticked every box for youth engaging in risky activities. And he had engaged in most of them. It was how he had landed himself at the ranch for troubled youths. He had been a youth. Who was very troubled.

Like you are in trouble now.

Maybe he was. But he didn't do or sell drugs anymore. So there was that. In fact, he'd left all petty criminal activity behind.

He was a respectable rancher. He had a good job. He had a

great family. It was just Lily. Lily was the only thing that reminded him that he didn't have everything. That things weren't perfect.

And he was stuck here with her.

Well, he could leave. He could head out and go to a motel in town, but that would violate his sworn internal oath to never let her see him sweat where she was concerned. Acting unbothered by her presence was his biggest skill set.

Well, one of them.

When he was in bed with other women, he might not feel half as much as he once had innocently kissing Lily, but he knew how to make them see God.

Detachment was the primary header most of his skills could be filed under.

He could do a lot of things without feeling much of anything, and no one with him would be any the wiser.

A blue-haired girl at his college had told him it was a trauma response.

Beth was one of his best friends now. He'd stayed with her and her girlfriend when he'd been in Portland. He liked to tell her men didn't have trauma. She liked to tell him he was gender essentialist. He pretended he didn't understand what that meant, like they hadn't gone to the same college and listened to the same people shouting into megaphones.

She said his enjoying making her mad was him testing boundaries, which was also a trauma response.

His eternal response was that people were too goddamned traumatized these days.

Who had that kind of time?

Secretly he wondered if she was right. But what did it matter if she was? What was the alternative? To lie down and cry about it?

Not likely.

It was best to just put your head down and get on with things.

He didn't hope for the best or the worst; he just dealt with the reality of it.

Whining about it wouldn't have helped him back when he'd been a legitimately traumatized kid, and it would seem damned ungrateful now that he was an adult who was *privileged* as hell. Another word he'd learned from Beth.

He didn't lie down. He didn't weep. He wouldn't be leaving this fucking *privileged* house to get away from his stepsister.

"Well," she said.

And he wondered if she was going to admit it was awkward or uncomfortable. For her. He didn't feel awkward. No, that wasn't the word that applied here.

But she didn't admit anything.

She wouldn't.

Which also annoyed him. Maybe that was the game. Maybe it was why he was so dedicated to not reacting to her. He was the one who deserved a reaction. She'd broken up with him and she tiptoed around him like a little church mouse, like she thought he was a cat who was going to eat her.

In many ways, he wouldn't be opposed.

The wreckage would be epic.

He did his best not to think about that too deeply.

"Well *what*?" he asked, in spite of himself.

"Nothing," she said. "I just…we don't hang out much."

"No," he said, deadpan. "We don't."

"Mom said grocery delivery was coming." She looked expectantly toward the door like she expected the delivery to come at any moment. Like she hoped it would.

"Did Marigold say when?"

He called his stepmother by her first name to emphasize the fact that she wasn't his mother. To emphasize the fact that Lily *wasn't* his sister.

"Uh. No," Lily said, skipping over his intent, because that was what they did.

They didn't call each other out, not ever. They didn't talk like they'd ever dated.

But it was there between them. Always. The biggest thing in the room.

"I'm starving," he said, moving past her and into the kitchen, slinging his bag onto the counter, along with his truck keys. "I might go out and grab something."

Not because he needed a break from her.

"Oh. Okay. I'm hungry too, actually."

"Do you want to come with me?"

He felt prodded into saying it. Like there was an unspoken dare in her proclamation of hunger.

She looked at him, her golden eyes round, her lips pressed into a flat line. "Yes. Yes I do."

"Don't sound so excited about it."

"I'm very excited," she said blandly.

"Come on, Lily, I'll get you some clam chowder." He turned away from the counter, grabbing his keys again, and he could hear her footsteps behind him.

"I need a coat," she said, and he heard her footsteps depart, scampering up the stairs.

He heard her come back down, and he challenged himself not to turn to her. He did that way too easily.

Turned to her like he was a plant looking for the sunshine.

If he said that to Beth, she'd say he had unresolved feelings.

He fucking knew that.

He opened up the door and didn't close it, and she walked out behind him, closing it. He got into his truck and she got into the passenger side. He knew he was being resolutely unfriendly in his friendliness. But it was how they were.

He started the engine and backed out of the driveway. "I really love clam chowder," she said, far too brightly.

"How nice," he said.

They weren't going far. There was a little local place their family always went to on the edge of town. The parking lot was packed. Unsurprising. The weather was terrible and the place was lit with a welcoming glow that warmed him just by looking at it. It stood to reason quite a few people in town had the same idea about where to get dinner.

He did the same routine going into the restaurant that he'd done to get out of the house. Got out of the truck, heard her but didn't look at her, and they walked into the restaurant with her a few paces behind.

The woman at the podium barely looked at them. "Booth okay?" she asked.

"Yeah," they answered at the same time.

Of course, when they were seated in the booth, they were directly across from each other, and he couldn't avoid looking at her anymore.

She was so damned beautiful, with her red hair and freckles, those golden eyes that had always made him think of her as a tiger. So gorgeous. So dangerous.

She always had been the prettiest girl he'd ever seen. And he was sure he must have seen women who were more beautiful by now. He must have.

But for some reason she was burned right into him. His appreciation for her beauty was branded into his soul and he couldn't seem to do a thing about it.

"What were you picking up in Portland?" she asked.

He was about to answer when the waitress came over. "Drinks?"

"Diet Coke," she said.

"Is Pepsi okay?"

He watched her chew her bottom lip. "Sure…"

He could tell it wasn't.

"Water is fine," he said.

The waitress was clearly annoyed that he would be a cheap bill. A lot of times people saw him in his ranch gear and expected him to start ordering beer. But Buck didn't drink, and given Colton's own background and the issues his birth mother had with substances, he'd always thought it was better to go ahead and abstain.

Before the waitress could clear out, he stopped her. "I think we're ready. I just want a clam chowder and a fish-and-chips."

"Me too," Lily said.

The waitress nodded and walked away.

"I think she might spit in the food," he said.

"Why?"

"I think she's annoyed her tip isn't going to be as big as it might be if we were drinking alcohol."

"Oh," Lily said. "I don't think so. I think she's just busy."

Lily had a kinder view of the world than he did. But she always had. She just hadn't lived the kind of life he had. Not that she'd had it easy. Her dad hadn't been in the picture or anything when she was growing up. She'd had a kind of stability he hadn't, though.

"Sure," he said.

The waitress returned a moment later with their drinks and with two bowls of clam chowder. She'd given him two bags of oyster crackers so maybe Lily was right and she wasn't mad.

Double oyster crackers was a pretty nice gesture.

Lily only had one bag.

She opened it up and poured her oyster crackers into her soup and stared at his extra bag.

"I was wrong," he said. "She thinks I'm cute."

She let out a harsh breath. "Oh sure."

"Women like me, Lily."

"Yeah, I know." She held his gaze for a beat, and it felt loaded. "So, why were you in Portland?"

"Picking up some supplies. I got a good deal on materials."

"For what?"

"As it happens, I'm getting chickens."

She frowned. "Why?"

"Eggs," he said.

"Why?" she pressed.

"I like eggs, Lily."

She sniffed. "Oh. So you had to go to Portland for that?"

"I got a deal on some supplies and I got to go and see Beth."

Her eyes sharpened. "Beth?"

Oh. She didn't know who Beth was. He hadn't intended to be vague or leading in any way by mentioning her, but the reaction to her name was…interesting.

"Yeah. I know her from college. I stayed with her."

Her shoulders shifted slightly as she took a bite of her soup. "How nice."

"It was," he said, slowly. "Very nice."

He was being a dick. He didn't care.

She ate her soup with more focus than it strictly required, and when their bowls were cleared and their fish-and-chips were put in front of them, she paid just as close attention to her fries.

"So you're working at the ranch."

"Yeah. My degree is in agribusiness, you might recall."

"I do."

"Unless I end up packing up and going elsewhere, I don't see why I'd work anywhere else. I'm making a smaller farm on my property, though. For my personal use. Hence the chickens."

She nodded. "That's great. Did you…buy a place?"

"Did Marigold and Dad not mention it?"

She pursed her lips and looked down, then back up. "Uh. Maybe they did."

He wanted to shake her. He wanted to yell at her and tell her it shouldn't be this awkward eating with a damned family member, and it wouldn't be if they were actual family members or didn't have unresolved sexual tension between them.

But he didn't say any of that because that would be breaking his personal set of rules.

They finished eating and when the check came, they reached for it at the same time. "Let me get it," he said.

"We'll split it," she said, frowning.

"No, we won't."

He picked up the receipt and put his card on it, then waved for the waitress, who came by and took it from him.

"Oh for God's sake," she muttered.

He signed the receipt quickly when the waitress brought it to him and got out of the booth. He returned to not looking at Lily, as they walked back through the restaurant and outside.

"I didn't know you bought the house," she said. "Because Mom and Buck don't talk to me about you because they know that we can't handle each other."

He turned to her, his heart rate picking up. "We can't?"

"No."

"And why is that, exactly, Lily?"

He wanted to hear her say it.

"Because we never recovered from our breakup. Because we don't act like stepsiblings, we act like exes. Because no matter how hard we try, it's what we are."

Chapter Three

She felt like an idiot. She had broken the most sacred, unspoken oath that she had ever taken. To never, ever signal to him that she wasn't over it. That she thought about him like that all the time. That she thought about *them*.

No. It wasn't supposed to be like this. She was supposed to be stronger, braver, smarter. But everything had gone sour inside of her when he had mentioned Beth. Was she really no better than that? Getting jealous because all of a sudden he had mentioned a woman by name?

That was hideous. Awful.

But she was stagnant. When it came to love and sex and moving on, she hadn't managed to figure out how to do that. She had known there would be a time when both of them would, when they had to. She had intentionally put herself in a holding pattern through college, and it had seemed reasonable. Her mom had instilled in her a fair amount of worry when it came to unexpected pregnancy, and that had been reason enough to focus on her studies instead of being sexually active. At least, that was what she told herself most days. Because telling the truth, making it about Colton, was too painful.

But the idea that he might have somebody else when she didn't, that stung.

Oh, she was certain there had been other women. But he had never mentioned any of them. And now there was a name. It made her real; it made her important.

He had someone else.

As long as Lily had played this game of chicken, as long as they had been engaged in a game where they didn't mention their past, she could believe he was as wound up as she was. She could believe he was as tangled up in all this as she was. But he had mentioned Beth, and Lily had swerved, so she was the loser. She was the one who oh so clearly couldn't deal with it. She was the one who wasn't over it.

And that was a significantly humiliating thing.

More than that, it ached. Like a lance straight to the heart.

But instead of acknowledging it, and instead of dealing with it, she got in his truck and slammed the door closed behind her. She could hear her own breathing echoing around her; she hated the silence. She hated all of it. She tried to take a breath, and her chest hurt. Everything hurt.

He got in the car, and he didn't say anything.

She recognized the game he was playing. This one where he didn't look at her so he could try to make her feel unimportant.

Or maybe it isn't a game. You just are unimportant to him. Because he has Beth, and he's normal, and he doesn't care about the fact that you thought you were in love with him when you were seventeen.

That was galling.

The drive back to the house was short, and neither of them said anything.

"Look," she said as they pulled up. "Groceries."

There was a stack of brown bags against the door, and she wished she hadn't said anything, because she really was doing the most to betray how disturbed she was by all of this.

She couldn't have made it more obvious if she had tried.

As soon as he put the truck in Park, she all but fell out of it, her shoes crunching on the icy gravel as she scampered up to grab the groceries, feigning an interest in them that simply didn't exist. Not on the level that she was trying to portray.

She was far too aware of him as he unlocked the door and opened it, picking up the majority of the groceries and following her inside.

"We gotta at least get the refrigerated stuff put away," she said.

"Yes, ma'am," he said.

"That's what you have to say? Yes, ma'am?"

Because he was still doing it. He wasn't commenting on what she had said, and if he was normal about it all, he would have. If it wasn't a game, he simply would have asked her if she was still bothered by their past relationship.

"You don't have anything to say?"

She made a decision then and there. She didn't have any pride left to salvage, so she might as well go all in. Because the truth was she was held back by all of this. Exceedingly. Ridiculously. She was.

And she was stuck here with him. If she had this venue, this moment, to vent her spleen without anybody else being around to hear it, then why shouldn't she take it? Why shouldn't she say it all?

The spell was broken. This silent vow to never speak of what had passed between them.

And it hung between them all the same.

So why not? Why not keep going?

"We've never been fine," she said.

"Sure we have been," he said, his eyes cool. "We've been just fine this whole time. We've never had to have a come-to-Jesus, we've never had to shout about it. We've been fine since the morning we caught our parents sleeping together and lectured them the way they did us and moved right on into being family. Just fine."

"That's a lie," she said. "And you know it. What we are is a mess of memory. And we won't even let ourselves have the memories. Because we're both just... In a stalemate. And I'm tired of it. I don't feel normal around you. I never have. It's been five years, and nothing feels normal. It doesn't feel okay. I'm not over it."

Suddenly, his unreadable eyes flashed with fire. It was like a veil had been torn away, and she could see him. She could really see him. Fury and all.

"What the hell am I supposed to do with that? You're the one who broke up with me, remember? I don't have shit to do with this awkwardness. I don't have anything to do with this," he said, moving his hand between them. "You didn't ask me what I wanted. You told me how it was going to be, and now you're angry? You think that somehow I've created the situation?"

"No," she sputtered. "But I... You just always acted like nothing happened. You always acted like you were fine."

"Oh, does that bother you, Lily? Did you want to break my heart? Would that have made things better for you? Easier? If you could have felt like you had power in the situation, would you be happier?"

"Of course not. I wanted things to be okay between us. I wanted to stop the relationship before we got in too deep. Before it was impossible for us to come back from it."

Yet it had been too late.

That was the thunderous, ridiculous realization she had right then. Because they had been in love. She had spent all this time gaslighting herself into believing they hadn't been. That they couldn't possibly. Because they were too young. That it hadn't been real. That they needed to go to college. That what they'd felt was a common thing. A useful connection that would be forgotten about in due time.

And instead, he was her defining heartbreak.

She thought of him that way sometimes, but not seriously. Her teenage heartbreak. How silly. How small. Except it had never been silly or small. It had left a crack inside of her that had never healed.

"I'm sorry," she said. "I realize now that what I thought was wrong. I just thought we could...end it, and then it wouldn't really be heartbreak. That we could end it, and then everything would be fine, because we were kids and we would get over it. But I'm not over it. I'm not. It isn't that I need you to have a broken heart about it, Colton, it's that I need to admit that I do. It's that I have never gotten over this. It's that I went to college and met other people, and I didn't feel interested in them at all. It's that I never even let anyone else kiss me. Because I couldn't handle it. It's because... I'm still a virgin, because I can't get over this, and I can't deal with it, because I've been lying to myself about what it is. It's because I never called it what it really was. It was love. And I broke my own heart. So what am I supposed to do with that?"

She was breathing hard, and she felt humiliated. Small. Maybe this was why small talk was so hard between them. They had nothing small to say to each other. But apparently there were a lot of big things.

"Don't tell me this shit," he said.

"Why not?"

He moved closer to her. "Because I can't know that you haven't touched another man. That you haven't kissed one, let alone had sex. I can't know that."

"Why not?" She pressed. She didn't care about Beth right then. Because what did Beth have to do with them? What could she possibly be next to the enormity of this? What could anything possibly be next to this?

Why had Lily been so quick to push aside her own feelings when she had been in the middle of this?

She couldn't answer that question right now, because the only thing was that heat rising up inside of her. The fire and determination to do something with the yawning ache inside of her.

She needed it. She needed him.

It was the only thing.

The only cure. The only possible answer.

"I can't know it," he said. "Because I'm going to end up taking it as a reason to do what I wanted to do for a long time."

"What is that?"

"Don't," he said.

"Tell me," she said. "I was brave enough to say all this—you be brave enough to tell me what you want."

"I want what I always wanted. I want you naked and underneath me. I want to corrupt you. That is what I want. It is what I've wanted since I first laid eyes on you. Because that was the whole point of it, wasn't it? The bad boy and the good girl? What is the fucking point if the bad boy doesn't take your virginity, Lily? Huh? What kind of fun fantasy was that?"

"Nothing about it was fun," she said.

"Damn straight," he said.

This felt dangerous. They were here, by themselves. There was no one around to stop them. No one around to make them think better of this. No one around to make them want to be better versions of themselves. No. There was only this.

Her heart was thundering hard at the base of her throat. She took a step toward him. "I guess I got all the heartbreak and none of the benefits."

"You broke your own heart, remember? I didn't do a damn thing."

She shook her head. "If it makes you feel better, you've broken my heart at least a dozen times since then. Every time I ever looked at you and couldn't... Couldn't be honest with you. Couldn't be close to you. It's never felt right. Having to live with you, treat you like a member of the family? What a joke. We're the reason they're together. We're the reason this family exists, and we're the only two that can never fully...feel like it's a family."

"What do you want, Lily?"

"Maybe I want what I lost? Maybe I want the opportunity that was taken from me."

"I'm going to need you to say it."

"Kiss me."

"We're not seventeen anymore. If you only want to kiss, you need to say that up front."

She shook her head. "I don't only want to kiss."

"Praise God," he said.

Then he closed the distance between them, and his mouth touched hers.

Chapter Four

It was a bad fucking idea. It was the dumbest thing he had done in his life, and he had done a lot of dumb things. It was incendiary. It was impossible. It was perfect.

It was inevitable.

They had been lying to each other all this time. That was definitive.

But everything had always been leading to this moment. All it took was the removal of their supervisors. It didn't take a hell of a lot to get back to that intense magical alchemy that had always existed between them. When their lips touched, it turned to gold. And there wasn't anything else like it.

God in heaven.

He had told himself that maybe he had built it all up in his mind. That it was an exaggeration. That for some reason, he had managed to build up a concept of attraction in his head that didn't exist.

Not in the real world. Except it did. Because right as soon as their lips touched, it was like being back home. It was like being back in the fire. In the center of the storm.

They had always somehow simultaneously been the most uncomfortable, comfortable trauma he had ever experienced.

They had never made much sense.

But it was real.

He couldn't deny that now as he moved his tongue against the seam of her lips and she parted them, granting him entry. As he tasted her, deep and long and perfect, soft and sweet as he remembered.

Yeah. There was no denying this.

And what the hell was there to be done about that?

Nothing but this.

Nothing but to kiss her, now that there was no danger of her mom walking in on them. Now that they weren't kids.

Now that they were adults who ought to have more control, but maybe had less.

Because she had said it was real. And he had always known it was.

There was an angry, bitter sort of triumph inside of him that sliced through his chest like a knife.

He would never fully be able to understand the hold she had on him.

He wasn't sure if he wanted to.

Not really.

But he wanted this.

So he kissed her. Deep and hard and long, with all the skill he had acquired in the years since his mouth had last touched hers. With all the feeling he had left behind the day she had broken his heart.

It was the first time he had ever kissed anyone with both of those things.

It was surreal.

It was a glory.

And at the same time, it was a sin. He was certain about that.

He cupped her face,—it was so soft. He couldn't find any anger, not anymore, not when this just felt so damned good.

It felt like his due. It felt like what he had been waiting for all these years.

Confirmation that it hadn't been a dream. The right to touch her again. The sound of her need, her pleasure, her demand for more.

It reminded him of being seventeen.

That day they had gotten caught by her mom. They hadn't meant to start kissing. Not in her bedroom. He hadn't meant to put his hand under her shirt. She hadn't meant to take his off. They hadn't meant to lie down on the bed. But they had been carried away in feelings, passion that was too big for them. Too advanced for their age.

And now, in this moment, it was right. They weren't too young, and there was no one else here.

There was magic in it.

And there had been spare little magic in his life, so he was bound and determined to claim what there was.

So he picked her up, held her in his arms, and started to walk her toward the stairs. She looped her arms around his neck, not breaking the kiss. Almost as if she was desperate to make sure the magic kept going. He could relate to the feeling. But he wasn't afraid of it vanishing quite so quickly.

He pushed open the door to the bedroom and looked down at the bed. There were too many pillows on it.

He had never understood what the hell all the extra pillows were for. It was a rich person thing, as far as he could tell. Most of his life he had been lucky to have one pillow. He had become a Carson, and suddenly there were pillows every fucking where. The couch, extras on the beds. It was unhinged.

"I don't... I don't have any protection or anything," she said.

"This is a Carson house," he said. "There have to be condoms somewhere."

He believed that to be true. They weren't the only branch of the family that used this place.

He went into the main bedroom and went into the bathroom, opening up the medicine cabinet and giving thanks he had been brought into a family who prioritized their needs. Because there was indeed a box of condoms.

He walked back into the bedroom, and she was sitting on the edge of the bed, her knees drawn up to her chest. She looked up at him with wide eyes.

"Second thoughts?"

She stood up and walked toward him, then she grabbed a fistful of his shirt and dragged him toward her, claiming his mouth. When they parted, she was breathing hard. "Hell no."

Chapter Five

They were past the point of no return. And she was so glad. So damned glad. All she wanted was to have him. To have this. Now that she had fully admitted it to herself, it was like the floodgates had opened. Need and desire were a driving force within her; there was no room for nerves.

It was actually like being young again. Because she had been completely inexperienced the first time she had made out with him. And she had still ended up getting him half-undressed.

She could still remember, with a rush of adrenaline, how she had gone down on him in his truck, in the driveway of his dad's place. She had never felt nervous. She had always just felt... Like she needed him. She had wondered if she might feel awkward her first time, since at this point, she had waited longer than she had intended. But she didn't. Instead, she felt like they were picking up right where they left off.

"I'm ready to get to home base," she said.

"What does that mean?"

"We went to third base, right?"

"I don't know," he said. "Do people still use that baseball metaphor?"

"I don't know. I don't do anything with anybody. So, I always have used it, but maybe it's outdated."

"Well, I don't care," he said. He pushed her down onto the bed, his weight over the top of her, and it was her turn to squeal like a 1930s movie heroine. She was a breath away from swooning.

She stripped his shirt up over his head and pushed him onto his back so she could look at him. He had changed. He was more muscular now; there was hair on his chest. Her heart skipped several beats.

He was just far too beautiful for his own good. For her own good. For anyone's sanity.

His golden good looks had always left her senseless, breathless. She kissed his neck, all the way down his chest, down to the waistband of his jeans, where she undid his belt, the button on his jeans, lowering the zipper.

"Indulge me," she said. "For nostalgia's sake."

Then she exposed him to her hungry gaze. Lord.

He was… She pressed her palm against his hardened length and dragged her hand down to the base of him. Then she leaned forward, tasting him with the tip of her tongue. He groaned and arched his hips upward, and, flushed with memory and need, she took him deep into her mouth.

He pushed his fingers through her hair; his hold wasn't tight or insistent. He let her direct the movements. Let her explore.

Somehow, she felt like this was about her. That his body was her playground, her domain. He was hers.

She knew that with certainty. Even though she knew she wasn't the only woman to ever touch him, to ever do this for him, she had the feeling so strongly then, and still, that it had never been the same for him. That it still wasn't *this*.

"Enough," he said, his breathing ragged.

"Why?" she said, raising her head, then she kissed his hip bone. "Because we've done this. I need you."

Then she found herself flipped onto her back as he shucked

his jeans off the rest of the way. As he stripped her shirt up over her head, unclipped her bra with expertise. He stripped her entirely bare, and she wasn't embarrassed at all. She felt powerful. She felt perfect.

And he looked at her like she was a treasure. He kissed her neck, her breast. He cupped her, sliding his thumb over her nipple, and she remembered how he used to do that in his truck. The first time he had touched her bare breasts. Only this time, he didn't stop there, he lowered his head and took her nipple into his mouth, sucking hard. She gasped, pleasure lancing her.

Then he moved his hand between her thighs and found her wet and ready for him. His touch was like white lightning against her flesh, and she arched against his hand as he pushed a finger inside her, making her shake with her desire for him. It was Colton.

How could she have ever thought of him as forbidden? When he was hers.

He had always belonged to her.

He kissed his way down her body, his hands still wreaking havoc between her thighs. Until his mouth found that sensitized pearl there, until he began to lick her like she was the most delicious thing he'd ever tasted.

He gripped her hips and pulled her firmly against his mouth, his tongue working her with firm strokes. She wanted to keep her head, not because she was afraid, just because she wanted to remember this in detail. Because this was a vacation out of time. Because this wasn't a declaration, it was only a reclamation, and eventually, their family would be here. And they would have to pretend this hadn't happened. So she was going to memorize it all in vivid detail, except she felt her grip on the earth begin to dissolve. She felt herself beginning to crack. And when he pushed two fingers inside of her while his tongue pleasured her, she shattered. Utterly and completely. And then he was over her, capturing her sounds of pleasure with a deep kiss. She could taste her own need on his mouth. He grabbed a condom, and he applied it with expert finesse, before cupping her chin and looking her in the eye. "Are you ready?"

"Yes," she said.

"This is a long time coming, Lily Rivers."

"It sure is," she said.

The blunt head of him pressed against the entrance to her body, and he pushed inside of her slowly. So slowly. And it felt amazing. She arched into him, urging him on, wrapping her legs around his hips as he thrust into her one last time. It hurt, but it didn't matter. Because she was finally with him. Like this. It felt like a reckoning. A homecoming. It felt like her due.

And then he began to move. And it was like the earth moved with him. And so did she.

She was caught up, completely enraptured by the moment. He drove them both to the heights, again and again, before setting them back down. And building it all over again. And when she felt herself getting close to the peak, when she couldn't possibly come back from it one more time, she jumped. And she took him with her. They both shuddered out their pleasure, and she could feel him pulsing deep inside of her as he gave himself over to the same madness that was overtaking her.

They held each other after that. Their skin slick, their hearts beating hard.

She put her hand on his chest, rested her face right next to it. She didn't feel awkward with him. Not now. It was the strangest thing. She would've thought that being naked with someone she felt unspeakably uncomfortable around 90 percent of the time would be worse. Instead, it was right.

Instead, it felt like everything.

Like this was where they were supposed to be all along.

"I've waited a long time for that," he said.

She wondered if she should be offended by what he said. If she should take it to mean that he had been waiting to make this conquest. But she didn't feel like being offended. She wanted to luxuriate in the moment. That was all.

"I feel the same way," she said.

"I didn't think I'd be giving thanks for bad weather."

"I didn't think I'd be giving thanks for being trapped here with you," she said.

"No. I guess not."

"I really did think that I was doing the right thing back then," she said. "I wanted to be doing the right thing. I hoped that I was. I wanted… I wanted everything to be perfect for my mom. Because she gave up so much to raise me. She never said that. She never acted like she was sacrificing, but I know she was. My dad… He was such an unforgivable asshole."

"Really? She never talks about him."

"She acts like she doesn't care. She acts like she doesn't care that he was never involved, and…that the way they hooked up wasn't super problematic. But I'm furious for her. I always have been. You know her brother died when she was a teenager? And she was hurting. Older men took advantage of her. The guy that got her pregnant was already in college. She was still in high school. And of course she plays it off. She acts like she was just as much at fault in it as he was. But… I remember when I fully realized how crazy it was that she got pregnant with me when she was sixteen. Sixteen."

"Maybe that's a little bit why you stayed away from men."

"It's a lot why," she said.

She wondered if it was partly why she had pushed him away initially too. That thought was a revelation. A strange, shocking one. She knew it was why her mother had been so nervous about Lily and Colton. Because they were getting too serious, too fast, too young. Because her mom wanted her to do something with her life.

"I don't envy my mom," she said. "I can't imagine the tightrope that she had to walk to make sure her child felt wanted, while trying to make sure I didn't make the same decisions she did. I mean, she did a great job. I never felt like she resented me. But I understood that her options were limited because of her circumstances. She had to work. She had to make her life about me. She wanted me to be able to live for myself longer than she did. But she also made it clear that having me changed her life for the better. I think she just never wanted my life to be as difficult as hers was. Of course she didn't. But it made me want to protect her. And maybe myself too."

"I just wanted to protect myself," he said. "I was lonely for so damned long. Everything in my life felt unstable and precarious."

"And then I dropped a bombshell on you at a school dance. I'm sorry."

"We were seventeen," he said.

"Yeah. That was how old my mom was when she was being a mom."

"Difficult to believe," he said.

"How old was your mom when she had you?"

He shook his head. "I don't really know. I mean, young. Probably sixteen, seventeen. But I don't know. I don't have much information about her. If any really. That's all right. It's not... It is what it is. I let that go a long time ago."

"Did you?"

"Yeah? I mean, I have a family. Regardless of things being occasionally difficult between you and me. I have more than most people who come out of my situation end up with."

She wasn't sure which thing was more mind-blowing. That she had just had sex with Colton, or that they were now having a conversation. All in all, it was difficult to say.

"I've never really heard everything about your childhood."

He chuckled. "There are things best left untalked about. At least, in my opinion."

"Why?" She rolled over onto her side and looked at him. At his strong profile. She didn't ask herself if there would ever be a moment in time when she didn't think he was gorgeous. Because... It was okay if this never went away. She didn't know why she felt that way, only that right now, it felt okay if this was how it was forever. Because he was that special. And it was that good. Because something felt deeply complete inside of her in a way that it hadn't before.

"We should go put the groceries away," he said.

He rolled away from her, and she grabbed his wrist. "I know that I'm the one who put a stop to things five years ago. So I feel like I have to say now… That can't be the only time."

"Sure. Until the road opens," he said.

That terrified her. Because that was just… Open-ended. Open-ended and impossible to sort through. It meant that everything could be over in a few hours, or in a few days.

She dressed slowly, and he put his jeans on, and nothing else.

She looked at the muscles in his back as she walked behind him down the stairs. Gave herself permission to really stare at him. It was a luxury she didn't usually allow herself. She kept her eyes trained on him while he put food into the fridge, into the cabinets.

"You can tell me, Colt. Everything."

"Why?"

"Who else are you going to tell? Maybe our connection is inconvenient, and maybe it doesn't make a lot of sense, but it has been real from the moment we first met each other. Why bother to deny it?"

"I don't think I was ever the one that denied it."

"Why are you so upset about it if you don't have any feelings for me? If it doesn't matter, why does it still bother you? We need to figure this out, otherwise everything is going to implode when everybody gets here. You realize that, right?"

"Why would it be any different now than it was before?"

"Because we…"

"You'd already seen my penis, Lily, and we somehow managed okay."

"We hadn't done *that*. And I was… I was an idiot, okay? So we have to figure out a different way to be. And there are no inconsequential things we need to know about each other.

We already know them. I know you ordered water at the diner because Buck doesn't drink, so you don't. And maybe it also ties to things with your mom, even though you haven't told me that. I know you went to school for agribusiness. I know you like fruit candy, and you hate cooked fruit. I know you didn't tell anybody you didn't like cooked fruit for years because you were afraid of seeming ungrateful, and I also wonder if it's a little bit because there were times in your life when you didn't have food at all. So your preferences didn't get to come into play. Why should we talk about small things, Colton? What's the point of it? You were just inside of me. Let's have a little bit of honesty."

"If you think you want that," he said, turning away from her.

"I know I do. Because this... These past few years sure as hell haven't worked. So let's... Let's talk about something real." She looked down. "I told you about my dad. Though... I didn't tell you that I found him."

"You what?" He looked at her.

She had never told her mother this. She wouldn't.

Because she knew that it would hurt her mom's feelings. That Lily had sought out her dad when her mother had made an effort to have there be a clean break between them. But she had been eighteen and out on her own, and she had been curious. She knew that her father lived near where she was going to school, and she did a little bit of digging and found him.

He hadn't been horrible; that was the worst part. He had been detached. He hadn't been cruel; that would've implied emotion. He just didn't seem to feel a thing.

"I went to his house. I told him who I was. He wasn't married or anything. He didn't have a whole other family. He didn't seem desperate to hide my existence. He's an engineer. He has a decent job, a nice house. He thought it was crazy that I was already in college. But that seemed more in regards to how old that made him. He wasn't impressed with me. He didn't seem to have any regrets. I think I was hoping he would. I was hoping he would regret that he wasn't part of my life, and it was clear he didn't. Worse, it was obvious I wasn't missing anything by not having him in my life. I was hoping I was.

"But then I felt guilty. Because Buck has been such a great father figure to me. And my mom sacrificed everything. She did the best job she possibly could, raising me without making me feel like I was missing anything. Also, it's a terrible thing to see the ways you look like somebody, to feel the connection, to feel that they're your flesh and blood and see that they don't feel it back. I hurt myself with that one. After my mom spent my life trying to protect me from it."

"It isn't weird that you wanted to find your dad," said Colton.

"You know where yours is?"

"He was in prison," Colt said.

"Oh."

"I think he's probably dead now. I could check. Look in some archives or something. But... I'm not sure I want to. Though I guess, either way, I know where he is. Safely tucked away in a jail cell or six feet under." He paused for a moment. "I find that to be a comfort. I have no idea where my mom is. I haven't for a long time. But it wouldn't be surprising if she were dead too. The way they both lived... Not conducive to long life spans."

"How old were you when you got taken away from your mom?"

"Six. The first time. I spent a few years bouncing back and forth. Foster homes for a while, and then she would get to have another try. See if she could get off meth long enough to be a parent. She couldn't. When I was ten, she lost her parental rights. And after that, I just didn't get the point. I felt like I had spent years trying to behave. Trying to be a decent kid so I could get put back with my mom. Like, if I were better, then she would have the inspiration she needed to get off the drugs. But once I knew there was no hope of going back to her, once she was just gone... I gave up. I started using. Thank God, nothing too serious. And thank God, I didn't take to it. Because that could have decided the entire trajectory of my life when I was way too young to be making decisions like that. I started dealing. To try and keep my head above water when I was out on the streets. I got arrested. I got sent to juvie. I got sent to group homes. Depending on the mood of the judge on a given day.

"Eventually, I exhausted my options locally. They decided to ship me out to Colorado. To Hope Ranch. My life changed because of that. If I hadn't gone there, I would be dead. Either because I ended up on the wrong end of somebody's gun, or because I took something. Maybe on purpose, and OD'd. Staying alive is just a lot of damned work when you live the way I did."

He shook his head. "And it's not even an interesting story. Not that part. That part is boring. That part is so common. It's a repeated cycle, one you don't know how to get yourself out of if nobody shows you how. And for a long time, there was nobody to show me how. And that was difficult. It was really difficult. But then I met Buck. And I learned that there was a different way to be a man. To be a person. He was honest. About his own struggles. Both with addiction and with just living through loss, violence. Your uncle's death, it changed him. He saw his friends die. Everybody in town blamed him. And if they didn't blame him directly, then at the very least there was a pall of suspicion cast over him. And combined with his own demons it was just too much. I don't ever want to be glad that somebody went through a hard time, and I really don't want to be glad that your uncle died. But I feel like Buck having gone through what he did… That's what saved me. He showed me a new way to be."

"I know you don't think it's interesting," she said, her heart squeezing tight. "But it's part of what makes you who you are. All the struggles that you've gone through. And I am grateful that Buck showed you a different path. But I don't think you would be dead, Colton. I think you would've found a different way. Because I think that's who you are."

"Why? Based on what? What have I ever done to show you that I am singular in some way?"

"You just are. I was so deeply suspicious of men. Why wouldn't I be? My dad was a shadowy figure who my mom had nothing to say about. And none of it meant anything to me. I didn't fantasize about having a romance because I had never seen one that was functioning. I met you, and something about you got to me right away."

He chuckled. "I think that's called hormones."

"I don't think it was just sex. Or I would've had sex with somebody else in the intervening years."

His face went blank. "I did."

It hurt her. She let it.

She had known that. She didn't think he was trying to be hurtful, though.

"Well, we weren't together." She winced. "Beth…"

"Is my friend. Not my girlfriend. I promise."

"She doesn't think…"

"No, she doesn't. There's no… There's no ambiguity there."

"Oh."

"Were you jealous?"

She looked down at her hands. "I was trying not to be. I don't have a claim on you. I never have. I mean, I have no right to be jealous, all things considered. But yes." She was rambling, stammering, going back over her words. "I guess I just thought it was okay if we were both stalled out. But if you had a girlfriend…"

"You didn't want me moving on and being happy, Lily?"

"That's not it," she said.

"What is it then?"

"I don't know. It just made things feel final. And I didn't want them to."

"Well. I guess they aren't so final."

"I guess not," she said.

They finished putting the food away, and Lily wandered into the living room and looked up at the tree. It was beautiful.

"Every year at Christmas I would get an orange in my stocking, and some chocolate. Like Laura Ingalls. Well, the chocolate was just because my grandpa wanted me to have it. Usually, I would get a present that my grandma made me and a small thing from my mom. It was just us. And it was happy. It was so different to suddenly be part of the Carson family. And to suddenly have you all in my family."

"Yeah. I can relate to that. We never really had Christmas. I mean, I never did. Not until I went to Hope Ranch. They did big Christmases there. They cooked us gigantic feasts, and we got presents sent to us from well-meaning people in the community. A lot of winter coats and gloves and things. But, damn, the nicest stuff I ever had. Before that, everything I owned I just kept in a black trash bag. I had a pair of shoes that were too small for about three years. There, I got some that fit. That was kind of a big deal. And once we became Carsons, it was like... I could have anything I wanted. My grandparents bought me a truck. I used to hate rich people. I still kind of do. But I guess I am one. I don't really know what to do with that."

"I don't think I've ever hated anybody for being rich. But I don't really think I knew that I was poor."

"That's because you were middle class," he said. "And you all don't talk about money that way. Your parents try to protect you from it. When you don't have food, nobody can protect you from that. When you're poor as shit, then you talk about it. I always knew. And then, when I got taken away from my mom, I was a foster kid. Bouncing around schools, and it was actually kind of a good thing, because at least it took a little while for people to find out that I had a foster family. It was so...embarrassing. Because then everybody knows that there's something wrong with your mom. And that kind of...made me sad. Because..."

He got a faraway look on his face. "I thought my mom was pretty. She got really skinny. Then sometimes she had wounds on her face. But... When she was fixed up, I thought she was just the prettiest lady. I liked her jewelry. She wore a lot of bracelets with charms. Stars and moons. She had long blond hair. I still think people who smoke smell kind of comforting. Because that was how my mom's sweatshirts always smelled. I really loved her, Lily. And I didn't want anybody else to think little of her. Because I didn't. I wanted to protect her, but I didn't even know where she was."

That was a terrible grief. She had an absentee father who didn't want to be in her life. It was clear to her that Colton's mother must have loved him. She was just trapped. Caught in the throes of an addiction she couldn't shake, in a cycle she couldn't break. Because she couldn't grasp a hand and get out the way that Colton had done.

Right then, Lily felt a profound amount of sadness for that woman. Because he was a wonderful man, and his mother didn't know it. Because someone else had brought her son into their family. After he had all but raised himself. Nobody dreams of that. It was a terrible thing to know that a woman who had, at one time, been a little girl with hopes and dreams for her life had grown into that reality.

"I bet she was pretty," Lily said. "And I bet she loved you a lot. Because she tried so many times."

He paused. "Thank you. For saying that."

"I mean it."

"A lot of people get mad when they hear about her. Buck did. And that's great. I mean, I get it. But I'm not mad at her. I'm just sad."

"I think that's really nice. But it makes me even sadder for her. To know she has a son who loves her unconditionally. When she probably doesn't know that."

"Well. There's not much to be done about it. Like I said. I have a good family. I just still have that feeling. Like I want to protect her."

"Well. Why would it go away? She's your mom. No matter how many years have passed."

"Well, like you, it feels kind of ungrateful. Especially given how Marigold has been such a great mother figure to me."

"But she would never resent you for caring for your birth mother. You know that."

He nodded.

She put her hand on his. Everything was put away now.

"Why don't we go back upstairs?"

"Sounds like a good plan."

He looked.

Chapter Six

When they woke up the next morning, they were tangled in each other. Colton had never slept with somebody all night before. Having Lily naked and wrapped around him was a surprise. A good one. It was Christmas Eve, and the roads hadn't opened up yet. The storm had, however, moved toward the coast, and when he got out of bed and looked out the window, he saw snow. On the beach.

"Look at that," he said.

She stirred and got out of bed, and for a moment, all his attention was on her. On her body. On how beautiful she was.

"What?"

"Snow on the beach," he said.

"Weird," she said, getting out of bed and making her way to the window.

He turned and looked at her. "Yeah. But fucking beautiful."

He mostly meant her. Even though the scene out there was stunning, it was nothing compared to Lily.

He grasped for the hurt he normally felt when he looked at her, because it was a talisman. A good one. One that served as a reminder for why he couldn't afford to have too many feelings. One that served as a reminder of what he was. Except, he had basically bled all his guts out to her last night, and she had still gone to bed with him. She was still here.

"Let's get some coffee and go for a walk," he said.

She lay back across the bed for a moment, stretching, and his heart lifted. Along with other things. She was so damned beautiful. He wanted her again.

But that was the problem. He had always wanted her. Wanting her was nothing new.

Having her, now that was an interesting turn of events.

He didn't know how to have her, that was the thing. For now, for this couple of days, maybe. But he was a tangle of dysfunction in his soul. And…

He would never make the mistake of believing everything was going to be okay again when it just wasn't going to be.

It just couldn't be.

Because that wasn't how life worked. You didn't get infinite good things. He had tricked himself into believing that back when he had been young. Like his luck had changed, his fortune altering itself entirely, which meant he would get everything. He had gotten a family, why not falling in love? Yeah. Well. He knew better than that now.

He didn't do wild, reckless hope.

It didn't end well.

He didn't want to know where his mother was. He didn't want to know how this ended.

This was going to be complicated. Because he didn't know how he was supposed to go back to not knowing how it felt to be inside of her. He had downplayed that last night, but he was good at downplaying how he felt.

Just detach. You know how to do that.

But he couldn't seem to do it right now. Right now he felt too much; right now he felt everything.

"I'm cozy," she said.

"You'll live," he said, reaching down and picking her up

around the waist, bringing her naked body up against his. "I can warm you back up."

"After the walk," she said.

He saw something like fear dancing through her eyes, and he wondered if she was trying to sort out how all this was going to end too.

Not the most pleasant thought process. But hell. What did you do about that?

They both dressed and walked out of the house. He looked up and saw that the snow was still falling. The sound of the waves was crashing in the distance. It was surreal. But then, the whole thing was. Being here with her.

He took her hand, and the two of them walked down the path that led to the sand.

Their feet sank in deep, a couple inches of snow, a couple inches of sand. The snow faded away where the waves touched the shore, but back further, the gray sand was covered in bright white.

"What the hell does this mean?" he asked. He hadn't realized he had asked it out loud. He hadn't meant to. He hadn't meant to marvel at it at all.

"What do you mean?"

"Well…" He cleared his throat. "It's a thing Buck talks about a lot. Watching for signs. Listening to your gut. I don't know. It sounds dumb and mystical when I say it. When he does it, it kinda makes sense. He says you have to always look around you. Figure out what the world is trying to tell you. I never did that, not when I was younger, because I was just trying to survive. I was just reacting. I wasn't… You don't pay attention to signs and wonders and all that shit when you're just running from a monster on your heels all day every day. But Buck made me try to be more mindful. Pay attention. Snow on the beach. It's weird. Unusual. And so was *this,* between us. I just wondered if it was something I needed to pay attention to."

He thought about his mom. How last night was the first time

he had thought of her in a while. The first time he'd talked about her. He wondered if this was a sign from her.

If that meant she was gone.

Or if he was supposed to look.

He had never really considered that he had something to give his mom. Not until Lily had said what she did. That perhaps knowing someone had loved her unconditionally all these years could make a difference to her.

Or maybe he was just supposed to be here with Lily. But he didn't know to what end.

She took his hand, her fingers laced gently with his, the kind of touch he hadn't had much in his life. Something sweet. Not demanding. A connection.

They walked along in silence. Until he thought something inside of him was going to burst. Then he turned to her and kissed her. Right there on the beach. He didn't care if anybody saw, but there was nobody out there with them anyway.

He held her close, kissed her deep. Until they were both gasping for air.

Then he walked with her, in their own footsteps, back up to the house. He brought her inside and walked upstairs with her, turned on the shower. "I'm going to make good on my promise keep you warm," he said.

He stripped his shirt off, the rest of his clothes.

She looked at him, her eyes filled with a kind of bashful hunger he found intoxicating.

As the water warmed, he went and grabbed a condom. Then he stripped her bare. He brought the condom into the shower with them, and she gazed at it wide-eyed.

"Oh come on," he said.

"I don't know. This seems like a really good way to die. And I don't really want to have to explain it to my mom."

"Well, in fairness, if you're dead, you don't have to explain it to your mom."

She choked a laugh. "I guess. But it's going to end up being news. It'll be on the internet."

"Have a little faith in me. In my skill set."

He moved the water over her soft skin, aroused her until all objections were lost. Her hands slick, gliding over his body, pushed him to a whole new place. One he'd never been to before. And he could talk about his skill set all he wanted, but this was uncharted territory for him. The feelings.

He pressed her against the wall and kissed her, moved his hands between her legs until she was crying out his name. And then he took hold of the condom, tore it open and rolled it over his hard length. He positioned himself between her thighs, lifted her up and pushed slowly inside of her.

She let her head fall back, but then forward, her eyes fluttering open. "Colton," she said.

His name on her lips like that, it set a fire off inside of him. Ignited something.

He was wild then, pushing them both to the brink. There were no skills here. It was just brute, driving need. And nothing else.

It was just all these years of wanting her and not having her. All these years of wishing it was her with him. Her and no one else.

His whole body felt raw with that realization.

You're always wishing for someone who isn't there.

He felt like that truth tore him open. Exposed the ugly part of his detachment.

He was holding on to himself, to his heart, to all the pieces inside of him, because he was never with the person he missed the most.

He was able to care for Buck. He cared for his brothers.

But there were parts of himself he held on to ferociously because he missed his mother.

Because whatever woman he had in bed with him wasn't Lily.

Love could be so painful.

And it felt significant to have this realization. With her, with the snow, with everything. Like it was meant to be. Because there shouldn't be snow here, and there shouldn't be snow on the roads, and he shouldn't be in the shower with his stepsister, but all those things were true, and they were happening.

There was no *should*. There was just this.

He was pretty damned cynical sometimes. He made a study of it. But he couldn't be cynical about this.

Worse, he didn't want to be.

He wanted to feel.

She clung to his shoulders, shouted out her climax, and he followed behind her. It wasn't only physical pleasure, it was something more. Something deeper. Something that left him feeling scarred. Ravaged.

And he wanted to feel it. The pleasure, the pain, all of it.

He wanted this.

He wanted it. But he didn't want to look too far ahead.

But he didn't know what to do with any of it, so he just clung to her.

Chapter Seven

They got up and made dinner—an unholy combination of cheese, crackers and summer sausage.

They brought it into the living room and sat by the fire. All the lights were off, the only glow coming from the fire. The house felt quiet and dark. Empty. She'd never been here before without the whole family filling it up. Not without Reggie cracking jokes and Marcus quietly egging him on.

Without her little half siblings running around, their feet heavy on the floor and her mom and Buck talking and laughing together.

Her and Colton navigating around each other like ships dodging sharp rocks.

But their family wasn't here.

And they were.

All of today had been a strange thing. Wonderful. But…sad in some ways.

She could feel something desperate coming from Colton, and she couldn't quite get a read on what it was.

She was beginning to come to terms with the fact that they were going to have to deal with this. Deal with each other.

Deal with the fact that it was still love.

She had realized that in the shower, with him inside of her. And maybe that was ill-advised for a woman who had been a virgin until yesterday, to go calling sex *love*, but for them, it had always been love.

From the day they had met.

It didn't matter if anybody else would be able to see it. Nothing mattered except how they felt about each other.

But she could sense that there was real fear, turmoil, going on inside of him.

She also knew that just because you got something good, just because you had a good thing, didn't mean you couldn't sometimes profoundly miss what you might have had. She'd spent the first seventeen years of her life with her wonderful mother, and then her family had expanded, and still, she had gone looking for her father. Colton had been denied a family for so long. Of course he must feel... He must feel terribly incomplete in some ways still.

She looked down at her plate, and she tried to figure out what to say. But she realized she only really had one thing left to say.

"I love you," she said.

He froze.

And she knew she had made a mistake. How was it that she always chose the wrong moment, the wrong words, with this man?

Was this her punishment? Her karmic debt that she had to pay? She had broken his heart, and so now he was going to break hers?

"I'm sorry," she said.

"No," he said, shaking his head. "Don't. Don't apologize."

"Well, what else am I supposed to do when you look at me that way?"

"You don't have to say you're sorry, dammit," he said.

"Well, I feel sorry. I feel very, very sorry."

"You don't even know what I'm going to say."

"Unless it's that you love me too, then, I'm sorry."

"It's not..." He sat up, tenting his fingers beneath his chin, looking straight ahead. "It's not that simple."

"Why not?"

"It's not that simple because... I just can't." He looked at her. "Don't look at me like that, Lily, because it's your fault. When we were seventeen, I thought everything was going to be okay. For the first time in my life, I thought it would be. I thought you and I were a sure thing. And yeah, that's a stupid thing to think when you're seventeen. But I did. I believed in it, I believed in you. You broke us. And it was like... The final nail in the coffin of me being able to have hope. I can't just resurrect it now."

"But I'm sorry," she said, her throat going tight. "I was... I was stupid then. And maybe I was afraid. Afraid because I thought I was going to make the same mistakes my mother did. Afraid because... Why wouldn't I be? What I knew about love was that it could leave you by yourself with all the pieces of your shattered self and a child to take care of. I was afraid. I wanted to make a future for myself. I wanted to have an independent life. I couldn't see a way around that. A way that...that included you. Not then. I was also afraid that if I did the wrong thing, then my mom would never be happy. I needed her to be happy. So much. So badly. I really wanted her to be happy."

"But you want to take it all back now, and you want to take the damage back with it, and it just is not simple."

"Maybe not. But what if I don't need you to say anything right now. We are...whether we want to be or not...we're stuck together, Colton. We are family." She laughed. "It has never mattered that these feelings hung between us—we still had to see each other. We still had to contend with each other. I thought it was love then, and I told myself it couldn't be. That I was too young. I talked myself out of it because I didn't want to be that serious that early. But it was love then, and it's love now. It is always love. It always has been."

"That's why it left such a deep scar. And I just... I don't want to."

She looked at him, and she saw years of loss. The kind she could never fully understand.

She had certainly been through her own pain, her own heartache, but it had never been this. Not what he had been through. She'd had stability. A mother who loved her.

He'd had heartbreak and all of these unclosed wounds. All of this unresolved trauma.

"I don't need you to answer me now," she said.

"I don't think I can. Not ever. Listen, I'm sorry. It's not you. It's everything. Yes, you were part of it. But since then, I've… figured out how to deal with things, but it isn't always healthy, or good. It isn't always in a way that makes me better. I'm not better. I'm just…limping along."

"You're not. You are so wonderful. You have come out of so much trauma with so much to offer. And I want to marry you. Colton. I really think it would be good and we could be happy."

He looked like she had struck him, his eyes full of pain, but he drew a shade down over his emotions, and he didn't let her look at him anymore.

"Colton…"

"Lily, I need you to listen to me. There's just too much wrong with it. With me."

"What about the snow? The snow on the beach. I thought… I thought you said it meant something. That it was special."

"It was. Something can be special without being forever. Maybe we just both have to accept that." He stood. "I think it's probably better if I don't stay."

"No. I want you to stay."

"Lily, I think it was a mistake. For us to indulge in a fantasy that isn't going anywhere."

"It's not going anywhere because you won't let it. Because you won't… Dammit, why can't you just be brave?"

"Because I've already had to be brave for too many years, for too long. Because I watched my mom sink deeper and deeper into addiction and not be able to get out of it. Because I went through too fucking much already. I won't do it again."

He walked through the kitchen and grabbed his keys off the counter. He didn't go upstairs, he didn't get his things. He just walked straight out of the house and drove off, leaving her there alone.

Chapter Eight

He was a fool. Maybe. It was entirely possible. She had been offering him what he wanted more than anything else in the entire world. At least, what he had wanted at one time. She had been offering him everything. And he...

He'd said no.

He could feel it. It was so close that his fingertips tingled with the desire to touch it, but he hadn't let himself.

He wanted her. He wanted that version of happy she seemed to think they could have, but the truth of it was... He was so tired. He was so tired of hoping. Hoping and not having. And what was the point of snow on the beach or fucking Christmas if you just felt this raw? He couldn't drive home, because the roads were closed. But he could drive back to Portland. He could go stay with Beth for a little bit. He could get a little...time away.

He showed up, and Beth answered the door, looking sleepy. "What are you doing here? I thought you were doing family Christmas."

"Yeah. I was. But do you have room for a guy with unre-solved trauma?"

"Always," she said.

"Thanks."

He stepped inside and looked around the apartment, which was put together, just like Beth. Which made him wonder, not for the first time, if she had the right of it. If dealing with your trauma was the only way to really live.

"What happened?" she asked.

"How do you know something happened?"

"Because you are normally with your family on Christmas Eve, and now you're not."

"Yeah I… It's complicated. In a way that you probably don't want to hear."

"I love complicated. But Luna will also want to hear this."

"Great. You might as well have a show out of my trauma. Did I tell you that I used to date my stepsister?"

"Luna!" Beth shouted. "You have to come hear Colton's batshit story."

"Yeah. It really is batshit."

He told both of them everything. The whole spiel.

"In fairness," Beth said, "that's not really dating your stepsister. I mean, you were with her first."

"That is true," he said. "I was. My dad poached on my territory."

"That's how I see it," Luna said. "So I think you have to take that out of the equation."

"But I can't. It's impossible. I still have to see her all the time. And if something goes wrong, it's going to screw up everything."

"But something already went wrong."

"I mean, if something goes wrong and…"

"You get your heart broken," Beth said. "That's what you're worried about."

"It's not even that. My heart is broken. What I'm worried about is spending all those years waiting for the other shoe to drop. I'd rather just leave them dropped."

"Trauma response," said Beth.

"Well thank you very fucking much, Beth. What should I do about it?"

"Go to a therapist."

"I need a quicker fix than that."

"Maybe you need to go back further?"

"How?"

"Your childhood," she said.

He thought about his mother. "I mean, I... I don't really want to."

"That's the problem, Colton. If you don't turn over the rocks inside your soul and start looking for the scorpions underneath, they're just going to bite you when you don't expect them to."

"What am I supposed to do with that metaphor?" he asked.

"What's the thing that scares you most?"

"Finding out my mom is dead."

"Maybe you need to find out," Luna said softly.

"But I... I want to be happy. I want to...pretend. I..."

"But it's keeping you from being happy. Obviously. It is so clear that you're in love with Lily. So whatever you have to do to fix this for yourself, you need to do it."

"How?"

Luna sighed. "Well, I work in mental health. I can see if she's passed through the system."

"Are you allowed to do that?" he asked.

"For family? Yes."

Luna disappeared and returned a few moments later. "She's in a mental health facility and care home downtown." She sat slowly and handed him a stack of papers. "She has some health issues, Colton. She requires a bit of care."

He nodded. "Oh. Well. Yeah, I mean she...she had it really hard."

"I think you did too."

He nodded. Yeah. It had been a hard road. But a good one too, eventually. But this...this felt like hope. Hard-won hope.

He was ready to go see his mom. He was ready to hope.

* * *

It was insanely snowy outside and the traffic was nuts. He got in his truck and drove to downtown Portland. It was dark, icy. Cold. When he pulled up to the institutional-looking place and saw the lights shining through the windows, he knew a strange sense of trepidation. Was his mother really here? Was it really that easy?

You have not because you ask not.

That old saying resonated somewhere down inside of him, and he thought of Lily, his mother, all these things he had wanted that he...hadn't reached out for.

Hadn't asked for.

That was the problem with living without hope. You didn't reach for the things you wanted most. You didn't go after what you wanted best and most dearly.

He had limited himself. All this time.

Maybe hope was the answer.

Hope for strange miracles and for a life that worked out, even though he'd been through so much that hurt.

He parked against the curb and got out of his truck, his boots sinking down into the snow.

And hope was what drove him inside.

He walked up to the front desk. "I'm here to see Olivia Sheldon."

"We only allow family to visit."

"I'm her son."

The woman behind the desk softened, and she looked at him with a strange sort of recognition.

"Colton?"

"How do you... How do you know?"

"Oh, Olivia talks about you. All the time."

He felt like he had been stabbed straight through the heart.

"She does?" he asked, his throat going tight.

"Yes. She's very proud of you."

"How does she...know anything about me?"

The woman's face softened. "Well, she doesn't share any details about you, but she's always said that you were the best son."

He nodded slowly. And he followed the woman into a recreation room. He saw her right away. She looked prematurely aged, sitting in a folding chair with oxygen on. She looked like an old woman, and she wasn't. She was just a woman whose body had lived several lifetimes, and who probably didn't have the strength to keep going much longer.

But she was beautiful. Just like she always had been. He walked across the room slowly.

And she looked up. "Colton?"

"Mom," he said, the word coming out strangled.

"How did you find me?"

"I looked up your name online. I... I miss you."

She smiled. "I miss you."

"Mom..." He sat down next to her in an empty folding chair. "I just want you to know something. I love you."

Tears filled her eyes. "Why? You shouldn't love me. I didn't even raise you."

"It doesn't matter. You're my mom. You did your best. I know that you did."

Tears spilled down her cheeks. "No one ever believed me when I said that. That I did the best I could. They just said it wasn't good enough."

It would be easy to get angry. To say it hadn't been. After all, she had lost her parental rights. He had been on his own. In the system. He had gotten into trouble. He had felt lost and scared. But so had she. And what good would it do? To be angry. Why choose anger when you can choose hope? Hope was the thing that built new bridges, that built new roads into different lives. And he hadn't been able to see that before. He had let his heartbreak with Lily, let his childhood become an excuse, a shield, so he could protect himself. So he didn't have to face the more difficult feelings. So he didn't have to risk. Looking at his mom, he could see that her years of drug use had ravaged her body. He didn't know what else was wrong with her. Loving her would hurt. Letting her back into his life would hurt. But maybe that was okay. Maybe sometimes it was all right to choose the harder thing because it meant more.

"It was enough," he said. "I'm okay."

"Do you have a family?"

"Yeah. I got adopted. I have a dad and stepmom. I have brothers."

She nodded. "I'm happy for you."

"I was taken care of. The whole time."

"You aren't on drugs," she said.

"No." He shook his head. "I went to college."

She grabbed his hand and pressed her face against it, tears spilling down her face now. "I couldn't have given you that."

"You gave me life," he said. "You were there for me when you could be."

She reached into the pocket of the sweater she was wearing and took out a small picture. It was him. A school photo, probably from second grade. "I show everyone this. But I guess I need a new one. You're grown-up."

"Yeah. I'm all right."

He stayed the whole evening. He ate Christmas dinner with her. And he made a decision.

He did love Lily. He had the whole time. He needed to get back to her. To hope. To love.

To that strange phenomenon he had tried to dismiss. Because sometimes it snowed on the beach. And sometimes a man really could get everything he wanted. Everything he needed most.

"Hopefully I'll be back soon to visit," he told his mom. "But…right now I have somebody I need to go see."

"Thank you for coming to visit me. It felt like a Christmas miracle."

"Everybody's allowed to have miracles," he said.

Even him.

Chapter Nine

The whole family arrived early the next morning. It was a beautiful, snowy day on the coast, a perfect white Christmas, and it was damaged because Colton wasn't there.

It could never be perfect. Not without him.

"Why exactly did Colton leave?" her mom asked, leaning against the counter, while the two of them were in the kitchen by themselves.

"It's complicated," Lily said.

"Did something happen with him?"

"How did you… How did you know that?"

"Because you look heartbroken. And I'm not surprised that he still has the power to do that to you, even though… Obviously I hoped it wasn't going to be like that with him. But… I always thought it was odd that the two of you broke up like you did. But you insisted everything was fine."

"Well. I lied. And we were here by ourselves, and… Well, you don't need to know the details."

"You declining to give me the details tells me enough."

"Well. At least I finished college. You don't have to worry about me getting pregnant and not finishing."

"But I have to worry about you having your heart broken."

"It's too late. So there's that."

There was a commotion in the other room, her half siblings were causing a ruckus, and she and her mom went to see what was happening. It was Colton. Coming through the door with a giant armload of gifts.

Lily felt dizzy. She could have been completely knocked over with a stick. "What are you doing here?" she asked.

"I'm here to fix things," he said. "I'm here to tell you that I'm sorry. And that I'm an idiot. Also I brought gifts. Because I figured everybody else might be mad at me too."

"Just me," said Marigold. "Nobody else has heard."

Buck came into the room then. "Heard what?"

"That I'm a dumbass," said Colton. "And a coward."

"Already knew that, bro," said Reggie.

"Well. I really fucked up. And I'm here to fix it. So thank God for miracles and snow on the beach. And stores that are open all night on Christmas Eve for people who don't have all the shopping done. And also hopefully for forgiveness."

Everyone turned to look at Lily, because he was looking at her. "Well, go on," she said, trembling a little bit inside.

"I love you. And I'm sorry."

That earned a whole lot of shocked looks all around.

"We were snowed in together for two days," Lily said. "Things happen."

"A lot of things," said Colton. "I found my mom."

"What?"

"I'll give more details later. But the important thing, the really important thing, is that I realized I've been trying to live without hope. And that is a damned foolish thing to do. I took a leap. I found my mother. I got to tell her how much she meant to me. I… I hoped, and it worked out. And so it makes me wonder why I don't just try to have everything. Including you. I love you, and I hope… I have hope. That everything is going to be wonderful." And then he got down on one knee, and her heart stopped. He had a small ring box. "This is just a stand-in," he said. "Because shockingly, places that are open twenty-four hours on Christmas Eve don't do the best with this kind of thing. But it's something."

He opened it up. It was a diamond ring. An honest to God diamond ring.

"We're still young. But we were young when we fell in love. And I just think it's right. I hope that... I mean, I can move where you are, I don't need to keep the chickens. I don't need to keep the farm."

"Yes you do," she said. "And it's okay. I've been wanting to come home anyway. But it was never going to be home unless it could be with you."

"Well, now it can be. I love you," he said. "I'm sorry that I was dumb."

"I forgive you for being dumb," she said.

And she threw herself into his arms and kissed him.

"Well, I am totally lost," said Buck.

"I'll explain it to you later," said Marigold, patting his arm.

"This is so weird," said Reggie.

"So weird," agreed Marcus. "Congratulations, bro."

"Technically, I was dating her before... Never mind."

"I'll marry you," she said. "I'm going to marry the hell out of you."

"Well, it's a Christmas miracle," said Marigold. "Everyone is finally, finally *together*."

Colton smiled, and Lily felt it echo in her soul.

Finally.

Epilogue

Next Christmas, they went to the beach house, and Lily and Colton were married. Colton's mother was able to make the trip.

It snowed on the beach again.

And that seemed about right to Colton, because his life was rare and beautiful. Because he got miracles. Because he had hope. So why shouldn't it snow on the beach?

Why shouldn't it?

* * * * *